PRAISE FOR THE ALASTAIR STONE

"The magic is believable, the characters c   the people you know
and the twists, turns and mysteries to be solved glue your eyes to
the page. You will never forget these characters or their world."
—*Jacqueline Lichtenberg, Hugo-nominated author of the Sime~Gen
series and* Star Trek Lives!

"Alastair Stone is like Harry Potter meets Harry Dresden with a bit
of Indiana Jones!"
—*Randler, Amazon reviewer*

"Somewhat reminiscent of the Dresden Files but with its own
distinct style."
—*John W. Ranken, Amazon reviewer*

"I am reminded of Jim Butcher here...Darker than most Urban
Fantasy, not quite horror, but with a touch of Lovecraftian."
—*Wulfstan, Amazon Top 500 reviewer*

"An absolute delight for 'urban fantasy' fans! Smart, witty and
compelling!"
—*gbc, Bookbub reviewer*

"In Alastair Stone, author R.L. King has a major winner on her
hands."
—*Mark Earls, Amazon reviewer*

"Once you enter the world of Alastair Stone, you won't want to
leave."
—*Awesome Indies*

"You will fall in love with this series!"
—*Amazon reviewer*

"It's getting hard to come up with something better than great to describe how good this book was."
—*Ted Camer, Amazon reviewer*

"You cannot go wrong with this series!"
—*Jim, Amazon reviewer*

"Warning—don't start reading this book if you have other things to do."
—*ARobertson, Amazon reviewer*

"Once you start, you need to get comfortable because you will stop reading all of a sudden and discover many hours have gone by."
—*John Scott, Amazon reviewer*

"R. L. King has my purchasing dollars with fun-to-read, suspenseful, character-driven stories…Damn fun reads."
—*Amazon reviewer*

"I have been hooked on this series from the first book."
—*Jim P. Ziller, Amazon reviewer*

"Awesome and exciting. Love this series."
—*Cynthia Morrison, Amazon reviewer*

"Amazing series. The characters are deep and identifiable. The magic is only a small part of what makes these books great. I can't wait for the next one!!"
—*Amazon reviewer*

ALSO BY R. L. KING

The Alastair Stone Chronicles

Stone and a Hard Place	*House of Stone*
The Forgotten	*Circle of Stone*
The Threshold	*The Madness Below*
The Source	*Boys' Night (Way) Out* (novella)
Core of Stone	*An Unexpected Truth* (novella)
Blood and Stone	*Death's Door*
Heart of Stone	*Blood Brothers*
Flesh and Stone	*Homecoming*
The Infernal Heart	*Mortal Imperative*
The Other Side	*Balance of Power*
Path of Stone	*Rite of Passage*
Necessary Sacrifices	*Winds of Change*
Game of Stone	*Shadows and Stone* (novella)
Steel and Stone	*Turn to Stone* (novella)
Stone and Claw	*Devil's Bargain* (standalone novel)
The Seventh Stone	*Stone for the Holidays* (short stories)
Gathering Storm	

Happenstance and Bron

The Soul Engine

Chariots of Wrath

By Demons Driven

Shadowrun (published by Catalyst Game Labs)

Shadowrun: Borrowed Time

Shadowrun: Wolf and Buffalo (novella)

Shadowrun: Big Dreams (novella)

Shadowrun: Veiled Extraction

WINDS OF CHANGE

ALASTAIR STONE CHRONICLES: BOOK TWENTY-SEVEN

R. L. KING

MAGESPACE
PRESS

Copyright ©2021, R. L. King

Winds of Change: Alastair Stone Chronicles Book Twenty-Seven
First Edition: September 2021
First Paperback Edition: November 2021
Magespace Press
Edited by John Helfers
Cover Art and Design by Gene Mollica Studio

ISBN: 978-1-953063-08-3

PROLOGUE

Darrell "Spunk" Gronsky always had a hard time returning to reality after a convention.

He sat at the Rochester airport, scrolling through photos on his phone as he waited for his flight to board, smiling as each one came up and brought back its own small memory. The memories were fresh now, only a couple days old, but the photos joined hundreds of others Spunk had taken at the dozens of cons he'd attended over the last several years.

Some of his coworkers at the bank back home in California where he worked as a new-account specialist razzed him about the conventions. "Are you serious, dude? You dress up like a wizard and wave around a pool noodle?" No doubt they thought he should be pursuing more "adult" pastimes, like fantasy football or trying to get into somebody's pants at their frequent beer bashes.

Spunk didn't mind, though. He'd met the best friends he'd ever had in his life during college, when he'd tried to combat his shyness by joining a gaming club. Now, five years after graduation, he still kept in contact with them even though they'd spread out all over the country. And at least once a year, they got together at a convention to share stories and play games. Spunk didn't care if his work friends thought he was immature. He thought getting excited about a bunch of oversized guys in tight pants throwing a ball around was a little silly too, but to each his own.

By this point, he didn't even remember the strange tingle he'd felt when he and his crew had taken a wrong turn into a dusty storeroom while searching for clues during their live-action roleplaying session. He'd barely even noticed it at the time.

And just as he wouldn't have noticed invisible virus particles wafting from his body if he'd been ill, he had no idea of a different sort of particles he was exuding into the air as he sat in his uncomfortable airport seat, grinning fondly at how stupid he'd looked in his fake beard and wizard hat.

If he *had* noticed, he'd probably have watched with fascination as the particles sluiced off him and crept along the floor like a ground-hugging fog. They crawled along, tentatively probing at other passengers' feet the same way a dog might sniff at an unfamiliar scent. Most of the time, they merely moved on. But as they continued ranging outward from Spunk, covering more space in the crowded gate area and its fifty-odd bored, waiting people, they paused.

The first time was near an older woman who was busily knitting a scarf and ignoring the world around her. The second was a teenage boy intent on a handheld video game. In both cases, the particles swirled around their feet in greater concentration, growing brighter and more agitated, and then flowed upward. The woman and the boy both felt the same brief tingling sensation Spunk had back in the storeroom, but both ignored it as he had. The woman had had several cups of coffee, and the boy had just finished an energy drink. These things happened.

By the time Spunk boarded his plane for San Diego thirty minutes later, the ground-hugging fog of particles had made it far enough to affect the crowds at the two adjacent gates—one to Seattle and one to Phoenix. It found what it was seeking in one case each.

That particular fog dissipated with Spunk's departure, but resumed when he settled into his seat in row 9A of his plane home.

This time, similar fogs from the knitting woman and the teen boy joined it.

On the Seattle and Phoenix planes, others crept eagerly outward, looking for receptive hosts.

CHAPTER ONE

ALASTAIR STONE'S FIRST IMPULSE when Aubrey left him a voicemail saying he had some news was a cold rush of terror.

Was the old caretaker's Parkinson's progressing already, despite Aubrey's assurances that it was under control? Why else wouldn't he tell Stone what was on his mind in the voicemail itself, rather than wanting to do it in person?

He forced himself to call back rather than popping over there right away. "What's going on?" he demanded, maybe a little too forcefully. "What's this news? Are you all right?"

"Oh, sir, I'm sorry." Aubrey *did* sound apologetic. "I'd completely forgotten that you might take my message wrong. I didn't mean to disturb you."

Well. That was encouraging, anyway. "You're all right?"

"Of course, sir. Doing very well, in fact."

Stone slumped in relief. "Well…that's brilliant, then. So, what's the news?"

"I'd rather tell you in person, if you don't mind. If you're not busy, perhaps you could come by tomorrow evening? I could have a lovely dinner prepared."

"Aubrey…"

"I know, sir, you're curious. But I'd rather tell you in person."

"You aren't retiring, are you? Found another position?"

"Oh, my, no, sir. Nothing like that. Will you come?"

"You haven't given me much of a choice, have you?" Before Aubrey could reply, he sighed fondly. "Yes, of course I'll come. But don't put yourself out fixing some fancy dinner on my account."

"It will be my pleasure as always, sir."

Stone was grateful he didn't have to use the portals to travel home anymore. But after three months had passed following the whole situation with Daphne, he was beginning to think about getting back to building the one he'd been working on in his basement. After a ritual had destroyed his previous work, he'd wondered if it was worth the effort to rebuild. He didn't *need* it to travel most places anymore, and there were very few locations where a public portal existed and a ley line didn't.

That meant the only time he'd need to use the public portal in Sunnyvale was if he wanted to take anyone with him. It was the one downside of his draconic travel method: he couldn't take passengers.

There was also the matter of Verity and Ian. His former apprentice had been looking forward to having a portal closer to her home in San Francisco—not to mention one she could use without alerting anyone—and it would be nice if his son could come straight to the Encantada house instead of having to pop in twenty miles away. Neither was a major consideration, but there *were* times when he'd like to bring someone to his place discreetly— Eddie and Ward, for example.

As he prepared the pattern that would take him to the Surrey house, he made a mental note to visit Madame Huan to see if she still had the vanazarite she'd been planning to sell him before. If not, he'd have no choice but to wait. His other source, an old woman named Oyunaa in Mongolia, was still fresh out, and his only other potential source—Stefan Kolinsky—had taken off for parts unknown recently, after telling Stone in no uncertain terms not to contact him unless the world was about to blow up. After everything they'd been through lately, Stone wasn't about to push things for a commodity he wasn't even sure he wanted.

Aubrey was waiting for him when he arrived, bustling around the kitchen putting the finishing touches on dinner. From the delightful aromas and the number of pots and pans spread out around the area, it seemed he had indeed planned a more elaborate meal than usual.

Stone lounged in the doorway. "Where's Susan? She won't be joining us tonight?" He offered Aubrey a sly grin.

"She will, sir." Aubrey's returning smile was less sly and more pleased with himself. "She's over at my flat, freshening up. I hope you don't mind I've invited her."

"Of course not." He gestured around him. "You two have mostly taken over the place in my absence anyway. I don't want to get in the way."

"Never, sir. Always happy to have you." The caretaker continued puttering around the kitchen. "Dinner will be ready in a few minutes, if you'd like to have a drink first."

"No, no. At least let me set the table or something." It felt strange to be eating dinner at what amounted to noon where he'd just been, but it was one of the things all portal-traveling mages had to get used to. "No arguments. I want to feel useful, at least."

Surreptitiously, he switched to magical sight to check out Aubrey's aura, scanning for anomalies. Not only didn't he see any, but the pleasant blue glow around him seemed a little brighter than usual. Almost *bouncy*. Stone relaxed a little more. That was not the aura of a man about to deliver bad news. In fact, he was beginning to suspect he knew what Aubrey's news was going to be. "Where's Selby?"

"Off today, sir. He's gone to London to spend time with some friends."

Stone wondered if Aubrey had asked him to make himself scarce, or arranged this little get-together on his night off, but didn't ask. At least the two of them were getting on—well, if the caretaker could be believed. Having the younger man around to take some of the strain off Aubrey had taken even more off Stone, so he was glad his decision to hire Selby had proven a good one.

"Really, sir—I've got everything under control here," Aubrey added.

Stone smiled. "That's your polite way to tell me to clear out until dinner's ready, isn't it?"

"I would never say such a thing, sir."

"You bloody well *would*. And I wouldn't have it any other way. Fine, then. I wanted to pick up a couple of things from my library anyway, so I'll do that. I'll try not to get too dusty in the meantime."

When he returned to the dining room fifteen minutes later with a book tucked under his arm, Susan had arrived. She and Aubrey had finished setting three places and laying out the serving plates on the long table. They stood on the other side, regarding him with twin happy, satisfied smiles.

"I'm not late, am I?"

"Not at all, Dr. Stone. Please, sit down." Susan indicated the spot at the head of the table.

Stone was now almost certain he knew what Aubrey's news would be, but he didn't plan to spoil it. "Smells wonderful. Please tell me you're not going to make me wait until dinner's over, though, before you tell me what's on your mind. My curiosity is killing me."

The two exchanged glances and settled into their chairs, Aubrey holding Susan's for her before seating himself.

To Stone's surprise, Aubrey looked suddenly nervous as they all passed around the roast beef and savory vegetables and served themselves. He deliberately focused on his plate, avoiding eye contact with the caretaker until he was ready to speak.

Finally, after a few bites and a long pull from his wineglass, Aubrey looked up. "Well, then, sir…" he began.

Susan, who was sitting next to him, reached over and clasped his hand, smiling encouragingly.

Stone couldn't take it anymore. He grinned. "Come on, Aubrey! Out with it!"

Aubrey exchanged a startled glance with Susan. "You…know already, don't you, sir?"

Finally! "You're not doing a very good job of keeping a secret."

Susan, apparently, had had enough of Aubrey's hesitation. Still holding his hand, her smile so wide it threatened to split her face, she said, "We've decided to get married, Dr. Stone."

Stone's grin widened too, as much from her words as from the look of consternation on Aubrey's face. "That is *brilliant.* Congratulations, you two. I'll admit I'd started to wonder why you've taken so long to get on with it."

Aubrey's expression went from apprehension to relief. "Thank you, sir. You're the first one we've told."

Stone tilted his head. "Did you think I wouldn't approve or something? Aubrey, come on! I can see how perfect you two are together. When's the happy occasion?"

"In a couple of months," Susan said. "We've still got some planning to do. We'll be having a little ceremony in the village, at our church—just a few family members and friends." She gave an almost girlish giggle. "A long engagement seems a bit silly at our ages."

Stone shook his head, still smiling. "I'm so happy for both of you. Will you be staying on here after at Aubrey's flat, or moving to

Susan's place in the village—or heading off to see the world together?"

"We haven't decided yet, sir." Aubrey started looking apprehensive again. "I want you to know, though, regardless of whether we live here or at Susan's place, it won't affect my duties here."

Stone snorted. "*Duties*. Aubrey, you should know by now that you can do as much or as little as you like around here—including nothing, if you'd rather spend time with Susan, pottering around your garden. Don't even worry about it. You should know by now that all I want is for you to be happy."

The old man's eyes glittered as crinkles appeared around the edges. "I know, sir. I know. But I *am* happy. I don't want to be anywhere else but here. And...I hope you'll stand with me at the ceremony."

Stone bowed his head, touched. "Just try to keep me away," he murmured. "I—" He paused as his phone buzzed in his pocket, indicating a text. As usual when traveling to England, he'd forgotten to swap it for one of his burners.

Aubrey must have spotted something, because he frowned. "Something wrong, sir?"

"No, no—just a text. It can wait."

"Go ahead," Susan said. "We don't mind."

"Sorry." He pulled out the phone and glanced at it.

The text was from Jason. *Got a few minutes? Got a new case, and it's a weird one.*

He tapped out a quick reply. *Busy now. Will call soon.*

Jason immediately replied with a thumbs-up emoji.

When he looked up at Aubrey, the old caretaker was smiling. "Something's come up, hasn't it, sir?"

"Am I so transparent?"

"I know you don't like me to remind you I've known you since you were born, but..."

"*Touché.*" He held up the phone. "That was Jason. He said he's got a 'weird' case he wants to talk about." He shot a sidelong look at Susan, wondering if Aubrey had clued her in yet. He still wondered how the old man explained Stone's frequent comings and goings if he hadn't told her anything, and supposed if the two of them were getting married, somebody would have to initiate her into the fold at some point soon.

Apparently, he hadn't done it yet, though. "You should…ring him, then, sir," Aubrey said.

It didn't escape Stone that he hadn't said *You should go home and talk to him.* "I probably should. But not before we finish this lovely dinner you've made. He can wait. I hope you don't mind, but I've got some business in London I've got to attend to this evening, so I won't be hanging about. You'll send me the details about the wedding and what you want me to do, right?"

"Of course, sir. And naturally, we hope Ian, Mr. and Ms. Thayer, and Mr. Thayer's wife can attend as well. I know it's short notice, but—"

"I'm sure they wouldn't miss it." Stone's mind was already on Jason's 'weird' case—it had to be weird indeed if his friend had come straight to him, since he usually tapped Verity to handle anything that required tracking rituals—but he nonetheless forced himself to remain present in the moment. Aubrey's happiness was more important than any case, weird or otherwise.

It wasn't easy for him to keep up light banter over the rest of the meal, but he thought he'd done a fairly good job. When the meal was over, he stood. "Thank you so much for everything. The food and the company were wonderful, and I'm serious that I couldn't be happier for you two lovebirds. Do you need any help with the washing-up?"

"Of course not, sir. Go." Aubrey made a shooing motion. "You're not fooling anyone, you know." Not only did he not look annoyed, he actually looked amused.

"I'm so glad you came, Dr. Stone," Susan said.

Stone chuckled. "Enough of that 'Dr. Stone' rubbish. If you're going to be part of the family, no more formality. Now, I'll be off so you two can have some time alone." He gave Aubrey a significant look. "Don't hesitate to call me if you need anything. I mean it."

"I promise, sir." Aubrey squeezed Susan's hand. "Now go, before you drive yourself mad with curiosity."

"Too late for madness, I'm afraid. Cheers, you two."

CHAPTER TWO

STONE FOUND JASON at his agency in San Jose.

"Hey, Al," he said from the doorway of his tiny office. "Thanks for coming. You had lunch yet?"

Stone winced. He'd eaten a bit too much of Aubrey's delicious cooking, and was still feeling it. "Er—yes, sort of."

"Hey, Doc," Gina called from her desk, waving without looking up from her computer screen.

"Mind coming with me, then?" Jason slung his messenger bag over his shoulder. "I'm starving. If you're okay with watching me eat…" He shot a glance toward Gina, his message clear: *this one isn't strictly on the books.*

"Yes, that's fine." Stone's curiosity about the "weird" case was growing by the minute, but if Jason didn't want to talk about it in front of Gina, he had to respect that.

As they headed off at a brisk pace down First Street, Stone hooked a thumb back toward the office. "You know, if she's going to keep working for you, it's probably best if we let her in on the secret."

Jason frowned. "You think she can handle it?"

"Do *you*?"

"I…don't know. I mean, I know she feeds you all those strange stories, and I know she suspects *something's* up because she asked me about it a couple times."

"What does she think?" Gina had asked Stone about it once too, and he'd managed to deflect her. He didn't know how much longer he could do that—or how much longer he wanted to.

"She knows what you teach, so I've been implying it's got to do with that. You know, gathering urban legends and stuff to add to your courses."

"Is she buying it?"

He shrugged. "Hard to say. Gina's smart—*really* smart. But she's also a skeptic."

"So, you think she wouldn't believe it if we told her."

"I do, actually—especially if you showed her, like you did with Stan. That's not what I'm worried about."

"What, then?"

Jason walked along in silence for a while before replying. "She's…her whole life is on the internet. She talks about it sometimes, when we're bullshitting during slow times. When she's not working, she hangs out online with her buddies, plays online games—she's pretty much a hermit on her off hours."

"So?"

"It's probably nothing. I mean, I trust her—I wouldn't have hired her if I didn't. But if you told her about the supernatural world and she couldn't keep it to herself…"

"I'm not that worried about it. Who's going to believe her? You know as well as I do that most mundanes aggressively deny even the evidence of their own senses. They want to *play* at the supernatural—watch their horror movies and television shows about sexy witches and vampires—but when faced with the real thing, they're having none of it."

"Yeah…" Jason didn't seem convinced.

"But…?"

"Hell, Al, I dunno. I know you don't spend much time online, but if something like that *did* get out, it would be all over the net. Even if people didn't believe it, they'd still be curious. At best, you'd have to deal with people bugging you, following you around, trying to spot you doing a trick."

Stone chuckled. "Well, I don't think we're there yet. There's no reason I can think of to tell Gina anything at present. But if that changes, I'm not worried. I already get followed around by nutters on occasion. It's part of my job. I'm used to it by now."

"Yeah. I guess. But don't forget, it's not just you. If anybody digs into your life, they'll turn up me and V too…and Amber." Jason paused in front of a sandwich shop before pushing open the door.

"Ah." Light dawned, and Stone nodded knowingly. "That's what you're worried about. You don't want any of my cast-off nutters bothering your wife."

Jason said nothing. Instead, he headed into the shop.

Stone followed him, content to wait. The place was crowded at lunchtime, with only a couple open tables. "I'll find us a spot while you order."

As he slipped through the crowd and claimed a tiny table under a collage of old license plates, Stone considered what his friend hadn't said. He didn't blame Jason—now that Amber was getting closer to her due date and decidedly showing, her husband's natural protective proclivities had ramped up to eleven. Never mind that her part-shifter heritage made her stronger, faster, and tougher than him, with heightened senses. Never mind that her mother-bear instincts meant she was even more formidable than usual these days. Jason acknowledged all that and wasn't intimidated by it, but that didn't mean he still didn't believe it was his job to keep her away from all harm whether she wanted him to or not. And that included potential nosy mundanes looking for supernatural dirt.

He watched Jason place his order and carry it back to the table, and decided to let the subject go for now unless his friend brought it up again. "So—what's this weird case you've got? And before you tell me, I've got a bit of news too." He leaned in closer and lowered his voice. "When I got your text, I was back home, at the Surrey house. Aubrey had an announcement."

Jason's eyes narrowed, and then a slow smile spread across his face. "Don't tell me—he and Susan are finally gonna get married."

"How did you guess?"

"I'm a detective, remember?" He took a bite of his sandwich and looked smug. "Plus you were smiling, which meant it couldn't be anything bad."

"Well, you got it in one. They don't have a date yet, but it will be soon—they said in the next couple of months, most likely. And they'd like you and Amber to be there, if you can manage it."

"We'll do our best. That's getting pretty close to the due date, but Amber's not worried." He shook his head in amazement. "She's not worried about anything. It's like this whole pregnancy process is no big deal to her."

"Probably a shifter thing."

"Yeah, probably. But it's a big deal to *me*." He took another bite. "Anyway, that's not why I texted you."

"Yes. You've got me intrigued. Tell me the details."

Jason paused for another bite and a swig of his root beer. "Okay, so we got this case a couple days ago. Missing guy."

"Okay…" Once again, Stone thought it odd that his friend would bring this to him. Amber was a wiz at hunting nearby people down, and Jason usually tapped Verity for anything requiring ritual tracking magic. He didn't say anything, but merely leaned back and waited.

"I know what you're thinking—why not ask V to help find him."

"That's what you usually do."

"I *did*. And she couldn't."

That perked Stone's attention. These days, Verity's tracking rituals were as good as his. The only thing she didn't have was his raw power, which sometimes made the difference. Especially if the target was behind wards or otherwise magically protected. "Indeed?" was all he said.

"Yeah. She had a good, solid tether object, but when she did the ritual yesterday, nothing came up."

"What do you mean by 'nothing'?"

"He's not dead, if that's what you're asking. She's sure of that. Well, pretty sure. But she said the results came back…weird."

There was that word again. It amused Stone sometimes that, even after all this time they'd known each other, Jason still wasn't entirely comfortable with the supernatural world. "Weird. A bit more specific explanation would be helpful."

"You can talk to her if you want, if you think it'll help. But all she said was that she was nearly positive he wasn't dead. The ritual got *something*, but she said it seemed to get confused."

"Like the target's protected, or out of her range?"

"She doesn't think it's out of her range. She said she knows what that feels like, and this wasn't it." He spread his hands. "I wish I could give you more detail."

Stone waved him off. "It's all right—I'll check with her when we're done here. Suppose you tell me about this person you're looking for."

"His name is Wayne Carter. Lives in Mountain View with his wife and three kids. He's the manager of a chain of local grocery stores."

"Okay. And you said he went missing a couple of days ago?"

"He's actually been gone for about a week. The wife reported it to the cops, but she doesn't think they're giving it the attention it deserves."

"Do you think she's right?"

Jason shrugged. "The cops are strapped, so she might be. That stuff you see on TV about a person needing to be missing a certain amount of time is bullshit, but what *isn't* bullshit is that the cops need to prioritize cases. And a guy with no enemies who leaves for work one morning and doesn't come home doesn't usually count as high priority."

"I assume they did the minimum—checked hospitals, morgues, accident reports—"

"They did, and so did we. Nobody matching his description."

"Did they find his vehicle?"

"Yeah. It was in the parking lot at his office. He did show up at work that day, but his admin said he left early. She didn't have any record of him having any appointments that afternoon, and she claims he didn't look stressed or say anything unexpected. In fact, she says he seemed unusually mellow."

Stone pondered. "Okay. I'll be honest with you, Jason—so far, I haven't heard anything that elevates this to 'weird.' It's not even all that unusual that Verity couldn't find him. He easily could have got out of her range in an afternoon. I know you said she doesn't think so, but tracking spells aren't foolproof. Do you have anything else?"

"Yeah. After his wife hired us, I took Amber and V to his office, since that's the last place he was seen."

"Amber's still working with you?" Stone didn't know much about pregnancy—it was, in all honesty, a topic he avoided—so he wasn't sure whether still working at six months was unusual.

Jason snorted. "Like I could stop her. Anyway, V didn't find anything—no sign of violence or agitation. But Amber did. She said he smelled odd."

"Odd? In what way? Fearful? Agitated?"

"No. We pulled the 'psychic' thing on the wife like we usually do, so we had a few items of his. Amber already had his scent, but she said the one at the office didn't quite smell the same." His brow furrowed. "She said he smelled…her words…'sexier.'"

Stone tilted his head. "What? What the hell does that mean?"

"She couldn't explain it, exactly. She said it was almost like he was putting out pheromones—but also that he didn't quite smell like himself, at least as far as the samples she had."

That *was* odd. As a part-bear shifter, Amber was highly sensitive to scents. "I assume she wasn't able to track him?"

"Nope. She said the scent was pretty strong and followed it out to the parking lot, but it petered out after that. That usually means he got in a vehicle of some kind."

"Hmm. So what do you want me to do? It sounds like you've got this fairly well in hand."

"I dunno—maybe try another tracking ritual? I know you've got more punch than V does. Maybe you can figure out where he's gone." Jason finished his sandwich. "I should probably head back—got some paperwork I need to deal with this afternoon. Anyway, will you do it?"

"Of course—you've got me intrigued now. I'll give Verity a call to see if I can get any other details from her."

"Yeah, magic consultation. I get it. Thanks, Al." He stood and grinned. "If this keeps up, I'm gonna have to put you on retainer."

"Eh, I'm easy to please. Just invite me over for a home-cooked dinner every now and then and I'm good to go."

CHAPTER THREE

STONE TEXTED VERITY as soon as he left the office. *Got a few minutes to discuss Jason's strange new case?*

Her reply came back almost instantly. *Sure. Can you come by the shop? We're doing inventory.*

Of course. Be there soon.

A couple months ago, Verity had gone into partnership with her friend, fellow Harpy, and alchemy mentor Hezzie. She'd used some of the funds she'd been saving from her work healing for magical tattoo artist Scuro to invest in the small shop, which had allowed them to afford a larger space on a funky side street in the Haight. The Harpies had helped move everything over last week, and Verity and Hezzie had been busily organizing the space ever since.

There weren't any ley lines near Jason's office, but one did run through the new shop—it was one of the reasons they'd chosen it. Stone left the car at the Encantada house and popped into an alley next door.

I'm outside, he texted. *Want to come out?*

No, you can come on in.

Are you sure? Hezzie was uncomfortable around men, and Stone respected that enough to avoid her when he could.

Yeah, it's fine. Hez is working on it.

Stone rounded the corner and paused to look up at the shop. The walls were sprayed with colorful, artistic graffiti. Above the door was a sign with *Sybil's Apothecary* painted in bright sky blue. When Stone shifted to magical sight, he immediately spotted the soft, pulsing glow around the magical sigils on either side of the name.

In the picture window to the left of the wooden door, Hezzie and Verity had arranged a tableau of "mystic-looking" objects: an iron cauldron, a rack of glass bottles with different-colored liquids, a few impressive-looking books, and a spread of tarot cards in front of a deep red velvet drape adorned with more subtle, gold-embroidered symbols. Aside from the sigils on the sign, none of it was truly magical, but it definitely had the appearance of it. Overall, the place looked much nicer than the tiny former shop, which had been narrow, dingy, and barely larger than a small bedroom.

A bell tinkled when Stone opened the door. Verity stood half-way up a rolling ladder, arranging vials and bottles on some built-in wooden shelving. She wore a dusty T-shirt and jeans, with a baseball cap perched on her head. Hezzie was nowhere to be seen.

"Hey, Doc." She hopped down from the ladder. "It's good to see you. I was hoping we'd have the place finished before you saw it, but we're getting there."

Stone looked around at the wooden display cases, floor-to-ceiling bookshelves, and curtained-off area in the back reserved for readings. A door at the back, presumably leading to the storeroom, was closed. "The place looks brilliant. You've done wonders with it." He'd offered to help them move when Verity had told him about it, but she'd said the Harpies had it under control.

"Thanks. We still have a lot of boxes in the back that need un-packing. I'm working out here while Hezzie gets the alchemy setup going in the back."

As if on cue, the storeroom door opened and Hezzie emerged. The slim, dark-haired witch stopped when she saw Stone, her whole body growing tense. "Hey," was all she said, though.

Stone noticed she wasn't glaring at him this time, which was an improvement. He wondered what Verity had meant by *she's working on it*. "Afternoon," he said in a neutral tone. "I was just telling Verity how good the place is looking."

"Thanks." Her plain face worked through several quick emotions, her large, dark eyes skating away from his gaze. "V, I'm goin' back to my place to grab some stuff. Be back in an hour or so. That cool?"

"Sure. I'll just keep doing what I'm doing."

Hezzie nodded curtly at Stone, then ducked back into the storeroom. A moment later, Stone heard the back door close.

"Sorry about that," Verity said. "I know she can be a little hard to deal with."

"It's quite all right. She seems…better, to be honest. At least this time I didn't get the feeling she wanted to gut me and leave me out back for the rats." There was no rancor in his tone. Verity had once told him Hezzie's reason for her distrust of men, and he had no desire to make the young woman's life any more stressful.

Verity nodded soberly, re-mounting the ladder. "She's been working with a therapist. She doesn't like it any more than you do, and she knows now that the shop's bigger, she can't just glare at the male customers until they leave. Bad for business."

"I see. Well, good for her. I hope it helps." He nodded toward the front door. "I've been meaning to ask you—who's 'Sybil'? Is that Hezzie's real name?"

Verity grinned. "Nope. Don't tell anybody, but she named the place after a cat she had when she was a little girl."

"Why does that not surprise me?"

"Yeah. We're actually thinking about getting a shop cat. There really are some rats around here, and some of our ingredients might attract them. Hey, hand me that box, will you?"

Stone levitated it to her. "I can help if you like."

"Nah, thanks. I got this. You wanted to talk about Jason's case?"

"I do. He told me you did a tracking ritual and got inconclusive results."

"Yeah. It was weird." She used magic to hold the box suspended next to her while she pulled out more bottles and lined them up along the upper shelf. "I'm certain he's not dead, and I'm pretty sure he's not far away. But something…I don't even know how to describe it. It's like I found him…but I didn't."

Stone frowned. "Not behind wards, or underground?"

"No, definitely not. I know how those feel." She finished placing the bottles, then dropped off the ladder and flattened the box, staring off into space. "Probably the closest thing I can equate it to—but not exactly—was the time we found the wild talent in Vegas. Remember him? The one who could completely change his appearance, his aura, everything?"

Stone remembered that all too well. "So you're saying you sensed two auras?"

"Not two. That's what I mean by 'not exactly'. It was more like I got a taste of the guy I was looking for, but he was different enough that the spell wouldn't latch on to him. Does that make sense?" Her brow furrowed. "Have you ever seen anything like it?"

"Not…really. That *is* unusual." He paced the shop, thinking. "You said you got something. Any sense of where he might be? Even something general?"

She gestured around the area. "Best I can do is that I think he's around here somewhere. In the San Francisco area, I mean. I showed the Harpies a photo and asked them to put the word out. Also my little mage group and Jason's mundane squad."

"Did you tell Blum?"

"Jason did. He said he'd do what he could, but it's not his case and they're pretty busy, so he can't spend much time on it."

Stone stopped his pacing and scanned the shelves Verity was stocking. Along with a collection of oils and essences, he spotted several items useful for alchemy rituals. "Sounds like you've done just about everything you can reasonably do."

"Yeah." She sounded discouraged. "I mean, Jason's still working the nonmagical end, of course, but there isn't much else I can do magically. You want to try a tracking ritual and see if there's something I missed?"

Stone shrugged. "I doubt there is, but I'm willing to give it a go if you think it will help."

"Couldn't hurt. We've got several tether objects from the guy's wife." She grinned. "Jason's agency is getting known for the psychic thing—it's why she picked him out of all the other places she could have called. So she was all ready with stuff when he asked."

"That's convenient." He scanned the shelves again. "Got any ritual materials here? I could pop home and collect some, if not."

She looked rueful. "Might not be a bad idea. I know we've got them *somewhere,* but—" She waved at the collection of boxes still needing to be unpacked. "—who knows exactly where."

"Not a problem. I—"

Verity's phone rang, with a snippet of a popular song. She held up a finger and answered. "Hey, Zel, what's up?" She listened a moment, her brow furrowing. "You sure?" Another pause. "Okay, can we meet her somewhere?"

Stone shot her a questioning glance, but she only frowned and shook her head.

"Yeah. Okay, that's cool. Can't go now anyway—gotta wait for Hez to get back. We'll head there, though. Doc's with me, so I'm gonna bring him along too if he wants to come. Thanks, Zel."

She ended the call and returned the phone to her back pocket, looking thoughtful. "That was…unexpected."

"What's that?"

"Remember I said I asked the Harpies to keep a lookout for our guy?"

"Did she find him?"

"No…but she found somebody who might have seen him."

"Brilliant. Who is it?"

"That's the strange part…or, I dunno, maybe it isn't. She's a friend of a friend of Zel's—a prostitute."

Stone tilted his head. "That's not terribly odd, is it? He certainly wouldn't be the first bloke who's deserted his family for the same reason."

"True…but Zel said the woman said there was something freaky going on. She wouldn't talk about it with her, but Zel said she's willing to talk to us as long as we don't bring the cops in."

"Now? Let's go."

"Not now. She's not available during the day. Zel says she's usually at a bar over on Polk Street after about nine." She glanced at her watch. "I've got a job with Scuro tonight at ten, but if we can find her there, we should talk to her."

"I'm happy to go along, but shouldn't you take Jason? It *is* his case, after all."

"True…but he can't come tonight. He's got some kind of class with Amber." She smiled. "My big brother's becoming positively domestic. It's cute."

"Ah." Stone kept forgetting all the things would-be parents had to do these days to prepare for their offspring's arrival. "Well, I wouldn't miss it. Do you still want me to do the ritual?"

"Might as well, I guess. I honestly don't think it's going to do much good, but we've got some time to kill. Tell you what—why don't you grab the stuff and go to my place to do the ritual? I've got a circle set up in the spare bedroom, and the wards won't stop you. I'll come home after we're done here, and we can go out later."

"Sounds like a plan." He narrowed his eyes. "Zel didn't say anything else about why this woman thought the situation was unusual?"

"Nope. Guess we're going to have to talk to her to find out." She laughed. "You're not fooling anybody, you know—you're dying to get your hooks into this mystery."

Stone didn't even bother to deny it.

CHAPTER FOUR

T HE BAR WAS ON A NARROW SIDE STREET in the Tenderloin district. This time of night, double-parked cars choked the area and people picked their way past the gauntlet of homeless people lined up in their tents and sleeping bags along the walls. A few scantily clad young women lounged in small groups near the corners, calmly watching the cars cruise by.

Verity scanned for a parking spot and grumbled, "I think we're gonna have to find a garage and walk."

"Probably a good idea, if we plan for the vehicle to be here when we return." Stone watched the traffic from the passenger seat. He liked San Francisco, but he didn't like the crowds.

"Too bad you couldn't find anything with your ritual. But I guess it makes me feel better in a way—now I'm sure I didn't screw up."

That afternoon, Stone had reached the same conclusions Verity had: after completing his own ritual, he was sure Wayne Carter was *somewhere* in the greater San Francisco area, but every time he tried to get a lock on the man, his aura had skated frustratingly away. It had almost felt as if the aura was deliberately hiding from him, but not in the manner of someone behind wards. He'd done scores of tracking rituals in his magical career, and none had come back like this one. After finally giving up, he'd taken copious notes and planned to send them to Eddie and Ward to see if they could make anything of them.

Verity had returned later bearing a tote full of alchemy supplies and two steaming bags from the Hmong restaurant up the street. They had lingered over the food while discussing the situation, then left early to make sure they had time to get to their destination by nine. It was a good thing, too, since they almost hadn't made it.

After circling the area twice, Verity found an open parking spot in a garage two blocks from their destination. They walked back, a disregarding spell helping them avoid attention from both the few homeless who were still awake and the streetwalkers.

The bar wasn't as seedy as Stone suspected it would be, given the character of the neighborhood. "Do you know anything more about this place?" he asked Verity.

"Just that it's a usual spot for prostitutes to pick up clients." She flashed him a sly smile. "So don't get too friendly with anybody. I'd hate to have to bail you out of jail."

"Not a problem. Not exactly my type."

Loud, bouncy dance music wafted into the street when they opened the door. The muscular, bored-looking man lounging just inside gave them both a quick look and then waved them inside. Stone blinked as aromas hit him: several clashing perfumes combined with the familiar, low-level funk of pot smoke.

Verity paused to look around. "Zel said she'd be at the bar, near the back. Her name's Nini. She's a tall black woman who likes red."

Stone scanned the bar, switching to magical sight. The auras were as bright and bouncy as the music, though he also wasn't surprised to detect the darker spots that probably indicated illness or substance abuse. Nobody seemed stressed or furtive; the overall vibe was relaxed, friendly, almost playful, with a strong overlay of sexual energy. A lot of people in here were hoping to get laid tonight.

Verity appeared to pick up on his thoughts. "I've seen places like this. The Harpies check them out occasionally—you know, to make sure nobody's hassling anybody. The cops usually leave them alone as long as nobody causes trouble. They—oh, wait. I think that's her over there." She didn't point, just nodded at the far end of the bar.

Stone studied the woman seated there, chatting with a friend. She did match the description, and he didn't see anybody else who did. Idly, he looked around for Wayne Carter, but wasn't surprised not to see him. "Shall we?"

"Why don't you get a table, and I'll see if she'll come talk to us."

The place was crowded, so it took Stone a while to find a spot. He watched Verity talk with the woman, then wave to the bartender. A moment later, the two of them approached Stone's table with fresh drinks. Verity also carried a Guinness. "Doc, this is Nini."

"Pleasure to meet you."

From behind Verity, Nini gave him a frank and obviously approving once-over. "Damn, girl. You didn't say your friend was that fine."

Verity grinned. "Slipped my mind, I guess."

They took seats across from him. "I can't talk long," Nini said, glancing back over toward the bar. "This is prime working time."

"Yeah, no problem. My friend said you might have seen somebody we're looking for." She nodded to Stone.

Taking his cue, he pulled out his phone and showed Nini the photo of Wayne Carter. "Do you recognize this man?"

Nini examined the photo. "Oh, yeah. For sure." Her brow furrowed. "He looks a little different, though."

"Different in what way?"

She thought about it. "I can't really say. He definitely looks like the same dude, but there's something…missing."

"Missing?" Verity leaned in for a look.

Nini continued to stare at the photo. "He's…how do I describe it? It's like he's *there,* but he's not *all* there."

This wasn't making any sense. "I still don't understand," Stone said. "Do you mean he had…what…some feature he didn't have before? Like facial hair, perhaps, or different clothes?"

"Naw." She shook her head emphatically. "Nothing like that. But this guy in the photo…he's just a guy, you know? Nothing special." A sly smile tugged at her bright-red lips. "Now the dude *we* were with…he was *definitely* somethin' special." She met Stone's gaze, and then her own shifted subtly downward toward his lap before coming back up. Her meaning about the way Wayne was "special" couldn't have been more obvious.

Stone remembered what Jason had said when they'd talked earlier—how Amber had said something about picking up Wayne Carter's scent, but *sexier*. "You're saying the man you saw was more attractive?"

"Oh, yeah. He didn't look any different, mind. It was something about the way he carried himself. You know, like he owned the world." Her gaze fuzzed out for a moment as she obviously replayed her time with Carter.

"You said 'we,'" Verity put in. "So it wasn't just you with him?"

Her smile widened. "Oh, no. There were three of us. And I will tell you, he had *no* trouble keeping us all satisfied, if you know what I mean."

Stone exchanged glances with Verity. "So…you had a foursome? And he…er…paid all of you?"

"For sure." She looked him over again. "We gave him a little discount, and not just 'cause he wanted three of us. Compared to the normal guys we party with, like I said, he was something special. He kept the party going all night long." She waggled her sculpted eyebrows suggestively. "You know, baby, I could give *you* a nice discount too, if you're looking for some fun."

"Er." Stone didn't want to admit that her blatant scrutiny was making him uncomfortable, so he indicated the phone on the table. "Do you have any idea where we might find him?"

"Why?" Her eyes narrowed. "He in trouble for something?"

"We…just want to talk to him," Verity said quickly. "No trouble."

"You sure? 'Cause I don't want to get nobody in trouble."

"Absolutely sure," Stone said. "He's a grown man, he can do what he likes."

"All we want to do is ask him a couple of questions," Verity added. "That's it."

Nini considered. "I'll put the word out and get back to you. From what I understand, he's been…let's say…sampling the offerings around town for the last few nights. Shouldn't be too hard to find him."

"Thank you." Stone prepared to rise. He wasn't sure what the etiquette was here, and didn't want to insult her by offering her money for helping them.

She seemed to pick up on his hesitation, because she waved him off. "You two don't owe me anything for this one." Her expression sobered as she turned to Verity. "A couple of you Harpies got a good friend of mine out of a bad situation a few weeks back. We don't forget stuff like that."

Outside, Stone walked along next to Verity on the way back to the garage. "You don't talk much these days about your Harpy outings."

She shrugged. "I don't go out with them that much lately, to be honest—not since Kyla and I broke up. But they do good work. I know that situation she was talking about. This guy was beating up working girls—had some kind of self-loathing thing going on, so he'd use their services and then 'punish' them after. A couple of the Harpies showed him what a bad idea that was. I think he ended up in the emergency room before getting turned over to the cops." She spoke matter-of-factly, with no regret.

"No doubt well deserved," he murmured. "But I'm still curious about what's going on with our Mr. Carter."

"Me too. It doesn't make a lot of sense. I mean, yeah, guys *do* sometimes do stuff like that, especially if they're having a mid-life crisis or something. But this whole 'sexier' thing...it's almost like he's got another personality. This might not be magic at all. He might just have had a mental breakdown."

"Possibly. That wouldn't be nearly as interesting, but it might be easier to treat."

"Yeah. Anyway, I'll call you if she gets back to me." They reached the garage, and she stopped to examine her black SUV for any signs of tampering. "You need me to drop you off anywhere? I have to get over to Scuro's if I don't want to be late."

"No, thanks. There's a ley line not far from here, so I can walk."

"Okay. Take care, and we'll talk tomorrow."

Stone watched her until the SUV disappeared around a corner, then raised his disregarding spell and set off at an unhurried pace toward the ley line. He kept an eye on his surroundings, but mostly he was deep in thought about what might be going on with Carter. He was already beginning to suspect Verity might be right: that this wasn't related to magic at all, which meant it ceased to be of much interest to him. Some random suburban dad deciding to ditch his family for a life of sybaritic excess in San Francisco was unfortunate, certainly, but it wasn't any of Stone's concern. Jason could take his case back, report his findings to Carter's wife, and that would be the end of it.

Except if that's true, why didn't he turn up to the tracking ritual?

That was the sticky part. Mundanes simply couldn't hide from magical tracking—not on purpose, anyway. If this was some kind of mundane wanderlust, it meant either somebody else was helping to conceal him (either with or without his knowledge), or he'd found a place to hide that was naturally resistant to magic. Both seemed unlikely. So what was—

A shadowy figure flashed across Stone's line of sight, half a block in front of him. It disappeared down a narrow alley to the left.

He stopped, all thoughts of Wayne Carter leaving his mind as he scanned the area for an imminent attack.

None came. A quick check with magical sight revealed no other signs of life around him, either on the street or along the roofs.

What had he seen? An animal? Whatever it was, it hadn't moved quite like a human. By the time he'd noticed it, it had already slipped out of his vision.

He picked up his pace, hurrying toward the side street. It was probably nothing—a big dog, maybe, or a homeless person running hunched over.

Homeless people don't move that fast, though…

Wouldn't hurt to check. Whatever it was, it hadn't appeared to notice him. It was probably long gone by now, ducking down the alley to avoid traffic. He'd been planning to turn left at the next side street anyway, so the alley would take him in the direction he was already heading.

He reached the alley, pausing at the edge to peer around the corner.

At first, he saw nothing out of the ordinary. The space was lined with rough tents, a few dumpsters, and trash pushed against the opposite wall, leaving a path barely wide enough for a single vehicle to pass.

A low, snuffling growl sounded from the opposite end.

Stone jerked his head up.

The figure was there, crouched over a huddled form on the ground. As he watched, it bent low. The form wasn't moving.

"Oi!" Stone called. "You down there! What are you doing?"

The figure tensed, rising from its crouch and looking toward him.

He was wrong: it *was* a human figure. He couldn't see any detail, but even from here he could tell it was a lanky male in a loose-fitting coat.

For a second, it hesitated. Then it leaped free of its prey and took off, moving low and fast.

Stone ran after it, even though he knew he was too far away to hope to catch it. As he did, he shifted to magical sight, hoping to at least get a look at its aura.

Bloody hell!

His shock slowed his headlong rush as his brain tried to make sense of what he'd just seen.

The figure had appeared entirely human to mundane sight—but his magical senses had revealed something else entirely.

As it disappeared around the corner and out of view, Stone stared at the last place he'd seen it—fur-covered, hunched, with large, clawed hands that had looked more like paws.

CHAPTER FIVE

STONE'S SHOCKED IMMOBILITY didn't last long. He launched himself forward again, running until he reached the end of the alley. He pulled up his shield as he went, in case the furred creature was lying in ambush around the corner, ready to leap upon him.

When he skidded to a stop at the corner and peered around, though, he saw nothing but a dark street and the far-off headlights of a car crossing at the next intersection.

No sign of a fast-moving, furry creature he'd sworn had looked like a human to normal sight.

A soft groan from behind him broke into his thoughts. With one more glance to make sure the creature wasn't preparing to pounce, he hurried back to the fallen figure.

As he'd suspected, it was a homeless man. His ragged coat lay open, revealing bloody slashes across his thin chest. His eyes were wide open, terrified, his harsh, gasping breathing the only sound in the alley. If anybody else was in the other tents, they were either asleep, drunk, or terrified to poke their heads out to see what was going on.

Stone crouched next to him and put a hand on his shoulder. "It's all right. It's gone. Let me help you."

The man raised a shaky hand and grasped Stone's arm with a surprisingly strong grip, raising a strong BO-and-unwashed-clothes funk. "It was crazy, man… Guy just started…like…*attacking* me."

"Shh…" Stone looked the man over, shifting back to magical sight. Aside from the slashes on his chest, which showed up as angry red blots on his muddy green aura, there didn't seem to be any other injuries. But the slashes looked bad enough, and Stone had no idea what had been on the furred creature's claws, or hands, or whatever. In the faint light of the streetlamp, the man looked pale and sweaty. Clearly, he needed medical attention. He pulled out his phone. "Let me call someone for you…"

The grip tightened. "No, man. Ain't nobody gonna come."

"Of course they will. I—"

By now, a few of the tent flaps were tentatively cracking open.

The man's breath hitched again. "If the ambulance…comes at all, it'll take its sweet time."

"They got a clinic two blocks over," another man called in a raspy voice from the dimness of one of the tents. He didn't seem inclined to come out, though.

Stone glanced at the tent, then back down at the man. The bleeding wasn't stopping; if something wasn't done about it soon, he could be in trouble. "Let me see if I can do something. Lie still."

He pulled the man's dirty shirt up to reveal his pale chest. More blood stained the sparse gray hair. He wished Verity were still with him, since her healing skills were miles better than his, but wishing was pointless. He was here, and he was all the old guy had.

With another quick look at the alley's end to make sure the creature hadn't decided to return, he shifted to magical sight and focused on the old man's wounds. Summoning the healing energy had never been easy for him, but at least the injury wasn't complex. These kinds of wounds were the simplest to heal—much easier than things like internal injuries or deeper slashes. He could do this if he kept his focus. But that was hard to do when half-expecting to get jumped by either the creature or the homeless guy's friends at any point.

Still, he managed. By concentrating hard and trying to remember all the tips Verity had given him, he formed the golden energy around the slashes, reminding himself not to force it. That was the most important thing Verity had taught him: the body wanted to be in harmony, and it was the healer's job to direct the energy only as much as necessary. Stone, who was used to shaping magic with the force of his will, had a hard time with that lesson.

Carefully, he maintained focus sufficiently to sustain the energy, and watched it as it flowed around the three slashes, rebuilding tissue and knitting the edges together.

It wasn't a great job—the guy would have scars, and there was nothing he could do about that—but at least it didn't seem he would die tonight. Unbidden, the long-ago memories of his failed healing attempts returned to him: Edwina Mortenson, her lower body crushed by rock, and Douglas Phelps, who'd been ravaged by ghouls. He'd made his peace with those, knowing even the best healers probably couldn't have saved either of them, but it was nice to have a win on his balance sheet every now and then, too.

The old man settled back, obviously still frightened but in less pain now.

"How do you feel?" Once more, Stone scanned the area. A few more people were peering out from behind their tent flaps, but no one had been brave enough to venture out. The creature was nowhere to be seen. Stone relaxed, if only a little. If it hadn't come back by now, it probably wasn't going to.

Unless it went to find friends...

He put that thought out of his mind and focused on the man, who was struggling to sit up.

"What did you do?" The old guy fixed Stone with a wide-eyed stare. He raised one hand to touch his chest. His shirt had dropped back down to cover it, torn and bloodstained, but he hesitantly prodded it in wonder. "It don't hurt no more."

Stone didn't answer. "Can you tell me what happened to you? What was that thing? Did you get a look at it before it attacked you?"

The man looked like he was going to push his question, but then shrugged. "I went out to take a piss." He pointed farther down the alley, away from the tents. "I was on my way back when that dude jumped me."

Stone narrowed his eyes. "Dude" didn't seem like the kind of definition anyone would use to describe a fur-covered creature with long claws. "Did you get a look at him?" he repeated. "Did you see his face at all?"

The man blinked a couple times, shaking his head like he was trying to clear cobwebs. "Not really. He was…a dude. White guy, I think, or maybe Mexican. Not much light, y'know? Young. Dark hair, scraggly beard. I wasn't exactly payin' attention, y'know, when he was tryin' to rip me apart." He looked past Stone, as if trying to remember something, and touched his chest again. "Musta had a knife or somethin'."

"A knife." Stone sat back on his haunches, recalling that when he'd first seen the creature, he'd looked human. It was only when he'd switched to magical sight that the fur and claws had appeared. Could it have been an illusion? Maybe the attacker *had* had a knife, or held metal claws between his fingers, and the wolf-like appearance had been nothing but a guise.

But why use an illusion that only shows up to senses almost nobody has?

He stood, still pondering. It didn't seem that there was much more he could do here. "Do you want me to call the police?"

The man shook his head quickly, fear showing on his face. "No, man. No cops."

Stone almost asked, *What if he comes back?* but didn't. The homeless generally didn't have a good relationship with the police—he remembered that from when he'd worked with the

Forgotten. Even if he called them to the scene, it was just as likely they'd either not show up at all, or spend more time hassling the people in the tents, than they'd try to solve the crime. He made a mental note to give Leo Blum a call.

"All right, then. You should probably get that looked at, just to be safe."

"I'll make sure he goes to the clinic t'morrow," said a voice.

Stone turned to find a stocky, older woman in sweatpants and a shapeless coat standing behind them. Her expression was wary but firm.

"Don't worry," she said, glaring at the man. "I'll make 'im go."

Satisfied, Stone left his patient in the woman's hands and hurried away. He kept a close watch on his surroundings for the rest of the way back to the ley line, but no other strange figures appeared.

CHAPTER SIX

STONE HAD TRIED TO CALL LEO BLUM as soon as he arrived home, but got voicemail.

The detective returned his call at eight the following morning, rousing him from a sound sleep. "What's this about some homeless guy getting beat up, and why are you telling me?"

Stone struggled to get his thoughts in order, sitting up in bed and tipping Raider off his chest. "Good morning to you too, Detective."

"Yeah, sorry. It's been crazy up here lately. I was on a stakeout when you called, and I haven't slept yet. I hate to sound callous, but one homeless guy gettin' rolled isn't high on my priority list—and I woulda thought it wouldn't be on yours, either."

"Normally that would be true. But then again, homeless people aren't usually attacked by people—or creatures, not sure which yet—that look like animals to magical sight."

There was a long pause on the other end, followed by a loud exhalation. "Shit."

Stone waited.

"That's just what I need right now. I got enough regular crime without bringin' in the magical kind, too."

"More than usual?" He swung out of bed and shrugged his robe on over his shorts.

"Oh, yeah. Lots more."

"What sort?"

"You name it. Burglaries, muggings, carjackings, sexual assaults, people freaking out in public places…all in the past month. I mean, yeah, it's summer and it's hot, which always leads to an uptick in crimes, but this is…I don't know what the hell it is, to be honest."

Stone digested that information as he padded downstairs, trying to avoid getting tripped by the insistent Raider. "So, no one has any theories?"

"Nope. Might just be a fluke. It does happen. But now you say we're adding magical stuff to the mix. Forgive me if I don't welcome that with open arms. How do you even know about this?"

"I was in San Francisco last night, helping Verity investigate a lead for one of Jason's cases." He described the situation, leaving out only the part about the ley line.

"Fuck." Blum sighed loudly. "What happened to the homeless guy?"

"He didn't want me to call anybody, so I used a little magical healing on him. He'll be all right."

"And obviously you didn't go after the attacker."

"He was too fast. By the time I had the victim stabilized, he was long gone."

"Okay. Can you describe him?"

"Not really. I didn't get close. When I initially saw him, he looked like a thin bloke in a long coat. The homeless man said he was either white or Mexican, with dark hair and a scraggly beard."

"That narrows it down," Blum said sourly. "But you said he looked different to magical sight?"

"Yes. He looked…furry."

"Furry."

"It was hard to miss. And his hands were bigger…more like paws, with claws."

"Come on, Stone—it sounds like you're telling me the guy got attacked by a werewolf or something." He paused. "*Are* there werewolves?"

"There are shapeshifters. I won't say there aren't werewolves, but I will say there hasn't been a credible report of any for a long time."

"So you don't know any socially or anything."

"Werewolves? No."

He sighed again. Stone got the impression he'd been doing a lot of that lately. "Okay. Well, thanks for the update. Honestly, I doubt I'll do much about it unless the guy turns up again, especially since your homeless guy doesn't want to make an official report. Keep me updated if you hear anything else."

"I will. And I'd appreciate it if you could do the same, at least about anything that might be supernatural in origin."

"You're the number-one guy on my Rolodex for weird shit, Stone."

One of the perks of Stone's elevated position in the Occult Studies department was that he didn't need to teach summer classes if he didn't want to. He'd signed up to present a couple of evening seminars, but aside from that his time was his own. Between renewing his work on his basement portal, Jason's case, and the bizarre attack, he was glad he didn't have to try fitting regular classes in as well.

Jason called later that morning, with Verity already conferenced in. She and Stone updated him on what they'd found regarding Wayne Carter.

"That's not what I expected," he said. "It sounds like the guy isn't even trying to hide."

"Yeah," Verity said. "From what Nini said, he's up there banging anything female and willing. You didn't see her face when she was talking about him. I could *see* her getting horny just thinking about him. Which…I know this is gonna sound kind of rude…doesn't make a lot of sense. I mean, you saw his photo, right? He's not exactly a movie star."

Stone pictured Carter's image: middle-aged, a little beer gut, with a receding hairline. Certainly not the type who could light up a bunch of jaded prostitutes who'd seen it all.

"My theory is that he had some kind of mental breakdown," Verity said. "Kind of a super-sized midlife crisis that changed his personality."

Jason made a noncommittal *hmm* noise. "I dunno. I talked to his wife yesterday afternoon, after you called me with the info about the prostitute. I asked if she'd ever suspected him of cheating on her. She said no. She said they got along fine. That he'd always had a higher libido than she did, but if he was cheating, he was being really discreet about it."

"What about drinking?" Stone asked. "Drugs?"

"She didn't mention them when I asked if there was anything I should know about him."

"Maybe we'll get more tonight, if we hear back from Nini," Verity said. "Maybe we can catch him in the act."

"I can't go up to San Francisco tonight," Jason's voice held a combination of apology and a little defensiveness. "Got another thing with Amber."

"Don't worry about it. Doc and I can handle it."

"Thanks, V. I owe you for this. You too, Al."

"Glad to help," Stone said. "You know I'm intrigued, although I'm not convinced this one has anything to do with magic. Unlike the *other* situation I encountered last night."

"Huh?" Both Jason and Verity sounded confused.

He quickly gave them a summary of his adventures with the homeless man and the furry attacker.

"Holy shit," Jason breathed. "That's freaky. You think it's a shifter?"

"If it is, it's an odd one. They don't normally show up only to magical sight."

"I'll ask Amber about it. Maybe she knows something."

"Good idea. And I think I'll pop by Kolinsky's place to see if he's back yet, and send a note to Eddie and Ward. *Somebody's* bound to have heard of this."

Kolinsky turned out to be a dead end. The sign was still on his shop door, and didn't appear to have been disturbed since Stone had come by last. He didn't bother going in. If the dragon didn't want to be bothered, this problem still didn't seem to be big enough to risk summoning him for.

If he'd even show up at all. Stone was beginning to suspect he might not.

By that evening, he still hadn't heard anything back from Eddie and Ward, beyond a quick message from Eddie acknowledging they'd received his note and would investigate as soon as possible.

He'd split the rest of the day between going up to the University gym, doing some last-minute research for a paper he was preparing to submit, and working on the new portal circle in the basement. He wasn't very far along with it yet, but he'd found it was moving faster this time.

When Verity called at nearly ten-thirty, he was crouched on the floor, carefully sketching out a series of sigils. "I didn't think you'd call tonight."

Her voice sounded wry. "People don't usually visit prostitutes at seven p.m., Doc. Not unless it's, like, the early-bird special or something."

Stone pictured a series of old men with canes and walkers, shuffling past a buffet of comely, scantily clad women. "Not really my area of expertise. Have you got something?"

"Yeah. Nini called back just now. She said one of her friends texted her—he's at a party with her and several other women. She says if we can get there soon, he'll probably still be there."

"Brilliant. Where?"

"The Razor's Edge. It's a dance club with a lot of that kind of action." She gave him an address. "How soon can you get there?"

He didn't have all the ley-line locations in San Francisco memorized, but he didn't think it was far. "Give me twenty minutes."

"Okay. There's a Peet's up the street. I'll meet you there. Dress for a party, so we'll blend in."

Stone was in luck this time: the nearest ley line crossed only a block from the Razor's Edge. He was waiting for her at the front of the coffee shop when she hurried in.

"Sorry." She sounded breathless. "Traffic was crap as usual. I sure wish you could teach me whatever you do to get places so fast." She wore a black, form-fitting dress and stilettos, and looked his stylish suit over approvingly.

"So do I."

Their destination was on the other side of the street: a trendy-looking lounge with a futuristic, cyberpunk theme. Verity touched

Stone's arm as they walked. "So, I talked to Jason today, before he left for his thing. He said we shouldn't confront Wayne."

"No?"

She shook her head. "All he was hired to do was find him. Technically, he's not doing anything wrong. Well, I mean, having sex with prostitutes is illegal, but you know as well as I do the cops here don't even bother enforcing it unless somebody gets hurt or cheated. He's a grown man, so what he does is none of our business. All Jason's supposed to do is report back to his wife if he finds anything."

"So we can't even talk to him?"

"Probably shouldn't. I'll snap a couple photos for proof, but that's it."

"All right. Fair enough." Stone didn't like it, but this wasn't his show. He was only helping a friend. "If there's nothing supernatural going on, I don't even care. Whether some bloke has something—or a few somethings—on the side is his business, not mine."

They crossed the street to the lounge. The beefy guy outside the door looked a lot like the one from before, except better dressed. He eyed Stone and Verity. "Private party. Got an invitation?"

"Right here." Stone handed him a hundred-dollar bill.

"Enjoy your evening." The man didn't even miss a beat as he palmed the money.

Verity grinned as they headed inside. "I'd really love to know how you'd cope with situations like that if you weren't loaded."

"Easy. Magic. Or natural charm."

Her grin widened. "Humility, too."

A short hallway lined with concert posters gave way to an open area dotted with semicircular, neon-edged booths on three different levels surrounding a spacious dance floor crowded with young people, both the men and the women dressed in skimpy, trendy styles. Loud, pounding music boomed through the room, and strips of colorful kinetic neon chased each other around the walls mimicking circuit-board designs. There didn't appear to be a band; instead, three strippers—two women and a man—gyrated on a stage beyond the dance floor, lip-syncing to the music while grinding suggestively against each other.

Stone touched Verity's arm and pointed discreetly. "Not hard to see what sort of party this is…"

All around them, couples and groups were all over each other in the booths, not seeming to care who saw them. As far as Stone could tell none of them were actually having sex, but in a few cases it didn't seem like it would take much to tip them over the edge.

"Not surprised." Verity was scanning the place too. "That does seem like what Wayne is into now. Do you see him?"

Stone switched to magical sight, though he didn't think it would do much good. This many people in a heightened emotional state meant the auras blazed brightly, joining together into a solid wall of color that made it difficult to pick out individuals. He switched back, shaking his head. "Can't see a bloody thing magically, but almost everyone in here looks a lot younger than Wayne."

"Yeah…" She moved in further, gracefully pivoting out of the way when partygoers approached her, obviously intending to invite her into one of their little sex pods. "Might work in our favor, though."

"How?" Stone hurried to keep up with her. He was getting his own share of attention, and did his best to project lack of interest. He liked sex as well as the next person, but didn't consider it a spectator sport.

"Means he'll stand out. We just have to figure out where he is. We—wait. Look!" She pointed up.

Stone glanced up. He hadn't noticed the shadowy alcoves beyond the booths on the second and third levels, but now that she pointed them out, he could see two of them on each level, for a total of four. Perhaps spots where those who wanted a more discreet experience could go?

"Should we split up?" Verity asked.

"I'd rather not, to be honest. If he's here, he's probably not going anywhere for a while."

She nodded and led the way to a set of clear steps ascending to the second level. It was too loud for any sustained discussion, so Stone followed her in silence. The walkways were packed with more people, holding drinks and leaning against the railing to watch the dancers and strippers below.

He touched her arm again. "Let's use disregarding spells, so we don't look like voyeurs."

In answer, she settled a spell around herself. She didn't look any different to Stone, but the others would see her as merely part of the scenery, just another horny partygoer. He cast his own spell and caught up with her.

The alcoves on the second level were a bust. Stone's guess about their function had been correct: instead of booths, the spaces included wide half-bed, half-couches surrounded by small tables for drinks. Several flat screens along the walls projected music videos, live feeds of the strippers below, and pornographic images, and speakers boomed the music at deafening volume. Bodies writhed—in both cases at least four—oblivious to anything going on outside. If they even noticed they were being watched, they clearly didn't care.

Stone hurried quickly past, and noticed Verity was doing the same thing. The participants could get up to anything they wanted to as long as everybody was consenting, but that didn't mean he wanted to watch. He felt like a pervert even pausing long enough to make sure Wayne Carter wasn't one of the writhing bodies.

Verity pointed up, heading for the stairs to the third level. It was getting warmer up here, and Stone got a brief mental image of

Dante's *Inferno*. All they needed were a few more circles. They certainly had Lust covered, anyway.

They reached the first third-floor alcove at the same time. Stone renewed his disregarding spell and paused at the edge.

This time, there were six people in the space, all of them lying in a jumble of naked arms and legs on a bed-couch the same size as the ones down below. The bodies were close enough together that Stone had to lean in closer to pick out the individual forms.

He didn't have any trouble picking out Wayne Carter in the middle of it all, though. He lay in the middle of the other five participants—two men and three women—a wide smile on his face. He looked like he was having the time of his life, with no hint of shame or hesitation. Nobody seemed to mind his paunchy, middle-aged form in the middle of all the young, taut bodies. In fact, he seemed to be the center of everybody's attention.

Stone and Verity exchanged glances.

"That is…not what I was expecting," Stone said.

"Yeah…no."

"You said we didn't have to engage him, right?" he asked hopefully. He had no interest in chatting with this man while he was very much *in flagrante delicto*. Or, really, any other time.

"Yeah. I feel weird about taking a photo, though. All these other people…"

A barely-dressed couple slipped past them, paying them no attention as they continued on their way to the other alcove.

"Just…make it quick, and use an illusion to hide the camera. Jason can obscure the others' faces before he sends it on to Mr. Carter's wife."

She nodded reluctantly and pulled her phone from her small bag, moving into position to get the shot.

While he waited, Stone idly shifted to magical sight, hoping he'd feel less like a peeping Tom if he watched the auras instead of the bodies.

What he saw made him stagger back a step and nearly drop his disregarding spell. "Bloody *hell,*" he muttered.

Verity had just finished snapping her photo and tucking her phone back in her bag. "What?"

"Verity…look at them with magical sight."

She narrowed her eyes at him in confusion, but turned back to the scene. An instant later, her whole body went stiff. "What the…hell?"

Stone hadn't shifted back to mundane senses yet. Any reluctance he'd had before about staring at the group in the alcove had dropped away.

Wayne Carter no longer looked like a middle-aged suburban husband and father in the middle of an orgy.

Instead, his whole image had transformed. A pelt of lush, reddish fur now covered his chest and forearms. His salt-and-pepper hair, which had been receding from a high forehead, had gone thick and shoulder-length, the same reddish color as the rest, and he now had a neatly-trimmed, pointed beard. As Stone leaned in for a better look, he spotted two small horns poking up through the hair above Carter's forehead. The rest of his body was obscured by the other people writhing on top of him, but a pair of cloven hooves stuck out from beneath a young woman's bare legs.

"What…*is* that?" Verity hissed into his ear.

Stone hesitated, not wanting to say it aloud. But the evidence of his senses was too hard to ignore. "If I had to speculate, I'd say…it's a satyr."

Her fuzzed expression cleared as she took another look. "But…how can that be? He looks totally normal to mundane sight."

Stone didn't answer, because he'd just noticed that Carter was looking straight at him. The man looked startled, his expression of mellow pleasure shifting to one of confusion and a little fear.

"Doc?"

Stone still didn't acknowledge Verity's presence. He wondered if Carter was about to jump up and run, and prepared to stop him if he did.

He didn't, though. Instead, he murmured something to his orgy-mates. They looked disappointed, but began disengaging their tangled limbs and rolling away, allowing him space to get up.

"Uh…" Verity said in Stone's ear.

Stone knew exactly what she was commenting on. He'd switched back to magical sight, and when the others had rolled off Carter, they'd revealed the rest of his naked body to the world.

He did indeed have cloven hooves, along with legs covered with a thicker pelt of the same red hair on his head and torso. With no apparent shame or modesty, he also displayed an endowment that would put porn stars to shame.

"Guess we know what the ladies are seeing in him…" Verity murmured from behind Stone. "Except…how can they even *see* it?"

The other orgy participants, sensing their good time was about to be interrupted, grabbed their minimal clothing and their drinks and drifted out, calling good-natured farewells to Carter.

When they were all gone, the man sat up, unselfconsciously pulling a thin sheet over his lap. When he spoke, his voice was pleasant and melodious, but held the unmistakable edge of confusion. "You…can see me, can't you? I mean, *really* see me."

Stone nodded. "Pleased to make your acquaintance, Mr. Carter."

CHAPTER SEVEN

C ARTER DIDN'T LOOK AT ALL SURPRISED that they knew who he was. Stone wasn't sure how he'd take the revelation that someone else could see his satyr guise—but out of all his possible guesses, relief wouldn't have been at the top.

Carter's shoulders slumped and his expression relaxed a little, but then turned suspicious again. "But…who are you? Why are you here?"

"I think we should have a little chat, don't you, Mr. Carter?"

The man looked longingly out the front of his alcove as if already missing his orgy-mates. He let out a long, resigned sigh. "Yeah. I guess we should. Give me a minute to get dressed." He tossed the sheet aside and swung his legs around so he could stand.

Stone focused on the screen showing a music video. Next to him, Verity turned to watch the dancers down below.

"Okay, let's go."

Carter now wore slacks and a button-down shirt, which covered him even though they seemed designed to fit his human form. When Stone switched back to normal sight, he was looking at the same chubby, middle-aged dad in their photo. He shot a quick glance at Verity, nodding for her to follow them while he led the way. He didn't think Carter would make a break for it, but he wasn't taking chances. At this point, this was no longer about a cheating husband running away from his wife. He didn't give a damn about that anymore.

As they headed downstairs, several of the party-goers—both female and male—flashed Carter salacious glances. Stone didn't turn back to see if he returned them, but continued to wonder if they could somehow see him even without magical sight. He remembered again what Amber had said about his scent seeming "sexier." Maybe it wasn't his appearance, but some kind of pheromones. He briefly entertained the idea that Carter could be like Elias Richter's late henchmen, Lane and Hugo—specialized beings designed to take sustenance from sexual energy, or more specifically, forced seduction and rape. But Wayne Carter didn't seem like he wanted to rape anyone, and while whatever pheromones he was emitting seemed to make him more sexually attractive to the people around him, everybody seemed consenting. Stone's gut told him they weren't dealing with the same kind of creature.

It was only when they reached an empty table near the wall that he remembered the situation from the previous night—the man, or creature, who'd attacked the homeless man. *He* had appeared different to magical sight, too.

Was he looking at a similar situation? But Carter didn't seem to want to attack anybody, either. He was wary but mellow, smelling of booze and pot smoke, eyeing the nearly-nude dancers with undisguised appreciation. Very clearly, all he wanted to do was have a good time.

"You...can really see me?" he asked Stone when they'd all sat. He still appeared skeptical.

"We both can," Verity told him.

"But...how?" His gaze shifted away from the strippers and back to them. "Nobody else can. It's crazy. I thought I was losing my mind at first. I thought everybody could, but they all just...ignore it." He gestured at his body, then his eyes narrowed. "What *are* you doing here? You're not planning to arrest me or anything, are you?"

"Farthest thing from our minds," Stone said. "I'm more inter-ested in your story. How long have you been...this way? When did you discover it?"

But Carter wasn't to be swayed. "Tell me who sent you. You know my name. I didn't use my real name anywhere up here. Did my wife send you?"

"Sort of," Verity said.

Stone tensed again, preparing to grab him if he tried to run.

Instead, his shoulders slumped. "I should've known she would. She doesn't deserve this. But I can't do it anymore."

"Deserve what?" Stone leaned closer. The pounding beat of the music made it hard to talk in here without yelling. "Do what anymore?"

Carter stared into the remains of his drink, swirling it around in silence.

"Mr. Carter?"

"Deserve what I'm doing to her." He tossed back the remainder of the drink and slammed the glass down on the table. "Don't you think I know it? I don't know what the fuck to do."

"Maybe you should go home and talk to her," Verity said.

"Talk to her." He shook his head. "And tell her what? That I've turned into some kind of...*thing*, and all I want to do now is drink and have sex and party? Yeah, that'll go over great." He looked up. "You said she 'sort of' sent you. What does that even mean?"

"We're associates of a private investigator she hired to find you when you disappeared," Stone said.

"She's worried about you," Verity added. "She thinks you were hurt or something."

"Yeah. Not surprised. Believe me, I didn't *want* to do it. But I can't go back now. I just...*can't.*"

"Why not?"

He spread his hands, indicating himself again. "Look at me, since you can apparently see me. I'm...different now. I have different priorities. I'm not proud of it. I kinda feel like shit about it, actually. But…"

"But what?" Stone watched him closely, shifting back to magical sight. His bearded satyr face looked as conflicted and frustrated as his human one had.

Carter's mouth worked, as if he wanted to say something but couldn't get it out. "Look. Like I said, I'm not proud of this. You're gonna think I'm an asshole for saying it. But…ever since I woke up and saw *this* in my bathroom mirror a few days ago, I…don't *care* anymore."

"Don't care about what?" Verity asked.

He bowed his head. "About my old life. It almost seems like it was somebody else's life, you know? My wife, my kids…it's like they're not even connected to me anymore. I don't feel…*anything* for them. Except maybe resentment. Like they're holding me back from what I really want to do."

"Which is carouse, have sex, and stay drunk off your arse," Stone said.

He nodded. "Yeah. I'm probably going to leave the area soon. Maybe leave the country, if I can. We've got good savings—my wife and kids will be okay."

Verity stared at him. "They're not going to be *okay,* Mr. Carter. Especially if you just…take off on them, without telling them where you went."

His face twisted. "What else am I supposed to do? Go back home and tell her I've turned into a…I don't even know what the hell to *call* this thing."

"Looks like a satyr to me," Stone said.

"A…*satyr*?" Carter glared at him. "What even *is* that? Wait…isn't that like some kind of mythological creature?"

"It is. Hairy-legged, cloven-hooved, with horns and…er…other impressive endowments. Known for being hedonists with a particular love for sex and drinking."

Carter had been watching him intently as he spoke. He looked down at himself. "That…does sound like me." Leaning back with an easy, lazy smile, he added, "Nice to have a name for it. At first, like I said, I was pretty freaked out. I mean, imagine getting up in the morning to brush your teeth and seeing *this* in the mirror. But it wasn't long before my feelings changed. It's hard to explain, but it was almost like I finally saw the light. I started feeling like this was what I'm *supposed* to be. You know, living the truth that's always been there. Does that make any sense?"

Stone exchanged glances with Verity. "I'm not sure, Mr. Carter. This is a new one to me."

"*You* don't seem very freaked out. How can you even see me? Nobody else seems to be able to. Except that one guy, a couple nights ago. The one that looked like some kind of weird ogre or something."

"One guy?" Stone leaned in closer. "Where?"

Carter shrugged. "On the light rail. We only saw each other for a second. I was getting off, and he was getting on a different car, and the doors closed before we could do anything else."

Stone pondered, going over every magical creature he'd encountered, either in person or in his research. There weren't many around these days. The prevailing theories among mages were split about fifty-fifty between the idea that modern-day magic wasn't strong enough to support them, and the one that they'd never existed at all and were merely twisted versions of naturally-occurring phenomena. Most of those he'd dealt with had been extradimensional entities like demons, but he'd also met ghouls, shifters, echoes, and a few magical animals.

And dragons, he reminded himself. *Mustn't forget about them.*

Even though, lately, they seemed to have forgotten about *him.*

The part that was throwing him, though, was that he'd never met any sort of magical creature that only looked like one to magical sight. Many of them could hide themselves or conceal their true natures when they chose to, and some gave clues when examined magically, but this was different.

The fact that he'd now seen two of the same sort of being in the past couple of days was pinging all kinds of warning bells on his arcane radar.

"I've got some questions for you, Mr. Carter," he said abruptly.

"Sorry, man—I've got to go." He pointed up toward the elevated alcoves. "I've got things to do and people to party with."

"They'll have to wait. I'm sorry, but I need these answers."

He glared. "Who the hell *are* you, anyway?" He pointed at Verity. "She said you guys were working for a detective my wife hired to find me. So, okay, you found me. Go back and tell her whatever you want. Tell her to keep the money, and I won't contest a divorce. She makes more money than I do anyway. Tell her I'm sorry, but I've…moved on."

Verity started to say something, but Stone held up a hand. "This has long ago ceased to have anything to do with your wife. I don't give a damn about your domestic situation. I want to know how this happened to you. Tell me everything."

"Doc—"

"I'm sorry, Verity, but this is important."

"Listen," Carter said, "it's been nice chatting with you, but I'm out of here." He started to rise.

With a subtle flick of magic, Stone shoved him back to his seat and held him there. "The sooner you start talking, Mr. Carter, the sooner you can get back to your fun."

Carter's eyes bugged out. He looked at Stone with new fear. "What…*are* you?"

"Let's just say I'm a bit closer to the world you're now inhabiting than I might appear. Start with what happened when you woke up that morning."

The satyr struggled, but it seemed more a token effort than anything. At last, he deflated and slumped back in his chair. "Fine. If I tell you, you'll let me go?"

"Of course. But don't lie. I'll know."

He stared into his drink for a few seconds, then looked back up. "Okay. A few days ago, I got up like usual, went into the bathroom to get ready for work. When I looked in the mirror, I saw...*this.*"

"Just like that? You didn't see anything like it before?"

He shot Stone a withering look. "Come on, man. Do you honestly think I would have missed it? When I brushed my teeth before bed the night before, I didn't have horns or a beard or..." He glanced down toward his lap. "Other stuff."

"Fair enough. What did you do?"

"Like I told you before, I freaked out. My first thought was, what's my wife gonna say when she sees it? The kids?"

"*Did* she see it?"

"No. I hid in the bathroom. When one of the kids came up to find out where I was, I told her I'd be down soon. She went downstairs and told my wife. Next thing I know, Margie's opening the bathroom door. We don't have locks, and she's not always good about knocking." He fidgeted in his chair. "I thought I was screwed. She'd get one look at me and run screaming from the room."

"But she didn't."

He shook his head. "Nope. Didn't even act like anything was strange. Just asked me what I wanted for breakfast before she left with the kids for school. I have no idea how I managed not to hyperventilate in front of her—remember, this was all pretty new to me, but even then I was already starting to be okay with it, you know? Maybe that's why she didn't get suspicious."

"What happened after that?"

"I took a chance. I wondered, if Margie couldn't see me, maybe the kids couldn't either. So I went downstairs with her."

"And the kids didn't see anything either," Verity said. She seemed to be getting into the story now.

"Not a damn thing. Everything was completely *normal,* which was pretty strange all on its own. They all finished their breakfast, said goodbye, and left for Margie to drop them off at school and go on to her job. Just like every other day."

"What did you do then?" Stone asked. "That was the day you left, right?"

"Yeah." He looked down again. "Like I said, I'm not proud of it…but I'm not ashamed of it, either. I know I should be, but for whatever reason, I'm not. I think it's been a long time coming, to be honest. I'd been feeling restless for a while, and especially the last few days before it happened. Seeing it was scary, but it was also a *relief.* This is what I'm meant to be. This is what I'm meant to do. I was never much of a family man. I did the wife-and-kids thing because that's what I thought I was supposed to do to succeed."

"When all you really wanted to do was drink, party, and have lots of sex?" Verity asked.

"Well…yeah." His gaze came up again, and the lazy smile came back. "I mean, why lie about it? That's what lots of guys want, but they won't admit it. But me—when I saw myself in the mirror that morning, I realized it's what I was made to do. You know how some people have spiritual revelations and get religion? Well, this was kind of like that."

He shifted his attention from Verity to Stone. "You get it, don't you? I mean, you're a good-looking guy, and I'll bet you're good in bed." His salacious expression suggested he wouldn't mind testing that theory.

"Er—"

"He doesn't bail on his responsibilities, though," Verity said.

Carter grinned knowingly, glancing between them. "Ah, okay, you *know* he's good in bed. Should have suspected that." He waggled his eyebrows at Stone. "See, you at least kind of get it."

Stone sighed. "We're talking about *you*, Mr. Carter."

"You asked me to tell you what happened. I told you. Now, can I go?"

"Not quite yet. One more thing. Tell me about this other man you saw, on the light rail. You said he looked like an 'ogre.' What did you mean by that?"

Carter shrugged. "Maybe that was the wrong term. It was at the Castro stop, around nine o'clock. He was a big dude—*really* big. Like seven feet tall, which was weird because he should have been all hunched over inside the light-rail car, but he wasn't. He had a big bald head, no shirt, jacked muscles. I mean *huge* muscles, bigger than those 'roided-up bodybuilder types." He pointed to his mouth. "And he had, like, these big teeth sticking up out of the lower part of his jaw. Whatever he was, he definitely didn't look like a normal guy. Any more than I do."

"Did you see what he did?"

"Nope. Like I said, the doors closed and the car took off before I could see anything else. Not that I'm sure I wanted to." He shivered. "Guy looked like he could take me apart, and he was putting out…I don't know…anger vibes. *Definitely* not somebody I'd want to party with."

"And no one seemed to notice anything unusual about him?"

"Nope, not a thing. And trust me, he would have drawn attention, if nothing else for the big teeth." He shifted in his chair again and finished his drink. "Come on, man. I did what you asked. Prime party time's wasting."

"Yes, yes, fine." Stone stood, releasing the spell he'd been holding on Carter. "You can go."

"Hang on," Verity said.

"What now?" Carter had already stood, and looked like he was ready to take off.

"Call your wife. Don't be a chickenshit. Don't make Jason do it. Even if you don't plan on ever going back to her, you owe her that, don't you think?"

He hesitated. "Maybe. I'll think about it. Have a good one, both of you." And then he was gone, disappearing back into the crowd. A moment later, Stone spotted him climbing the stairs toward the alcoves.

"Let's go," he told Verity. "I've had quite enough of this place, and we've got some things to discuss."

CHAPTER EIGHT

THEY MET AT JASON'S AGENCY the following day, when Gina was out to lunch.

"You're shittin' me." Jason's eyes widened when Stone and Verity filled him in on what they'd found. "You're saying he's a…*satyr*? He just…turned into some kind of mythological creature overnight? One mundanes can't see?"

"That's what it appears." Stone paced the small office. "And the thing that troubles me about it is that I've never heard of anything like this happening. I popped home earlier today and had a chat with Eddie and Ward. *They've* never heard of it either. Eddie says he can't think of anything he's ever seen in the library that describes something like this."

"So…it's new?" Verity asked. She and Stone had chatted for a bit the previous evening before he left for home, but they hadn't reached any conclusions.

"It appears so. Damn, I wish Kolinsky hadn't picked now to take off for parts unknown." He'd stopped by the shop before heading to England, and it was closed as tightly as before. He had no idea if the dragon was specifically avoiding him, or if he was simply off dealing with other important business and didn't want to be disturbed. But if this phenomenon had occurred before, the dragons were the only beings he knew of who might have remembered it.

"What about Madame Huan? Do you think she'd know anything?"

Stone hadn't considered her, because she was gone so often and wasn't usually the person he went to with these kinds of issues. "Good thought. I'll check her shop later, when we finish here."

"So what am I supposed to tell his wife?" Jason ran a hand through his hair. He had the usual long-suffering look he got when dealing with new versions of what he'd come to identify as "MFM"—*more fucking magic.*

Verity pulled out her phone. "I snapped a pic so you'll have something to show his wife. Don't worry, he just looks like his regular self in it."

He waited for her to send the photo, then studied it. "Yeah, I don't see any sign of weird stuff here—well, aside from the six-person orgy. That's almost worse, though. She's not gonna be happy when I tell her that her husband's hanging out in sketchy clubs organizing gangbangs with hookers."

"Yeah, but that's not your problem, right? She's paying you to find him, not to explain what he's up to."

"Yeah…" He opened a file on his computer and tapped in some notes. "I guess as far as I'm concerned, the whole magic thing isn't relevant. Do the job, report the findings, get paid. That's all I'm on the hook for. I still don't like it, though. I mean, I talked to this woman quite a bit. Carter wasn't exactly father of the year, but this is gonna blindside her."

Stone was only half-listening. He still wasn't interested in Wayne Carter's domestic issues, or his wife's either. "I'm more intrigued by why we couldn't find him."

"Huh?" Jason looked up from his screen.

He nodded toward Verity. "Both of us did tracking rituals, with good solid tether objects in both cases. He wasn't out of our range, but the spells didn't locate him."

"Got any theories?" Verity had picked up a puzzle box from her brother's desk and was trying to open it.

"I do, actually, but there's no way to prove it."

"Give it a shot," Jason said.

"Well...obviously Mr. Carter went through a fairly profound change. I've never seen anything quite like it. The satyr persona didn't look like any kind of illusion. It was clearly there, but yet his normal body was obviously still there too, because his clothes fit him."

"Almost like a kind of...overlay," Verity added. "But a really solid one. When I looked at him with magical sight, all I could see was the satyr. No sign of the regular guy."

"Yes." Stone stared off into space, thinking. "And his aura was strong, regardless of whether I was looking at the human or the satyr form. Bright red, and not indicating any underlying illness or disturbance."

"Just that he was drunk off his ass and horny as hell," Verity said with a grimace. "What are you getting at, Doc?"

"Well...we never saw his aura *before,* which is why there's no way to prove my hypothesis at present."

"Before?" Her eyes narrowed. "Wait...are you saying you think his aura *changed?*"

"It's a possibility. I didn't think it was possible before, but we've got precedent right here in this room." He was referring to Jason's switch from medium blue to deep indigo, but there was also his own case, where his aura had sprouted a third color following his return from Calanar.

Jason frowned. "Okay...let's assume for the moment that *is* what happened. Why would it mean you couldn't find him? And how could it even happen? In my case, I had to get injected with a mage's blood and put through a fairly complicated ritual. That couldn't have happened to Wayne, right? You said he woke up one morning with the satyr thing going on, but his wife didn't mention any suspicious disappearances before that."

Stone held up a hand. "Hold on, slow down. One question at a time. Why it meant we couldn't find him is easy. A tracking spell locks on to an individual aura, using the tether object to locate its like energy out in the world. If Carter's aura changed when he became a satyr, he wouldn't have worn the clothes his wife gave you to use as tethers—which means they were associated with his *original* aura."

"So the spell wouldn't find him because it was looking for the old aura, and the new one didn't give it anything to latch onto?"

"Precisely. It makes quite a lot of sense, actually."

"So what about the other thing? *How* would his aura change? You said that's a huge deal, right? Life-changing huge. Not something that could just…happen without something causing it?"

"Clearly something *did* cause it. But I haven't got a bloody idea *what.*" He stood and began pacing. "And what disturbs me even more is that Mr. Carter doesn't seem to be alone."

"Huh?" Jason turned away from his screen, confused, but then his expression sharpened. "Wait—you're talking about the werewolf thing you saw attack the homeless guy, right?"

"Yes, but not just him. Mr. Carter mentioned seeing a man who looked like an 'ogre'—his word—getting on a MUNI train a couple nights ago."

"He *saw* this?"

Stone nodded, satisfied he was keeping up. "Yes. You begin to see where I'm going. Mr. Carter—as far as I know, one hundred percent mundane aside from suddenly taking on the magical appearance and personality of a satyr—spotted another of these odd beings without making any effort to do so. And the other man spotted *him.*"

"So…they can see each other, somehow." Verity finished opening the puzzle box and began putting it back together.

"Apparently."

Jason looked troubled. "Do you think there are…more of these things out there, running around San Francisco?"

"No idea. But it does make sense. I think the odds that we somehow managed to encounter or hear about the only three in existence are fairly low."

"So what do we do about it?"

"You? Probably nothing, at this point. You report back to Mrs. Carter about her husband, leaving out the satyr bit."

"What about you?"

"I'm going to consult a few people, assuming I can find some of them. I've already mentioned the situation to Eddie and Ward, so I'll pop over there periodically and update them with any new information. If I can find Kolinsky, I'll tell him as well, and Madame Huan. And perhaps I'll head back up to San Francisco and look around a bit."

"I can do that too," Verity said. "Let me know if you see any others, and I'll do the same."

Jason still appeared pensive. He made a noncommittal noise and stared at his desk.

"What is it?" Stone asked. "I know that look. You've still got something on your mind."

"Not really. I just can't help worrying this is the beginning of something big, if we don't figure out what's causing it. Big like the Evil. And—maybe I'm gonna sound like a dick for sayin' anything about it, but I don't want to deal with any big magical bad stuff right now."

Stone nodded sympathetically. "Of course you don't. You've got far more important things on your mind. My advice is not to worry about it if you'd rather not. Even if there *are* more of these creatures around, you haven't got any chance to identify them. So far, they seem to be confined to San Francisco, and need magical sight to spot. Let me deal with this—and Verity, if she wants to. You focus on Amber."

Jason didn't meet his gaze. "Thanks, Al. I feel like I'm letting you down, but—"

"But your family is more important. I get it. You're not letting us down. If you did anything else, I'd wonder what had got into you."

"He's right," Verity added. "It's all good, Jase. Let us handle this one."

"Yeah. Okay. But if you *do* end up needing help, you have to promise you'll call."

"Absolutely," Stone said. "Let's hope it doesn't come to that."

CHAPTER NINE

STONE CONTINUED TO THINK about the San Francisco situation as he returned to his Encantada house. He was in the middle of cleaning Raider's downstairs litter box and setting out fresh food and water for the cat when a chilling thought struck him—one he mentally kicked himself for not thinking about earlier.

What if this was yet another consequence of the periodic dimensional-intersection rifts he and Kolinsky had been keeping tabs on for the last two years? He hadn't been checking on them recently, but if another one had popped up somewhere in San Francisco, it was possible it could cause unexpected changes like this in people who got near it.

So far, the only thing the rifts seemed to have in common was that they came into existence due to this dimension drifting into brief contact with others. Aside from that, every one Stone had personally encountered had different effects, from enhancing magical ability, to bestowing odd, wild-talent-like powers, to shifting an entire small town out of phase with reality. Kolinsky had explained to him that the different effects were due to the varying characteristics of the intersecting dimensions combining with the constant of their home plane. To apply a simple metaphor, mixing milk with chocolate flavoring got you a different result than mixing it with flour. Since every other dimension that might drift into proximity had different characteristics, the results would always be unpredictable by nature.

After his initial frustration at not thinking of this idea, the thought energized Stone. He immediately popped over to the London house, where William Desmond's massive magical globe displayed, among other things, the locations of any rifts currently active around the planet. He still felt guilty for doing nothing to close them, but by now he'd accepted Kolinsky's admonition that closing them would do more harm than letting them run their course naturally. So far, they'd been mostly behaving, causing only minimal disturbances, or appearing in remote locations where humans would be unlikely to encounter them. By the time he crouched next to the globe with the magical magnifying glass and spun it to display North America, he was convinced he had to be right.

His excitement quickly turned to disappointment, though. Not only did no current active rifts exist anywhere in San Francisco, there weren't even any in California. In fact, the only one near the west coast was in the middle of the Arizona desert, miles from any inhabited areas.

He sighed, frustrated, and sank lower into his crouch. "Well, bugger," he murmured under his breath. "That's a bust."

Ah, well. At least it eliminated one potential hypothesis—but given that it was the only credible one he had, it didn't make him feel any better.

Before heading home, he popped up to Caventhorne to give Eddie and Ward the latest information.

They both looked intrigued, but didn't have any new ideas for him.

"I've been diggin' through the library ever since we talked last," Eddie told him ruefully. "You'd think there'd be *somethin'* there somewhere, but nothin's turnin' up at all. Mind if I ask a few other folks? Fellow researchers and summat? You never know what somebody might have floatin' 'round in the back o' their 'eads."

"No, go ahead. I'll take anything at this point. Ask them to be discreet, though. I suppose there isn't much to worry about with this getting out, since it seems to be confined to San Francisco so far, and nobody can see it but our lot—when we look for it—and the ones affected. But even so—"

"Don't worry yer pretty little 'ead," Eddie assured him. "Discretion is my middle name."

"I thought it was Hubert."

"Yeah, well, we don't let that get around too much."

Reluctant to let this go and for lack of anything else to do, Stone decided to head to San Francisco that night and look around for any other signs of oddness. He texted Verity to ask if she wanted to come with him.

Sorry, she sent back. *Can't tonight. Got a thing with Scuro.*

That's fine. See anything today?

Nope, but been working in the shop most of the time. We're reopening next week.

He was about to put the phone away when it buzzed again with another text.

Tell me if you find anything, Verity sent. *And be careful.*

He considered driving, since he wanted to look around various parts of the city, but getting anywhere in San Francisco was a nightmare and parking was worse. If he *did* spot anything, he'd need to go after it quickly. Fortunately, the pair of ley lines that crossed through the town provided enough locations so he could cover several different areas, and if he needed to go anywhere else, he could call a cab or a rideshare. At least, for the first time in a while, he was actually in a place he could be reasonably expected to be, so he could use his electronics without worrying about Big Brother adding another entry to his no-doubt-growing profile.

He decided to start in the Mission district, partially because it was near a ley line and partially because it was one of the City's less savory neighborhoods. He had no idea if someone who woke up one morning to discover they'd sprouted horns or full-body fur might gravitate to a more shadowy part of town, but he had to start somewhere.

He used a disregarding spell to keep from being noticed, but didn't bother with a disguise amulet. Nobody around here knew him—and besides, he wasn't doing anything wrong. He had as much right to wander around San Francisco after dark as anyone else did, and it wasn't as if he had to worry about anyone messing with him.

He kept up a confident pace, choosing his direction mostly at random. Every couple minutes, he shifted briefly to magical sight and scanned the people walking along the street, but after half an hour he spotted nothing out of the ordinary. He saw what he expected to see: normal humans with normal human auras, many of them marred with the dark patches indicating illness or substance abuse.

He gravitated north, heading toward SOMA and the Tenderloin district. Still, nothing interesting turned up. He saw his share of homeless people, shadowy groups consummating furtive drug deals in alleyways, and working girls lounging on street corners scanning for customers, but all of them still looked one hundred percent human. Most paid him no attention, thanks to the disregarding spell. He picked up his pace a bit, beginning to think this had been a bad idea—or at least a pointless one. The more he thought about it, the more it occurred to him that he'd barely seen the man he'd come to think of as "the werewolf," and had nothing but Wayne Carter's word about "the ogre." Wayne had been the only one of these strange beings he'd got a good look at, but that didn't mean there were a lot more of them out there. And even if there *were* more, unless there were a lot more than he expected, the odds he'd run into one while on his aimless path through San Francisco's bad neighborhoods were fairly low.

He'd made it most of the way to the Tenderloin when he realized he was being observed.

He had turned left off Mission Street and onto Hyde. As he crossed Turk Street, he spotted movement to his left as he passed a small, gated park or playground to his left. The area was clearly closed this late, so he assumed at first that homeless, stoners, or teenagers had climbed over the fence. He shifted to magical sight almost idly, expecting more of the unsettled but normal-human auras he'd been seeing all night.

The figure crouching next to a play structure didn't look like a normal human.

For one thing, its limbs seemed to be too long and skinny. For another, the way it crouched looked almost spiderlike. It was too dark to see it clearly, but its green aura had strange, spiky edges.

It was looking right at him.

For a second it looked startled that he'd noticed it. Then it spun and took off, moving in a hunched-over way that made it look even more like some kind of four-legged spider creature. As Stone continued to watch, it leaped up, caught the edge of the building next to the park, and scrambled around the corner.

Intrigued, he checked to be sure nobody was watching him, then called up an invisibility spell and levitated over the fence. He couldn't stay invisible for long, so he hurried to the same corner as fast as the spell would take him and peered around, still using magical sight.

For a moment, he thought he'd lost the creature. Then he looked up and spotted it clambering up the side of a rundown building, as nimble as a monkey. He caught a brief glimpse of it before it climbed into an open window on the building's fourth floor. It did look more like a monkey than a spider, long-limbed and furry. Before it disappeared into the darkness, it poked its head out as if checking to make sure Stone wasn't still following it.

He waited for it to pull back before dropping the spell, puffing. No matter how long he practiced, he never seemed to get much better with the invisibility spell. Even switching to Calanarian magic had only added another minute or so to the maximum time he could sustain it before having to rest. It was inconvenient, but every mage had weaknesses.

After his breathing returned to normal, he evaluated his next move. The monkey-like creature was probably long gone by now. It had to know the area better than he did, so it had likely used the building as a shortcut on its way to wherever it was headed.

But what if it hadn't?

What if it was still inside, secure in the knowledge that it had lost him? Stone didn't think it could see past the invisibility spell, judging by its apparent satisfaction that nobody was following it.

He'd come to San Francisco tonight trying to find more of the strange creatures. He hadn't switched to mundane sight when he'd spotted it, afraid he'd lose it in the darkness if he couldn't see its aura, but he'd bet a lot of money that he'd found another one. If it was still in the building, he might be able to corner it long enough to ask it some questions. He needed more data points, and the only way he'd get them was to go to the source.

Decision made, he re-applied the disregarding spell and levitated over the park's back fence.

The building where the creature had disappeared was across a narrow alley. It had five stories, accessible from the outside by a rickety, rusting fire escape. The place didn't look completely abandoned, but most of the windows were dark. The one where the creature had entered glowed with a faint light.

Stone didn't waste time trying to climb the fire escape. The ladder to the ground was pulled up, and even if he trusted the rest of it to hold his weight, he didn't trust it not to make enough noise to announce his presence to people on the next block. Instead, he drifted up, keeping to one side of the windows so nobody would see him unless they were specifically looking for him.

Nobody bothered him. No heads appeared at any of the windows, and when he glanced up with magical sight, he didn't see any auras glowing from the roof.

First guess was probably right. Whatever it was, it's long gone.

He swapped the disregarding spell for invisibility when he reached the fourth-floor window, then drifted over and carefully lowered himself to the fire escape, prepared move again if it made any noise.

It didn't. Despite its dilapidated appearance, it felt surprisingly strong under his feet.

There wasn't much room to the side of the window, but he pressed himself back as far as he could manage before peering inside.

He didn't expect to see anything but an empty room. What he *did* see made him tense.

The room had the look of a semi-permanent squat, with strewn sleeping bags, boxes, and a few clothes draped over broken furniture. The dim glow Stone had spotted came from a small camping lantern on a wooden box.

It illuminated not one, but three figures.

Two were seated on sleeping bags. The third, obviously the long-limbed, furry creature Stone had initially spotted in the park, paced around restlessly. It held something in its hand, which closer inspection revealed to be a soda can.

The other two looked odd too, but not in the same way. One was large and bulky, dwarfing a sleeping bag obviously too small for it. The other was hunched and looked bald, with pointed ears. Its long, nimble fingers moved as it gestured. The lantern light gave its skin a greenish tinge.

Stone concentrated. It would be tough to hold the invisibility spell while switching back and forth to magical sight, but he had to know. He waited until the pacing creature had its back to him, then dropped the sight.

Instantly, the bizarre figures faded away, revealing three normal humans—two men and a woman. The large, bulky creature became a hefty young woman with green hair. The hunched one with pointed ears was a young man with sharp features and a sly grin. The furry, monkey-like creature changed to a tall, loose-limbed teenager in sweatpants and an oversized hoodie.

Bloody hell. There are *more of them. And now they're finding each other.*

Stone was already breathing hard. He couldn't keep the invisibility spell going much longer. He willed the young man to sit down, but he didn't. Instead, he continued pacing. Any moment, he might turn toward the window.

"You sure he didn't see where you went?" the woman was asking. Now *she* turned toward the window. She had rough, blockish features, and was older than Stone had initially thought.

Stone ducked out of visibility, reluctantly releasing his hold on the spell. If he tried to maintain it much longer, they might hear his harsh breathing. This way, with the disregarding spell, he might at least be able to hear something useful before he confronted them.

The teenager laughed. "Naw, no way. S'prised he spotted me before, though."

"Maybe we should go somewhere else for a while anyway," the seated man said.

"Don't be such a chickenshit. They can't see us. Who gives a fuck if some normie spotted me? Ain't no way he knows what I really look like, or that I got up here that fast."

"Yeah, you're right." But the man sounded reluctant.

Stone wished he could still see them, wondering if they were all looking toward the window now. It wasn't as if he couldn't deal with them if they decided to come after him, but he didn't want to have to. He wanted answers, not a confrontation. He pressed his ear against the side of the building, trying to filter out the street noise from below.

Later, he assumed he must have been focused so hard on trying to make out the conversation inside that he wasn't paying attention to anything else. Whatever happened, he didn't hear anyone approaching from behind. The only thing that saved him—partially, at least—was a faint disturbance in the air behind him.

He immediately flung himself sideways, which meant the club that had been aimed at the top of his head instead glanced off the back.

Pain lit him up. He staggered sideways, crashing into the fire escape's railing, which gave way under his weight.

Then he was falling.

"Oh, shit!" The voice behind him sounded young and scared. He got a quick impression of another dark figure standing on the same level he'd been, and then it dived through the window and was gone.

His brain too scrambled from even the glancing blow to summon a levitation spell, Stone twisted his body and lashed out with both hands. By some miracle, one flailing hand came into contact with the third-floor railing. Acting on nothing but instinct, he locked his fingers around it and gripped tight.

The momentum continued carrying him down, though, wrenching his shoulder so hard it almost ripped his hold loose. He hung there for a couple seconds, fighting pain on two fronts, but managed to swing himself forward over the second-floor platform. He dropped ungracefully down, panting, but quickly scrambled to his knees despite the growing pain. If anyone else was coming after him, he needed to be ready for them.

It didn't seem as if they were, though. As he crouched there, still breathing hard, his head and shoulder throbbing in time with his racing heartbeat, nobody else approached him.

He remembered the voice. Whoever had hit him, they'd sounded frightened. Why? Had they not meant for him to fall? Were they afraid they'd killed him?

He didn't have time to think about it now. Neither of the injuries were severe—the head blow had been glancing, and thanks to his regular gym routine he didn't think his shoulder was dislocated—but they still hurt and they were still distracting. He needed to get out of here and find a place to hole up.

His thoughts were moving more slowly than usual, but as he dropped to the ground and staggered back toward the park, he remembered why Verity couldn't join him tonight: because she had a session with Scuro, healing one of his magical-tattoo clients. Scuro's shop was in the Castro district, which wasn't far from where he was now.

At least his phone hadn't broken when he landed. That was something.

It took fifteen minutes before a rideshare car showed up to pick him up, and when the guy got a look at him, he almost declined the ride.

"You look messed up, man," the nervous, hipster-looking driver said. "You drunk? I don't want any drunks pukin' in my car. I just had it cleaned."

"No." Stone pushed himself off the wall. He hadn't tried to heal his injuries himself, since he knew Verity would do a much better and more thorough job. "Just—took a little fall. Not drunk, I promise."

The guy looked him up and down. "I dunno—"

"Look—I'll give you an extra fifty in cash. It's only a few blocks." He pulled out the cash and offered it to prove he wasn't lying.

That swayed it. "Yeah, okay. Get in. But I'm warnin' you, if you puke back there, I'm givin' you a one-star rating."

Stone didn't reply. He settled into the back seat with a grunt when his shoulder lit up again and closed the door.

The driver kept snatching glances at him in the rear-view mirror, all the way to their destination. He seemed quite relieved when he finally double-parked in front of Scuro's shop, and wasted no time pulling back into traffic as soon as his fare was out.

Stone had texted Verity on the way over, barely managing to tap out *On my way over, need healing* with shaking fingers, but it was enough. She was waiting for him in the doorway, and hurried out to take his arm. She must have been looking with magical sight, because she avoided the injured one.

"What happened?" she demanded as she helped him inside and settled him on the soft leather couch in the lobby. Nobody else was here, so Stone assumed the client was already in the back with Scuro. Pounding heavy metal played from a speaker behind the reception desk.

"Long story. Could I trouble you for the healing first? My head feels like someone hit it with a club. Which could be because they did."

"Someone hit you with a *club?*"

He gestured weakly. "Healing, please. Then talk."

"Okay. Okay. Sit back and stay quiet."

The sofa's soft cushion felt great on his throbbing head. He closed his eyes and tried to focus on nothing while Verity gently and efficiently ministered to his injuries—first his head, then his shoulder. He relaxed as the warm energy coalesced around him, gradually replacing the pain with a sense of peace.

Damn, she's good. No wonder Scuro pays her so well.

A few minutes later, she let her breath out in satisfaction. "There. How's that?"

Stone sat up, trying his arm first. The wrenching pain was gone as if it had never been, leaving only the faintest sensation of tightness. He raised his hand and touched the back of his head, wincing in anticipation, but nothing happened. There wasn't even any blood.

He relaxed again, smiling contentedly. "Good job, apprentice. Brilliant work."

When he opened his eyes, she was regarding him with narrowed eyes. "Want to tell me what got you into that state? Were you serious about getting hit with a club?"

He looked around the lobby, half-expecting Scuro to be coming out from the back wondering where his healer was. "Have you got time?"

"Yeah. He's gonna be working for another half-hour or so before I need to do anything. Start talking. You want a drink?"

"I'd love one. Got any Scotch?"

"We have bottled water and fruit juice."

"Beggars can't be choosers, I suppose. Either one is fine."

She brought him a bottle of water and plopped back down on the sofa next to him. "I'm having a hard time believing you got mugged."

Stone drank half the bottle before speaking. "I didn't. I found more of them, Verity."

"More? You mean like Wayne Carter?"

"Yes."

"Satyrs?"

"No. Not this time. I'm not sure *what* they were, to be honest. One was some kind of monkey creature—furry and very agile. One was a large, muscular woman. And one looked like a sort of…goblin, I guess. Pointed ears, long fingers, long nose."

"Wow." She looked surprised. "You found *three* of them? Where? Were they together? Did one of them hit you?"

"I think I found four." He quickly told her the rest of the story.

She listened with growing, shocked interest. "So you think this fourth one snuck up behind you and hit you?"

"Yes, which isn't supposed to be possible. Well—to be fair, I was paying more attention to their conversation than my surroundings. But to sneak up on me while I was on a small, precarious fire escape—that would take more than human ability, I think."

She rubbed her chin, pondering. "And you're sure these are more like Wayne? You looked at them with normal sight too?"

"I did, and I am."

"So they're…finding each other? Banding together? I guess it makes sense—if they're the only ones who can see each other, aside from mages with magical sight, then it's not surprising they're grouping up. But why would they *hit* you? You said the one who did seemed scared?"

"I think they were just trying to protect themselves, honestly. They didn't come after me, and I suppose I can't blame them for being wary. If *I* had suddenly changed into something I couldn't explain, I wouldn't want anyone following me."

"So what do we do now? You aren't going to go look for more of them tonight, are you?"

"No. I think I've had about enough of that for the night. But we need more information. We've got to find more of them and talk to them, if they'll let us."

"What makes you think they will? It doesn't seem like most of them want to talk."

Stone shrugged. It felt good to do that without a small bomb going off in his right shoulder. "Who knows how many of them there are? Though I'm beginning to suspect there might be more than we think, given how many of them I've managed to blunder

WINDS OF CHANGE | 87

into proximity with. Unless I'm some sort of magnet for them—which I doubt—it suggests there are a lot more out there we're *not* seeing."

"Yeah…maybe." Verity took his empty bottle and tossed it in the recycle bin. "Anyway, I should probably get back. You're okay to go home, right?"

"Thanks to your first-rate healing, I feel better than ever." He stood, taking in the shop with its black-and-white tile floor and walls covered in tattoo art. "Thanks again."

"No problem. Kind of what I do. But what are you going to do next?"

"Good question. I'll have to give it some thought. I suppose the next step is to see if the phenomenon really *is* confined to San Francisco."

"You don't have any idea what's causing it, do you?"

"Not a bit, and that's what troubles me most."

CHAPTER TEN

STONE DIDN'T SPOT ANY MORE of the creatures over the next few days, despite spending a couple hours each night driving around Palo Alto, parts of San Jose, and Sunnyvale near A Passage to India. He even returned to San Francisco and, along with Verity, patrolled some other areas in the city. In every case, he turned up nothing. A check of the original group's fourth-floor squat in the Tenderloin revealed it had been cleared out. Obviously, they'd moved their home after finding him spying on them. He hardly blamed them.

Kolinsky remained unavailable. Though he wasn't sure it was a good idea, Stone finally decided to enter the shop despite the warning, and call for him. It might make Stefan grumpy, but enduring a grumpy dragon to get some answers was an acceptable risk.

He needn't have bothered, though. Not only did Kolinsky not respond to his call, but when Stone reached the downstairs area where the shabby shop normally resided, he found nothing but concrete walls and threadbare carpet. It was the same brief view he'd seen one time for an instant—what the place looked like when the dragon's powerful illusions weren't maintaining its usual façade.

Stone stood there in the middle of the space. Did this mean Stefan had vacated the premises permanently, or only that he couldn't be arsed anymore to keep up the charade when he knew he no longer needed to? Unfortunately, there was no reliable way to find out.

Wait…maybe there is.

He hadn't visited Madame Huan's eclectic junk shop in a while. As usual, it didn't look any different, at least on the macro level: the narrow, dusty shelves were still lined with a crazy amalgamation of unrelated items, most of which looked like they'd not only seen better days, but likely weren't anything anyone would ever want to buy. Also as usual, none of the items were the same as they'd ever been before. Stone had tested that one time, entering the shop on two consecutive days, and discovered the entire selection of items had changed—even those he would have bet a lot of money nobody would ever have wanted to purchase. He found it amusing, never sure if the whole place was an elaborate illusion like Kolinsky's shop, or if Madame Huan merely found it entertaining to mess with people's heads. Before he'd found out his old friend's true nature, he thought it had to be the latter, because unlike Kolinsky's place, he did sometimes see customers here. He'd even spoken with them on occasion. But now, he wouldn't put it past the kindly, mischievous dragon to entertain herself by creating not only the shop's wares, but its clientele out of illusionary whole cloth.

You never could tell with dragons.

Today, Madame Huan's cheerful assistant was running the shop. A couple customers wandered up and down, examining the bizarre items on the packed shelves with interest. Stone ignored both, striding up the narrow aisle to the back.

The assistant flashed him a smile. "Oh, good morning." Unlike the products and the customers, she didn't change, and had met Stone before on several occasions. "How are you today, Dr. Stone?"

Stone mentally cycled through several responses: *Busy? Confused? Frustrated?* before finally settling on, "Fine. Is Madame Huan around?" He glanced hopefully at the beaded curtain behind the desk. As usual, from here it appeared to separate the front of the shop from a cluttered supply room. In reality, it was another strong illusion that hid a cozy sitting area where Stone and the dragon had shared many conversations and cups of tea.

"Oh, I'm sorry, she's not." She looked apologetic.

Damn. "Do you know when she'll be back?"

"I don't. But I'll let her know you were here."

Stone fought to hide his frustration. This didn't necessarily mean anything. Madame Huan was gone a lot, and ever since he'd found out she was a dragon and could travel via ley line in the same way they'd taught him to do, he knew she could easily be anywhere in the world. "Thank you. Please ask her to contact me. It's…I suppose it's rather important."

Even if she didn't know anything about the hidden beings popping up, he still needed to ask her about the vanazarite. He still had some time before his portal was ready for it, but if she'd sold the last bit and had to get more, it was best to let her know early.

"I'll do that. I don't know when she'll be back, but I promise I'll pass the message along as soon as I can."

He thanked her and left the shop in a state of despondent frustration. It was absurd to think Kolinsky and Madame Huan were avoiding him over this new development, if they even knew about it at all. For the most part, dragons didn't involve themselves with human affairs much. They had agreements in place that made it difficult for them to do so. Apparently, they were a rather contentious lot if allowed to get out of hand, and the agreements ensured everybody made nice with each other.

Probably a good thing, Stone decided as he got back in his car. Having a bunch of ultra-powerful magical beings going to war over gods knew what dragons got their pants in a knot about would surely result in a lot of collateral damage.

He just wished they were a bit less secretive about the whole business.

With nothing else to do, he drove down to Jason's agency. He didn't call ahead, and was surprised to see Gina's desk empty when he entered. Instead of the usual drift of papers and anime-based screensaver on her computer, the desk was clean and the computer turned off.

Stone stopped in the waiting area. "Jason? Are you back there?"

Jason immediately appeared in the doorway of his tiny office at the rear. "Hey, Al. What's up?"

"Just thought I'd stop by and see if you wanted to have lunch."

He shook his head ruefully. "Can't. I brought something from home today. Crazy busy. Gina's been out sick for a couple days and things are piling up."

"Sorry to hear that. Hope it's nothing serious."

"Yeah, me too. She didn't volunteer anything, and I didn't ask. None of my business. But it's making it tough around here."

"Perhaps you should hire someone else to help out. You're getting fairly successful now, aren't you?"

Jason looked amused. "You never read the reports we send you, do you?"

"Er...no. I think I remember seeing something a couple weeks ago, but Raider probably knocked it on the floor." As an investor in the agency, Stone was entitled to such information, but that didn't mean he gave a damn about it one way or the other. He had bankrolled Thayer Investigations to help his friend, not because he cared about making money from the venture.

"Why am I not surprised? But yeah, we're doing pretty well. I'm actually thinking about looking for a bigger place—somewhere I can have an office that isn't the size of a broom closet. It was one of the things on Gina's list for this week. I guess it's gonna have to wait, though. I don't have time to do it myself."

Stone nodded. "I won't keep you long. How did the Wayne Carter situation go? Did you tell his wife what he was up to?"

"As much as I could, yeah. I blurred all the other faces in V's orgy photo and showed it to her."

"How did she take it?"

"Not so well, as you might have guessed. She wanted to know if we found out anything about *why* he did it."

"I assume you didn't tell her he's transformed into a mythological sex addict."

"Good guess. I told her I had no idea. I felt bad, but all she paid me for was to find him, not psychoanalyze him. She did ask me if I knew any good divorce lawyers, though, so I'm guessing it won't end well."

"Shame, but I'm not surprised."

Jason half-leaned, half-sat against Gina's desk. "V told me you found some more of those…creatures? People? I don't even know what to call them."

"Yes. At least three, maybe four—and that doesn't include the werewolf and the 'ogre' Mr. Carter claims to have seen. But I haven't seen any others since. Either they're lying low or somehow I managed to blunder into the only ones in existence."

"It's your weirdness magnet. You attract it."

"Probably." But Stone didn't mean it. Weirdness magnets were one thing, but this was simply too coincidental to be possible. He was certain there were more of the creatures out there, but that didn't get him any closer to figuring out *why* they were out there. Or, for that matter, how long they'd been around. For all he knew, they weren't new—this was just the first time he'd ever encountered them. There were a lot of things out there in the magical world that were very good at staying hidden.

Jason glanced at his watch and looked apologetic. "Anyway, I hate to run off, but I have to be in court in forty-five minutes, so I've got about ten to eat lunch before I have to go."

"No, no, it's fine. I haven't got anything else to report. If you talk to Gina, tell her I hope she's feeling better soon."

Stone returned home, more disappointed and frustrated than before. On the way, he caught himself shifting to magical sight at stoplights, scanning the streets for unusual beings, but wasn't surprised when he didn't see any. He decided, for lack of anything better to do, that he might as well use the downtime to catch up on some of the research he'd been putting off. It was better than sitting on the sofa in front of mindless television, drinking too much, and letting his mind chew itself to bits trying to work out any more angles to pursue.

When he came up for air, it was after nine p.m. He ran his hand through his hair and glanced over at Raider, who'd draped himself over the back of the sofa. *I wish I could relax like you,* he thought, amused that he was jealous of a cat.

He couldn't stand the idea of spending any more time on his research, but it was far too early to go to bed, so he gathered his papers and stood. Perhaps he'd go down to the basement and work on the portal circle some more. In his current state of distraction it was probably best if he didn't focus on any of the complex bits, but there was still a lot of basic stuff that needed doing. That kind of work he could do in his sleep.

His phone buzzed with an incoming text as he reached the doorway. He pulled it out, heart already beating faster in anticipation. Maybe it was Verity with another sighting, or Eddie with research updates.

　　　　　　　　　　　　　　　　　　　R. L. KING

Hey Doc.

Ah. It *was* Verity. But then he glanced at the sender name at the top and narrowed his eyes.

Gina R.

Gina was sending him texts? Why was Jason's assistant contacting him this late? But of course—if she was home sick, that didn't mean she probably wasn't still glued to her computer screen. Maybe she'd located another weird-stuff story to send him.

Like I need another *weird-stuff story right now.*

He returned to the office and sat on the sofa. Raider stretched, purred, and went back to sleep.

Hello, Gina. Feeling better?

There was a long pause, even though *Read* appeared almost instantly below his message. It was nearly two full minutes before her reply came back: *I need to talk to you about something.*

Odder and odder. *About what?*

I know this sounds weird but can you come here?

Stone looked at Raider. *Here? To your place?*

Yeah.

Now?

Like I said, I know it sounds weird. But I need help.

Now it was Stone's turn to pause. *Is something wrong? Jason said you were ill.*

The dots cycled. *Please Doc.*

He had no idea what to make of this. If she was sick, there wasn't much he could do to help her. But he could feel the urgency coming from her typed words. *All right. Give me the address and I'll be there as soon as I can.*

She sent an address near downtown San Jose. *Thanks Doc. Didn't know who else to ask.*

That was strange in and of itself. He didn't know how many friends she had from her online activities, but normally it would make more sense for her to contact Jason if she needed help with something. If she was bypassing her boss and going straight to him—

Gina, is this "my" sort of problem?

This time, the answer came back right away. *Yeah. Just please come ASAP.*

CHAPTER ELEVEN

G INA'S APARTMENT was off Delmas Street, on the top floor of a small building that looked like it had once, many years ago, been a single-family residence. He texted her from the lobby, trying to quell his growing curiosity. *I'm downstairs.*

She'd obviously been waiting for his text, because she answered instantly. *I'll buzz you up. Hang on.* A few seconds later, a faint *bzzt* sounded from the door next to the mailboxes.

Stone hurried up the two flights of stairs. Gina's place was the only apartment on this floor, so it was easy to find. He knocked twice on the door, refusing to speculate about what might be going on. If this was "his" kind of issue, it could be just about anything.

She answered as if she'd been standing on the other side of the door, ready to pounce as soon as he arrived.

For a moment she did nothing but stand there, looking at him in an almost challenging manner. She wore cutoff shorts and an oversized T-shirt with the logo from a gaming convention, and her hair was disheveled. From somewhere inside the apartment came the sound of a television show.

Stone tilted his head. "Er…hello, Gina."

Her eyes narrowed, and a look that was half-surprise, half-relief crossed her face. She almost looked startled. "Hi, Doc. Thanks again for coming. I know this is weirder than weird, but you were the only one I could think of to call."

This was getting odder by the moment. "Do…you want me to come in?"

"Oh!" She gave a slightly manic laugh, then stepped back and swung the door wide. "Sorry the place is kind of a mess."

Kind of a mess was an understatement. The apartment was small, with only a living room, kitchen, and two other doors that no doubt led to Gina's bedroom and bathroom. Stone swept the area with his gaze, taking in the sofa in front of a large flatscreen TV, another table brimming with computer equipment, and a kitchen table with two chairs. Every flat surface was covered with papers, books, toys, more bits of computer equipment including a VR rig, and scattered clothes. It looked like a geeky whirlwind had ripped through the place. A superhero movie played on the TV, and the computer screen showed some kind of online game she'd obviously been playing before he'd arrived. The place smelled like fast food, but surprisingly there was no odor of unwashed clothes. Aside from the glows from the TV and the computer screen, there were no other lights on.

"Can I get you anything?" Gina backed further into the room, giving him space. She was still looking at him with anticipation, as if expecting him to notice something. It couldn't have been more obvious she was nervous.

"No, thank you." Stone entered slowly, careful not to step on anything on the floor. "Gina, I don't mind telling you, you've got me confused. What did you need my help with, and why couldn't it have waited until tomorrow?"

"Um." She dropped into her desk chair and spun it around to face him, taking a big swig from a can of Red Bull next to her computer. She fidgeted, not meeting his gaze. "I…kinda thought it would be obvious, actually."

He tilted his head. "I've got no idea what you're talking about. Jason said you were ill, but you don't look ill to me. Just…nervous about something." With a quick, suspicious look around the apartment, he dropped his voice to a near whisper. "Is someone here? Is someone threatening you?"

She barked another manic laugh. "No, nothing like that. Nobody's bothering me. But…you can't see it? You really can't?"

"See what?"

But then, before she could answer, a sudden thought struck him.

Still focusing on her, he shifted to magical sight.

"Bloody hell…" he murmured.

"You *can* see it?" She sounded eager now, though still nervous.

He didn't reply. He barely heard her.

As soon as he'd shifted to his magical senses, Gina's chubby, dark-haired figure had melted away, replaced by…

By what he could only describe as a human-sized, bipedal cat.

Fur now covered her body, the same dark color as her hair had been. She now had two large, pointed ears extending from the top of her head, and her eyes, normally big and dark brown, were now even larger and a faintly glowing yellow. Her furry arms and legs now ended in clawed paws, and a long tail curled around her. Her aura was a swirling, luminous yellow—completely unlike the orange one he'd seen previously.

"Doc?"

Stone jolted himself back to awareness, but he still didn't say anything.

"Earth to Doc Stone." She waved a paw in front of him, looking for all the world like Raider taking a swipe at a laser pointer.

"Er." He shifted back to mundane sight, revealing Gina's familiar, T-shirt-and-shorts-clad form. She was leaning forward, staring hard at him.

"You…*can* see it, can't you?"

He swallowed. "I…can."

"But you didn't before, right? When I came to the door, you didn't see it?"

"No."

She flung herself out of the chair. "Doc, I have no *idea* what's going on. I haven't been out of my apartment in two days. Ever since—"

"Don't tell me: ever since you woke up one morning and looked at yourself in the mirror."

She snatched up something from the table next to the computer and shoved it toward him. It was a stuffed pink cat with jaunty tentacles where its legs should be. "Doc, how are you not freaking *out*? I'm a freakin' *catgirl*. I know you're used to dealing with the weird shit, but…this is kinda off the charts. I honestly thought I was going crazy. I *still* think I might be going crazy."

She looked back and forth, settling her gaze on the window. The blinds were closed. "I mean—you can *see* me, but you couldn't right away. What's that even mean? Can *other* people see me? Do they have to be around me for a while before it works? Or are we both having some kind of crazy hallucination?" She threw the stuffed cat into a nearby chair. "What's going *on*, Doc?"

Stone could tell from her aura that she was a lot more agitated than she appeared. "Okay," he said, raising his hands and keeping his voice even. "First, calm down."

"Calm down, he says." She glared at him, then indicated herself. "This isn't exactly the kind of thing you calm down from."

He had to give her that. Maybe it would be better to try taking her mind off her current predicament. "Why did you call me? I'm sure you've got other people you're closer to. Jason, Verity—"

She slumped in her chair. "I dunno. Because of all the strange stuff you have me find for you, I guess. Because of that conversation we had a while ago."

"Which conversation was that?"

"You know, where I asked you if there was more to your interest in this stuff than some connection to your job, and you said there was." She spread her hands. "I dunno, Doc. You just seemed like the most logical person to call. The one least likely to get freaked out and call the cops—or...I dunno...the animal-control people."

"Well, you got that part right. I'm not going to call anybody."

She spun her chair slowly around. "I don't know what to do. How is it that you couldn't see me before but then you could? I'm scared to death that if I go out there, *everybody*'s gonna be able to see this."

"They won't."

She thrust a furry paw down and stopped the chair, her head jerking up. "How do you know that?"

Stone got up and began pacing. There had been previous instances when he'd considered letting Gina in on the secrets of the magical world. Given how closely she worked with Jason and how many times his cases overlapped with the supernatural, it was getting harder and harder to keep her in the dark while still making use of her computer skills to hunt down useful information. He remembered the discussion he'd had with Jason, who'd talked him out of it because he was afraid if she let anything slip to her online friends, the inevitable fallout might affect him and his family.

But now, things were different. Gina had a stake in keeping things quiet now, too.

"Doc?"

He returned to his chair and sank into it, focusing his attention on her but not using magical sight. "Gina..."

"How do you know nobody else will be able to see me if I go out? How can I believe you?"

He felt sorry for her. She was normally so confident, almost cocky, and now it seemed she might fall apart right here on her cluttered couch. But he had to tell her the truth—at least as much of it as he knew. "I didn't say *nobody* else would be able to see you."

"What do you mean?"

"I can't tell you much yet, because I'm still investigating. But I know of situations where this has happened before."

"You do?" Her eyes widened in surprise. "You're kidding. Who? When?"

"Recently. One of them is one of Jason's cases."

"What?" She leaned forward, drawing her legs up under her until she was sitting cross-legged in the chair. "Which one?"

"Do you remember Mr. Carter, the man whose wife wanted your agency to find him?"

"Yeah. Jason handled that one on his own, but I processed some of the paperwork for it." She swallowed hard. "Are you telling me he turned into a catgirl—er—catboy too?"

"No."

"Then how do you know it's the same thing?"

"Because I saw him, and now I've seen you. In both cases, the affected person could see it, and I could see it, but almost nobody else could."

"*Almost* nobody else?"

"It seems, at least so far, that anyone affected by the condition can see others who are also affected."

Her gaze sharpened. "Does that mean *you're* affected too?" She looked him over, obviously trying to spot signs of fur or a tail.

"No."

"But how can you—"

"Gina. Listen." He paused, trying to decide how he wanted to do this. He hoped it would get easier with each subsequent time he did it, but so far that hadn't proven to be the case. Every time was different, with different variables. "There's something I think it's time to tell you."

"Yeah?" Once again, she leaned forward. Curiosity radiated off her so hard Stone could see it even without magical sight. "What? Are you going to tell me the *real* reason why you're looking for all the weird stuff you ask me to track down for you?"

"I suppose I am."

She almost seemed to have forgotten about her current problem. "Let me guess. You work for some super-secret organization investigating the paranormal."

He chuckled. "Not exactly. I *am* the paranormal."

"What? What's that mean?"

"Before I tell you, I've got to have your word that you won't spread this around. It's not the sort of thing I want getting out. It could cause a lot of trouble for me, and for those close to me." He eyed her sternly. "I hate to sound like an arse about it, but if you want me to help you, you've got to agree."

"Of course," she said immediately.

"I know you spend a lot of time online—"

She waved him off. "I spend a lot of time playing online games and hanging out with other computer geeks. Trust me, none of them would believe me even if I told them. The only reason I check out those crazy conspiracy-theory sites is to hunt up stuff for you. Not gonna lie, half the time I'm laughing my ass off at some of the stuff I find there."

He watched her aura as she spoke, and didn't see any obvious signs of subterfuge. Auras weren't lie detectors, but he'd gotten fairly good at reading them—enough, at least, to believe Gina wasn't deliberately deceiving him.

Plus, she *was* a catgirl now, which kind of gave her skin—or fur—in the game.

"Okay," he said. "The reason why I'm interested in those odd occurrences I have you send me is because I'm a mage."

Her eyes widened even further. "A mage?"

"Yes. It's a—"

"Oh, I know what it is!" She spoke faster, with obvious enthusiasm. "I play one in *World of Warcraft*. Her name's Arabella. She's an Orc. She's not my main, but—wait, let me show you!" She started to spin the chair again, back toward the computer, and reached for her mouse.

"Gina—"

"Oh! Sorry." She spun back, looking sheepish, but her excitement and curiosity quickly overshadowed it and she regarded him in a new light. "But…you're serious? You can do magic? Magic is *real*?"

"Yes, yes, and yes."

"That is…so freakin' *cool!*"

That was *not* the reaction Stone had been expecting. Every other time he'd spilled the supernatural beans to an unwitting mundane, he'd had to convince them he wasn't crazy or delusional, usually by giving them a demonstration that left them astonished and confused.

"Can you show me magic? Can you do it here, or do you need…I don't know…a wand or a magic circle or something?"

"I don't need a wand. Real mages don't use wands."

"But you do use magic circles?"

"Only for rituals. I think we're getting a bit off the subject—"

"Oh, right." She settled back. "So, can you?"

"Can I what?"

"Show me some magic. Please?" Her yellow cat eyes glowed with excitement.

Stone sighed. Clearly, they weren't going to get any further until he did a trick, but he supposed he couldn't blame her for wanting to see. He raised a hand, made a gesture, and the stuffed tentacle cat rose from where Gina had tossed it and landed in her lap.

She looked like a kid on Christmas morning who'd just unwrapped the best present ever. "Holy…shit…" she breathed, her furry hand closing around the stuffed toy. "That's…" She raised her head and looked at him with near-reverence. "What else can you do? Can you throw fireballs? Fly? Teleport? Go invisible?"

"Er. Let's not discuss specifics now, shall we? If I've sufficiently convinced you I can do what I claim—"

"Oh, yeah. I believe you. To be honest, I've kinda thought there was something odd about you for a while now. It's nice to see I wasn't wrong."

"Yes. Well. Let's get back to your situation."

"Right. Catgirl." She shifted in her seat, curling her legs even tighter under her. "So…if I'm understanding you right, you can see me because you're a mage—how does that work, anyway?"

"We have a special kind of sight that lets us see things normal people can't."

"Oh, cool. That makes sense. So you weren't using it when you first saw me, but then you used it and that's when you saw the whole cat thing."

"Yes."

She nodded, filing that away. "So…you can see it with this special sight, *I* can see it because it's me, and…the only other people who can see it are ones who have it too?"

"So far, that seems to be true. This is still a very new phenomenon. I've only become aware of it in the past few days."

"Whoa…" She unfurled her legs and leaned forward, propping her elbows on her knees. "So you don't know what causes it? Did somebody put a curse on me? Did I wander into some kind of magic field? Did somebody put magic catnip on my In 'n' Out burger?"

Stone noticed she seemed to be moving more gracefully than normal, even when he wasn't using magical sight. Gina had been chubby since he'd met her, with the typical sort of build one might expect from someone who spent a lot of time in a chair and existed on junk food and caffeine. Now, though, her movements were more fluid.

Dare he say…catlike?

"I don't know," he said in answer to her question. "I've got a couple of theories, which I can't share with you because I'm not allowed to, but…"

"Not allowed to?" Her gaze sharpened again. "You mean because the Wizards' Council won't let you?"

"No."

"No, that's not the reason, or no, they won't let you?"

"That's not the reason."

"*Is* there a Wizards' Council?"

"No. Do you think we could—"

But there was no deterring her now. "Why not? Shouldn't there be some kind of organization? You know, like in the *Dresden Files* books, or *Harry Potter*? One that's only purpose seems to be to get in the way of everything you're trying to do?"

Maybe this *wasn't* going to be as easy as he thought. "No. There isn't any Wizards' Council, or any other kind of council. Can we please stay on topic?"

"Sure. But you said you weren't allowed to tell me. So who won't allow you?"

Brilliant. Another smart and perceptive friend. Just what I need. "I can't tell you that, either. But the point is, I'm investigating to see whether it might be the cause." He pondered. "Have you been anywhere unusual in the past month or so?"

"Define 'unusual.'"

"I don't know—have you been out of the country? Traveled out of the area at all?"

She snorted. "I don't travel much, Doc. Ask Jason." She spun her chair around and picked up her VR headset. "All my traveling is with virtual reality. Safer that way. And cheaper. I'd rather spend my spare cash on pimping out my rig."

Stone rose from his chair and resumed pacing, picking his way with care around the items strewn on the floor. "Have you attended any unusual events? Or have you been to San Francisco in the last couple of months?"

"No on both." She stared off into space as she thought. "There was a kind of rave thing last month in a warehouse in Hayward. I went with some friends to help work on the lightshow. Oh, and I did AnimeCon in San Jose a couple months ago. But aside from that, I'm pretty much a hermit when I'm not working. I prefer interacting with people virtually." She held up her hands, staring at her furry paws. "You know…like I said, this really freaked me out when I first saw it. But the more I think about it, the more I'm thinking it's kinda cool. Especially if everybody in the world can't see me. Did you know I can do stuff I couldn't do before?"

"What sort of stuff?"

Her smile grew self-deprecating. "As you might have noticed, I'm not exactly the most optimal physical specimen. Let's be blunt about it—I'm a bit of a chonk."

Stone didn't reply. It had always been his experience that commenting on a woman's weight—even when she did it first—was a reliable path to ruin.

She seemed to notice his hesitation, and laughed. "Don't worry about it, Doc. I know I'm not a stick, and I'm cool with it. That's why I play Orcs in *WoW*. But the point is, I can move better now. I can jump higher, and I think maybe I might even be able to actually *climb*. She held up a paw. "Can you see the claws?"

"I can."

"I haven't tried it yet, but I wonder if they're functional. I definitely feel like my muscles are stronger. And I can see in the dark! How cool is that?"

Stone had to smile at her enthusiasm, but he still didn't reply.

She wrinkled her nose. "I don't know if I'm more curious now than before, because I've always been crazy curious. But I definitely want to take more naps. I'm gonna have to talk to Jason about working something out. It was hard enough being out in the daytime before, but now all I want to do is curl up in a sunbeam and sleep." She jerked, startled. "Holy shit. Jason. Does *he* know? About you, I mean? That you're a mage?"

"He does."

"Is *he* a mage?"

"No."

"What about Verity and Amber? Are they?"

"Gina—those things aren't for me to tell. I'm sorry, but I can't reveal that kind of information."

Her eyes were shining. "They *are*."

He sighed, annoyed that she'd maneuvered him so deftly.

"I promise I won't say anything to them."

"They aren't. Well—both of them aren't, anyway."

"Ooh. Hmm…let's see. If I had to guess, I'd say if it's only one of them, it's got to be Verity. She's always had kind of a witchy vibe, and she helps Jason out with the 'psychic' missing-person cases." Her eyes widened. "Oh, wow. I don't have to put that in air quotes anymore, do I? Is she *really* psychic? Are *you*?"

Clearly, this whole conversation wasn't going to go anywhere near as quickly or efficiently as Stone had hoped. Such was the price of progress, he supposed. "Sort of. But psychic powers have nothing to do with how we find missing people. That involves a ritual. Can we please stay on topic for now, though? I promise, I'll answer your other questions later."

She looked disappointed, but nodded and held up her hands. "I still can't get my mind around this. I was so worried my life was over—I mean, how can I go out in public with fur and pointed ears? I thought I'd end up in somebody's exotic zoo somewhere. But if most people really *can't* see me, it's kind of the best of both worlds, isn't it? I get to have all the cool cat stuff, but nobody sees me." She broke into a wide grin. "It's kind of like having a secret identity. And superpowers! I'm Catwoman! Oh, wait—that's taken, isn't it? And Catgirl sounds too much like something out of an anime. Let's see—"

"Gina—"

She deflated in her chair, obviously still more than halfway caught up in her careening thoughts, but she made an effort to focus on him. "Fine. Okay. What?" She frowned. "You don't think I'll start coughing up hairballs, do you?"

Stone sighed.

"Okay, I'll get it out of my system. I really *am* glad I decided to call you tonight. You took a real load off me. So, what do you want me to do?"

He pondered. "Well…you do plan to continue working for Jason, right?"

"Oh, hell yeah. I wouldn't think of quitting now that I'm not just hunting for weird stuff—I *am* weird stuff. It makes sense to stay close to the other weird stuff. Are there other ways I can help now?"

"Possibly." He was glad to hear her say that.

"I guess I'll have to tell him, right? And Verity, and Amber?"

"Verity and Amber will probably figure it out on their own when they see you."

Her eyes narrowed. "Really? I thought you said they weren't both mages."

"They aren't. But…there are other factors too. And don't ask me to tell you, because it really *isn't* my place. I suspect you'll find out soon enough."

"Oh, wow, more cool secrets." She spun her chair around almost giddily.

"Gina—do you mind if I examine you?"

She stopped spinning and shot him a suspicious look. "Examine?"

"Magically. No touching involved. I just want to look at your aura in depth."

"I have an aura?"

"You do. Everybody does. And it's changed since you changed."

She looked intrigued. "Changed how? What does an aura look like?"

"It's like…a nimbus of colored energy that surrounds every living thing."

"Whoa. Is everybody's the same color?"

"No."

"What color is mine?" She leaned forward in anticipation, like a little girl waiting for a good story.

"Right now, it's yellow."

"And what was it before?"

"Orange."

"Whoa," she repeated. "So it totally changed when I got catified."

"Yes, and you're the first person I've seen with your condition where I knew them before they changed. So as you might guess, you might provide some valuable data if you let me examine you."

Her suspicious look returned. "Wait—you've been sneaking peeks at my aura before?"

He snorted. "Don't make it sound so lascivious. I look at *everyone's* aura when I interact with them. It's…just a mage thing."

"You can't…you know…see through my clothes, can you?" She crossed her arms protectively over her chest. "Like those old X-Ray Specs from the comics?"

"I give you my word, I can't see anything of the sort. And I wouldn't, even if I could. I'm not a teenage boy, Gina."

"Okay," she grumbled, reluctantly uncrossing her arms. Still, her obvious enthusiasm quickly overshadowed her suspicion. "I wish I could see what an aura looks like…"

"If I show you, will you let me do my examination? I promise, I won't touch you and I won't see anything you'd object to."

"How can you show me?"

Stone raised a hand, forming an illusion in the middle of the room. He'd gotten better at these kinds of illusions since his Calanar days, and now he created a three-dimensional replica of Gina standing in the open space. Another gesture, and the swirling yellow aura sprang from the figure. "That's what yours looks like now."

She nearly fell off her chair. "Oh...*wow*..." she whispered. "What *is* that? How did you do it?"

"A simple illusion." He didn't bother telling her it wasn't actually so simple, since that wasn't the point.

"Wow..." She stood and walked around the illusion, examining it from all angles. "It looks like when R2-D2 showed Luke the hologram of Princess Leia in *Star Wars.* Only bigger." Tearing her gaze away to look back at Stone, she added, "So...that's what I look like to you?"

"Only when I use my magical senses. And right now, you look more like this." He gestured again, and Gina's familiar human form morphed into the bipedal, dark-furred cat.

She studied it. "Yeah, that's what I see now when I look in the mirror. I really have to concentrate to do things like get dressed. I've already learned to do it by feel rather than sight, but if I work hard at it, I can still kind of see my human form."

"All right—I've shown you what your aura looks like. Will you let me do my examination?"

"Uh—sure." She shot him a quizzical look. "What do I have to do?"

"You can sit back down. It will only take a minute or two."

She resumed her seat. "Okay. Go for it."

Stone dropped the illusion, shifted back to magical sight, and paced slowly around the chair. He wished Verity were here, and planned to ask her to do another examination if Gina allowed it, but right now anything he could see would be more than he had.

He concentrated, entering the deeper, meditative state that allowed him to get better readings.

He lost track of time, but eventually he stepped back and let his breath out.

"You done?" Gina asked.

"Yes." He settled back on the couch.

"What did you find out? Anything interesting?"

Before answering, he pulled out his notebook and jotted a few thoughts. Only then did he face her. "It's…hard to say. I never did a full examination on you before, obviously, so I haven't got any solid data to compare with. But I can say with a reasonable amount of certainty that something about you has fundamentally changed."

She snickered. "Uh…no offense, but *duh*. I've got fur, pointed ears, and a tail. I'd say that's pretty fundamental."

"That's not what I meant." Stone refused to take the bait. "I'm talking *fundamental*. Down at the auric level."

"Sounds scary. Is the auric level deeper than, say, the cellular level?"

"Yes and no. The cellular level is purely physical. You haven't changed there, which is interesting. At least I don't think you have. Verity is much better at this sort of thing than I am, so with your permission, I'm going to ask her to take a look at you as well." He rose and began pacing again. "As far as I can tell, physically you're still human."

"You mean, if I went to the doctor and they examined me, they wouldn't find I've got cat innards?"

"I doubt it."

"That's comforting, I guess. Okay, so what's this auric thing? What's it mean?"

He considered his words, dropping into 'professor mode' as he always did when explaining magical concepts to mundanes or apprentices. "Your aura is…your essence. What it means to be *you*, on the most basic possible level. It's much more related to your mind and your psyche than anything physical. If you were to, say, fall pregnant or lose a leg or something, your aura would remain the same."

She frowned. "So you're saying…if my aura changed, I'm not *me* anymore? I still *feel* like me. I mean, aside from looking like a refugee from a Meow Mix commercial, I still like the same things. I still have all my memories and knowledge."

"Yes. I think in this case it's not as much a change as a sort of…enhancement. An overlay. You mentioned before that once you got over the shock, you felt like your change was in line with your personality, right?"

"Well…yeah. I guess. I mean, I've always been curious, I've always been a night person, I love naps, I'm kinda scatterbrained when I'm not focused on something…All those things are cat traits, right?"

Stone thought about Raider and smiled. "Oh, yes. And what you've said lines up with the only other affected person I've been able to question—the man we were trying to find for Jason's case."

"You found him? And he changed too?"

"Yes."

"Into what?"

"A satyr."

Her eyes got big again. "You're kidding. Like, a mythological creature? Furry legs, horns, cloven hooves, great big…uh…"

"Yes." Stone didn't meet her gaze. "And sexual stamina that would put most porn stars to shame."

She gave him a sideways glance. "I'm not sure I want to know how you found *that* out. But anyway…he was like that before? That's why he became a satyr?"

"Who knows? Jason told me his wife said he had quite an active libido, but nothing like this."

She leaned back, picking up the tentacle cat and gazing down at it. "So, you're kind of saying that people who change into something like this do it in line with their…what…basic personality?"

"I've only got two solid data points so far, but it seems so. You're intelligent, highly curious, and—forgive me—a bit lazy—"

She laughed. "No forgiveness needed. I'm lazy as hell."

"And Mr. Carter claims to have felt tied down by his responsibilities, and frustrated because his sexual needs weren't being met. With nothing else to go on, it seems a logical initial hypothesis."

"Listen to you, sounding all sciency."

Stone ignored that, thinking. If this idea *were* true, how did that explain the others he'd seen? What kinds of personality traits made someone an ogre, a werewolf, or a goblin? And, even more importantly, what had *caused* the change? His initial thought that the catalyst must be confined to San Francisco was obviously not correct, since Gina hadn't visited there in recent memory.

Did that mean this was happening all over the area? Perhaps even all over the country…or more?

"You look like you're deep in thought about something," Gina said.

"I am." He stood. "I don't think there's much else I can do tonight, though. If you'll excuse me, I've got some work to do. Are you all right here on your own?"

She waved him off. "Oh, yeah. Now that I know I'm not going crazy or gonna freak out the normies if I bop over to 7-Eleven to restock my Red Bull stash, I'm cool." Her expression sobered. "Hey, thanks, Doc. I really appreciate you coming by, and I'm glad I was right about you not losing your shit over this. It makes me feel a lot better."

"Glad to be of help. And believe me—it will take a lot more than this to rattle me at this point." He gave her a jaunty wave as he headed for the door. "Are you planning to go back to work tomorrow?"

"Might as well, I guess. That seems to be where the action is."

"I'll see about popping by as well, and I'll ask Jason to call Verity and Amber. Best if we get this out of the way quickly."

"Doc?"

Stone stopped in the act of reaching for the doorknob. "Yes?"

"How many people do you think we're talking about? Am I gonna start seeing cat-people and satyrs and…I dunno…orcs and elves on every street corner?"

"I don't have an answer for that yet, Gina. But if you *do* happen to see any, please let me know."

He turned to leave again, but she still looked like she had something on her mind. "Something else?"

"I was just wondering…is this a permanent thing, or is it gonna wear off?"

Stone hadn't thought of that. "I don't have an answer for that either, unfortunately. But it's a good question."

"Yeah. 'Cause you know…this is gonna sound really strange, but…I'm not sure I *want* it to wear off. It just feels…*right,* you know?"

CHAPTER TWELVE

WHEN STONE SHOWED UP at Jason's agency the next morning, Jason and Amber were already there, but Verity and Gina hadn't arrived yet.

"What's this about, Al?" Jason offered him a cup of coffee and held out a box of Psycho Donuts.

Stone took the coffee and waved off the donuts. "Gina didn't say anything yet?" He noticed Amber, who was showing significantly now, had a bottle of water and also hadn't touched the donuts.

"Gina? What's this got to do with her? Is she coming back to work today?"

"That's what she said." He supposed he wasn't surprised she hadn't mentioned anything about her news—it was another catlike trait to be secretive. Stone sympathized, amused at the thought that if he were to be afflicted by the condition, based on his personality and habits, he'd probably end up as a cat as well. The amusement didn't last long, though—so far, he had no reason to believe he *wouldn't*. And as fond as he was of Raider, he had no desire to become his feline roommate's brother in fur.

Could Gina's condition be contagious? He looked warily at Jason and Amber, hoping if it was, he hadn't inadvertently passed it on to one or both of them.

"How do you know that?" Amber asked. "Did you talk to her?" Her eyes narrowed. "Why would she tell you and not Jason?"

"Let's...just wait until she gets here, shall we?" Despite both of them giving him the eye, Stone would say nothing more.

Verity breezed in five minutes later, looking frazzled, and threw her bag down on the couch in the lobby. "Traffic was *terrible*," she grumbled. "Somebody forgot to tell the three accidents I passed that this is supposed to be the reverse commute direction." She flashed Stone a weak glare. "I hope this is worth it."

"Oh, I think it will be."

Fortunately, Gina chose that moment to come in. "Morning, guys. Ooh, donuts!" She tossed her patch-covered backpack next to Verity's bag, plucked a Cereal Killer from the box, and took a big bite. She scanned the faces around her while she chewed, settling on Stone with a questioning glance.

He shrugged and shook his head.

"Okay," Jason said, "we're all here. What's this about, Al?"

Stone was about to answer when Amber sniffed the air and frowned. "Something's strange."

"Strange?" Jason hurried over to her, ever the solicitous husband and would-be father, and glanced around suspiciously as if trying to identify a threat.

"Don't worry, boss," Gina said with a grin. "That would be me. I guess Doc Stone didn't say anything yet."

"Say anything about what?"

But now Verity was frowning too. She had the characteristic fuzzed-out look that clearly indicated magical sight. "Hoooly *shit!*" she breathed, her eyes going huge.

Gina preened, satisfied.

Jason's gaze darted between them. "Does somebody want to tell me what the hell is going on?"

"Yeah—me too," Amber said, glaring. "Something's up. I can smell it. Gina's changed, but I can't tell how."

"She's a freakin' *cat!*" Verity still sounded shellshocked. "Holy shit, she's a cat!" She dragged her attention from Gina and leveled it on Stone. "Wait. Doc—she's got it, doesn't she? She's got the same thing Wayne Carter has."

"So it would appear. Gina, if you'd be so kind as to fill everyone in…" Stone pushed Verity's and Gina's bags aside and took a seat on the sofa, crossing his ankle over his knee and leaning back as if preparing for a good show.

Gina seemed to be enjoying the attention. She told Jason, Amber, and Verity about what she'd discovered a couple days ago, how it had scared her, and how she finally called Stone to see if he had any insights. Then, grinning, she shrugged. "I'm cool with it, to be honest. Took me a little while to get used to it, but now that I know most people can't see me, I don't see a lot of downsides." Her grin widened. "And who knew Doc here was some kind of badass wizard? That's even cooler!"

Jason shot Stone a narrow-eyed look. "You told her?"

"I sort of had to. How else could I explain things to her?"

"Don't worry, boss," Gina assured him. "I promised him I wouldn't say anything to anybody, and I mean it. Your secret's safe with me. Cat, remember? We love secrets." She turned her smug attention to Verity. "And you're one too, which is cooler still. And no, Doc Stone didn't tell me. I sorta figured it out on my own."

Verity looked like she didn't quite know how to react to that.

"*You,* on the other hand…" Gina stalked over to Amber, but stopped far enough away not to incur Jason's protective instincts. "You're something different." She sniffed delicately at the air. "You said you could smell that I've changed, but you can't be like me. Doc said I'd be able to see it if you are." She leaned in closer. "And I can smell there's something interesting about you too, and I don't think it's that you're pregnant. What do you say—I told you mine. Will you tell me yours?"

Jason and Amber exchanged glances. "Uh…" Jason said. It was clear all this was moving too fast for him, and he was trying to get his feet back under him.

But Amber didn't seem disturbed. "What the hell," she said as if it didn't matter. "I guess if you're going to join the team for real, you need to know. I'm part-shifter."

"Shifter?" Gina cocked her head. "You mean like a werewolf or something?"

"No," she growled. "Not a werewolf. Most shifters hate being called were-whatevers. And anyway, I'm not part wolf. I'm part bear."

"Whoa." Her eyes shone. "This day just keeps getting cooler. Who knew I've been surrounded by all this awesome stuff and I *missed* it? So you're saying you can turn into a bear?"

"No. I'm *part* shifter, not full. I can't change, but I got a lot of the other perks. Fantastic sense of smell, strength, toughness…"

Gina's gaze dropped to Amber's belly. "Mama bear."

"Damn straight," Jason's voice took on a dangerous edge. "You might wanna back off."

Gina leaped back, startled but far more graceful than she'd ever done as a human. "Sorry, sorry! I'm still learning the ropes, so don't get too mad at me if I blow my weird-people etiquette rolls for a while." She took another big chomp from her donut and grabbed her pack from next to Stone. "Anyway, I'm sorry about taking the last two days off, but I didn't know nobody could see me. I thought waltzing in here like this wouldn't be a career-advancing move, y'know?"

Jason was still looking like he hadn't come to terms with all the new information yet. "So…what do we do now?"

"What do you mean?" Stone uncrossed his ankle and leaned forward.

In answer, Jason waved mutely at Gina.

"Why do we have to *do* anything? Gina, you still want to work here, right?"

"Oh, yeah."

"And Jason, you still *want* her to work here, right?"

Jason shifted his gaze between Gina and Amber, and didn't answer right away.

"Of course he does," Amber said firmly. She patted Jason's shoulder. "Come on, Jase—she's not a threat or anything. She's just…a little furrier than she was before. And most of us can't even see *that*."

Gina shot her a grateful look. "Seriously," she agreed. "I'm still me. I might need to curl up under my desk and take a quick nap in the afternoon, and I might want to get in a little later and do more work at night, but it's not like I'm gonna need an ADA litterbox or anything." She plopped down in her chair and did a happy little butt-wriggle, looking at each of the others in turn. "I'm still getting my mind around how cool this place is. Two wizards, a mama bear, and…the world's best boss," she finished a little lamely.

"Hey, I've got something too," Jason protested quickly.

Amber laughed. "He doesn't want to be left out."

"You do?" Gina spun her chair back toward him. "What?"

He appeared to regret that he'd spoken up. "Uh…it's hard to explain. And not nearly as cool as the rest of these guys."

"By the way, we're not *wizards*," Verity said.

"Oh. Sorry. Blew my roll again. See, it's gonna take some time."

"Okay. I should have known the MFM train hasn't stopped yet," Jason grumbled.

"MFM?" Gina asked.

"*More Fucking Magic,*" Jason, Verity, and Amber responded in unison.

"You have a *term* for it? That's awesome."

"*Anyway,*" Jason continued with a long-suffering look, "I guess it kinda is a good thing to have you fully on the team. It'll make a lot of things easier."

"Ooh, do we have a bunch of secret cases where we hunt down supernatural threats or something?"

"Uh…no. Maybe a few. Mostly we hunt down insurance fraud and tail cheating spouses, just like before. But at least this way we can tell you *why* you're looking up the strange stuff." His expression turned stern. "And I was serious before—I hope Al got it through to you that you need to keep your mouth shut about this stuff with the rest of the world. No blabbing to your internet buddies. Got it?"

She looked mildly miffed, but nodded soberly. "Yeah. I get it. And you don't have to worry." She made a zipped-lip gesture. "You think I want to piss off real, honest-to-goodness wiz—er—mages?"

Stone stood. "Right, then. That's that sorted. Gina, I'll probably want to chat with you some more about this, since you're the only person I've got access to who's been…er…afflicted."

"We've *got* to come up with a better name for it than that," Verity said dryly.

"Enhanced," Gina offered.

"Whatever," Stone said. "I assume you're willing?"

"Oh, sure. Ask away. And you have my email address."

"Hey, I just had a thought," Verity spoke up. "Gina…I know this is going to sound creepy, but…would you let me have a little of your blood?"

"My…blood? Why?"

"One of my magical specialties is alchemy."

"You mean like turning lead into gold? Or like *Warcraft,* you know, making potions?"

"More the second one." She glanced at Stone. "Maybe Hez and I can examine her blood and see if we can find anything showing where this might have come from."

"Brilliant idea."

"Except for the whole *my blood* thing." Gina still didn't look convinced.

"I promise, I won't use it for anything but an examination," Verity said. "I'll destroy whatever's left when we're done. You have my word."

"Whoa…you mean you could *do* things with it?" Her expression grew even more apprehensive. "I didn't know that. All I meant was that I hate needles."

"Mages *can* do things with blood," Stone said. "So you want to be careful about who has access to it. But you can trust Verity. She was my apprentice, and I'll vouch for her."

She shifted her gaze between the two of them, clearly soaking up every bit of new information about the magical world like a sponge. "Well…"

"It's up to you," Verity said. "But it would really help us out, especially if we find something."

It took her a while to respond, and she obviously still wasn't crazy about the idea. "Okay," she finally said. "If it'll help." She shrugged out of her jacket and offered an arm. "It won't hurt, will it?"

Verity fished in her bag and pulled out a capped syringe and a sterile alcohol wipe. "Just a little pinprick. I'm good at this."

Gina turned away from the syringe. "I'm not sure how I feel about the fact that you carry that kind of stuff in your bag. Do you *often* go around taking blood samples from random people?"

"Nah. But it's always good to be prepared." She pulled up a chair next to Gina and deftly but gently drew a syringeful of blood. "There. That wasn't so bad, was it?"

"I'm not gonna answer that. Shouldn't I…you know…get back to work or something?"

"Yeah," Jason said. "I still need that info on the Bonetti case, remember? We're already overdue."

Gina looked relieved to have something to do. "Let me know when the next meeting of the Scooby Gang happens, okay? I'll even bring the refreshments."

Stone moved off to the waiting area with Verity. "Let me know what you find out," he said under his breath, indicating the syringe she'd stuck back in her bag. "I hope you *do* get something. This is starting to alarm me, if I'm being honest."

"Because we're encountering so many of them?"

"Exactly. I don't believe the 'weirdness magnet' thing in this case. I'm more inclined to think that if this many of them are turning up in our circles, that must mean there are a lot more of them out there we *haven't* seen. I want to know where they're coming from—and how to stop them."

Verity looked pensive. "Why?"

"What do you mean, why?"

"Let's step outside for a minute, okay?"

Stone glanced toward the interior of the room. Gina was already tapping away on her computer, and Jason and Amber had disappeared into Jason's office. He allowed Verity to lead him outside, where they stood and watched the heavy morning traffic crawling by on First Street. "What's on your mind?"

She leaned against the building. "Why do you want to stop them?"

He narrowed his eyes. "Why *wouldn't* I want to stop them? Or, more precisely, stop whatever it is that's causing this."

"But why?"

"You're not making sense."

She shook her head. "No, Doc. *You're* not making sense. You talked to Gina more than the rest of us did. Does she seem unhappy about what's happened to her?"

"No, but—"

"But nothing. Mr. Carter didn't seem unhappy, either. They both said the same thing—that whatever this is, it felt like it was meant to be. Like they were discovering a part of themselves they didn't even know they were missing. They *like* it. So what right do we, or anybody else, have to think we can take it away from them?"

Stone pondered, glancing at her. Her words reminded him of the arguments they'd had in the past about magical oversight and how much of it there should be. She didn't sound blindly passionate or angry now, though, but merely calm and firm. She'd done a lot of growing up since last summer. "So you're saying we should just…not even try to figure out where this is coming from? Verity, we know next to nothing about it. We don't even know if it's permanent, or whether it might lead to something harmful."

"In the first place, why is it up to *us* to figure anything out? I mean, yeah, I want to know too. I'm not arguing that it won't be valuable to know where it's coming from, if we can. But it's not our job to *do* anything about it."

He narrowed his eyes. "Aren't you saying the exact opposite of what you said before?"

"How so?"

"Before, you wanted to create some kind of central authority to round up mages who used their talent to exploit mundanes. Now you're saying we should just…allow this to continue unchecked? You don't honestly think some of these people won't use their new forms for nefarious purposes, do you?"

Now it was her turn to ponder. "Maybe they will," she admitted. "I'm just saying it's more complicated than either 'we've got to stop it before it spreads' or 'we've got to let it happen and do nothing about it.' It's not really our call. If this is as widespread as you're afraid it is—and we don't know that yet, because all the cases we know of are in the Bay Area—then this might be time to consider letting the other mages know about it."

"That is a very good point. I've already got Eddie and Ward researching it. If they turn up anything, we can go through Caventhorne to get the word out to the UK mages. Not sure how successful that will be here, though."

"First things first," Verity said. "Maybe if it comes to that, I can talk to Bron's Nana. Their group has contact with a lot of mages all over the country. What about your friend Kolinsky?"

"I can't find him. He's made himself scarce again. So has Madame Huan."

"You think that's related to this?"

"Who the hell knows? Stefan sits on a lot of information, but if he doesn't care about something, he doesn't bother expending effort on it." If the phenomenon *was* confined to the Bay Area and both Kolinsky and Madame Huan were elsewhere, it was entirely possible they didn't know about it yet. But if it was more widespread, then how was he supposed to find out what they knew if he couldn't even—

A sudden thought struck him. "Listen," he said quickly, "I've got to go. Can you say my goodbyes for me? I need to check on something."

"What?" She looked at him suspiciously.

"A research source I hadn't thought of before. Keep me updated on the blood, will you?"

"Yeah." Obviously, she'd realized asking more questions would get her nowhere. "I sure wish I could travel like you do, though. The drive home's gonna be a bitch."

CHAPTER THIRTEEN

S TONE WAITED UNTIL HE GOT HOME before sending a text. *Are you around?* He had no idea when he'd get a response—it could be a few seconds, or it could be a couple days. There was never any telling.

To his relief, this time it skewed toward the near end of the spectrum. He'd stuck the phone back in his pocket and was putting out a bowl of food for Raider when it buzzed.

What's up?

Stone smiled. He hadn't heard from Ian in a couple weeks—the last message had been that his son was deep-sea diving off the coast of Africa—and it was always a pleasure to get a message. By now, he'd come to terms with the fact that their relationship wasn't going to be one of constant contact. *Where are you?*

Prague.

Stone did a quick mental calculation. It was noon in California, which meant it was nine p.m. there. *Out at a club?*

Not yet. Why?

Need to talk to your master. He always felt odd referring to Gabriel as Ian's "boyfriend"—not because he had any problem with the relationship, but because Ian, despite all the outward indications, claimed he wasn't. *Is he around?*

Yeah, he's in town. Why?

Long story. Can I come over?

Sure. Pick you up at the portal?

R. L. KING

Sounds good. Meet you in an hour. It was a good thing there was a public portal in Prague—it meant he didn't have to arouse Ian's suspicions if he turned up too quickly.

Prague's public portal was in the basement of a small, trendy nightclub in the Prague 1 district in the heart of the city. Stone made a point to arrive ten minutes early, in case his son was watching for him to come through. Fortunately, the portal was on a ley line, so he had no trouble popping in. Ian was never early for anything, but there was always a first time.

When Ian arrived, Stone was seated at a shadowy table, listening to a frenetic, blue-haired DJ spinning edgy electronic music. Stone watched his son slip through the crowd and take the seat opposite him.

"Hey, Dad. It's good to see you." As usual, Ian looked like he'd just stepped out of a fashion magazine, his slim, muscular frame clothed in a skintight T-shirt, designer jeans, and an expensive black denim jacket. He'd grown his hair a little longer over the past year and artful stubble defined his sharp jawline.

"Always good to see you." They'd remained in communication via text and occasional video calls since the situation with the ghouls, but hadn't seen each other in person since then. "How did the deep-sea diving go?"

"Fantastic." Ian's face lit up. "We were off Pemba Island in Tanzania. Gabriel taught me a spell so we could breathe underwater, and the disregarding spell meant we could get a lot closer to the hammerhead sharks. You should try it, Dad. It's amazing."

Stone smiled at his son's enthusiasm. "That's all right—I'll live vicariously through you. I get my excitement a little closer to dry land."

"Fair enough. We're going mountain climbing in Nepal next month—you're welcome to come along if you want."

"I appreciate the offer, but I'll leave that sort of thing to you, I think." He could hardly begrudge his son his jet-setting, daredevil lifestyle—he'd certainly earned it after enduring a difficult childhood with his single mother and her tyrannical, homophobic husband, not to mention being brainwashed into nearly killing his own father when they'd barely had a chance to know each other. That didn't mean he didn't wish Ian would get it out of his system at some point, though.

Ian gave him an easy grin. "Okay, I get it. I'll stop trying to drag you along on my adventures."

"More fun with two anyway. Speaking of—" He glanced around the club. "You said Gabriel was around? I do need to chat with him."

"He's back at the flat. We've got a party at midnight, but he should be there for another hour or so. Come on—I'll show you the place."

Stone shifted uncomfortably in his chair. He didn't want to say his next words, but there was no helping it. "Ian—I do want to see you. You know I do. I hope we can get together and catch up a bit before I head back. But…I've got to talk to Gabriel alone."

Ian's eyes narrowed. "Why?'

"Nothing to do with you, I promise."

He didn't look convinced. "Then why keep it a secret from me?"

Stone was definitely getting tired of keeping people in the dark about various aspects of his life. "Because I need to talk to him about some things I'm not at liberty to reveal. If he wants to tell you, that's none of my business. But I…can't," he finished a little lamely.

"You can't."

"No." He glanced at the DJ to avoid meeting Ian's eyes. "Some of it, I can tell you after I've chatted with Gabriel. That part's not a secret, and I actually could use your help with it. But the rest…" He spread his hands in a *what can I do?* gesture and looked back at his son.

Ian held his gaze for a long few seconds before finally nodding. "Okay. Fine. Come on—I'll take you to him."

Stone didn't miss the slight chill in his son's voice, and it sliced through him. *Damn these dragons anyway.* Knowing about them had made some things in his life easier, but there was always a flipside.

He followed Ian outside, where he hailed a cab. They sat in silence as the driver picked his way through the heavy downtown traffic and eventually pulled up in front of a handsome, old-fashioned seven-story building on Pařížská Street in the heart of the ultra-pricey Old Town district. When it stopped, Ian made no move to get out.

"He's on the top floor. Can't miss it—it's the only apartment on that level. I'll text him that you'll be up."

"You're not coming?"

Ian shrugged. "Why? Send me a text if you need me for something. I've got a couple clubs I can hit up in the meantime."

"Ian—"

"It's all good, Dad. We'll talk later." He pulled the door shut, and the cab rolled smoothly off into the night.

Well. That could have gone better.

No helping it now, though. Best to get what he came for over with, and then afterward he could try to smooth things over with Ian before he headed home.

The building was very old. The interior maintained its old-world charm, but Stone didn't miss signs that the place had been subtly updated and renovated to increase its appeal to residents who were both wealthy and unconventional. Though the elevator looked like a freight lift from the early part of the previous century, when Stone stepped inside and touched the button for the top floor, the door slid shut and the cubicle ascended with quiet efficiency. Stone was sure he'd never have been allowed to even enter it without Ian's text informing Gabriel of his imminent arrival.

The door opened not on a hallway, but on the apartment itself. Stone stepped out before it closed behind him, taking in the soaring ceilings, walls of old, weathered brick, and tall windows affording a commanding view of the city.

"Welcome, Dr. Stone," came a voice from the darkness. A familiar figure strolled out of the shadows. "I must say, I didn't expect to ever see you here."

"Nice place you've got." Stone studied Gabriel. He didn't look much different than last time he'd seen him: slim and impossibly handsome, no older than twenty, with spiky, white-blond hair and snug-fitting jeans and T-shirt that showed off his ripped physique. He moved with a sensual grace that invited anyone around him— male, female, or otherwise—to put aside their inhibitions and see what kind of pleasures he could open up for them.

In other words, he couldn't have looked more different than his father, Stefan Kolinsky.

"Thank you. Can I get you something?" He himself held a glass of some jewel-green liquid.

"No. Thank you. I won't stay long. I know you and Ian have a function to attend later."

"A function." Gabriel smiled lazily. "That's one way to put it, I suppose. But that's not for a couple of hours. What is it you wanted to discuss that you didn't want Ian to hear?"

"I'm sorry about that. I think I might have offended him, and that wasn't my intention. I hope we can smooth it over before I go, but I'm sure you'll understand why I left him out when you hear what I have to say."

"Let's have it, then." He waved Stone toward a butter-soft, brown-leather sofa. He himself stretched languidly in a chair across from it, hooking one leg over the arm and raising his glass as if to say, *go on, I'm listening.*

Stone wanted to pace, but instead he took the offered seat, which faced the spectacular view. "I'll get right to it, then. I'm looking for your father."

"What makes you think I'd know where my father is?" Gabriel's smile didn't falter; it gave him the aspect of a cat playing with a toy mouse.

"I know you two don't get on, but he's disappeared and I need to talk to him."

"Hmm. Interesting. But I ask you again—why do you think I'd know where he is? As you said, we don't...see eye to eye on much."

"I think you might see eye to eye on more than you might admit to, actually."

Gabriel raised his glass and sipped. "Do tell."

Stone wished he'd taken the young man up on his offer of a drink. "I know what your father is, Gabriel. And I know what you are."

"Is that right?" He still appeared amused and utterly unruffled by Stone's words. "What are we, then?"

"Dragons." Stone met his gaze with a direct one of his own, and spoke in an even, firm tone.

Gabriel chuckled. "Ah, so he's told you. He wasn't supposed to do that."

"You didn't know?" That surprised Stone. He thought all the dragons had some kind of network where they kept each other up to date on recent developments.

"I didn't. I don't really...keep up with their goings-on. Not interested."

"I didn't think that was allowed."

Gabriel waved it off. "I stay out of the whole business, and they don't bother with me because I'm a bit of a disgrace. As long as I keep their secrets, they don't care what I do."

"A disgrace?"

He indicated the apartment, and himself. "I've gone native. Over the wall, as you humans say. I don't bother with the things they consider important—the agreements they maintain to keep them from killing each other, their overcomplicated rules and protocols and etiquettes. I'm simply not interested."

"Not interested in what? Being a dragon?"

"Exactly." He stretched on the chair, twisting his body so he was lying with his back against one arm and both legs draped over the other. "I hardly see the point. I don't know how much my father told you, and how much trouble he's in for doing it—"

"I don't think he's in trouble. He wasn't the only one who told me. They got together and discussed it, and they revealed certain things to me to prevent me from causing problems with my investigations."

Gabriel's smile widened. He did a slow golf clap. "Bravo, Dr. Stone. I'm impressed. You must have done something truly impressive to get that affiliation of hidebound fossils to un-knot their underwear enough to agree on something so momentous. I'd love to hear the story if you're willing to share it."

"There isn't much to tell." Stone wondered how much Gabriel was lying to him about what he knew. Unfortunately, whether the young man chose to claim his draconic heritage or not, he still possessed all the immense magical power of his species. That meant his aura was impossible to read—or even if it wasn't, Stone couldn't be sure he wasn't spoofing it.

He thought back to what he'd discussed with Kolinsky and the other dragons. Nowhere could he remember them ever telling him he couldn't share what he knew with other dragons—or anyone else, for that matter. He'd chosen to keep the secret from his human friends because he didn't want to open them up to the dragons' scrutiny. But that didn't apply to Gabriel.

He wondered if Kolinsky's oath about the rifts would prevent him from revealing his knowledge to another dragon, but decided not to push it yet. "You know I'm a scion, right? And so is Ian?"

"Of course."

Here goes... "And you know about the interdimensional rifts?"

The words came out with no hesitation. Apparently, other dragons *were* exempt from the oath. Even ones who didn't want anything to do with their own kind.

"I do, yes." He didn't seem concerned about them.

"Well, that's what I stumbled into. I was closing them, and the other dragons didn't think that was a good idea. So your father explained to me why I shouldn't do it anymore."

Gabriel nodded, still not seeming concerned. "That still doesn't explain why they revealed their true nature to you. That isn't something they do lightly."

No bloody kidding. "I think it was your father's idea. He convinced the others that I could be of use to them—helping deal with situations they'd prefer not to involve themselves in directly."

"I see." He stretched again, drained his glass, and used magic to levitate it to a nearby table. "And now you say my father's disappeared?"

"Yes. And so has Madame Huan. I don't know if the other dragons have too, since I haven't got any way to contact the rest of them." He shrugged. "I also don't know if there's anything to be concerned about. As far as I know, they could be off on some kind of...dragon retreat or something. It's probably none of my business, and even your father doesn't make a point of sharing his plans with me unless I'm directly involved in them. But something's...come up, and I need to discuss it with him. So if you've got a way to reach him—"

"I don't. I actually *do* know where he is, but it wouldn't be advisable to try reaching him, even if I had any desire to do it. I doubt he'd want to talk to me anyway." He twisted around until he was sitting upright. "What's this thing that's 'come up'? Anything I can help with?"

Stone considered. "That's hard to say. I suppose it's worth asking, anyway. I'm guessing that, even though you don't want to be in the Dragon Club, you've still been around a hell of a lot longer than any of us humans have."

"That's a reasonable assumption."

Stone wished Gabriel would stop looking so damned amused, like this whole thing was a big game for him—even though it probably was. He forged ahead, determined to play it straight. "Something's happening. People are turning up who look normal to mundanes, but to magical sight—or to others who've been afflicted with the same condition—they look like…something else."

"Something else." For the first time, Gabriel seemed interested in Stone's words.

"Yes. So far, I've encountered seven of them, including a group of four together. All but one were in San Francisco. In every case, to magical sight they look like supernatural creatures. Werewolves, goblins, cat-people, satyrs…" Stone watched Gabriel's face carefully for any reaction.

There was none, except for a slight furrowing of his brow. Either he didn't know what Stone was talking about, or he was hiding it *very* well. He said nothing.

"You don't know anything about this, do you?" A little shiver ran up Stone's spine. Gabriel might not be the most representative sample of dragonkind, but he was still a dragon, and that meant he was old. If this phenomenon had occurred before, it made sense he'd have at least heard rumors of it.

"I don't."

"So, you haven't seen anything like it?"

"Not in the past, no. And not that I'm aware of in the present. But then again, I haven't been in the United States in quite some time. Ian and I have been dividing our time between magical studies and…entertainment." His smile turned lascivious, but only for a moment. "You have no idea what's causing the condition, or how widespread it is?"

"None whatsoever. One of the afflicted people works for a friend of mine, so she's allowing Verity and me to do a few experiments. But aside from that…nothing. I was hoping you—or your father—might have more information."

"He might, but I doubt it. Just because I don't spend much time with my own kind doesn't mean I haven't been around. And it doesn't mean I'm not curious about magic."

"So you're saying, if it had been around before, you'd have seen it. Or at least heard about it."

"Most likely, yes." He smiled. "There are some aspects of dragonkind that even *I* can't avoid, and one of them is that most of us fancy ourselves the protectors of this world from magical incursions."

Stone blinked. Even Kolinsky hadn't come right out and said *that*. "You're serious."

"Oh, quite serious. For some of us—my father included, if we're being honest with each other—mostly it has to do with the fact that we're stuck here with no way to return home, so we've got a vested interest in keeping it from being overrun by things humans couldn't hope to deal with. It's not so much that they're interested in protecting you. That's more like a side effect."

"What about the rest of you?" Once again, Stone met Gabriel's gaze head on.

He shrugged lazily. "What can I say? I can't speak for the others, but I've gotten attached to you hairless apes over the years. Especially since I've had to become one of you. You're a lot more fun than my bunch, I'll say that for you. You'd be astounded at all the ways humans have invented to experience pleasure."

Stone didn't answer.

"Does it surprise you so much, that a dragon would admit to preferring humans? It shouldn't. I was very young when we were exiled. Do you know about the exile? Did my father tell you that part?"

"He...did, yes."

Gabriel made a little clucking sound. "He's gotten positively *chatty* with you. If I didn't know better, I'd swear he had a crush. Or, more likely, since I can't conceive of Father having a crush on *anyone,* he considers you a surrogate son to take the place of the one he's given up on. But no matter. The point is, I was barely more than a hatchling when we got sent here. I grew up as much among the humans as among the dragons. I barely had any time to experience life in my true form before it was taken from me."

"I suppose that makes sense." Stone sighed. "So here I am back at square one. This is happening, but I don't know why, or how widespread it is, or how to stop it."

"I wish I could help you." Surprisingly, Gabriel sounded sincere now, and no longer gently mocking. "As it is, I'll keep an eye out for the phenomenon, and if I discover it, I'll see about trying to figure out what's causing it. But that's all I can promise."

"Thank you. I'd appreciate it if you'd contact me if you *do* find anyone—especially outside the U.S. I'm trying to determine how widespread it is. As I said, right now I've only seen it in the Bay Area, but that's more likely because I haven't been to many other places since first spotting it than because it doesn't exist anywhere else."

"If I see anything, I'll let you know." He stood. "Is that everything? I do need to get ready for the party tonight. You're welcome to come along, if you want to. It's going to be quite the experience, so I'm told."

"Thank you, but I'll pass. I should go find Ian and try to explain to him, as much as I can, anyway." He shot a faint glare at Gabriel. "Are you ever going to tell him what you are?"

The dragon shrugged. "I don't see that it's relevant, honestly. And even if it were, that's the one thing even I'm not willing to defy the agreements on. If the others revealed themselves to you, they doubtless had a good reason. I don't."

Stone couldn't help feeling a little disappointment. Not only would such a revelation go a long way toward explaining why he'd had to be so secretive, it would also mean that, as a scion, Ian could possibly learn the ley-line travel method. "And I suppose I'd be in a world of trouble if *I* told him."

"Who knows? I wouldn't chance it if I were you, though. That group, especially the older ones, have no sense of humor when it comes to their secrets getting out."

"I suppose so. In any case, I'm not sure Ian wants to talk to me right now. Will you tell him about the new affliction and ask him to keep an eye out as well? And tell him I'll be in touch?"

"I'll tell him. You've got me fascinated, and that's hard to do these days. Take care, Dr. Stone."

CHAPTER FOURTEEN

ANOTHER WEEK PASSED without any new information. Stone continued his evening patrols around the Bay Area to search for more of the hidden creatures, but didn't find any. Gabriel didn't contact him, though he did get a call—not just a text—from Ian the day after he spoke with the dragon in Prague.

"Sorry I got pissed last night," he'd said. "I just don't like it when people go over my head and keep me in the dark about stuff that might affect me. Reminds me of my childhood, I guess. You know, 'kids should be seen and not heard' kind of thing. Bobby was big into that."

"I quite understand. I'm sorry I had to do it, but unfortunately nothing's changed. I still can't tell you some of what Gabriel and I discussed."

"That's fine. I get it. Not everything's my business. He *did* tell me about the people you saw, though. I've been looking around for them, but haven't seen any." His voice took on amusement. "I'm kinda disappointed, to be honest. I was hoping to see a hot satyr at a party or something."

Stone chuckled. "Well, keep looking. So, we're good?"

"We're good. Hopefully we can get together soon."

"Maybe sooner than you think. I forgot to tell you last night— Aubrey and Susan are getting married next month."

"Oh, wow, that's awesome. About time, too."

"That's exactly what I said. And I hate to start sounding overly parental, but—please make it a point not to be off with Gabriel digging for fossils on Mars or something when the date comes. Aubrey will be gutted if you don't turn up."

When Stone got a text from Verity later that week, he'd begun to get discouraged about finding any more of the creatures. Eddie and Ward hadn't come back with anything, much to their disappointment. He still hadn't heard from either Kolinsky or Madame Huan, neither of whom had returned to their shops. And Jason had reported that Gina had resumed work as if nothing had changed, aside from getting sleepier than usual in the late afternoon and bringing rare roast-beef sandwiches for lunch. Reluctantly, Stone had turned his focus to putting the finishing touches on his seminar presentation, and gone back to working on his portal circle.

The text came mid-morning on Thursday. *Hey Doc. You want to come up here? We might have some info for you. We're at the shop. You need to come now, though—the grand opening's today so we'll be busy after ten.*

Stone didn't even bother pretending to allow commute time. Fifteen minutes later he pushed open the door of Sybil's Apothecary and hurried inside. He stopped and looked around. "Wow. You've really got the place in shape since I was last here, haven't you?"

Verity looked up from wiping down a display case and grinned. "Thanks. We've been working hard."

By now, all the visible boxes had been unpacked. Bottles, vials, crystals, candles, and books lined the wooden shelves, while several other free-standing display cases in the middle of the space contained everything from tarot decks to collections of herbs and bundled-together plants. Posters and framed prints on the walls and eerie music playing softly through unseen speakers completed the pagan, 'witchy' vibe. The whole place had a pleasantly earthy smell, like an herb garden that had lain undisturbed for years and been allowed to go wild.

"So, what have you got for me? Did you find out anything interesting?"

"Maybe. Hang on, let me get Hezzie. You want anything?"

"No, thanks."

Verity disappeared into the back. Stone paced, examining the wares and wondering if Hezzie's curiosity about their findings was finally going to overcome her dislike of being around him.

They returned a few moments later. Verity carried a sheaf of notebook paper, and Hezzie had a rack with several vials on it. Verity hurried over and locked the front door, pulling the shade down so no early birds looking for bargains could peer inside. Hezzie, meanwhile, shot Stone a nervous, suspicious look and quickly put the counter between him and herself. She set the rack containing the vials on the countertop.

"Okay," Verity said. "I gotta tell you, Doc, this is weird. Weirder than usual, I mean." She indicated the vials. "Hez and I even took a quick trip down to Ojai to see Edna about it."

Stone frowned. He hadn't visited Edna Soren in a long time. The old woman had been Verity's teacher for a while during her apprenticeship, with a focus on nature-based and healing magic that had aligned with her interests and talents. "How is she doing these days?"

"Pretty much the same. Grumpy and wants to be left alone." Verity grinned. "But she liked Hezzie, go figure—I guess the terminally cranky and misanthropic gravitate toward each other."

Stone snatched a quick glance at Hezzie to see if Verity's words had offended her, but she was smiling smugly. He noticed she still refused to make eye contact with him, though.

"Right, then," he said quickly. "What did you find out?"

"We did a bunch of alchemical tests on Gina's blood." Verity picked up one of the vials, which contained a green liquid that didn't look anything like blood unless Gina had turned not only feline but Vulcan. "Obviously we don't have serious medical equipment so we couldn't do a lot, but that wasn't really what we were looking for anyway. We were more concerned with magic."

"Plus," Hezzie said, her gaze still firmly fixed on the vials, "we didn't have a sample of Gina's blood from *before* she changed to compare it with, which limits what was possible to discover."

Stone merely nodded, examining the other vials. Two looked like they contained normal blood, while the liquid in the fourth and final one was a murky gold.

"Bottom line," Verity said, "there's *definitely* something magical going on in there."

"Well…that's not really a surprise, is it? People don't completely change not only their astral appearance but their auras without some kind of significant catalyst."

"Yeah, that's true." She picked up the gold vial and jiggled it, sloshing the liquid back and forth. "But that's not the weird part. Or the weird*est* part. That's why it took us so long to get back to you—we wanted to be as sure as we could be before we reported our findings."

"So, what is it?" Stone didn't mind that they were drawing out the reveal. He'd be a hypocrite if he did, given his propensity to do the same thing.

"We think it might be contagious."

Stone took a quick, involuntary step back. "Contagious? You mean, like a disease?"

"Yeah, exactly. We still need to go see Gina again, but based on what we've discovered so far, we think the people who have it are…shedding whatever causes it. Kind of like a mundane contagious disease."

"So…does that mean any of us could get it?" Stone shivered, taking another step back. He had no desire to change into anything *else* supernatural.

"Well…maybe. But that's another interesting thing we discovered." She nodded toward Hezzie.

"We don't have it," the other woman said.

"You…don't have it." Stone tilted his head. "You mean, you and Verity."

"Yeah. Naturally, once we found out it might be contagious and we were exposed, we checked our own blood. No sign of the same magical factor."

"Hmm. Interesting." Stone didn't know that much about magic-based medicine, but one of the things he *did* know was that magical talent didn't show up in the blood. There was no known way to test for it, other than by doing the kind of in-depth astral examination that even most mages didn't know how to do. "What does that mean? That you're immune? Obviously at least Verity has been exposed, since she was around both Carter and Gina."

"We don't know yet," Verity said. "We can't tell this soon. We're not sure whether we're immune, we didn't get a high enough dose to trip it, or it just has an incubation period longer than a few days." She looked up at Stone, her expression serious. "There's a lot of stuff we don't know, Doc, and that scares me. We don't have the facilities or the expertise to do the kind of in-depth testing that needs to be done. Not to mention the test subjects. Are mages immune? Can it affect all mundanes, or only some subset? Who knows?"

"So…we could be looking at some kind of magical plague," Stone said grimly.

"Sort of," Hezzie said. Though she still wasn't looking directly at Stone, she seemed to be warming to her subject. "So far, it doesn't seem to be causing harm, even to the people it affects. It just…changes them."

"And you don't call that *harm?*" Stone demanded. "Bloody hell, we're talking about something that can alter humans at an auric level. That's pretty damned significant."

"Yeah," Verity said, "but so far, at least the ones we've met personally don't seem to mind it. Almost the contrary—both Gina and Wayne Carter talk like they've had some kind of epiphany about what they're meant to be. Like it's not so much a disease as...I dunno...an enlightenment. An awakening."

"That's only two data points," Stone said stubbornly. "We don't know about the others—or how many *more* people were afflicted." He began pacing around the open floor. "You say it's like a disease—does that mean it might be possible to cure it?"

"Whoa, Doc." Verity held up a hand. "We're nowhere near that far along yet. Like I told you—Hez and I are just a couple of small-time alchemists. This is way above our pay grade. If you're serious about studying this, we're gonna need to bring in some heavier hitters."

"Like who?" Stone paused his pacing and considered, trying to remember if he knew any other alchemists. At first, the only one he could think of was Marciela Garra, the mad old woman who'd kidnapped shifters to steal their blood for her super-soldier potions. But she was currently worm food, sans her head, which made her a poor choice. "I don't—" Another memory surfaced. "Wait—I do know another alchemist, though I haven't got a clue how to contact him these days. And I can check with Eddie and Ward. They might know some people in the UK or somewhere else in Europe."

"This might be a case where we want to get some people together," Verity said. "If we want to figure out what's causing this and how to prevent other people from getting it, we can't have a bunch of people working on their own without some kind of collaboration."

"Agreed." Stone considered. "Caventhorne would be an ideal place for that kind of research. They have all sorts of resources, and what they don't have, they can buy." He looked at the rack of vials again. "Anything else you've found out? Any speculation on who or where our Patient Zero is? This has to have started somewhere, so maybe another good idea is to try figuring out where."

Verity looked dubious. "I'm not sure that would be possible. I know I'm just a layman and we should probably talk to some real experts—maybe even mundane experts—but my feeling for where to start is to try growing this ourselves and seeing how long it takes to mature. If we know the incubation period, we might be able to track back. Of course, doing that increases the chance of us getting exposed, too, if we're not immune." She shook her head ruefully. "Now I kinda wish the Whitworths were still alive. Melvin might have been an arrogant ass, but he was a mage and a damn good medical researcher—which is exactly the combination we need right now."

"Okay. I'm not going to presume to tell you to take safety pre-cautions, because I know you're already doing that. I'll contact Eddie and Ward and ask them if they know anyone who can help—and if they can set up some kind of isolated lab somewhere in an out-of-the-way corner of Caventhorne. Hezzie, if you know any other alchemists, this might be a good time to contact them too."

"Yeah, I got that." Her eyes came up in a quick glare.

Stone refused to let her annoy him. Instead, he spoke softly. "Listen—I know you don't think much of me, and you'd rather I kept well away from you. I can do that if it will make you more comfortable, but I've got to stay involved in this. Especially in light of the new information you two have turned up, I think it's got the potential to be a huge disruption in the magical world. If you like, I'll communicate through Verity."

To his surprise, Hezzie looked down and shifted uncomforta-bly. "I…it's not you. Not specifically."

"I know that too. But does it matter?"

Verity gently gripped Hezzie's shoulder. "I hope you don't mind," she said softly. "I…told him a little bit about why you get uncomfortable around guys. He gets it."

She didn't seem angry at the breach of confidence. "I know. I—" With obvious effort, she dragged her gaze back up and met Stone's. "It's still hard, and I hate that. But I'm working on it. I'm trying."

"I understand. And I won't make it more difficult for you, I promise." He backed off, putting more distance between them. "I'll clear out of here now, and I wish you both the best on your grand opening. I'll even be your first customer, since I need to restock some of my ritual materials. But please keep me updated about anything you find. I'll do the same. As hypocritical as I might sound to say it, this isn't one of those situations that will be helped by everyone going off to do their own thing."

Stone used the ley line to return to Encantada, then drove down to Jason's agency. He could have sent the update by text or called him, but he wanted to ask Gina if she'd allow him to do another astral scan. Verity and Hezzie's hypothesis that the new condition might be contagious had rattled him, and while he didn't have Verity's level of auric sensitivity, he hoped his greater power and experience might turn up something she'd missed.

It was worth a try, anyway.

Gina looked up from her screen when he entered. "Hi, Doc. How's it going?"

To mundane sight, she didn't look any different than she ever did. Dressed in her usual casual-but-professional working style of blouse, dark jeans, and black Chuck Taylors, she'd added only a cheeky cat pin to her collar as a nod to her new status.

"Moving along," he told her. "How have you been?" Neither she nor Jason had given him any update on her status, which led him to believe nothing new had turned up.

She shrugged. "About the same, really." She glanced at the door to make sure nobody else was coming in. "It's surprisingly boring, being a secret catgirl. A few things to get used to, like things smell a lot stronger now—nice aftershave, by the way—and I keep getting these huge cravings for meat." She tapped a couple more things on her keyboard and turned to face him. "So…anything new?"

"That's why I'm here, actually. Where's Jason?"

"Not here. He went out with Amber. I think they've got another doctor's appointment." She grinned. "They're so cute—especially him. He's treating her like she's made out of glass or something, and she's just rolling along like everything's fine and there's nothing at all to worry about. When that baby comes, Jason's gonna wrap it in bubble wrap, just you wait and see."

Stone chuckled, but his mind wasn't on Jason's upcoming parenthood. "Damn. I was hoping he'd be here. I need to update both of you."

"Go for it—I'll pass on the info, and you can call him later to make sure I didn't miss anything. I don't think he's gonna be back today."

It wasn't what he wanted, but he was here now. He told her about Verity and Hezzie's examination of her blood, and what they suspected about the condition being contagious.

"Whoa." She frowned. "You think I got it from somebody else? And I can maybe pass it around to other people like a case of the flu?"

"Who knows? We still don't have enough information to know for sure. If it *is* contagious, you could have got it anywhere. From the party you attended, the convention, or even interacting with someone in a shop. It's far too early to consider taking any action about it."

"That's a relief. I know I'm kind of a hermit, but telling me I have to stay in my apartment is the easiest way to make me want to go out. You know, like a cat who can't decide whether it wants to be in or out." She looked away, a clear indication to Stone that she had something else on her mind.

"Something wrong?"

She jerked her head up as if surprised he'd caught that. "No, not wrong. I have something I wanted to tell you. But I don't want you to be mad at me."

"Why would I be?"

"Because of what we talked about the other night."

Stone tilted his head. "I've got no idea what you're on about, Gina."

She glanced at the screen, then back at Stone. "I...uh...found more."

"More?"

"Of us. Of me."

"What?" Stone hurried over to check her screen, almost as if expecting to see someone watching them.

"Yeah. I couldn't help it. I promise I didn't reveal anything," she added hastily. "Everything was completely anonymous, with no names and no way to trace it back. Trust me, Doc—this is what I'm good at, and I'm one hundred percent certain nobody can follow it back to me or even my location."

Stone's heart beat faster. "Follow *what* back? What did you mean, you found more? How?"

Gina leaned back in her chair. "I got curious a couple days ago, back home. Figuring if you knew about a few of us, there were probably more out there you *didn't* know about. So I started poking around a little, using proxies and anonymizers and all the tricks I know to make sure I stay stealthed."

"And what did you find?"

"At first, nothing. I put in a few search terms and waited for them to come back, hoping somebody out there was talking about this stuff. But as far as I could tell, nobody was, except for a few scattered stories of crimes or situations that might *possibly* be caused by one of us. No way to tell, though, not for sure, since hardly anybody can see us and the people who can obviously aren't blabbing it to the world."

"Okay..." Stone barely noticed he'd begun pacing around in front of her desk. "But you said you found more."

"Yeah. That happened after I got a little more proactive." Idly, she swung her chair around to follow his path. "I sent out some carefully worded messages in a few places—the kind of places people like me hang out because we like privacy."

"And?" Stone wasn't sure what to make of this, except that he was rapidly heading out of his element. He was as comfortable using the internet for basic functions as the average person, but Gina's online activity was as incomprehensible to him as his magical activity was to a mundane.

"And I got some hits. People responding, saying they thought they were going crazy because they'd changed, and *they* could see it but nobody else could. There was a lot of relief in those notes, Doc. *Lot* of relief. I mean, think about it—what if something like this happened to a person who doesn't have any access to people like you to tell them what's going on. You know, like some poor kid in the Midwest, or a housewife in Dallas."

Stone narrowed his eyes. "I thought you said this place where you put out these messages wasn't accessible to people like that."

"It's not. Mostly it's hackers, IT people, some college students." She swung around to face him. "That's the *point*, Doc. I'm finding a few of us among *that* group, which isn't all that large compared to the general public. And the ones I'm finding are all over the place, not just around here. Mostly in the US, but a few in Canada, Mexico...a couple in Europe, and even one in Africa."

"Bloody hell…" he murmured. If the condition had already ranged out that far, then his theory that it had originated in the Bay Area was probably wrong. "How many are we talking?"

"About twenty so far, and that's just the ones who responded. I haven't checked my query today because I don't want to take any chances on connecting it with the agency. But they're out there, Doc."

Stone stopped pacing, staring off into space as his mind raced. "What did you do about them?"

"What do you mean?"

"Did you respond to the messages? Did you connect them with each other?"

"I and a couple of the others set up a message board for us. Still one hundred percent anonymous and untraceable. Nobody uses real names, and locations are super vague, like California or Vancouver or whatever. And a couple of them have admitted to seeing other ones out in the wild. Now that they know they're not alone, they're going to look for others to bring in."

Stone wasn't sure this was a good idea, but there wasn't anything he could do about it. If the condition was this widespread, there was no way he could hope to contain it. "Did any of them say what their particular…manifestation was? Were there any commonalities?"

"A couple, but not really. One guy turned into, like, a lizard-person. A woman said she looks like some kind of faerie creature—drop-dead gorgeous but weird, like with pale skin and long fingers and purple eyes. One guy's a goblin-looking dude with greenish skin and pointed ears. One's a fox-person. The one thing they all have in common is that they all feel like it was supposed to happen. Like they've turned into…*more* of themselves." She met his gaze, looking serious. "That was the story, over and over. They were initially freaked out and scared, but once they got over it, they felt like it just…made sense. Like it did with me."

Stone wasn't sure how to respond to that. If this condition *was* contagious, and spreading to more and more people, there had to be something in common among those who were afflicted. Obviously, it wasn't affecting everyone it came into contact with—or even the majority of them. So what was it about *these* particular people that made them susceptible? Even if he wanted to ask Gina to pose that question to the people she'd gathered, he didn't know what to ask. He couldn't very well say, "*Hey! What do all you people have in common?*"

She was looking at him nervously. "So…are you pissed at me? I promise, I didn't say anything at all about magic or mages."

He shook his head. "No. As long as no one can connect it back to us—or, more specifically, myself and Jason's family—I haven't got any right to ask you not to look for more answers."

Her shoulders slumped in relief. "I'm glad. I was worried all night, but I can't just keep this a secret. Not completely." She tapped something on her keyboard and turned back to him. "So…was the update all you came down for? I'll pass it along to Jason tomorrow if you don't want to just call him tonight."

"Fine, yes." He spoke distractedly, already moving on to the next thought. "Actually, I was hoping you'd let me do another scan on you."

"Another one? No more blood, right?"

"Not by me. Verity and Hezzie are the ones who want the blood. But if they're right and this condition *is* contagious, I wasn't looking for signs of that before."

She glanced toward the door again. "Uh…sure. But we might want to go into Jason's office. It'll look weird if somebody sees us through the window."

The new scan didn't reveal much that Stone hadn't already seen in the old one. Aside from the aura change, there was definitely something magic-based going on in Gina's system. He even checked for latent magical talent, but found none. Whatever these manifestations were, they didn't necessarily convey magical ability. He wished he had more test subjects to study.

"Find anything?"

He popped out of his trance with a start, realizing he'd taken more time than he'd planned. "No, unfortunately."

"So you don't see any…I don't know…little magical virus particles running through my veins?"

"Not that I can tell, but that's not really my specialty." He stood, running a hand through his hair, frustrated that this was going on all around him but he wasn't any closer to an answer. This was the first time in a long while when he'd felt out of his league when dealing with a magical problem. What concerned him was not knowing whether this *was* more of a magical problem, or more of a medical one, not to mention having no idea how fast it spread or how contagious it actually *was*.

"So what's the plan going forward? Do you want me to keep looking for more folks?"

He wanted to say no, but that was his old self talking. Trying to stuff an oversized feline back in a tiny bag wouldn't get them anywhere. "I think so, yes." A sudden thought struck him. "Gina…" he said contemplatively.

"Yeah?"

"Do you think you could connect me with this group? Even just let me read the responses? Is there a way you could set it up so no one would know it was me?"

She grinned. "This is me you're talking to, Doc. Sure I can."

"Brilliant."

"I can even fix it so you can post if you want, though I'm not sure how cool it is for you to pretend to be one of us, and I'm also not sure how else you'd explain why you're there if you didn't."

"Let's deal with that if it becomes a problem. Right now, I just want to read what people have to say. Maybe it will give me some insights."

"Sure thing. I'll do it tonight and send you the info. Right now, though, I'd better get back to work. If I don't get stuff ready for Jason's court date tomorrow, he's gonna spray me with a water bottle or something."

CHAPTER FIFTEEN

STONE TEXTED EDDIE on his way back to the car. *Anything new from your end?*

Not much. Still got nothing from the library or the C. archives.

I have some new information for you. Shall I come over?

Sure, if you want to go to the pub with us. We were about to knock off and head back to London.

I'll meet you at the Dragon. I'm buying.

Too right you are.

It was after nine when he arrived at the Dancing Dragon Inn. The place was crowded, though Stone didn't recognize any other mages. He hoped it was just that he was out of touch with the younger generation of magical Brits. The alternative—that the local mundanes, or even worse, the tourists, had discovered the place—was unthinkable. On a hunch, he scanned the area for anyone afflicted with the new condition, but didn't see any of those either. That was less of a surprise, though.

Eddie and Arthur were already there, seated at their customary table in the back. "'Bout time," Eddie called cheerfully. "We were about to 'ave to buy our own pints, and that would've been a shame."

Stone waved to Gus, indicating for the old bartender to start a tab and keep the pints flowing. He carried the first round to the table and dropped down across from them.

"Almost feel like we 'aven't earned these." Eddie nonetheless grabbed his and took a long pull. "We 'aven't got bugger-all for you yet."

"And that disturbs us," Ward added. "I think this might be the first time Eddie hasn't been able to put his hands on something at the Library."

"Slipping, are you?" Stone asked, but their usual banter felt almost rote tonight.

"I 'ope so, actually." Eddie looked almost as serious as Ward.

"You do? Why?"

"Because the alternative is that there isn't anything *in* the Library about this. And I've never encountered that before."

"That can't be true." Stone thought back to the other things he'd asked his friends to research. "You didn't find anything about necromancy. Or much about other dimensions."

"Nothin' useful, true. But at least they're both *mentioned*. Nowhere that I can remember ever seeing says anything about people taking on new forms that alter their auras. That's big. If it 'appened before, it should be in there somewhere. If not in the Library, then at Caventhorne." He cocked his head at Stone and narrowed his eyes. "You're not 'oldin' out on us, are you? I know you kept back some of the books old Desmond left you."

"I'm not holding them back from *you*. You've got access to everything I do. The only things I'm keeping back are things I don't want to share with the general magical public."

Stone wondered if there was anything about dragons in the Library, but didn't ask. He wasn't sure he wanted the answer—and he was *definitely* sure he didn't want to put tenacious Eddie onto that particular scent. "Anyway—you might not have anything, but I do."

"Let's 'ear it, then. Maybe it'll trip somethin' in my nut."

The two of them listened with growing fascination and apprehension as Stone caught them up on the latest news. He didn't identify Gina by name, but he did tell them about her affliction, the scan he'd done, and the blood test Verity and Hezzie had finished.

"Contagious?" Ward looked astonished. "That's…troubling."

"You always did have a way with understatement," Stone said. "But yes, it is. Especially since we know nothing about what causes it, how it's transmitted if it is contagious, and how long the incubation period is."

"We also don't know what other effects it has on the people affected," Ward said. "We've barely scratched the surface of this yet."

"We need to bring in some more experts." Stone sipped his pint and glanced around the room to make sure nobody was listening to them. "Experts in magical medicine, biochemistry…and we've got to start putting the word out to the other mages. I thought we could set something up somewhere at Caventhorne. What do you think?"

Eddie was already nodding. "You read my mind, mate. I know just the place. There's a group o' rooms in the east wing on the second floor that we're not currently usin' for anything. We could set them up there. And there's still an arseload of money sitting in the various accounts Desmond left to keep the place runnin'. I'd say this is a good reason to dip into some of 'em, wouldn't you?"

"I can't think of a better one. Oh—forgot to tell you the other thing I learned." He described Gina's message board, and how she'd located several more people.

"Not just in your neck o' the woods, then?" Eddie asked. "That's not good. Gonna make it a lot 'arder to track down if it's all over the place."

"If it is contagious," Ward added, "people traveling around, by plane especially, will spread it efficiently. That's doubly true if it has a long enough incubation period that people don't realize they've got it until—"

"Until they wake up one morning and end up looking at a completely different face in the mirror," Stone finished. "Gi—my friend mentioned she'd been feeling a bit off for a few days prior, but not like she was ill. She's *happy* with the change. So is Carter, the other one I spoke to directly. Even if someone finds a cure, I'm not sure all of them will take it."

Eddie patted his arm. "Let's not get ahead of ourselves. First things first—we need to figure out where it's comin' from. You leave it to us on this end. I know several folks who can be 'elpful, assuming they're willing. Truth is, I think I'll have to 'old 'em off with sticks if they get wind of a problem this interesting."

"I know some as well," Ward said. "We'll get in touch with them. I assume we have leeway to access the funds we need for equipment and renovation of the space?"

Stone waved it off. "Setting up a research center for an obviously magic-related affliction is well within the purview of Desmond's bequest." He finished his pint and let his shoulders slump. "Thanks, both of you. You've taken some of this load off me. Keep me posted on what you find, and I'll do the same."

"You are gonna stick around and 'ave a few with us, aren't you?" Eddie had already polished off his first pint and was rising to get a second.

"Can't. Still got some things to do back in California. But I've got you covered for as many as you want."

"Oh, sure, give us a brain-bender we need our wits to deal with, *then* offer unlimited pints." Eddie glared at him in mock annoyance.

"More where those came from, especially if you solve this."

Before he headed back to California, Stone decided to pop down to the Surrey house and check his own library. He was almost certain he'd find nothing, but he had a better idea what to look for now.

Aubrey wasn't in the house, which didn't surprise him given the lateness of the hour. When he glanced at the caretaker's apartment over the garage, he saw a light in the front window, and Susan Fletcher's serviceable old Vauxhall parked out front. He smiled as he passed by. It was the first time in recent memory that Aubrey's sixth sense about his arrival hadn't tripped.

Or maybe he's got better things to do these days.

He made it to the hidden basement library without encountering Selby, who'd probably retired to his rooms for the night, but it didn't matter. It quickly became apparent that he hadn't forgotten the contents of any of his library, and he still didn't have anything covering the new condition. The closest thing was a couple references to an old disease that diminished magical ability, but that one had only affected mages of advanced years, and been wiped out centuries ago.

Stone swiped his hair off his forehead. For the first time since the days of the Evil, he found himself wishing the world's mages were better organized. This was the kind of problem that lent itself to a group effort, and if he'd learned anything over the years, it was to rely on experts instead of trying to solve problems on his own. He also wished Kolinsky and Madame Huan hadn't chosen right now to disappear without leaving contact information, and once again he wondered if their disappearance had anything to do with the affliction.

Got to stop calling it 'the affliction,' he thought sourly. *Makes it sound like they've got leprosy or something.*

He floated up to reshelve the book he was examining and left the library. There was nothing else he could do here tonight. Remaining and continuing to look through books he knew wouldn't help was nothing more than spinning his wheels.

He decided he'd take a quick detour to the London house to check Desmond's globe for any suspicious new rifts, then head home. He needed to put the finishing touches on his seminar, which was next week, and if he got that finished early enough, he might have time for at least one patrol to look for more creatures.

Standing in the center of the room, Stone visualized the pattern for the London sitting room, closed his eyes, and released the energy.

He knew before he opened them again that he wasn't where he'd intended to go.

CHAPTER SIXTEEN

H E WASN'T SURE *HOW* HE KNEW IT. Perhaps the smell was different, or something subtle in the air currents, or just the kind of feeling it was impossible to quantify.

Regardless of why, though, he was definitely not in the London sitting room.

He also wasn't alone.

He spun around, pulling up his shield, and glared at the shadowy figure seated in the chair on the other side of the small room. With sudden clarity, he knew exactly who it was, even if he didn't know *where* he was.

"Aldwyn."

The lights came up, revealing the familiar, broad-shouldered figure of his dragon ancestor. Aldwyn Stone looked much the same as the last time he'd pulled his descendent into this windowless, doorless room, his brown hair with its gray temples neatly combed, his posture relaxed, his tailored suit perfect. He watched Stone with mild curiosity. "Good afternoon, Alastair. It is good to see you again."

"You could have sent a bloody invitation, instead of—" He stopped, his whole body growing cold as the realization settled over him: this time, Aldwyn hadn't somehow hijacked his teleportation portal.

He'd redirected his ley-line travel.

How powerful *was* this guy?

Be careful…

The hell with that.

"What do you want?" He spared a quick glance, taking in the room. He wasn't positive it was the same one as before, but it definitely had the same look: fine hardwood floor covered with an intricately woven rug, a pair of antique chairs, no-doubt-priceless paintings in elaborate frames on the walls. But was any of it real? The last time Stone had spoken with Aldwyn in person, he hadn't known his ancestor's true nature—only that he was a very powerful mage who'd somehow managed to survive being interred in an underground prison for two hundred years with no ill effects.

Now, he knew better.

Aldwyn was a dragon, and every bit as dangerous as Kolinsky and the others.

Perhaps more so, if Kolinsky could be believed.

Aldwyn gave a thin smile that didn't make it to his eyes. "Why do you always think I *want* something?" His voice was soft and amused.

"Oh, I don't know—why else would you drag me here against my will?"

"So suspicious. I suppose I can't blame you for that, especially given the way your mind's been poisoned."

"What are you talking about?" Stone didn't release the shield; it wasn't visible, but he was sure Aldwyn knew it was there. He didn't care.

Aldwyn's gaze sharpened, but he still looked relaxed. "Come now, boy. Let's be honest with each other. I'm well aware you've come into certain knowledge since we last spoke."

That didn't surprise Stone, though he did wonder if the other dragons had shared the information with him, or if he'd found out through some stealthier method. "You mean that you're a dragon?"

"Indeed. I'm surprised they shared that with you, truthfully. They aren't usually forthcoming with that sort of revelation."

Stone remembered the recent, similar conversation he'd had with Gabriel, who *hadn't* known about it. "What can I say? I guess I've got an honest face."

Aldwyn showed no visible reaction. "It does seem, though, that your old friends have forsaken you."

"What's that supposed to mean?"

His right shoulder shrugged minimally. "I believe I told you before—because you're my descendant—"

"And your scion, let's not forget about that."

"—I devote a bit of time to remaining aware of your activities," he continued as if Stone hadn't spoken. "I'm also aware that your friends Stefan Kolinsky and Madame Huan have disappeared, without informing you of their whereabouts. Or why they have departed."

"So? They don't exactly give me detailed itineraries of their plans. Nor would I expect them to, any more than I give them mine." Stone tried hard not to react to the fact that Aldwyn had admitted to watching him. That disturbed him more than he was prepared to admit.

"But you're curious. And more than a bit annoyed, I think." When Stone glared at him, his smile widened and raised a hand. "There's no point in trying to deny it. You're very good at hiding your true feelings, even from other mages. But I am not merely another mage."

Stone didn't answer. Damn dragons, anyway. At least Kolinsky and Madame Huan had the good manners not to wave it in his face that they could read him like a book.

"Don't you want to know *why* they've disappeared?"

"Would it matter if I said I didn't?"

"Not really. You can lie to me—or yourself—if you like, but I hardly see how it's serving any reasonable purpose." He indicated the other chair with a nod. "Please—sit. Would you care for a refreshment?"

It was useless to argue with him. Stone threw himself into the chair, but shook his head. "This isn't a social call, and it's not a bloody cocktail party. I can see things too—and one of them is that you're practically gagging to spill the dirt on your fellow dragons. So let's hear it, then."

Aldwyn flashed him a sharp look. "Have a care, boy. You may be my blood and my scion, but I won't stand for being spoken to in such a manner."

Stone spread his hands and glared right back. "Go ahead—have a go at me, then, if you think it will get you anywhere. I don't make a habit of groveling in front of people who grab me against my will, even if they *are* dragons. At least Stefan has the grace to send me invitations."

For a moment, he thought the dragon would do just that. He steeled himself, his invisible shield up. But Aldwyn merely settled back in his chair. "You are young, and I suppose a certain amount of rudeness must be tolerated in the young. I advise you not to abuse that tolerance, however."

"You were going to tell me about why Stefan and Madame Huan have disappeared. Is it related to me?" He remembered last time the two dragons had made themselves scarce, to prevent him from asking too many questions about their activities and the interdimensional rifts. But as far as he was aware, he hadn't learned anything new about dragon society.

Unless…

With effort, he kept his reaction from his face and fixed Aldwyn with a blank, attentive stare.

"I do not believe their absence is related to you. Nor is it unique. Many of our kind have left their homes to convene a conclave."

"A conclave? You mean they're getting together for a meeting about something? Is that common?" In spite of his reluctance to trust Aldwyn, Stone found himself curious. *Be careful,* he told himself sternly. *He lies. He'll tell you anything you want to hear.*

He wondered if that was true, though. So far, at least as much as he could tell, Aldwyn hadn't lied to him. Obscured the truth, perhaps, but all the dragons did that. Even Madame Huan.

"It is not common." Aldwyn sipped his drink and set it on the table next to him. "I do not believe another such gathering has occurred since before I was interred in your catacombs."

A tiny thought poked at the corner of Stone's mind at the mention of the catacombs, but he left it alone for now. "So why aren't you there too? Are they on a break? Or didn't they invite you?"

"They did, in fact, invite me. I chose not to attend. I find such things tiresome, and most of my kind find my company...distasteful. The feeling, I assure you, is mutual. But I am not without my agents, who report back to me with information I might find interesting."

Stone wondered if all dragons took this long to spit out what they were trying to say. So far, the only one who didn't seem to fit the mold was Gabriel, the only one who had deliberately distanced himself from dragonkind. Had *he* been invited to the conclave and chosen not to attend either, or had they left him out because he was too young? "So, what is this interesting information? And why are you telling me? I'm just a lowly scion."

"Not so lowly as you might pretend to be, I think."

"What's that supposed to mean?" Again, Stone tried not to let his concern show. Was there any possible way his ancestor could know about things like his apparent inability to die, or his connection with Trevor Harrison and Calanar? Even Kolinsky didn't know those things—or at least if he did, he'd never spoken of them.

Aldwyn waved it off. "No matter. It isn't relevant. But as you may or may not be aware, something new has come into the world."

A little shiver passed through Stone. "You're not talking about the dimensional intersection rifts, are you?"

"No. Those are not new."

"What, then?"

"I think you might already know."

And he did, of course. "The new...affliction. The one that's changing people's essences."

Aldwyn inclined his head.

"So the dragons know about that. And they're worried enough about it to have the kind of get-together they haven't had in over two hundred years?"

"Yes."

The little shiver became a big shiver. "You're telling me they've got no idea what's going on either."

"According to my agents, that is correct."

Stone narrowed his eyes. "Why are you sharing this with me?"

Aldwyn leaned in closer. "I wanted you to consider that perhaps those you've chosen to trust don't have your best interests in mind, nor hold you in as high regard as you might think. You have developed a close relationship with Stefan—even closer, now that he and some of the others have revealed new truths to you—but yet neither he nor your old friend Madame Huan has chosen to reveal this information to you."

"Why should that matter?" But in the back of his mind, Stone felt a tiny sliver of doubt. Kolinsky and Madame Huan had been his allies ever since he'd met them—hell, Madame Huan had told him their meeting when he was a teenager had not been coincidental, nor was her presence in the Bay Area—but how much did they truly share with him?

He shook off the feeling. *Don't let him get into your head.* "What difference does it make? They're bloody *dragons.* They're hundreds, maybe thousands of years old. I might be a scion, but I'm a blip on their timeline." *Maybe not so much of one going forward, but they don't know that.* "Why should I care what they do and don't tell me?"

"In this case, because it affects you." Aldwyn rose and began pacing the room, pausing to study each painting for a few seconds before moving on. "All I am trying to tell you is that among dragons, blood is important, and holds a great deal of power. You are my blood. You are not theirs."

Stone snorted. "You *do* know about most of my family, right? They're rubbish, almost to a man—or woman. Hell, one of them betrayed *you*. If you knew anything about me, you'd know I don't take blood into much consideration when choosing the people I trust."

"And in most cases, you would be justified. But our bond is different."

"No, it isn't." He glared at Aldwyn. "Don't try to fool me. I've done my research, and I saw what was in those catacombs. You're a monster, Aldwyn. You murdered at least forty-one people—and those are only the ones I know about—to power your rituals. You don't give a damn about mundanes."

Aldwyn didn't seem angry, or even disturbed, by Stone's words. "I don't deny it, nor do I offer a defense. I will say only this: times were different then, and I am not such a unique monster as you might try to convince yourself I am."

"'Times were different.'" Stone shook his head in disgust. "Do you know how many people use that excuse to explain horrible things they've done? *'Things were different,'* or *'That was ancient history,'* or *'Everybody was doing it,'* or *'I was just following orders.'* I've heard them all. Believe me, some mundanes can be as bad as you lot when it comes to justifying the unjustifiable."

He gave Stone a cool, appraising look. "You may be correct. Perhaps that is how you justified killing your twin sister. Or the woman who attempted to turn your son against you."

Stone glared harder. "That's different. The people you killed were innocents."

"I thought, among your kind, murder was considered murder, regardless of the extenuating circumstances." Before Stone could sputter a reply, he waved a languid hand. "No matter. We are getting off track. I do not fault you for killing those people. They no doubt deserved it. And whether or not those in my past also deserved it, you would be naïve to think that times have *not* changed. We dragons are nothing if not adaptable. It is a necessary condition, given how long we live. As long as we are confined to this world and forced to operate under our overly-restrictive covenants, situations such as that are unlikely to occur in modern times."

"You got away with it before," Stone said stubbornly. "Maybe that was why Cyrus and Brathwaite took the risk to put you down. I'm surprised the other dragons didn't come after you for breaking their laws."

"But, you see, I *didn't* break their laws." Aldwyn's smile was sharklike. "*I've* never killed anyone. Not directly. That is the beauty of our agreements, and I don't for a moment believe it was an oversight. We are not permitted to involve ourselves directly in human affairs—but *indirect* involvement is not only allowed but tolerated. Perhaps even encouraged, in some circumstances."

"I see. So you didn't kill them, but you arranged for *other* people to kill them. That's much better." Contempt dripped from Stone's voice.

"We will get nowhere rehashing the past." Aldwyn returned to his chair. "I don't believe you want to remain here any longer than necessary, so I will get to the point. Whether you believe it or not, I have not lied to you—either about myself or about Stefan. We are a manipulative lot, every last one of us, including the kind and saintly Madame Huan. As long as your interests and ours converge, we can be valuable allies. We can also be dangerous enemies."

"Is that a threat?"

"Not at all. A warning, perhaps—but not about me. Just remember to keep your wits about you when dealing with any of our kind, and always look for ulterior motives. And to keep in mind that we are blood, and you will find me a valuable ally, should you choose to align yourself with me."

"Noted. And the ally thing? That isn't going to happen, so you might as well stop wasting both our time trying to lure me to the dark side. Are you quite finished?"

Aldwyn studied him a moment longer, then inclined his head. "For now."

"Brilliant." Stone stood. "Next time you want to chat—which won't get you any farther than this one—call me on the phone. Send a text, or even an engraved invitation like Stefan does. No more yanking me out of the ley-stream."

"I shall consider it." He pulled a card from his inner pocket and offered it to Stone. "If you should ever wish to reach me, you can do so using this."

Stone almost didn't take the card, but his curiosity got the better of him. It was black, the size of a business card, and utterly blank. Even magical sight revealed nothing. He looked up, confused.

"Press your thumb to the center of the card and picture my name in your mind. I will respond at my earliest convenience."

"Yes, well, don't hold your breath." He stuck the card in his pocket. "Ready to let me go home now?"

Aldwyn nodded toward the other side of the room, and a swirling portal appeared. "I apologize, but I cannot allow ley-line travel from here, as it would require revealing my location."

"I thought we were family." Again, Stone infused his voice with contempt. "I guess that trust you're asking for only goes one way. Color me surprised."

The dragon didn't respond. "Good day, Alastair. I do hope to hear from you again."

Stone turned toward the portal, but stopped when the same small thought as before resurfaced. Without turning back, he said in a conversational tone, "He's alive, you know."

"Who is alive?"

"James Brathwaite."

The silence behind him made him wonder if Aldwyn *didn't* know. He smiled thinly. Perhaps the dragon didn't have his scaly finger on *every* bit of his business.

"How do you know this?" The voice behind him sounded different now—less amused, more focused.

"Because I've met him, on several occasions. If you hate him so much, perhaps it might be a better use of your time to hunt him down and eliminate him, which I'm sure would be something all of us would agree with. His echo survived being sealed in that sarcophagus in my catacombs, when Cyrus betrayed him. He's taken over the body of his descendant, a woman named Miriam Padgett, and re-started the family necromancy business." Stone did turn then, curious about how his words were affecting Aldwyn.

The dragon's gaze was fixed on him, his expression no longer relaxed and mocking. Stone still couldn't tell whether he knew and was stringing him along to get more information, or if this was a new revelation.

"Where is he?" Aldwyn asked.

"I don't know, and that's the truth. The last I heard he was working with a powerful mage named Elias Richter—head of the European branch of Ordo Purpuratus, if you remember *that* lot from your day. Richter's probably dead now, but I wouldn't be the least bit surprised if that old snake Brathwaite slithered out of our little trap." He shrugged. "Do with that information as you will. I'm sure you can see by my aura, or whatever other connection you have with me, that I'm telling the truth. Perhaps you might be better served focusing on rooting that particular bit of filth out of the world instead of spying on me and trying to recruit me to your nasty little cause."

Aldwyn didn't reply. In fact, he appeared to have forgotten Stone was in the room. His stared off into the middle distance, obviously deep in thought.

"Right, then," Stone said, satisfied he'd finally scored a point on the old dragon. "I'll be off. Hope not to see you soon."

Before Aldwyn could reply—though it appeared he didn't intend to—Stone stepped through the swirling portal.

CHAPTER SEVENTEEN

BY THE TIME the evening of his seminar rolled around a few days later, Stone was glad he'd remembered to include a reminder on his phone's calendar. If he hadn't, he'd probably have forgotten about it.

Reports were finally starting to come in from his various sources, and every new one disturbed him even more. Whatever this was, it wasn't isolated, and it wasn't small.

Locally, Verity and Hezzie had told him they'd seen three of the creatures—a scaled reptilian being, a fox, and what they described as a "beautiful elf"—during their normal travel around San Francisco. The elf had actually entered their shop two days after their grand opening, looking for a tarot deck to give a friend. She'd seen surprised when they spotted her "difference," but didn't have a problem chatting with them about it. Like the others, she admitted to being shocked and scared at first, but quickly feeling like the change was something she'd been waiting for all her life without realizing it.

Gina's anonymous mailing list turned up even more unsettling information. She'd provided Stone with a login and showed him how to access the list untraceably from his home computer, and every morning when he checked it, more posts had been added. They came from all over the country, and in several cases other countries, and all of them told essentially the same story: they'd awakened one recent morning to discover they'd changed into some kind of nonhuman creature only they could see. Some were surprised to find out others like them existed and could also see them—they'd been holing up in their homes, afraid to leave in fear of being noticed. After the second day, Stone began plotting their numbers, dates of discovery, and approximate locations on a map. By the third day, there were more than a hundred of them. There didn't seem to be any rhyme or reason to where they were, other than larger concentrations in more populous areas.

The disturbing bottom line seemed to be that the phenomenon was not only not slowing down, it appeared to be growing.

Eddie and Ward had thrown themselves into the task of organizing experts in magical biology at Caventhorne. As they'd predicted, the researchers they'd contacted had been happy to have a new puzzle to sink their teeth into, to the point where some who didn't live near convenient portals had chosen to temporarily relocate to the Hertfordshire area.

Some of the preliminary findings they reported back were equally worrisome. Stone had met with Eddie and Ward the night before at the Dragon, using a "cone of silence" spell to ensure nobody overheard them.

"It's scary, I've got to say," Eddie told him. "I mean, they've only been at it for a few days so obviously we don't 'ave much yet, but these blokes and birds are tops in their fields."

"What's scary?" Stone hadn't touched his pint yet.

"They think it's permanent," Ward said soberly. He hadn't touched his either.

"Permanent? What do you mean, permanent?"

"Just what 'e said." Eddie, on the other hand, had not only touched his pint, but already downed half of it. "They agree that it's likely contagious, but it's not a disease. Not exactly, anyway. They think it's more likely the folks who get it 'ave come into contact with some sort of…catalyst, I guess it is. Something that reacts with something inside them and changes them."

"Bloody hell," Stone murmured. "You're saying that once they get it, there's no way to cure it?"

"They're still working on that," Ward said. "It's far too soon for those kinds of solutions. It could take months or years before they know."

"But what they *do* know," Eddie added, "especially after we managed to find a couple of test subjects willin' to be examined, is that whatever this is, it's not 'urtin' the people who 'ave it."

"How can that be?" Stone narrowed his eyes and frowned. "It's changing their *auras*. It's changing something fundamental in their bodies."

"Yes," Ward said, "but what we're saying is that doesn't appear to be doing any damage or physical harm. Every mundane medical test has come back negative. It's not harming their organs, causing undue stress on their systems, or anything like that. In fact, in some of the cases, the contrary seems to be true."

"What do you mean, the contrary?" Stone was having a hard time getting his mind around this.

"Some of them are reporting lower blood pressure readings, the clearing up of conditions they 'ad before they changed, that sort o' thing," Eddie said. "The researchers are sayin' some of it's consistent with a general lowering of stress." He leaned forward. "I didn't want t' say this yet because like Ward said, it's way too early for any kind o' definitive findings, but it fits with what the folks are saying—that whatever this is, they feel like it was there inside them all along, deep down."

Stone pondered. "So you're saying every single person who's got this is over the moon about it? That mostly fits with the information I've got from my friend's anonymous online message board—but in a couple of cases there, people have reported their friends having mental breakdowns. One young man said his brother had some sort of psychotic break, claiming he'd turned into a bat-creature. He ended up attempting suicide and they had to put him in a facility for treatment."

"Well…" Ward looked pensive. "In the case of any sort of change, there will be a subset of people who don't cope well with it. But at least in our limited research, so far the vast majority of those afflicted are pleased with the result."

"But what's *causing* it?" Stone remembered his pint, and grabbed it with enough force to slosh a bit over the glass. "You said they think there's some catalyst that's making this happen. Have they identified *anything* it might be?"

"Not yet," Eddie said. "Unfortunately, they can't get too far without more test subjects. It's a lot easier to get somebody to answer a few questions than to show up and let a bunch of egg'eads poke and prod at them."

"Damn. I can't believe this just…popped up spontaneously, in so many different areas." He thought about what Kolinsky had said about the rifts. Mages had speculated for a long time that magic levels in the world used to be higher in the past, using the existence of artifact-level magic items that could no longer be produced as proof. The mages didn't know about the dragons, of course, but they added credence to these theories. Could that be what was going on here?

As compelling as the theory was, though, Stone's gut told him that wasn't it. If the ambient level of magic power in the world had suddenly taken a big jump, he would have felt it. The ley lines would be stronger, for one thing, and so far they didn't seem to be. Hell, even if *he* hadn't felt it, the dragons would have. Gabriel, at least, would have said something.

"We're thinkin' along the same lines," Eddie said. "Right now, the researchers are focused on tryin' to identify three things: what the catalyst is, 'ow it's changin' people, and 'ow long it takes from initial exposure to manifestation o' the changes. But at last report we got, which was yesterday, they're not gettin' very far. It would 'elp if there were distinct clusters, but we're not showin' that. Like we said before, it's possible this is a spontaneous thing poppin' up all over the place, or if it's got a long incubation period, it might be gettin' spread through people travelin'. No way to know yet."

Stone had been passing along his own research results, including the data from plotting the instances of the affliction. "It sounds like the next step is to identify more people willing to get tested. I'm hoping that might lead to some commonality among them. Obviously, there's got to be something determining who gets it and who doesn't, or we'd be seeing it on every streetcorner. Even as disturbing as this is getting, it's still quite rare compared to the general population."

Ward nodded soberly. "All we can do is continue what we're doing. The researchers are definitely engaged, and they're starting to pull in others—even mundanes. We can't bring mundanes to Caventhorne, obviously, unless they're already familiar with magic. But we can take advantage of their expertise for mundane-style medical research."

Going over this conversation again occupied Stone's mind as he crossed the campus toward the lecture hall where he'd be delivering his seminar. As he drew close to the building, he made an effort to put the whole thing temporarily out of his head. Judging from the signups, the talk would be well attended, and he owed it to the attendees to be fully focused on his presentation. He paused outside the door, taking a few deep breaths to center his thoughts.

This is what you love, he reminded himself. And it was true. This was what had compelled him to complete the years of education to become a professor, despite both his magic and his wealth— even before he'd inherited the fortune from William Desmond— ensuring he'd never needed to work a day in his life. He loved imparting knowledge to students, seeing their eyes light up as they made connections or some topic lit a fire under them.

This was the time to remember that. Tonight wasn't for magic.

The lecture *was* well attended—impressively so, as it turned out. Every seat in the large, tiered hall was full, with more people lined up along the back wall. Stone watched them through the little window in the hall's antechamber door as they filtered in and took their places, recognizing several of his Occult Studies students and more from the wider Cultural Anthropology department, but a good sixty percent of the attendees were unfamiliar. Some looked the right age to be grad students or even undergrads, while quite a few appeared to be from the community at large. The talk wasn't limited to enrolled students, so anyone who wanted to pay the modest fee could sign up.

Apparently, his reputation as a lecturer had grown larger than he'd thought.

He smiled, putting all his magical-world problems firmly out of mind, and opened the door.

"Good evening," he called to the crowd. "As you no doubt already know—at least I hope you do, unless you've wandered into the wrong place—I'm Alastair Stone. I'm happy to be here tonight, and I hope for the next hour or so I can educate—and with any luck, entertain—you with some of my personal experiences with occult practices around the world. So sit back, get comfortable, and please hold your questions until the end of the presentation."

The applause that followed was nowhere near what some music or sports star might have received, or even what The Cardinal Sin got on a good night. Stone had no illusions about that. But it *was* significantly more enthusiastic than the average scholarly lecturer's reception. Stone flashed them a conspiratorial smile, raised his hands for silence, and stepped around the podium to begin his usual circuit around the hall.

It was showtime.

The hour—it ended up being more like an hour and half, but nobody seemed to mind—passed so fast Stone barely had time to notice it. As almost always happened when he was talking about something he was passionate about, he slipped into "lecture mode." But the reason he was such a popular professor, with consistent student evaluations at the top of the charts, was because his lecture mode wasn't dry and pedantic. Students had told him in the past that he reminded them of one of those successful motivational speakers, with the rare ability to pull the audience into his orbit and convince each and every one of them that he was delivering his talk directly to them. Tonight he was constantly moving, prowling up and down the aisles of the lecture hall, pausing to address someone who appeared particularly interested in one of his points, and punctuating his words with enthusiastic gestures. His burning interest in his topic couldn't have been more obvious to his listeners, and they were happy to come along for the ride. When he finally finished, as always timing the end of the talk with a seemingly careless return to the podium where he'd begun, the entire hall erupted in applause even louder than they'd given him when he'd first arrived. He smiled back at them, tired but also energized.

"So," he said, coming back around the podium to perch on the desk next to it. "I said I'd allow a question-and-answer session, though we've gone a bit over our time and I do apologize for that."

Once again, nobody seemed bothered. Nobody got up, either, and a few hands immediately shot into the air.

Stone handled their questions—from the scholarly to the silly—with equal aplomb. The truth was, he could have stayed there for another couple hours, but when he glanced at his watch and discovered it was already after nine, he raised his hands to the crowd.

"I'm afraid that's going to have to be all for tonight. I know you're all too polite to tell me you've got cats to feed and children waiting to be tucked in, so I'll call it there. I've got my email address on the board, though, so if you think of any other questions I didn't address tonight, please feel free to send them on. Thank you so much for coming, and have a safe trip home."

The audience gave him another round of applause and began filing out. As he expected, a few of them filtered up toward the podium. There were always last-minute questions or comments people didn't want to reveal in front of a hall full of people, so he lingered as he gathered his notes into his leather briefcase.

Most of the questions were quick—a couple of his students wanted clarifications on esoteric points that would have bored a general audience, one woman wanted to talk to him about writing a book (he took her card and thanked her, but told her he was unlikely to follow up on her offer), and a scruffy young man turned out to be a reporter from the *Daily*, who was writing a story about the seminar. One by one they got what they wanted and left through the door nearest the front.

Stone was about to pick up his briefcase and follow them when he realized he wasn't alone yet. One more figure held back, almost as if unsure about whether to approach him.

Glancing up, he saw it was a woman—an undergrad who had taken his introductory Occult in America course last quarter. He didn't technically need to teach that course anymore, especially with his protégé Brandon Greene having recently accepted a full-time position in the department to teach lower-level courses while continuing to pursue his doctorate, but he enjoyed the enthusiasm of the newer students so he made time to do it when his schedule permitted.

He recognized the woman, noting she looked somewhat different—more put together—than she had when she'd been a mousy sophomore. He couldn't remember her name, though. "Er—hello. Have you got a question?"

She smiled. "I do, Dr. Stone. Do you remember me? I took your class last quarter."

When she moved closer, he saw she was dressed better than the average student, in a silky blouse, snug-fitting designer jeans, heels, and full makeup. Her long, blond hair hung loose around her shoulders. It struck him as odd, since most students didn't bother doing themselves up to sit in a stuffy lecture hall. When she'd been in his class, she'd worn the same casual gear as most of the others. Maybe she was meeting someone afterward.

"I do remember you," he said. "I hope you'll forgive me if I can't recall your name, though."

"That's okay. I know you have a lot of names to remember. I'm Michele Berry."

The name rang a bit of a bell, but not much. She hadn't stood out to him as impressive in any way, being average and unmemorable in both scholarship and appearance. As a professor, he wasn't supposed to notice students' appearances, but he was human and the attractive women did catch his eye. Never more than that, though. Women that young didn't appeal to him even if *had* been appropriate. Verity had been an aberration for many reasons, and one he realized now had been a mistake.

Now, though, he hadn't been mistaken—she'd definitely upped her game. Maybe she had a boy- or girlfriend now, and a reason to make herself more attractive. Not that it mattered to him one way or the other, though. He immediately put it out of his mind and spoke briskly. "What can I do for you, Ms. Berry? I've got to clear out of here—the janitors will be along soon to tidy up."

"It won't take long." She moved even closer, her gaze locked on his.

Okay, this was getting awkward, but it wasn't anything Stone hadn't dealt with many times before. Every young, even marginally good-looking professor, both male and female, had experience with it, and if they knew what was good for them, they figured out fast how to deflect it.

He deftly put the podium between himself and her, pretending to be searching for something in his briefcase. "What's your question, then?"

"It's not really a question, actually. More of an...observation."

He jerked his head up. He hadn't been mistaken: there was a sultry purr in her voice that had never been there before. She was still looking straight into his eyes.

This could be inconvenient.

He shoved the last of his notes into the briefcase and snapped it shut. "I'm sorry, but I've got to run. If it's something you can tell me quickly—" He stepped away from the table and turned toward the nearest door.

She immediately drifted in front of him, never taking her eyes off him. "You're very attractive, Dr. Stone. I bet a lot of girls tell you that, don't they?"

"Ms. Berry, please. I'm flattered, but—"

"You probably didn't even notice me when I was in your class, did you? I don't blame you. I was a real mess back then. Hopeless."

Stone considered his options. She was standing between him and the door, meaning if he tried walking around her and she continued blocking him, he'd either have to make an awkward run for it—a bad idea—or push her out of the way—an even worse one. Touching students in any way beyond a professional handshake was heavily discouraged, for just this reason. Even an encouraging clap on the shoulder could be misconstrued.

Instead, he went for his stern "professor stare"—the one he aimed at students who tried to convince him to give them extra credit assignments when they were behind, or allow them to hand in work late. "Please excuse me. As I said, I've got to be off."

She didn't move. "You can stay just a couple of minutes, can't you? I loved your lecture, by the way. You're an amazing speaker. A lot better than most of the other boring professors around here. Easier on the eyes, too. Trust me, a lot of girls notice that. Some guys, too. You'd probably get embarrassed if you heard some of the things people say about you."

Stone had never thought about that, and now it made him uncomfortable. "Er—"

She laughed. "You're so cute when you're acting shy. I don't think you're shy at all, though, are you? You have quite a reputation." Her smile grew conspiratorial. "My roommate's in a sorority. Did you know they keep lists of the hottest male professors? Want to know where you are on it?"

"I do not, actually. Ms. Berry, I—" He tried to sidle sideways and get around her, but she drifted over again.

She seemed amused by his discomfort. "Number three. Number one's in Theater Arts, and number two is in the Music department. A lot of girls want to do you, Dr. Stone. And some boys. My roommate said her boyfriend told her the frats keep lists too, and some of the gay frat bros have their own version."

The back of Stone's neck was growing hot. He wanted to get the hell out of here, but there didn't seem to be an easy way to do it. He could use magic, of course—but even then, there wasn't much he could do with her standing so close to him.

The worst of it was, her proximity and seductive expression were beginning to affect him. She wasn't precisely his type, but she *was* quite attractive, and she obviously wanted to—

He caught himself leaning in closer to her, and jerked back. *Bloody hell, Stone, get a grip on yourself!*

Her smile widened further. "You want it too, don't you?" she murmured. "I can see it." Her gaze drifted downward, then back up. She took a step toward him.

He took one back, and quickly found his back pressed against the side of the podium.

"I've always had this fantasy about making it with a hot professor right there in his lecture hall, where just *anybody* might come in. That sounds like it ought to be a really good porno, doesn't it?

And I know how much you older guys want hot young girls. It's a win-win, the way I see it."

Stone swallowed hard, trying to decide how awkward he'd look if he scooted sideways along the podium. Despite the heat growing in his body, he struggled for his stern tone. "Stop it, Ms. Berry. You know as well as I do that this isn't appropriate."

"Appropriate." Her gaze wandered, starting at a point over his shoulder, traveling down his body, and then returning to his eyes. "That's silly. We're both adults. Why should we let any stupid rules get in the way of something we both want?"

Her eyes narrowed, and a smile tugged at the corners of her lips. "Be honest, Dr. Stone—you'd like to, wouldn't you? I get it—you're being good because you'll get in trouble if anybody catches you. But why would they catch you? It's late. Everybody's gone. The doors are closed." She leaned in closer. "You *do* want it, don't you?"

Later, Stone would be annoyed at himself for not catching on sooner. In his defense, he'd had to deal with similar situations—a few female students and a couple of males who tried coming on to him over the years, albeit usually not nearly so aggressively—but even so, he should have figured it out before he did.

He should have noticed there was more going on here than merely an overzealous undergrad trying to seduce a professor she had a crush on. Especially since he was actually tempted to respond to her advances, which was normally unthinkable.

As she leaned in closer, he switched to magical sight, intending to check her aura for any signs of outside influence.

Instead, his eyes widened and he stared at her in shock, momentarily forgetting about his attempt to get out of her way.

She still looked mostly like herself, true—her features were still recognizable, and she still wore the same clothes—but that was where the resemblance ended. To magical sight, her skin was flawless and porcelain-pale, her blond hair a shimmering gold that reflected the hall's buzzing fluorescents, her figure slimmer, taller, and curvier. The fingers on the hands she was extending toward him were longer and more graceful, with long, painted nails. Her eyes, which had been a lackluster shade of moss green before, were now a bright, sparkling violet, ringed by long, curving lashes, and her lips were fuller and redder. Oddest of all, her ears swept up to slight points. To his magical senses, her breathtaking beauty was strangely compelling.

He hadn't seen a woman this beautiful since Deirdre Lanier. And she had been—

Almost as if thinking of Deirdre's name had flipped a switch in his mind, his growing desire dropped instantly away, replaced by swelling anger.

How *dare* this woman try something like this on him?

He straightened abruptly, stepping to the side and shrugging out of her grip with no further regard for how she would react to his rebuff. "Get away from me, Ms. Berry," he snapped. "I don't know what you're playing at, but it's not going to work."

Her eyes went wide with shock, almost as if she couldn't believe he had resisted her advances, but recovered quickly. She regarded him with sultry eyes and seductive, half-open lips. "Come on, Dr. Stone…or can I call you Alastair? Don't be like that." She took another step toward him, reaching out as if to pull him into an embrace. "I can't believe you don't want it. Want to hear a secret? I've had a thing for you since I first saw you in that class last quarter, but I was too scared to go for it. I never thought you'd want somebody like me. Isn't that funny? Of course you do. I can tell."

"I said, get *away*." He kept his voice calm, implacable, and stern. How could he have desired this woman, even for a moment? He'd definitely been slipping if he'd let whatever strange magic had come with her transformation seep through his defenses. "I think you'd better go, Ms. Berry." He picked up his briefcase and snapped it shut. "And I wouldn't try that on anyone else if I were you."

"Come on…" She flowed closer, moving with preternatural grace, her smile never faltering. "I promise, it will be amazing." She put her hands on his shoulders and leaned in again.

"No, damn you. I know what you are, and I know what you think you can do. But it won't work on me." Stone was still seething with anger, mostly at himself for not seeing the truth sooner, and that was where he made his mistake. He jerked back, pushing her away from him with a gentle shove.

To see her reaction, though, it was far from gentle. She staggered backward, barely catching herself on the edge of the podium before she fell over. Her eyes narrowed, her seductive expression turning hard. All traces of the flirtatious amusement had departed as she scrambled back from him with her hands defensively raised. "You stay away from me, Dr. Stone. Don't even think of trying that again! And you can bet I'm going to report your ass for not keeping your hands to yourself!"

It took a moment for her words to sink in. *Oh, bloody hell…* "Don't be absurd! We both know that isn't how—"

Her smile was back, but now it was calculating. "Nobody here but us. And who are they going to believe? A hot professor with a reputation for sleeping around, or a poor, innocent young student who got in over her head?"

A core of cold dread was growing in the pit of Stone's stomach. She was right, of course—absent any proof, he had little defense. The system in place was designed to protect the students, especially the women, because overwhelmingly it *was* the one in the position of power who tried taking advantage. That was the way it should be—but in this case, it could do nothing but work against him. "Ms. Berry, why are you doing this? What do you want?"

"Want?" She laughed. "I didn't *want* anything…except you. I wasn't kidding that I had a crush on you since last quarter. It would have been fun. But hey, it's okay." She gave an airy wave and headed for the door. "Guess you'll be hearing from your boss soon. G'night!"

"Wait!" he called after her. "I wasn't kidding—I know what you are."

Her laugh was mocking now, her hand on the doorhandle. "I don't think so. And even if you do, so what? Nobody will believe you." She flashed him a cruel grin. "Hope you liked your job, Dr. Stone. Later!"

And then she was gone, the door swinging shut behind her with a final *click*.

He watched the closed door for a few seconds, then slumped to the edge of the table and plowed his hands through his spiky hair.

This was bad.

And, worst of all, he didn't see a way magic could get him out of it. Not one he was willing to take, anyway.

CHAPTER EIGHTEEN

H E COULDN'T THINK OF WHAT ELSE TO DO and he knew his brain wasn't firing on all cylinders, so when he reached his car in the darkened parking lot, he texted Verity. *Are you busy?* He didn't have much hope: she was probably working for Scuro, or out with friends, or even working late at the Sybil's Apothecary.

To his surprise, she answered right away. *Nah, just home doing some reading. What's up?*

Mind if I pop up there? I need your perspective on something.

Sure, come on up. Something wrong?

Yes, but I'll tell you when I get there.

He drove home and immediately teleported to San Francisco. The two-block walk from the ley line to her apartment seemed to take forever. He barely paid attention to his surroundings, so if anyone had been lurking in the shadows waiting to mug some unwitting victim, he wouldn't have noticed until they were on top of him. Fortunately, the muggers seemed to be taking the night off.

Verity met him at the door, looking immediately concerned when she saw him. "Come on in." She eyed him critically as if looking for blood, torn clothes, or any other indication of physical injury. "Want a cup of coffee? Tea?"

What he wanted was a stiff drink, but that didn't seem appropriate at the moment. "Coffee's fine, thanks." He trudged inside and dropped onto her old, overstuffed couch with a loud sigh.

She puttered in the kitchen and returned with two steaming cups of coffee. When he accepted one gratefully, she sat in the chair opposite him and leaned forward, propping her elbows on her knees. "So, what's up? You said something was wrong, but you don't look hurt. Is this about the…changes?"

He stared into his cup. "Indirectly, yes. But that's not the bad part." Speaking slowly and deliberately, almost as if he were telling a story about someone else, he related what had happened after the seminar.

Her eyes widened as she listened. She said nothing until he was finished, then let out a loud blast of air. "Wow."

"Yes." He set the cup down on the table and threw himself backward, gazing up at the wood-beamed ceiling. "I haven't got a clue what to do about this, Verity. If she goes to Martinez with this story—"

"Will Martinez believe her?" Verity's voice was steady, firm but comforting.

"How the hell should I know? Why wouldn't she? I've been through the training. The overwhelming majority of women who report things like this are telling the truth. The default, barring evidence to the contrary, is to believe the accuser. I get that, and I support it. I haven't got any illusions that it happens. Professors *do* sometimes behave inappropriately around students—even the ones you'd never suspect of it. That sort of abuse of power shouldn't be tolerated."

"But you *didn't* do it."

"No, I didn't. I've never acted inappropriately with a student. But—" He spread his hands. "I do have a reputation of seeing a lot of women." With a snort, he added, "She told me the sororities keep a list of so-called 'hot professors.'"

The corner of her lip quirked in a smile. "So, are you on it?"

"What difference does *that* make?"

"You're right. Sorry. Back to the problem. Do you have any idea what you're planning to do about it? Do you think she really will go to Martinez, or was she just trying to scare you?"

Stone was having a hard time staying still, but he forced himself not to leap up and stalk around the room. "I've got no idea. Before, I would have said no. I remember her from the class she took. She was a mousy little thing, quiet, the sort that doesn't get noticed. But now…"

"Now she's turned into…what?"

"I don't know. I've never seen whatever she is before. She was quite beautiful, and had some sort of…seduction aura around her."

"Sorry for bringing it up, but…like Deirdre?"

He bowed his head. "Sort of. But not the same thing. She was definitely one of the new changed people, because all of this was only visible to magical sight. Except the seduction aura, of course. That was functioning quite nicely even without it." He glanced back up as he considered something he hadn't thought about before. "She'd never have come on to me like that before, even if she did fancy me. She was never that assertive. I wonder if something changed her personality, too—made her more confident because her new abilities make men respond to her more strongly. Hell, she almost got *me* before I realized something was up and took a look, and I'm usually fairly well inoculated against that sort of thing."

"So, you're saying this change might be…innate? Like it made her more sexually predatory?"

"Possibly. That's sort of what happened with Wayne Carter when he became a satyr…except I wouldn't call him 'predatory,' exactly. With him it was all consensual, but a lot more people were consenting."

"Hmm." She sipped her coffee. "Maybe it could be a personality thing—Wayne was horny but not predatory—or it could be a function of whatever kind of thing they changed into. Though satyrs do have a reputation for being…a bit rapey, at least in mythology, right?"

Stone wasn't sure this line of conversation was helping, but he didn't have a better one. "If I had to offer a guess, I'd say whatever they change into *affects* them, but doesn't necessarily *define* them."

"What do you mean?"

He shrugged. "Perhaps it amplifies what's already there. So Carter, who has a high libido but is otherwise fairly easygoing, becomes more of a Dionysus-style satyr—you know, drinking, carousing, and having lots of sex. While Ms. Berry…perhaps she had all this sexual energy all along, but didn't get a lot of chance to express it due to her innate repression."

"That sounds like a lot of unsupported psychological diagnosis," Verity said. "You could be right, but damn…if Eddie and Ward's researchers are right about this change probably being permanent, it's going to take years to unpack all the implications." She leaned back in her chair and set her cup down. "But that's not the important part right now."

"Not to me," Stone agreed morosely. Even though he'd been entertaining the idea of leaving the University for quite some time, he'd never seriously considered it. Despite it being inconvenient and frustrating sometimes, he still liked his job. He certainly didn't want to leave it with this sort of thing hanging over his head—and the implication of inappropriate conduct with students was one of the few things that could get him sacked, even with full tenure, if he didn't find a way to deal with it.

"What if you…head it off?"

"Head it off?" Stone tilted his head.

"You know—go to Martinez first. Tell her what happened, so she gets your story before the girl's."

"That's one option…though it's possible it might backfire on me if she doesn't believe me."

"Why wouldn't she believe you?"

"I don't know. I *do* have a reputation. Sometimes I think some of my colleagues have a betting pool going for when I'm going to trip up."

"I doubt that." She was watching him soberly now. "Come on, Doc—you've never even gotten near a student."

"Of course not. But don't think I didn't hear the whispers when you and I were seeing each other. It's not hard to extrapolate, especially for someone who doesn't know me very well."

She bowed her head. "Yeah...I guess you have a point here. And I know how serious this is. I still think you should talk to Martinez, though. Do you think there's a *chance* she'll believe you?"

"Of course. But I've also got it going against me that as far as she's likely to remember—if she remembers at all—Ms. Berry was a quiet, unassuming girl who never spoke up in class. Hardly the vengeful *femme fatale* type."

Verity was silent for a while, her gaze fixed somewhere in the middle distance as Stone watched the wheels in her mind turning. "She's not trying to blackmail you, is she?"

"No. I asked her what she wanted, but she said all she wanted was me. I honestly think if I'd gone along with her, let her indulge her fantasy, that would have been it."

"But you couldn't do that."

"Of course not. I wouldn't give in to such a thing in the first place, even if I *were* inclined to take advantage of a student." He shook his head. "I'm not sure that even *was* what she wanted, anyway. This...affliction might have changed her, but deep down I suspect she's still the same person. I mean, look at Gina. She's still Gina, even if astrally she looks like a humanoid cat."

She gave a sage nod. "I think I get it now."

"Get what?"

"What's going on with this girl."

Stone frowned. "Do share. Because I haven't got a clue."

"I think you do—the only reason you're not seeing it is because you're right in the middle of it. Honestly, I see it more with guys than women, but nobody's immune."

"What are you on about, Verity?"

"Think about it. What do a lot of people—especially younger people who aren't very experienced in dealing with rejection—do when their advances get rebuffed?"

Stone was about to say he didn't know, but then it dawned. "They get angry."

She nodded. "Not just angry. *Pissed.* They lash out. They want to hurt the person who hurt them by rejecting them. Just the other day, I was walking down the street not far from the new shop, and some asshole catcalled me. When I didn't respond, he called me a 'stuck-up bitch.'"

"I hope you showed him the error of his ways."

"I may or may not have made him drop his sandwich in the gutter. But that's beside the point."

Now that she'd said it, it made more sense. "So, she's lashing out at me because she's taking my rejection personally."

"I'd bet a lot of money on that."

"But what's it mean? How can it help me? I think going to talk to her would be a very bad idea. If she's still angry, she could accuse me of trying to intimidate her. Hell, she could even secretly record or film me."

"Yeah…you have a point there. And I guess it wouldn't do any good for somebody else to talk to her—like, say, me." She thought some more, then focused on him. "How did you reject her?"

The change of topic startled him. "What?"

"You know—were you nice about it, or did you say anything mean?"

He repeated the conversation in his mind. "I didn't insult her or anything, if that's what you mean. This is me we're talking about. I try to be professional, though she did catch me off guard. Oh—and I told her I knew what she was."

"How did she react to that?"

"She said it didn't matter, because nobody would believe me. Which she's right about, of course." He remembered the rest. "And damn, I also gave her a little shove when she got too close to me. Not hard at all—but she's got a future as a football player, because she responded like I tried to push her through a wall."

"Hmm. That's not good."

"No. It's not. If she accuses me of not only trying to take advantage of her sexually, but actually *assaulting* her..." His mind spun, wondering now if getting sacked was the worst thing that could happen. If she managed to get anyone to believe the assault thing, he could end up in jail. Perhaps he should ask Jason for advice—or Leo Blum.

Verity finished her coffee. "Even so, you still might get lucky."

"How could I possibly get lucky?"

"She might get home, think about it, and decide not to do anything after all. People say a lot of things when they're angry and feeling hurt, but they don't always act on them. Especially if you're right, and she's so hot and confident now that she could get any guy she wants. If you want my advice, talk to Martinez—give her a heads-up before the girl can tell her story, but otherwise just wait. She might let it go and not say anything about it."

That was a lot of ifs, and a lot of trusting other people to do the right thing. Stone didn't like it at all, but his other options were all even less appealing. He stood heavily. "Thank you, Verity. I appreciate your help. I just hope I don't need to call my solicitor."

"Let's not get lawyers involved yet. I know girls like that. I can't promise you she's all talk and no action, but remember—you *didn't* do anything. She knows that. And she doesn't hate you from before. Maybe her better nature will shine through."

Stone made a noncommittal noise. In his experience, staking your future on other people's better natures was rarely a good bet.

CHAPTER NINETEEN

STONE KNEW IT WAS POINTLESS to try sleeping when he returned home, but he made the effort nonetheless. If he intended to go to Martinez tomorrow, he couldn't show up looking like he'd been out drinking all night. While the thought of doing just that crossed his mind more than once, he didn't indulge.

In the end, he spent most of the night haunted by uneasy thoughts of how this situation might go down. Verity was right: Michele Berry might have been all sizzle and no steak, consumed by hurt feelings and anger that would fade when she got away from him. He had always treated her with the same respect he used on all his students, which meant if he was lucky, she'd realize she'd been the one out of line and let the whole thing drop.

That was one possibility. But he had no idea how her particular change had altered her way of thinking. Wayne Carter no longer cared about his commitment to his wife and children, preferring to pursue his hedonistic lifestyle instead. Michele might have experienced a similar shift in priorities. Even though her only reasonable motive for going after him was revenge, it was possible Michele 2.0 might consider it a perfectly valid one.

What was she, anyway? Verity and Hezzie had mentioned the "beautiful elf" they'd seen at the shop, but Michele hadn't looked like an elf, exactly. He wondered how many different forms the people affected by the change would ultimately take. Was there a finite number, or would each person's manifestation be highly personal and individual? Would it be like the Forgotten, where some types would be more common than others?

Stone growled softly, tired of all these questions he couldn't answer and problems he couldn't solve. Raider, curled on his chest, raised his head curiously but then settled back again.

Stone envied him. Cats didn't have to worry about anything but mealtimes, sleeping in sunbeams, and knocking things off counters. Right now, that sounded appealing.

Finally, after tossing and turning for several hours, he gave up and rose from bed, gently tipping Raider off. The cat, deep in slumber, barely noticed, immediately rearranging himself into a tight, purring ball in the warm spot his human left behind.

As long as he was up, Stone decided to check the message board Gina had given him access to. Every day there were more posts, and his count of distinct cases had risen to close to two hundred. Whatever this was, it was escalating, whether because the incubation period was catching up with people or because more of them were getting exposed. He hadn't been tracking the specific manifestations yet, but thought it might be useful to start doing that. Maybe some patterns would emerge, with clusters of similar types in specific areas.

Before pulling up the message board, he clicked his email almost unconsciously. He didn't get much email in his personal account usually, and since he was off work for the summer he only checked his University account every two or three days.

Now, though, a subject line caught his eye amid the usual smattering of updates from the department:

MB

The message was marked *Important*, and the sender was listed as *A Friend*.

He stared at it, his hand tensing on the mouse. *MB* could be nothing but *Michele Berry*. Who could be sending him something about her? Did someone else know what had happened?

He clicked the link, and the email popped up.

The first thing he noticed was it was from a throwaway account. Either the sender didn't want to be traced, or they wanted to maintain plausible deniability. He quickly scanned the lines of text:

I want to talk to you about what happened with MB. I have important information you'll want to hear before you talk to anyone else. Come to Mitzi's on University tomorrow morning at 7 a.m. Please reply so I'll know you got this.
—A Friend

Stone sat still in his chair, reading the note over and over until he'd burned its every word into his brain. Who was this person? How did they know about what happened? Could it possibly be Michele herself, suffering a change of heart and wanting to make things right?

Or maybe trying to trap him into trying to coerce her not to pursue the matter?

No, he couldn't think like that. If he did, he'd paralyze himself. And besides, he was still a mage. Maybe it wasn't ethical to use his magic to get him out of this situation, but there was nothing wrong with a little recon. Mitzi's Café was a small restaurant across the street from the Stanford Theatre, which only served breakfast and lunch. He could show up a little early, check the place out, and decide what he wanted to do if he spotted Michele there.

Quickly, before he could change his mind, he clicked *Reply* and sent a three-word answer: *I'll be there.*

He wasn't entirely sure it was the best course of action, but his curiosity wouldn't let him miss the meeting.

At least he had something to do now.

Seven a.m. was far earlier than Stone was usually up and about, let alone coherent, but a shower and a strong cup of coffee before he left the house roused him sufficiently to get him moving. He arrived outside Mitzi's Café, his illusionary amulet disguising him as a young undergrad in a Stanford hoodie and jeans. Lingering outside, he peered in through the display window.

The place was doing a brisk business, but most of the people loitering around inside were waiting for takeout orders. About half the tables were occupied, and it was easy to see Michele Berry wasn't among them. Magical sight confirmed this. As far as he could tell, no one inside the restaurant was magically disguised or one of the changed people. Relieved, he glanced around to make sure no one was looking at him, then dropped the illusion and headed inside. He took a seat at the rearmost available table, picked up the menu, and pretended to peruse it while surreptitiously observing the area around him.

"Hi, Dr. Stone."

The unfamiliar voice had spoken from behind him. He jerked, startled, and twisted in his seat.

He didn't recognize the woman standing there, but he definitely recognized the type: she was a student, probably an undergrad like Michele Berry. Athletically built, with short, light-brown hair, she wore a Stanford Softball sweatshirt, skinny jeans, and colorful athletic shoes.

"Er…good morning. I'm afraid you've got me at a disadvantage."

"Okay if I sit down?"

It was hard to miss that she clearly didn't want to give her name. "Of course." He waved her toward the open seat opposite him. "I'm guessing you're the one who sent the email last night."

He looked around to make sure nobody else was paying attention to them, but no one seemed to be.

"Yeah." She appeared nervous, as if she wasn't sure she wanted to be here.

He indicated the menu. "Would you like anything? Cup of coffee? Breakfast?"

"Coffee's good, thanks. I don't want to stay long."

The server came by and they each ordered a cup. While they waited for her to leave, the woman watched Stone with an odd, pensive look.

"What can I do for you?" he asked. "Your email said this was about last night. I assume my guess about who *MB* might be is accurate."

Their coffees arrived quickly; the service here was quite brisk. The woman stared into hers, swirling it around before taking a long sip. "I didn't want to do this," she said at last, raising her gaze to meet hers. "But I'm worried about Michele."

He frowned. "Worried about her?" *She's not the one potentially in hot water here.* "You two know each other, then?"

"Yeah. She's one of my housemates."

"I see." Stone kept his voice noncommittal. He had no idea where this was going.

She took a long, deep breath. "Like I said, I'm worried about her. She's been acting…different lately."

"Different in what way?"

"It's hard to say. She's…I don't know if you know what she used to be like…" She paused, looking at him expectantly.

"She took one of my courses earlier this year. She was…I would say she kept to herself. Quiet, shy, not the sort who spoke up in class."

"Exactly." She nodded vigorously. "That's the way she's always been, as long as I've known her. But then, a month or so ago, she…changed."

"Changed." Stone switched briefly to magical sight and studied the woman. To his relief, she looked the same as she did to mundane sight, except for the addition of her healthy, bright-blue aura. Good. Michele Berry might have been afflicted by the change, but this woman hadn't been.

"Yeah. I can't really explain it, except that she got a lot more…confident. And a lot more successful with guys. She'd always been super shy, and guys didn't look twice at her, but the last month or so it's like a switch flipped. She's been taking better care of herself, dressing better, wearing makeup…and it seems like she's seeing a different guy three or four times a week."

Stone pondered that. It made sense: if her change had made her more beautiful, confident, and seductive, it followed that she'd flex her new muscles after too long as a reluctant wallflower. "I…noticed that."

"Yeah." She looked at her hands around her coffee cup. "The thing is, Dr. Stone, she's had a crush on you ever since she took your class. She talks about you a lot. It was kind of embarrassing to listen to, to be honest. I mean, yeah, girls get crushes on their professors. It happens all the time. Hell, I think my art history professor is pretty hot. But that doesn't mean I follow him around and try to bend him over the lecture-hall table."

Stone winced, as her blunt words brought back the visceral memory of the previous evening. "Yes. Well. I concur, but I don't see what this has to do with—"

She looked around to verify nobody was paying attention to them. "The thing is, I'm pretty sure she went to that lecture last night intending to do exactly what she did. And I'm also sure it freaked her out when it didn't work out the way she expected."

"That doesn't surprise me either. But how do you know all this?"

"I was there."

Stone blinked. "I didn't see you there."

She gave him a wry smile. "Did you look? There were a lot of people in the audience, and I'm guessing you didn't notice all of them. You probably didn't even notice Michele until she came up to talk to you after."

He had to concede that she had a point. Despite his talent for making each audience member feel like he was lecturing directly to them, he didn't necessarily pay attention to the individual people. The tiered part of the hall had been dimly lit to allow the visual parts of his presentation. The woman had been just another face in the crowd.

"I was in the back," she was saying. "I hadn't planned to go, but I guess I kind of had a hunch she'd try something with you."

"Why did you care?"

She shrugged. "I still care about Michele, but like I said, she's changed. I heard the way she talked a couple times when she didn't think a guy was as into her as she thought he should be. I wanted to see what would happen."

"Where were you? You certainly weren't there when Michele was…making her move."

"No. I went out with everybody else, through the door in the back. But I hung around after the rest were gone. I had the door a little way open and was watching."

He frowned at her. "If that's true, then why didn't you—"

"Why didn't I come in and stop it?" At his nod, she gave a nervous chuckle. "Because that would have been super awkward, you know? Walking in on the middle of that?"

Stone didn't agree, and wished she'd been a little less worried about awkwardness, but what was done was done. "Why did you email me about it, then?"

She fumbled in her small leather purse and pulled out her phone. "I didn't bust in on you guys…but I did get a video of what happened."

A cold shiver ran down Stone's back, and he froze. "You…took video."

"Yeah. The picture's not great since I was so far away, but trust me, it's good enough. And the audio is solid." It was still obvious she wasn't happy about what she was saying. She looked up at him almost pleadingly. "Dr. Stone, I don't want Michele to get in trouble. She's a good kid. I think something's wrong with her, making her act like this, and I want her to get help. But…" She swallowed hard. "I don't want her to get anyone *else* in trouble, either. I don't want you to get hurt because she can't deal with…whatever it is that's happening to her." Her hand tightened on the phone.

Stone didn't answer right away. His mind spun with possibilities, and he didn't want to handle this wrong. Doing that might get him in more trouble than he could already be in. "What…do you plan to do with that?" he asked carefully, nodding toward her hand.

She looked miserable. "I don't know. If she goes to anybody and claims you were inappropriate with her, I could show this to them to make them see you didn't do anything wrong. But if I do that, she'll get in big trouble. She could get expelled. Maybe even arrested."

His first impulse was to protest, to say *Never mind her, what about what will happen to* me *if she does that?* But he didn't say that. Instead, he paused again, considering. "So…what do you propose, then?"

"I could send you the video, I guess." She still didn't sound certain. "But it's the same deal. She could get in big trouble if you share it, and you could get in big trouble if you don't."

Stone couldn't remain silent any longer. "You've got to understand—this is potentially my career we're talking about here. If she claims I assaulted her, I could be arrested. You know they'll believe her over me if there's no evidence—which is what they should do. I've got no illusions—I've got a lot of money and good solicitors, so I doubt anything will stick. But my reputation would be tarnished to the point I'd probably have to resign. And I'm not the one in the wrong here. We both know that."

"Yeah. We do." She stared at her hands. "That's why I'm here now. I guess...I was hoping you'd have some ideas. Some way we could do this where neither of you will get in trouble. I don't know what's wrong with Michele, Dr. Stone, but I know it's something. Either she's taking drugs, or the stress of trying to keep up with her schedule has messed up her head, or...something," she finished lamely. "She needs help."

Stone, of course, knew exactly what was wrong with her, but he couldn't tell this woman. Despite what Michele had threatened to do to him, he didn't particularly feel compelled to punish her. If he could get out of this without implicating her, he'd be satisfied.

"Could you talk to her?" the woman asked hopefully. "May-be...let her know the video exists? I don't think she's talked to anybody yet. She usually sleeps pretty late."

"I'm not sure that's the best idea." A little shiver ran up Stone's back. "Can you imagine what that might look like—the professor she's claiming harassed her showing up on her doorstep to try to dissuade her from doing it?"

"Good point." Her gaze returned to her phone, which she was turning over nervously in her hands. "Do you think it would do any good for *me* to talk to her? You know, show it to her and tell her if she takes this to anyone, I'll reveal the truth?"

A glimmer of hope flickered. He wouldn't have proposed that, but he was glad she'd suggested it. "It might be better, yes. Though it would probably make your life awkward if you're housemates."

"I don't care about that." She looked up at him with more re-solve. "Here's the thing, Dr. Stone. I had this happen to me once. It was in high school, and nothing really terrible happened, but when I told the school authorities about it, they brushed it off. I know they don't do that around here, and I'm really glad about that. But I don't want the girls who *really* have a complaint to get doubted because Michele's feeling rejected. You know?"

"I do," he said softly. "Thank you for coming to me with this. It took a lot of courage, and it will take more to do what you're proposing."

"It's the right thing to do." She still didn't appear entirely happy about it, but a quick look at her aura told Stone her reluctance didn't come from what she would be doing, but merely that she wished none of this had happened in the first place.

She picked up her phone and stood. "I'll send you a copy of the video, just in case things don't go like I hope they do. Take care, Dr. Stone."

Before he could reply, she quickly slipped away from the table and hurried out the door.

He watched her go, deep in thought. He didn't dare assume this situation might resolve itself yet, but he allowed himself a bit of hope.

It was all up to this unknown student, and that made him nervous.

CHAPTER TWENTY

TWO DAYS PASSED.

Stone checked his email, texts, and phone messages often, almost obsessively, convinced any moment he would hear from Beatrice Martinez, calling him into her office. He tried to keep busy by concentrating on his studies of the affliction, adding data points to his list, checking Gina's message board, and keeping in touch with Eddie and Ward, but his mind wasn't on it. The number of afflicted was growing steadily, but so far the researchers hadn't come up with any breakthrough ideas to explain the phenomenon.

Verity checked in with him a couple times a day. He'd told her about the meeting at Mitzi's, and she'd been cautiously optimistic that the lack of news was a good thing. When he'd shown her the video the woman had sent him, she'd agreed that, if it came out, there was no way anybody could have called him the aggressor in the situation.

He hadn't mentioned anything about it to Jason or Amber. They had enough to worry about with their baby due soon, so he didn't want to concern them with anything else—especially something that didn't involve them.

Late Tuesday afternoon, he stopped in to Jason's agency without calling ahead. He found his friend deep in conversation with Gina at her desk, an open folder full of papers in front of them. Both looked up when he came in.

"Al. Didn't expect to see you today." Jason dropped the page he'd been examining.

"I was in the area. Actually came to see Gina."

"That's good, since I'm on my way out." He indicated the drift of other folders. "Got three different cases going at once, and with Amber not helping out as much for a while, it's keeping me hopping."

"You need to hire another investigator." Stone smiled, proud that his friend's agency was doing so well.

"Thinking about it, but that's not gonna help me now. I gotta fly down to L.A. to tail a guy who's suspected of selling company secrets."

"Don't let me keep you, then. We can chat when you get back if you like."

"Yeah. Sucks that I have to miss going with Amber to Tahoe, though."

"She's going to Tahoe?"

"Yeah. Her brothers' wives and some other friends are throwing her a baby shower."

Stone didn't miss the reluctance in his voice. "You're not in favor of it?"

"Eh, it's not up to me, but that's a long drive. I just wish she'd at least fly, but she says she likes driving and I know she hates planes." He flashed a tight smile. "I know, I'm overprotective, and she's not exactly a delicate flower. She laughs at me when I worry too much. Says pregnancy is a lot easier for shifters than for us vanilla human types. But she's only one-quarter shifter."

"I'm sure she'll be fine." Stone didn't bother reminding Jason that his wife, under normal circumstances, was both stronger and tougher than he was. The only time the situation got closer to equal was when Jason's new, adrenaline-based magical enhancements took hold.

"Oh, yeah, of course she will. She's still planning for us to be at Aubrey's wedding, even though it'll be close to the due date by then. She's something, that's for damn sure."

Stone grinned at his combination of exasperation and affection. "She is indeed." He made a shooing motion. "Anyway, off you go. Don't miss your plane on my account."

"Yeah. See you later, Al. Gina, you might as well head out after you update the active cases. We can't take on any more work until I clear a couple of these."

"You got it, boss."

She waited until he'd swept out, the door swinging closed behind him, before addressing Stone. "So, what's up?"

"That's what I wanted to ask *you*. How are you doing?"

"You mean how's life as a furball?" Her grin was cheeky.

"Well…yes." He switched to magical sight, still not quite used to the way she and others like her changed so completely. When he looked at her astrally, no sign of her human form remained unless he specifically tried focusing on it. Even then, it was nothing more than a faint trace. He wondered if lesser-powered mages would even see that. "How has your research been going?"

"Good. I'm pretty obsessed with this, actually." She swung her chair around, indicating her screen. "I'm not technically supposed to be doing this at work, but I've set up some safeguards so I can't be traced. Jason doesn't mind as long as it doesn't interfere with what I'm supposed to be doing."

He glanced over her shoulder as she pulled up a map of the world and zoomed it in on the USA. It was clustered with dots, most of them in and around major cities.

"I've been tracking as many of them as I can," she said. "I've found a couple other spots online where they're starting to congregate, and any time they reveal a location, I plot it on the map here."

Stone leaned in closer, surprised. There were a *lot* of dots—he estimated at least a thousand, probably more. Most of them were red, but a subset were other colors. "Why are they different colors?"

"Just something I was trying—tracking them by the date when they noticed the change. The red ones didn't reveal anything. The blue ones are within the last week, the green two weeks ago, and the orange, three."

"Three is the longest?"

"So far, yeah. The oldest one I tagged was this guy in San Diego." She pointed at an orange dot in southern California. "But don't get excited about that. As you can see, the vast majority haven't specified yet. I started threads on a couple of the groups asking people to tell when they changed, but that was just a couple days ago. Not a lot of response so far."

Stone studied the map, noting the positions of the orange dots. Several of them were in the northern Midwest, but the rest were scattered all over the country. "That doesn't help much, though, unless we know what the incubation period is. If it's long enough, we might never trace this back to a catalyst, or a Patient Zero."

She narrowed her eyes. "Your brainiacs back in England still trying to cure it?"

"I don't think they're anywhere near that yet." He backed up and paced the room. "So far, all they've determined is that it doesn't seem to be causing anyone physical harm."

He thought about Michele Berry, and wondered about other kinds of harm. If she tried her seduction trick on the wrong person, it could backfire in her face and get her in trouble. Hell, if he'd been less of a gentleman, the outcome of her attempt might have been a lot less benign.

"Yeah, I think I could've told you that." She turned away from her screen. "I've met some others locally, by the way."

"Is that right?" He stopped pacing, interested.

"Yeah. There are several of us around the area. We got together the other night at a Round Table in Mountain View." She grinned wickedly. "*That* was trippy, I'll tell you. All the normies just going about their business while a cat, a fox, a fairy-looking girl with wings, and a goblin chowed down on an extra-large Wombo Combo and a pitcher of beer."

Stone leaned against the counter, shaking his head in wonder. "I'm still marveling at how you lot are so *comfortable* with this so quickly. I mean, this has got to be a massive upheaval in your lives, but yet here you are, less than a month after it happens, casually getting together for pizza."

"Right?" She lazily spun her chair around. "It's freaking me out a little too, but it's like I keep telling you—it just feels *right*. I can't explain it better than that, but no matter how much I rationally think I should be in therapy about it, I can't help feeling deep down like I've *always* been like this." She indicated her body, decidedly normal-human-looking to mundane sight. "Like some part of me always knew this was the real me, and I've been repressing it. Does that make any sense at all?"

"Not...really," he admitted. "I'm not doubting you, but I suppose it's not possible to truly understand it unless I experienced it."

"Yeah, I hear that." She fixed an earnest stare on him. "But even if you don't get it, Doc, you have to believe me: a lot of us don't *want* to be cured. You aren't gonna find too many people willing to work with you if you tell them you're trying to make this go away. For a lot of us, it's the best thing that ever happened to us."

Stone didn't answer right away. As hard as he tried, he couldn't get his mind around personally being happy if he woke up one morning and found he'd turned into something...else. "I suppose I'll have to take your word for it. Unless I get it myself, at least."

"Maybe you will." She laughed, stopping the chair's spin to face him. "You never know, Doc. If it *is* contagious, maybe you'll be next. Unless magic guys like you are immune. Maybe you already have too much magic floating around in your blood to let it take hold."

He almost gave a flippant reply, but then stared hard at her. "You know, you might be on to something there." He remembered what Verity and Hezzie had said before—that they didn't have it. Obviously he didn't have it either, and neither did Eddie, Ward, or any of the magical researchers at Caventhorne, despite being exposed. *Were* mages immune, or perhaps less likely to be affected because of the same unknown factor that made them mages?

"How so?"

"I think I need to talk to Eddie and Ward. I'm wondering if any of the afflicted—"

"Dude, *please* stop calling us that."

"Sorry, sorry. The…er…affected, then. I wonder if any of them are mages."

"Dunno. That's not something I can track, for obvious reasons. I doubt any of your bunch are gonna reveal their magic status to some message board, even if it *is* anonymous."

"That's all right. I think this is more my thing—but thank you for the idea. It might give us another data point, anyway. I—"

In his pocket, his phone buzzed, indicating a text.

"Excuse me a moment." He pulled it out and glanced at it, expecting something he could put off.

"Doc?" Gina sounded concerned. "Everything okay?"

He realized he was staring, and jerked his head up. "Er—sorry. I've got to deal with this. Thank you for the insights, Gina. I'm sure we'll talk again soon."

"Yeah, happy to help, as long as you stop trying to mess with my cathood."

Stone barely responded, except for a vague wave. He didn't look at the phone again until he got outside, realizing his heart was beating fast.

We need to talk, the message said.

It was signed, *MB*.

CHAPTER TWENTY-ONE

STONE KNEW IT WAS A BAD IDEA to meet Michele Berry alone. He had no idea if she'd gone to anyone with her story yet, nor if her housemate had talked to her and revealed the existence of the video. But he did it anyway, because he'd always trusted his gut in the past and didn't intend to stop now.

He'd replied to her text with a simple *Yes?*, leaving her the opening to provide more information.

Her own reply had come quickly, as if she was sitting somewhere, hunched over her phone and hoping he would respond. *Can you meet me at the mausoleum on campus in an hour?*

It was an odd spot for a meeting, but the place didn't get a lot of visitors except during the annual Halloween party. The crypt was located on the north side of campus, near a cactus garden originally created for the Stanford family. If he left now, he could easily make it in an hour—or even earlier, so he could arrive before she did. *Yes, I'll be there.*

Thanks. There was none of the sneering confidence from before. It could all be an act, but Stone didn't think so.

He drove fast, but it took him a while to find parking so he didn't reach the mausoleum until ten minutes before the appointed time. He paced the area, studying the white building with its classical columns and doorway flanked by two Sphinx statues, and wondered what Michele had in mind.

"Dr. Stone?"

He turned quickly. She was standing there, ten feet away from him, her expression pensive. There was nothing seductive about her appearance now: she had her hair tied back in a ponytail, and wore an oversized sweater, jeans, and red Chuck Taylors. Still, a certain unquantifiable quality hung around her, even now making Stone want to look at her. She made no move to approach him.

"Hello, Ms. Berry," he said, keeping his voice even.

"Don't worry. This isn't a trap or anything. I promise. I just...wanted to talk to you."

"Possibly not the wisest thing, given what happened last night."

"Yeah..." She looked at her feet. "Listen...Jennifer came to see me today."

"Jennifer?"

"My housemate. She said she met with you this morning."

Stone glanced around to make sure no one else was in the area. "She did. She cares about you, Michele."

"Yeah. I know." Her gaze remained downcast for several seconds, and then she looked up at him. "I'm not going to tell anybody about what happened. I know you didn't do anything."

"That's...a relief. I know that too."

"Just so you know...I wasn't going to anyway. Even before Jen showed me she had a video."

Stone wasn't sure he believed that, but he didn't reply.

"I was just...mad, you know?"

"I'm not sure I do."

She met his gaze, but couldn't hold it.

Stone got the impression there was something else she had to say, but she wasn't sure she wanted to say it. He switched to magical sight. As he expected, her dejected form immediately morphed into the willowy, curvaceous figure from last night, complete with silky golden hair, violet eyes, and gently upswept ears. Her breathtaking beauty stirred him even now, when he knew what was causing it. He immediately switched back to mundane sight. "Is there something else you wanted to discuss, Ms. Berry?"

She licked her lips, swallowed hard, and looked at him again. "You said something last night."

"I said a lot of things last night."

"I know. But…this was something strange. You said… 'I know what you are.'"

"Yes." Still, he kept his own tone even and steady. She needed to say this herself, without help or encouragement.

"What did you mean by that?"

"Exactly what I said."

"What…am I, then?"

Stone picked up the unspoken overtones of her words. She not only wanted to know if he was aware of her new status, but *she* wasn't even sure what she was and wanted him to give her answers.

Before he could answer, though, tears sprang to her eyes. Her breath hitched, and her shoulders slumped. "I don't know what to do, Dr. Stone."

He remained where he was, but spoke more softly. "I can see you. Your…other form."

She jerked her head up. "You…can?"

He inclined his head. "I can. That was why I got angry with you, when you…did what you did. Because I knew it wasn't entirely you."

"What do you mean, not entirely me?" Her eyes widened. "Is *that* what's going on? Because I don't know, and it's scaring me. I don't know how to stop it."

"Stop it?"

She nodded miserably. "I can't turn it off. At first I didn't want to, but now…"

"How long have you been like this?"

"A couple weeks." She approached him, but veered away at the last moment and slumped to sit on the steps leading to the mausoleum's door. "At first I thought it was the best thing ever. Guys never even noticed me before, but now...all of a sudden, a *lot* of them were noticing. That was scary...until I realized I could control them." Her breath hitched again, and she swiped the back of her hand across her face. "It was like having the perfect boyfriends—they'd do what I wanted, but if I didn't want to keep going, I could make them stop."

Stone paced away from her. "I'm glad you came to me—though I wish you hadn't done what you did last night."

"Yeah...me too. I'm sorry, Dr. Stone. I wasn't lying when I said I had a crush on you, but lots of girls have crushes on their professors. That doesn't mean they should—"

"No...it doesn't. But it's all right. I believe you when you say you aren't going to do anything about it."

"You do?" She dared to look hopeful.

"I do."

"So...you won't tell on me? You won't show anybody the video? Jennifer said she sent you a copy. If anybody sees that, I could get expelled."

A tiny, vindictive part of Stone was glad she was experiencing a little of the dread he'd spent the last night dealing with—but she was a student and he was a professor. He should be better than that. "I won't show it to anyone. As far as I'm concerned, as long as you don't pursue it, the matter's closed."

A momentary relief passed across her face, but dejection quickly replaced it. "I just hope I don't do it again. Sometimes I...can't control myself. When I'm attracted to somebody, it's like there's a...connection. Something that wants me to use...whatever this is...on them." She spread her hands in a gesture of futility, indicating her body. "What *am* I, Dr. Stone? What happened to me? *Why* did it happen?"

"I can't answer that. Not yet. But I do know you're not alone."

"I'm not?" She stared at him in shock. "You mean…there are other people…like me?"

"I haven't met any specifically like you. But there are others who have changed. I'm surprised you haven't seen any of them." Perhaps not, though—he hadn't seen any others on campus either, but he hadn't been here much this summer. Plus, he didn't make a habit of looking around with magical sight when he was working.

"Why would you say that?"

"From what I understand, those who are affected can see each other."

Her eyes got even bigger. "Oh, wow…that explains it."

"Explains what?"

"The other day, when I was walking across campus back toward my place, I thought I saw this…I don't even know what it was. It had fur, and a tail. I only saw it for a second. I thought I was crazy."

"You aren't crazy." He paused, trying to decide how he wanted to proceed, and made a decision. "Will you excuse me for a moment, Ms. Berry?"

"Why?" Her eyes narrowed with nervous suspicion.

"I want to contact someone. Someone who might be able to help you."

"Help me? You mean…help me get rid of this?"

"No. That isn't something anyone knows how to do yet, as far as I'm aware."

"Wait. You mean…somebody else who's like me?"

"Yes."

Her reluctance was clear, but so was her hope. "Uh…Okay. I guess."

He quickly turned away and texted Gina. *I've met another one, and she's having a difficult time. Mind if I put her in touch with you?*

The answer came back quickly. *No prob. Tell her to text me.*

Stone turned back to find Michele watching him closely. "Right, then. I'm going to send you the number of someone you can text. She's coordinating a group of you." He pulled up her text and sent Gina's number.

"Thanks, Dr. Stone." She sighed. "I'm still scared, but also...kind of excited. I'm not sure how I feel about this. I'm just glad I'm not crazy."

"You aren't crazy. But you'd best work on your control before you get yourself into trouble. Not everyone will be susceptible to your...unique charms. You're lucky it was me you tested them on, instead of someone less forgiving."

CHAPTER TWENTY-TWO

FOR THE NEXT COUPLE DAYS Stone felt lighter, as if a weight had been lifted from his shoulders. He still shuddered when he thought about the bullet he'd dodged, and how much it could have upended his life, but at this point he was reasonably certain Michele Berry wouldn't cause him any more trouble. He hoped Gina and her group could help her.

To take his mind off the situation, he popped over to Caventhorne early the following evening to check in with Eddie and Ward.

He knew they would both be working late, and he wasn't wrong. Even though it was one a.m. in England, he found both of them in one of the larger conference rooms, wrapping up a discussion with a pair of researchers. He waited until the researchers had filed out before he made his presence known.

"Looks like you two have been busy." He glanced around the room. Almost every spare bit of wall had been covered with super-sized sheets of note-scribbled paper. Two big whiteboards, likewise covered, were stationed at either end of the room, and the conference table was barely visible beneath piles of reference books, drifts of papers, and a pair of open laptops. A large, flat-panel monitor affixed to the only part of the wall not covered by papers displayed what appeared to be the screen of one of the laptops.

"Too bloody right, mate." Eddie, in jeans and his West Ham football jersey, looked like he hadn't slept for at least two days, but

Stone recognized the manic gleam in his eyes. He lived for this kind of thing.

"Care to update me on the latest?"

"Go ahead, Ward." Eddie began pawing through a stack of papers. "I need to write up a couple things before I forget 'em."

Stone snorted. "Like you ever forget *anything*."

Ward, seated at the far end of the table and surrounded by more papers, pulled off his wire-rimmed glasses and swiped a hand across his forehead. "To start with, the phenomenon is growing—or at least we're getting a better idea of its extent."

"Growing. How much?"

Ward indicated the flat-panel monitor, and clicked something on his laptop. The scene changed from columns of figures to a world map. Like Gina's, a series of dots peppered it. There were a lot more dots on this one, though, and they were all the same color. "We've now got documented cases on every continent save Antarctica. We've put the word out to mages all over the world, and they're contacting others. The data is starting to come in fast now."

Stone let his breath out. "Bloody hell. Does anyone know what's causing it yet? Is it biological? Magical? A combination of the two? Are some people more susceptible than others? How is it spread?"

Eddie laughed and raised his hands. "'Old on there, Stone. Slow down. We're all impatient for results, but you know this isn't a fast process."

Stone forced himself to ramp down his speeding thoughts. "Okay. Okay. Tell me what you *do* know, and what you suspect. I assume your people are still testing affected volunteers."

"Oh, yeah. We've managed to persuade several of 'em to come in, or at least to let us take a blood sample." He indicated the room, his eyes gleaming with pride. "Some'ow, we seem to 'ave become the central repository for information about this phenomenon. We're working with groups of researchers in the US—upstate New York, to be precise—and Germany, but everything's flowin' in 'ere.

Probably because we got the jump on it before anybody else did, plus we've got the best facilities."

"That's brilliant, Eddie. But what do we *know*?"

"Not much yet," Ward said soberly. "But there are a couple of strong hypotheses, one of which was helped considerably by the fact that we're doing our work here in England."

"What's that mean?"

"It means," Eddie said, "that you lot over in the States are bloody disorganized—at least your magical society is. Everybody's a bleedin' maverick, doin' their own thing and not keepin' in touch to maintain proper records. Nobody knows anything about anybody over there."

"They like it that way. But what's it got to do with—"

The librarian picked up a thick, leather-bound tome and opened it to a page he'd marked. "Over 'ere, we keep records. Genealogies of magical lines. Okay, sure, it's mostly just the wealthier families like yours, but we've got enough of the others that a pattern's startin' to emerge. There's not enough to be sure, but our egg'eads are beginnin' to think they might be on to summat."

"Don't keep me in suspense, Eddie. Out with it."

It wasn't Eddie who spoke, though, but Ward. "We think it might be affecting people who have magical blood, but didn't inherit the Talent."

"Not all of 'em," Eddie added. "But so far, we've identified quite a few."

Stone stared at them. "So...you're saying mundanes—true mundanes—aren't affected?"

"That's our current working hypothesis," Ward said. "Of course, there's no way to be absolutely sure, because there isn't any way we know of to identify magical blood. It's not the same as those who have the Talent, who can be identified with an astral scan."

Stone knew this already. Magical science hadn't discovered any way to reliably confirm if someone belonged to a magical line but didn't inherit the ability to use magic. The only way to know was if the person's lineage could be traced to a mage. And since many mages never learned of their potential, that was often impossible. Not to mention that the Talent was notoriously fickle, sometimes skipping two or more generations before manifesting again, or eventually petering out until the magical spark died and the line became fully mundane.

He paced for a moment, staring at the map on the monitor, then turned back to his friends. "Do your people know how it's transmitted? What the incubation period is?"

"It's still all speculation," Eddie said. "Since it's not ethical to round up folks from magical families and stick 'em in a room with somebody who's already got it, that limits our options. Especially since they can't identify anything in the bodies of the affected people."

"That seems odd, doesn't it?"

"It does if you think of it as biological," said a German-accented voice from the doorway.

Stone looked up to see a stout, dark-skinned woman in a white coat standing there.

"Who's this, then?" she asked Eddie and Ward, nodding toward Stone.

Eddie strode over. "Matilda, this is Alastair Stone. Stone, this is Dr. Matilda Schubert, from Berlin. She's over 'ere today meetin' with some of our people."

She nodded as if she recognized the name. "Pleasure to meet you, Dr. Stone."

"Er—likewise. But what were you saying about assuming it's biological?"

Her eyes held the same gleam Eddie's had—working on this project was obviously energizing her. "What I mean is, what you say makes sense if you look at it like a biological affliction. A virus, or a bacterial infection, say. In those cases, there would be something detectable in the body: a growing bacterial colony, viral load…you've got to understand, I'm simplifying this significantly."

"Simplify away. I haven't taken a biology class since my undergrad days, so speak slowly and use small words."

She chuckled. "The point is, yes, if that were the case, we should be able to see it. We've scanned enough of the affected people that if there was something biological going on, we should have spotted it."

"So you don't think there is."

"No."

"So…something magical? You *are* a mage, right?"

"Oh, *ja*. I am. As for the first part of your question…that's harder to say. Needless to say, we've also done full astral scans on our volunteer subjects, but we haven't found anything new."

Stone narrowed his eyes. "Please forgive me, Dr. Schubert, but could that be because—"

"Because we're not sensitive enough? Possibly." She didn't sound offended. "Most of our researchers are not at the top of the power scale, magically speaking. But we *do* have a lot of experience and we know what to look for. You're welcome, of course, to do your own scans—"

Stone remembered Gina. He and Verity had both scanned her in depth, and their sensitivities were at the top end of the charts. The only way they might get better results was to ask Gabriel or one of the other dragons to do it.

"No, that's all right." He waved her off. "I believe you. So…if it's not magical, and it's not biological, then what *is* it?"

She raised a hand. "I didn't say it wasn't magical." Nodding toward Eddie and Ward, she added, "So far, the existing research concurs with Mr. Monkton's and Mr. Ward's initial hypothesis: that something catalyzed the change. Set it off, set the transformation into motion, and then disappeared, either burning out or simply ebbing away when its work was done."

Stone began pacing again, rubbing his chin. "They also said they didn't think it was reversible—curable. Does your research concur with that as well?"

"It does," she answered immediately. "This isn't a disease, Dr. Stone. That much, we're nearly certain of. Whatever it is, it's changed the subjects at the auric level. That's rare—or at least it used to be—but once the aura has been transformed, there's no going back. At least none that current magical science knows about." She paused, looking thoughtful. "And in any case, so far our examinations have indicated that in the vast majority of cases, the subjects don't *want* to be cured. Of the nearly sixty we've studied, ninety-two percent claim they not only don't want to change back, but they feel more comfortable with themselves now than they did before they changed."

"We've brought in a couple of psychologists familiar with magical society," Ward said. "They've spoken with a few of the subjects, and they agree that their mental health not only hasn't suffered due to the change, but in some cases it has demonstrably improved."

"Brilliant," Stone muttered. This was all well and good, and he was happy that the affected people weren't having breakdowns over changing into cats and elves and lizard-people, but it still wasn't getting him the answers he was looking for.

He thought about his conversation with Gina, remembering her map and the different-colored dots. "Have you done anything to trace dates of…for lack of a better word, infection? Gina back home has."

"Yeah, she's been sharing 'er data with us, from those message boards," Eddie said. "'Ang on, we're expectin' a new drop from 'er, but I got busy and forgot to check." He hurried over to the other laptop and tapped a few keys. "Yeah, 'ere we go. Lemme shoot this over to you, Ward, and you can plot it on our map."

Stone watched them work. Dr. Schubert had already left to return to her research, so the three of them were alone in the conference room. He paced around the table, peering at the various charts on the walls and listening to his two friends tap away at their keyboards until Eddie finally called, "'Ere we go. Watch the monitor."

Stone returned and leaned against the table as more dots, this time in multiple colors, appeared on the darkened world map. A larger number of the ones that had already been there switched color, changing from red to green, blue, or orange. Some, apparently those with no associated time data, remained red.

"Interesting," Eddie said, getting up for a closer look.

Stone joined him. They'd apparently retained Gina's color-coding system, meaning the orange dots represented the oldest cases. A sprinkling of them appeared around the world, but the vast majority were in North America.

"It appears that, at least according to this data," Ward said, "the phenomenon started in the States."

"Yeah, that's a good guess," Eddie agreed. He took another step closer to the monitor, pointing. "The biggest concentration looks like it's around 'ere." He returned to his laptop and clicked on something. The map zoomed in on the USA, and an overlay appeared to show the state boundaries. "You know where that is, Stone? I'm afraid my US geography is a bit pants, especially in the middle part. All those bloody states look alike to me."

Stone's was too, but after more than ten years in the country, he was getting better. In this case, though, he didn't need to. A cold shiver ran down his spine as he stared at the map. To be certain, he pulled out his phone, called up a labeled map of the USA, and held it up to compare it to the bigger one.

"Bloody hell..." he whispered.

"What?" Eddie and Ward were staring at him now, like a pair of dogs on a scent. "You see somethin'?"

"It can't be...it's got to be a coincidence."

"Stone..." Eddie growled.

Stone held up his phone again and double-checked his findings, hoping he'd been wrong.

He wasn't wrong.

The largest concentration of orange dots was centered on three states: Minnesota, Wisconsin, and Illinois.

He'd forgotten his two friends were there until Eddie gripped his arm, hard. "Stone! Come on, mate. If you see something, tell us!"

"I've got to check something."

"What?" Ward, normally easygoing, was looking as intense as Eddie now.

"I...think I might know where the epicenter of this whole thing is."

They gaped. "But...'ow?" Eddie pointed at the map. "'Ow does that tell you? Are you talkin' about the concentration of orange dots in the northern US? Even if that's it, it's a 'uge area. 'Ow can you—"

"Because I think I might have been around when it was created." His heart was beating faster, his whole body going alternately hot and cold. Could it be possible? It was farfetched, out of the question—

—but then again, *was* it? The oldest incidences of the phenomenon were less than a month old...and Daphne Weldon and her son Jeremy had returned to their home dimension only a couple months before that. From that exact area. If Jeremy had opened another rift, one none of them had seen or thought to look for—

"I've got to go," he said again, more urgently. "I need to check something back home."

"Stone—"

"If you've got something, let us come with you," Ward said.

"No. It's a crazy idea, and I'm almost certainly wrong. You two need to stay here and coordinate the real research, not be off chasing hare-brained notions. If I find anything, I'll get back to you as soon as I—"

In his hand, his phone rang. The map of the US winked out, replaced by Jason's familiar number. "Hang on a moment," he told his friends, walking to the far corner of the room before taking the call. "Jason. Little busy at the moment. What can I—"

"Al." Jason cut him off, his voice heavy and full of stress. "I need your help."

Another frozen bolt passed through Stone's body. "What's wrong?"

"Amber's missing."

CHAPTER TWENTY-THREE

"MISSING? WHAT ARE YOU TALKING ABOUT?" Stone shot a glance over his shoulder at Eddie and Ward, who were watching him with concern and curiosity.

"Remember I told you she was driving to Tahoe, to that baby shower her sisters-in-law were throwing for her?"

"Yes…"

"She never arrived. They called half an hour ago, wondering where she was."

"Bloody hell." He took a deep breath, trying to organize his thoughts. "All right—let's think. I assume you've tried all the mundane options."

"Yeah. She's not answerin' her phone—but a lot of that area can have spotty service. I tried tracking it, but that's not working either. And I've called the cops to keep a lookout for her, even though I haven't got a fucking clue where to tell them to look. It's like two hundred miles from our place to Tahoe." Jason was obviously doing his best to remain calm, but Stone didn't miss the tense edge in his voice.

"Okay. What about Verity? Have you called her?"

"Yeah. She was workin' with Hezzie at the shop. She's on her way down, but she said Tahoe's out of her range. If the car went off the road or something, she won't be able to find her unless she's a lot closer to here than there." He pulled a deep, shuddering breath. "Al, can you help? Are you home right now?"

"I'm in England, at Caventhorne."

"Damn." Now his despair was on full display. "So there's no way you can get back in time to—"

"Yes, I can. You sit tight, Jason. I'll be there before you know it. Where are you?"

"Still in L.A. I'm tryin' to get the next plane home, but it'll take time."

"Okay. Get there as soon as you can. Tell Verity to go to my house, and bring something of Amber's if she has it. We know how to combine forces on a tracking spell now, remember? Between the two of us, we should be able to find her." *Assuming she's alive,* his perverse little mental voice spoke up, but he quashed it immediately.

"But how are you going to—"

"Don't *worry* about it, Jason. Just get there." He softened his tone. "We'll find her."

"Yeah. Okay. Thanks, Al."

Stone turned slowly back to Eddie and Ward, who were still watching him. "I'm sorry," he said softly. "We've got an emergency back home. This business will have to wait."

He could tell they were both brimming with questions, but Ward shook his head. "You go. I hope everything turns out all right."

"Yeah," Eddie added. "Let us know if we can 'elp, mate."

Stone gave them a grateful nod. They were good friends. But already his mind was far away, visualizing the narrow, winding roads leading to Amber's family's compound near Lake Tahoe. If something had gone wrong and she'd lost control of her car, she could be anywhere—and she could be hurt.

He refused to let himself think about how much losing her—losing the baby—would devastate Jason. Right now, until he knew otherwise, Amber was alive.

And he was going to find her.

When Verity reached his house forty minutes later, he was already there, setting up a circle in the basement. She didn't bother knocking on the door since she still had a key, so she appeared, breathless, at the bottom of the stairs. "Anything?"

He didn't look up from what he was doing. "Almost done here. Have you got something that belongs to her?"

"Yeah. She left a jacket at my place last time she visited." She paused. "Doc…what if—"

"None of that," he said firmly. "Amber's bloody tough, and strong, and resourceful. We'll find her."

"Yeah." She didn't sound as certain as he did. "But…"

"But what?" He put the finishing touches on the circle and rose to face her.

"Even if we find her, it'll take a long time to get there. Even if we tell the searchers where to look, we won't be able to give them an exact location."

"Let's find her first, then deal with that. Are you ready?"

"Yeah. Let's do this."

He stepped into the circle's center, where he'd left enough room for both himself and Verity. "You remember how to do the combined ritual, right?" He indicated an open notebook on one of the side tables. "Some notes there, if you need to refresh your memory."

"I remember." But she drifted over to the notes and gave them a quick scan. This was too important to leave to chance. Afterward, she joined Stone in the circle and placed the jacket, a zip-up hooded sweatshirt with TAHOE across the front, into the brazier.

Stone looked into her eyes. They were big and scared, and her face was pale. He could almost see her thoughts swirling, as she considered all the implications of her beloved brother potentially losing his wife and his baby before it was even born. He gripped her hand. "We'll find her," he murmured.

Maybe if he said it enough, he'd believe it himself.

He couldn't let his worry affect his focus, though. He took several deep, centering breaths and lowered himself to a seated position, facing the brazier. Verity did the same, and sat across from him. He switched to magical sight, noting her aura was disturbed but controlled. He'd taught her well, emphasizing discipline during magical techniques, and she was using all that training now. "We've got this."

She reached out to clasp hands with him. Hers were cold. They met each other's eyes and began the ritual.

It was a little harder and took a little longer than a standard, single-person tracking ritual, but Stone was glad he had decided to combine forces with Verity. The first thing they got, to their immense relief, was that Amber was still alive. The tendril, which had been searching seemingly aimlessly, locked on to its target barely five minutes into the ritual, and shot up through the basement ceiling.

Stone gripped Verity's hands tighter. "Keep it together…"

The tendril ranged out, at first confused, but then more confidently. "She's definitely out of my range," Verity said, her voice tight with concentration.

"Out of mine, too. She must have got fairly close to her destination before something happened. Don't lose it now…"

Stone's range, when he pushed it, was about a hundred and fifty miles, which meant whatever had happened to Amber, it had likely happened in the last fifty miles of her journey. That wasn't necessarily good news, though: Amber's part-shifter family didn't live near any major roads or towns. Stone had never visited them, but Jason had told him once that their remote family compound was located deep in the woods, up some fairly winding roads that rose to a higher elevation.

He looked at Verity across the circle, and was sure she'd come to the same conclusion he had: if Amber had an accident and her car had gone off the road, she and the car were likely hidden by heavy forest and would be difficult for mundane emergency personnel to find.

They weren't done yet, though. Tightly gripping each other's hands, they continued to focus on the tendril, willing it to get them as close as possible to where they'd need to go to find her. Stone had placed a large map next to him, just outside the circle, ready to pinpoint the location as soon as the ritual completed.

The tendril hesitated again, sniffing around like a bloodhound suddenly uncertain about a scent. "Come on…" Verity whispered. "Find her…"

And then it was moving again, surging forward. Although there was nothing alive about it, the tendril always seemed to Stone to give a little dance of triumph when it found its target. "There!" he nearly shouted as the tendril collapsed. "Got her!"

He leaped to his feet and pounced on the map, snatching up the red Sharpie he'd placed next to it. With the results of the spell fresh in his mind, he quickly scanned the area closer to Tahoe, double-checked that he had the right spot, and stabbed the point of the marker down. "That's what I got. Do you concur?"

Verity had already joined him. "Yeah. That's what I got too." She let her breath out. "That's really remote—and it's a good thirty miles from her family's place."

"Yes." Stone pulled out his phone and snapped a photo of the map, close enough to show the location of the dot. "I'll send this to Jason and he can contact the authorities, but you're right—it's going to take them a while." That was especially true since, despite his and Verity's agreement about where to place the dot, it didn't mean they could zero in on the exact point. It could represent at least two or three miles of terrain from this distance. The longer the range on a tracking spell, the less precise the results were.

"What do we do?" Verity was looking agitated again.

"Not much else we *can* do." Stone felt as stressed and helpless as she did. He wondered if she'd noticed the same thing he had: that the lifeforce the tendril had locked on to was flickering, and not as strong as he'd hoped. He was certain Amber was injured, though there was no way to tell how badly. "I'll call Jason with this information, and—"

He stopped.

"What?" Verity demanded.

"Just a moment!" He jerked up from his crouch, vaulting across the room to a bookshelf.

"Doc, we have to tell Jason so he can—"

"This will only take a moment!" He scanned the shelf until he located a large tome, which he yanked from its shelf and slammed down on a nearby table. He wasn't a praying man, but he put out a call to the Universe for things to go his way, just this once.

She hurried over to join him, eyes narrowed. "What's that? Why are you—"

He threw the book open and quickly turned to the page he was looking for, ignoring her.

"A ley line map? Doc, what the hell—"

"Bring that map over here!"

"Doc—"

"*Now,* Verity!"

She glared at him—he rarely used that tone on her—but hurried over to grab it. "What are you looking for?"

He pulled the map to him and compared it to the book page, which showed details of ley lines running through the western

United States. "Yes!" he snapped in triumph, jamming his finger down on a spot.

Verity finally got it. "Oh, my God," she breathed. "There's a ley line close to where she is. That means you can—"

"I can get to her faster than anyone else. Yes!" He studied the two maps again, fixing the location in his mind. "It might not be right on top of the spot, but it's bloody close." He pointed at their map. "Snap a photo of that map and send it on to Jason. I've got to go. No time to waste." With a gesture, he pulled his black overcoat to him and shrugged into it. "Damn, I wish I could take you with me."

"She's hurt, isn't she?" Verity asked soberly.

"I think so, yes."

She gripped his arm. "You got this, Doc. I know you can do it. You remember what I told you about healing, right?"

"I hope so. Haven't got much choice, have I?" Now that the initial elation about finding her and realizing he could get to her was ebbing, it was quickly replaced by terror. He'd never been strong with healing magic. Verity was orders of magnitude better, but he couldn't take passengers when using the ley-line travel method.

He would be all Amber had until the professionals arrived.

"Go," she urged. "I'll call Jason. If you can call when you get there, do it."

He gave a tight little nod, already focusing on what he had to do. "Tell Jason I won't let him down."

"We all know that, Doc. Go."

He stepped away from her, struggling to concentrate, to form the pattern in his mind that would take him to the spot along the ley line where he needed to be. It was harder than usual; he hoped he didn't end up in the wrong place. *You've done this dozens of times. You're not going to get it wrong.*

With one final look at Verity, who mouthed *good luck,* he disappeared.

CHAPTER TWENTY-FOUR

THE SUN HAD ALMOST COMPLETED its descent, so the sky was mostly dark when he reappeared on a pine-needle-strewn hillside, surrounded by towering trees.

He stopped, getting his bearings, and looked around with magical sight active, hoping to spot Amber's telltale aura. That would have been far too easy, though—the odds of him popping in at the exact correct spot were vanishingly low, and he knew it.

That was all right, though. He cast a levitation spell and, still keeping magical sight up, floated above the trees. The darkness was actually an advantage—it would make an aura easier to spot, though the green auras surrounding the trees provided a lot of interference.

He sniffed the air. His senses were merely human, but there was always the chance he might catch a whiff of spilled gasoline or even smoke. He didn't expect the latter, though: she'd been missing for at least an hour, so if her car had caught fire, the whole forest in this area would be ablaze by now.

And Amber would no longer be alive.

Roads, he told himself. She'd been driving on a road, which meant if her Jeep had gone off, it had to be fairly close to one. He pulled out his phone again, hoping to call up Google Maps for a view of the area, but *NO SERVICE* showed at the top. *Bugger.* He'd been afraid of that, but hoping for a bit of luck.

He turned in the air, scanning the area below. The spot they'd located with the ritual had to be fairly close. Despite the flickering of Amber's aura, the signal had been strong, and his and Verity's combined sensitivity in the ritual meant they couldn't have been off by much. All he had to do was be patient and make sure he didn't range too far from the spot where he'd appeared.

There. Below him, a narrow road snaked between the trees, snug along the edge of a hillside. That had to be the one she'd taken. He drifted over to it and dropped lower, following along its path. To his dismay, no other headlights appeared anywhere within his line of vision. He supposed that wasn't unexpected: this was fairly remote territory, and not the sort of place tourists would visit, especially at night.

There were no lights along the road, either, which meant Stone had to make a decision. If he dropped still lower and used a light spell, he might spot a break in the guardrail indicating where a car had left the road, but it would make it harder for him to see any signs of Amber's aura.

Trying to push aside the stress of indecision—if he made the wrong choice, he might doom Amber—he decided to focus on the road. The solid guardrail separating it from the drop-off meant if she *had* gone over the edge, it would be broken. He lowered himself until he was ten feet above the road, summoned a powerful light spell around his hand, and continued forward.

As he kept scanning and no break appeared in the rail, he began to doubt himself. His head was throbbing—normally, the effort of keeping two simple spells going wouldn't have affected him at all, but combined with the leftover tiredness from the tracking spell and his growing worry about Amber, he knew he couldn't keep this up much longer without a rest.

To hell with that. She's out there somewhere, and you're going to find her. They're all counting on you. She—

Wait.

Cruising along on autopilot, he'd almost missed the spot—a rough, twisted break in the metal rail, wide enough for a vehicle to have passed through. Heart pounding, he stopped and turned back, floating above the break. He dropped the light spell and shifted to magical sight again, but not before he saw how steep the drop was. *If she went over here, it's got to be bad.*

Stop it. Deal with what is. No speculation.

He didn't spot any sign of an aura, save for those of the trees and underbrush. He didn't even see any small animals.

This wasn't good.

"Amber!" he boomed into the night, using magic to amplify his voice. "Are you here? It's Alastair! If you're out there, say something!"

He went silent, hovering there, holding his breath so he wouldn't miss any faint sounds.

For a time, he thought there wouldn't be any. But then, after nearly thirty seconds had passed, he heard three distant *clangs*— what sounded like metal on metal.

He jerked around to face the sound—or at least where he *thought* it was coming from. Out here, sounds echoed oddly. "Amber! If that was you, do it again! Keep doing it so I can home in on you!"

Another interminable few seconds passed, and then the sound repeated: *Clang. Clang. Clang.*

This time, Stone got a better sense of where it was coming from: off to his left. He flung himself toward it, pausing again to re-orient himself when it came again. Was it weaker this time? He couldn't tell, and refused to let himself consider it.

"I'm coming, Amber!" he yelled, dropping lower to follow the slope of the hill.

Clang. Clang.

Definitely weaker—but also closer. There was no third *clang*.

Stone focused his magical sight, swiveling his head back and forth, breathing hard. *Come on...come on...*

No blue-green light flickered—but up ahead, he spotted the dark bulk of something large against the side of a tree. When he switched back to mundane sight and re-cast the light spell, he saw it was a vehicle lying on its roof, its undercarriage and tires— including one that had shredded around its wheel—pointed toward the sky.

"No, no..." he muttered, increasing speed. He dropped down on the other side of the vehicle and immediately summoned a light spell. What he saw made him wince, a hard pit forming in his stomach.

"Amber..."

She lay there, looking up at him with the dull expression of someone who barely believed what she was seeing was real. Her face was pale and blood-streaked, but that wasn't the worst. Her legs disappeared beneath the Jeep's roof, pinned to the ground.

Bloody hell...

Stone flung himself to the ground next to her, gently gripping her shoulder. "Amber, can you hear me? It's Alastair. I'm here, and we're going to get you out of here."

She moaned, but her gaze grew more lucid. "Alastair...?" she whispered, her voice a dry croak.

"It's all right." He glanced down at her legs, images of Edwina Mortenson coming unbidden to his mind. But this wasn't Edwina. For one thing, a Jeep roof was a lot lighter than a multi-ton rock. For another, the Jeep covered only the lower part of her legs, not her torso. *Thank the gods,* he thought, remembering the baby.

"Where's...Jason?" She looked around, as if trying to spot the remainder of the rescue party.

"I'm afraid I'm all you've got at present, love." He fought to keep his voice as calm and comforting as possible. "But don't you worry—we'll get you sorted straight away."

"Please…water…in back…"

For a moment he didn't know what she was talking about. Then he realized she was gesturing toward the back part of the Jeep. He scrambled around, peering in through the shattered rear window, and saw several plastic water bottles strewn throughout the space along with her bag and a hefty first-aid kit. He grabbed a bottle and the kit and hurried back to her.

"Here we are…" He took the cap off the bottle and handed it to her.

She swallowed it in slow, measured swigs, her hand shaking. "Thanks." She sounded a little stronger now.

"What happened to you? Did your tire blow?" That seemed odd—Jason and Amber both kept their vehicles in great repair.

She nodded weakly. "Big deer darted out in front of me. Couldn't get out of the way. Hit it, then the tire went and I went over the edge."

"Okay…okay…" Stone's mind spun fast. He pulled his phone out and checked to see if, by some miracle, he had any bars, but the *NO SERVICE* message still haunted him. "Let's start by seeing if we can get you out from under that Jeep, shall we?" He frowned, vaguely remembering something he'd seen on a TV show about issues that could arise after removing a crushing weight. "Is it safe?"

"I'll…start regenerating once I'm free." She winced. "Won't be fast, but it'll work."

"Okay. Good. Hang on, then. Do you think you can pull your-self free if I lift the Jeep?"

She gave him a sideways look, her message clear: *You're* gonna lift a Jeep?

He made a mocking muscle, then waggled his fingers. "What I lack in physical prowess, I more than make up for with magic. Do you think you can do it? If not, I'll use magic to pull you out too, but it's a bit riskier."

"No. I'll…do it. Just tell me when."

"Good." He rose and took a few steps back so he could see the whole Jeep. He wouldn't need to lift the entire vehicle, just rock it backward to take the weight off her legs. Grateful once again for his Calanarian training, he focused his concentration, took hold of the Jeep's side, and lifted it a few inches from the ground. "Go!"

Clearly, even injured, she was stronger than she looked. She moved instantly at his order, yanking her body free of the Jeep's roof. Immediately, she gave a sharp wince followed by a moan and lay still.

As soon as her feet were clear, Stone dropped the Jeep and hurried over to her. "Amber? Are you still with me?" Under the light spell, her legs were streaked with blood. More stained her shirt.

"*Damn*, that hurt." She twisted around until she was lying on her back.

Stone slipped out of his overcoat, folded it into a hasty pillow, and gently put it under her head. "I'm sorry. Is that better?"

"Yeah…some." She met his gaze. "Is…anyone else coming?"

That was the important question, wasn't it? "I…hope so. Eventually. They know you're missing, and Verity has the general idea where you are. We did a tracking ritual."

"I thought I was…too far away for that."

"Verity and I combined forces."

She nodded wearily. "Oh…right. I remember. Like with the ghouls. But…how did you get here so fast?"

"Long story. Right now, I should see about trying to heal you." His gaze traveled nervously down to her middle. He had visions of having to reprise what happened on practically every TV show in existence, if it stayed on the air long enough: the hero ended up having to deliver a baby under less-than-optimal circumstances. That thought terrified him more than anything else he'd done tonight. "The…er…baby is all right, isn't it?"

She snorted. "Don't worry, Alastair. You won't have to deliver it."

"Cue my heartfelt sigh of relief." He was pleased she was joking now—perhaps it meant her shifter regeneration was taking hold. She was only part shifter, which meant it wouldn't work nearly as fast, but at least she seemed to be stable at the moment. "I'm at a bit of a loss about what to do now, though. My phone's got no service, so I can't call anyone and tell them I've found you." He moved the light spell down to study her blood-streaked legs. "I can try to heal your legs, though I'm not sure how well it will work. Can you tell if anything's broken?"

She closed her eyes. "Not sure. Might have cracked a couple of ribs, and wouldn't be surprised if my lower legs aren't at least fractured."

"How did you get under that Jeep in the first place?" His mind finally settled on what had been bothering him: her position didn't make sense. If she'd been wearing a seatbelt, she should still be inside the vehicle. And of course she would have been belted—if not for her own safety, then for the baby's.

She shot him a sheepish look. "Yeah…about that. The Jeep rolled down the hill and landed on its side. I popped my belt and tried crawling out through the sunroof, but I guess I was hurt worse than I thought. When it started to go over, I couldn't get out of the way in time."

He patted her shoulder. "Don't worry. I'm just glad we could find you. I wish I could signal the rescuers somehow. I'm afraid to start a fire out here…"

She gestured toward the Jeep. "Look in the back. There's an emergency flasher. Set it up and hopefully somebody will notice it."

"You *are* resourceful, aren't you?" Stone was impressed. Sometimes he forgot about how good mundanes were at dealing with emergency situations without magic. He crawled to the back of the Jeep and looked around until he found the flasher, along with some flares. When he switched the flasher on, a powerful red light began strobing. He set it near Amber and contemplated the flares. He couldn't light those here—too much chance of catching something on fire. But then he had an idea.

"Hang on," he told her. "Let me take the flares up to the break in the railing. They can't miss them there. It's not far."

At her weary nod—she was still obviously not doing as well as she was trying to pretend—he levitated back to the road, noting there was still no sign of any vehicles. He lit three of the flares and placed them in an arrow formation pointed toward the Jeep, then floated back down to Amber. "There," he said, forcing a breezy edge into his tone. "Shouldn't be long now. Let me see what I can do with those—"

Her loud wince, followed by a sharp gasp of pain, cut him off.

"What is it?" He dropped to his knees next to her, and the hard pit in his stomach returned when he saw she was clutching her middle. "Amber? What's going on? Where does it hurt?"

Her eyes were haunted. She swallowed hard against gritted teeth. "The baby…"

Oh, gods… "What about the baby? Is it—" Stone knew next to nothing about babies and their attendant processes, but he remembered something about their arrival being preceded by water breaking. He redirected the light spell down toward her jeans, but they looked as dry as ever. "Amber, talk to me. Is it coming?"

"I think it's…hurt," she got out on a rush of air. She gripped his wrist so hard she threatened to break it. "Alastair…I think something's wrong with her!"

*No…*Stone fought not to panic. He was bad enough at healing full-grown adults. What was he going to do for an unborn baby? Why wasn't Verity here? She'd know what to do. If only she were—

Enough, he told himself sternly as Amber's desperate grip tightened on his wrist. *Verity's not here. You're here. Which means you're going to have to buck up and do something. Now.*

"Please, Alastair…" Amber's hand slipped off his wrist and joined her other ones, both clutched around her midsection. "Help her…please…oh, God, don't let her die…"

Stone barely registered that somewhere along the line, she'd stopped referring to her child as "it" and was now calling it "her." He shook the thought free and took several deep breaths.

"I'll do my best," he told her, surprised his own voice was shaking. *Gods, please let this be enough. Let me be enough…*

Driving away all thoughts of Jason, of his friends' excitement about their upcoming child, of the fact that his meager healing talents might possibly be the only thing standing between life and death for this baby, he knelt next to Amber's belly and reached out with his magical senses. He tried to remember everything Verity had ever told him about healing. Did it even apply in this case? She'd always gone on about systems and how they had a natural state they wanted to return to, and how a healer's job was to nudge them back into that natural state. But a baby was different. Was the child still part of Amber's system, or one of its own? If the latter, how would he reach it?

Stop thinking. This isn't about thinking. That was the other thing Verity had tried to pound into his head: healing wasn't a cerebral process. It was why he had so much trouble with it—because he'd always been much better with thoughts than with feelings. He'd gotten better over the years, helped by his friends, but would it be enough? This wouldn't be an easy job, even for Verity.

Amber moaned again and then cried out, jolting him from his reeling thoughts. *That's it. No more stalling. Let's do this.*

He took a few more deep breaths, closed his eyes to center his thoughts, and then reached out with his magical senses. "Please try not to move…" he murmured. "I need all my concentration for this…"

At that point, any sound she might have made dropped away as he fell into the deeper state of meditation he used for delicate magic. He could no longer feel the faint chill of the night or the pain in his knees from his uncomfortable position. Every shred of his focus was now on Amber's blue-green aura—and on the tiny, bright-yellow one drifting at its middle. Barely formed and nebulous, the aura hadn't yet formed into a fully human shape. It was so tied up with Amber's own protective aura that Stone had a hard time picking it out. Only when he fought to deepen his concentration even more did he see the angry red knot in the pure, otherwise unsullied yellow.

He couldn't tell exactly what it was—whether one of Amber's cracked ribs had somehow injured the child, or whether yanking herself free of the Jeep had jarred something in there, or something else entirely. All he knew was that the tiny life inside her was in distress, its lifeforce draining away through that red knot, and if he didn't do something about it fast, the baby would die.

Remember the system, Verity's voice spoke in his head. *Don't fight it. Don't force it. Work in harmony with it.*

He'd done this once before, with Edwina Mortenson, blocking the pain from her ravaged lower half.

But Edwina died, his perverse mental voice responded.

She died, yes, he agreed firmly. *But you took her pain away. You gave her a peaceful passing. There was nothing you could have done to save her then. Nothing* anyone *could have done. But this time, you* can.

The tiny lifeforce was surprisingly potent. Even as it faded, it fought. This little girl didn't want to die before she even got her first glimpse of the world.

Stone hardened his resolve. Nobody was going to die today. His own inadequacies were no excuse.

Oblivious to anything around him, he reached out to the yellow aura first, and then narrowed to the red knot. He still didn't know what it was, not exactly, but that didn't matter. He gathered magical power and carefully fed it into the little system—*not too much, or you'll overwhelm her*—reminding himself not to try directing it anywhere. That was where the force came in, where his every instinct and every shred of training told him to use his will to shape the power, but he fought against them.

This isn't about power. It's about feeling. Empathy. Hope. Give her the power and let her do what she will with it.

It seemed to take forever. The little life wanted so much power. It siphoned off every bit he could give it and demanded more. But slowly, ever so slowly, the red knot began to shrink. Stone kept at it, refusing to stop even as somewhere in another world he felt his body begin to slump.

Keep it going…not much longer…it can't be much longer…

And then it was gone. The last of the red knot dissipated and faded, leaving nothing behind but the strong, pulsing yellow. Before he pulled back and disengaged, Stone got the faintest, briefest glimpse of the tiny, curled infant relaxing into easy slumber as she floated, effortless and uninjured once more, in her mother's body's protective embrace.

As he returned to reality and all the sensations he'd been ignoring flowed back at once, he barely managed to wrench his body sideways when he slumped, so he didn't pitch forward onto Amber. He lay, panting and spent, body drenched in sweat and heart pounding.

"Alastair…?" Amber's voice was tentative.

He dragged his head up, afraid he'd somehow failed. "The baby—" he whispered.

She swallowed, her fingers gently probing her belly. "It…doesn't hurt anymore. I think…she's okay."

"I'm glad to hear it…" His voice barely had any strength behind it. As the faint sound of sirens became audible in the distance, he offered her a manic grin. "I'm afraid, though, that if you're planning one of those frightful gender reveal parties, we've just spoiled the surprise."

CHAPTER TWENTY-FIVE

EVERYTHING HAPPENED IN A BLUR AFTER THAT.
The emergency personnel arrived: a fire truck, ambulance, and two police cars, all stopping at the break in the guard-rail. Stone had reclaimed his coat and faded into the background, using a disregarding spell to hide in the shadows as the EMTs and others slid carefully down the hillside and clustered around Amber.

As soon as he was sure she was safe and in good hands, he levi-tated away toward the ley line. He'd already told her it would be better if nobody knew he'd been there, and he hoped she remem-bered and didn't let anything slip. He was certain that between his magical healing, her natural regeneration abilities, and the medical care she'd be getting, she would be fine in short order. There might be a bit of explaining to do regarding just how *fast* she healed, but he was sure she and her family were used to dealing with things like that.

The first thing he did when he arrived at the Encantada house was call Verity.

"They found her!" she said breathlessly before he even had a chance to speak. "Her car went off the road. She's hurt, but she's gonna be okay."

"Yes…I know."

"You sound exhausted. Did *you* find her?"

"I did…and I am. Remind me I owe you a posh dinner sometime."

"For what?"

"Doing your best to teach me healing, even though I'm so rubbish at it." He slumped back on the sofa, and immediately a concerned Raider leaped into his lap. "Does Jason know?"

"Oh, yeah. They called him straight away when they found her, and he called me. She's gonna be okay, Doc. They're still worried about her, but they said her injuries were relatively minor for such a bad crash." She paused. "How much of that was you?"

"Some. I suspect most of it is her own natural regenerative healing ability, once I got the Jeep off her legs."

She gasped. "And…the baby? Is it okay too?"

It seemed odd that she was calling the child 'it,' but he remembered she didn't know that bit of information yet. "I think so. I'm not a physician, but everything looked all right." He was far too tired to explain the whole situation to her. He was sure once the doctors let her and Jason see Amber, she'd provide her own explanations. "Where are you now?"

"Heading to the airport. Jason hadn't got on his flight yet, so he talked them into letting him switch to one going to Truckee. They're taking her there and we're gonna meet her. Her brothers and their wives, too. Are you coming?"

"Brilliant. And…no, if you don't mind. I'm shattered right now. Healing is hard work—for me, at least. Please give everyone my best. I'll pop over tomorrow."

"Yeah. I will. And…thanks, Doc. Whatever that weird thing is you have that lets you travel all over the place without portals…I'm glad you have it. It might have saved Amber's life."

Score one for dragon magic, he thought, but already his eyelids were drooping. Raider curled on his chest, purring, was lulling him to sleep. "Glad I could help. Talk to you soon."

As he drifted off, his conversation with Eddie and Ward from earlier last night came back to him. The whole situation with Amber had understandably driven it from his mind, but now that he knew she and the baby would be all right, it returned. However, much as he wanted to head immediately to Minnesota and search for any stray extradimensional fissures, his tired brain was having none of it.

First things first, he told himself. *If it's there at all, it's waited this long. It can wait another day or two until this is fully sorted.*

He slept late the following morning, waking up on the sofa. Sometime in the night he'd twisted around and sprawled out the long way, and Raider had readjusted himself to remain splayed across his chest. He fumbled for his phone and texted Verity. *How is Amber?*

She didn't answer until a few minutes later, when he was preparing to get in the shower. *She's better. They're making her stay til tomorrow, mostly to keep an eye on the baby.*

Tired of tapping out messages, he called her. "Are you still in Truckee?"

"Yeah. Jason's at the hospital, sleeping in the waiting room. I got a motel room. Amber's bros and their wives are here too. It's quite the family reunion over there."

"Would it do me any good to pop over?"

"Yeah, if you can. I think Jason wants to talk to you."

"All right. Give me an hour to make myself presentable and locate a ley line, and I'll be there."

To his good fortune, the ley line running through Truckee wasn't far from the hospital. The walk in the brisk, early-afternoon air finished the job the shower had started, clearing the last of the cobwebs from his brain.

Jason wasn't in the waiting room when he entered; in fact, he didn't see any of Amber's family or Verity there, only an older couple having an earnest conversation near the front window. The nurse at the reception desk told him Amber was in room 210.

He was about to text Verity when a familiar voice called to him from the other side of the room. "Al."

Jason stood there, holding the open the swinging door that led to the back part of the hospital. He wore jeans and a rumpled T-shirt, and looked like he'd neither shaved nor slept.

"Hello, Jason. I'm glad to see you. I—"

He didn't get anything else out before Jason crossed the room in three long, swift strides and engulfed him in a bone-crushing embrace.

"Er—I'm glad to see you too," Stone sputtered.

"Thank you, Al…" His voice, his whole body shook with emotion, and when Stone pulled back a little to get a look at his face, he was surprised to see tears glittering in his friend's eyes. "Oh, God, thank you. If you hadn't been there…if you hadn't gotten to her so fast…"

Stone gave up trying to pull free, since it was a fruitless effort. Jason's arms around him felt like spring steel. Instead, he awkwardly returned the hug. "I'm…glad I could help. I truly am."

"I don't know how you did it, man…I don't fucking care. You keep your secrets." He swallowed hard, choked a little, and pulled back, his intense gaze fixed on Stone. He dropped his voice to a shaky whisper. "Amber told me what you did. How you got her out from under the Jeep…healed her…and how you saved our baby."

Stone managed a chuckle. "You can thank your sister for teaching me that…and I'm bloody grateful it's all I had to do. I was terrified I was going to have to deliver the little sprog, and that wouldn't have ended well for anybody. Not to mention being the world's biggest cliché."

Jason looked like he wanted to hug him again, but instead pulled back and swiped a tanned forearm over his face. "Al…bro…I owe you…*everything*. Every time I think of what could have happened if you hadn't—"

This whole conversation was making Stone increasingly uncomfortable. "It was my pleasure, Jason. Really. I'm dead chuffed about the whole thing. I assume everything's all right now?"

Jason indicated for Stone to follow him to the other side of the room, where he continued to whisper. "By the time they got her here, her shifter regeneration had taken care of most of the damage. The doctors said she was really lucky, but…she wasn't, was she?"

"Well…she was, really. She's a tough lady. Her legs were injured, and she had some cracked ribs and general cuts and bruises. But given how far that Jeep went over, she fared a lot better than she could have, even without my intervention."

He dropped his gaze. "But not the baby."

Stone considered his answer before speaking. "I…don't know. It's far too early to tell whether it—"

"She. I know you know, so no secrets."

"—whether *she* inherited her mother's shifter abilities."

"Amber said she was in bad shape. That…" His voice hitched again. "…that she might have died if you hadn't done what you did. Is that right?"

Stone didn't look at him. "I suppose it could be."

And then he was struggling against another steel-armed hug. "I owe my daughter's life to you, Al. I'm never, *ever* gonna forget that. Anything you want, all you have to do is ask. I'll find a way to make it happen."

"Well…right now, I'd like it if you wouldn't crush me into powder. And a nice cup of coffee would be lovely. I didn't get a chance to have one before I left to come here."

Jason disengaged reluctantly, still looking shellshocked from everything that had happened.

"Can I see her?" Stone asked. "Verity said they're keeping her until tomorrow."

"Yeah." He visibly pulled himself together. "She already wants to go home, but I talked her into humoring them." Indicating the door he'd come through, he motioned for Stone to follow him.

"Where are the others? Verity, her brothers—"

"You just missed the brothers and their wives. They headed out like half an hour ago. Amber convinced them she's fine and said she just wanted to get some rest before she heads home. V's off getting lunch since Amber refuses to eat the hospital food." He gave a damp chuckle. "Nobody argues with Amber."

"Yes, I'd got that impression."

They reached room 210. Jason knocked on the frame. "Hey, babe, you have a visitor."

Amber was in the bed next to the window, the sun filtering in through the tall trees outside. She'd been reading something on a tablet, but looked up as Jason came in. She smiled when she spotted Stone. "Hi, you."

Stone looked her over with both mundane and magical sight. Most of the injuries from last night were nearly healed. There was still a bit of angry red energy near her lower legs, but it looked much better than the previous night. She was well on her way to healing. The energy around her belly was serene and untroubled. "It's good to see you looking so well. I hear you've got the nurses hopping."

"Yeah. I want to get out of here, but Overprotective Hubby here won't let me until the doctors say it's okay." She patted her belly and smiled. "Plus, my little soccer star is making it hard to get much rest."

Stone returned the smile. "Yes, well, she got knocked around a bit, so I'm not surprised she's making her displeasure known. She probably wants out as much as you do."

"Not for a couple more months." Jason pulled up the chair next to the bed and dropped into it, then looked up at Stone. "You doing okay, Al? V said you were pretty tired last night."

"I'm fine. Healing takes quite a bit out of me since I'm so bad at it. I'm sure your sister would have done a much better job."

"I'm not," Amber said soberly. "I didn't get a chance to thank you last night, Alastair. So…thank you."

Stone was spared another awkward answer by Verity's appearance in the doorway. She carried two bulging bags from a local sub shop, but stopped in surprise when she spotted Stone. "Doc!"

"Hello, Verity."

"I'm glad you came. Hang on a sec, let me feed the hungry mama bear before she jumps out of bed and attacks me." Grinning, she started pulling wrapped sandwiches from the bag and handing them around. "You want one? I got some extras for Amber, but I bet if you asked nicely she could spare one."

"He can have as many as he wants, no asking nicely required." Amber held up the one she was already ripping the wrapping from. "Except for this one."

Stone realized he hadn't had any breakfast, so he gratefully accepted a sandwich. For a while, everyone was silent except for the sounds of crackling wrappers and chewing, but then Amber swallowed, glanced toward the door, and grinned at Stone.

"So…you got out of there and nobody saw you, so that's good. But the rescuers were baffled about how those flares got up by the road. They figured I might've gotten the flasher out of the back, but I didn't bother trying to convince them I crawled all the way up the hill. Even though it would have made me look pretty badass."

Stone winced. "Bugger. Wasn't even thinking about that."

"I didn't tell them anything. I think they figure some driver came by and spotted the break, but that doesn't explain why nobody stopped to call anybody about it."

"Yeah," Verity said. "And we had a hard time explaining how it was me who called to tell them where Amber was. Somebody's probably going to have questions about that, but I'm just gonna keep my head down until it blows over. If they push me, I'll tell them I had a psychic vision again."

"I always wonder when they're going to stop believing that." Stone crumpled his sandwich wrapper and tossed it into the trash can by the door.

"They did find the deer she hit," Jason said. "So that confirms her story about what happened. I don't think anybody thinks it was attempted murder or anything." He shrugged. "I'm not gonna worry about it. We're heading home tomorrow, and if they have any other questions, they can call us."

"I'll have to get a new Jeep, though." Amber finished one sandwich and started on another. "Hope our insurance covers Acts of Deer."

Stone stood. Now that he could see, with both mundane and magical vision, that Amber was well on the road to recovery, his thoughts were once again turning to his suspicions about the cause of the strange affliction. "I'm glad to see you're doing well. If there's anything else I can do to make things easier for you, don't hesitate to ask."

Jason squeezed Amber's hand. "I think you're good there for a long time, Al."

"Verity—could I borrow you outside for a moment?"

She tilted her head in confusion, but quickly stood. "Be right back, guys." When they got outside, she frowned at him. "What's up? Something wrong?"

"Not…wrong, exactly. I was over at Caventhorne last night— that's where I was when I got the call about Amber—talking with Eddie and Ward. They've got quite a lot of people working on our little problem now. The word's getting out all over the magical community."

"That's…uh…great. But what's it got to do with—"

"After we looked at some of Gina's data, combined with theirs, I'm very much afraid I might know where the source is."

Her eyes widened. "The source? You mean…what caused it?"

"Yes. It's just a speculation at this point and I haven't had a chance to check it yet, but when we analyzed the cases we know about based on when they were affected, a statistically significant number of them clustered in the same general area."

"What area is that?"

"The northern Midwest. Specifically Minnesota and Wisconsin."

For a second, she didn't make the connection. But then she gaped. "Holy shit, Doc. Are you saying what I think you're saying?"

"If what you think I'm saying is that Jeremy might have popped another fissure that no one knows about…then yes, I am."

"Holy *shit*," she repeated. "But…could that be possible? The other ones all grew. This was more than two months ago. If it's been growing all this time, *somebody* must have noticed it. Right?"

He shrugged. "Who knows? This is all new territory. Possibly it *is* growing, but since they're invisible to mundane sight, nobody's noticed it yet. Or perhaps this one is a different type. The others didn't behave consistently. The one in North Carolina popped in and then receded on its own, while some of the others remained and grew larger. Perhaps this one showed up, affected some people, and then disappeared again. There's no way to know for sure without out more information."

"So…what are you going to do?"

"As soon as I leave here, I'm going to head to Minnesota and see if I can find it."

She glanced back toward the closed door to Amber's room. "Can I come with you?"

"Verity, I—"

"Come on, Doc. I won't get in your way. I was in on the end of things back there, so if there's something else, I want to see it through. Besides, if you find it, I can help you close it."

He considered, but then shook his head. "You can't get there fast enough. I don't want to wait while you find a flight—"

"What flight?" she asked with a snort, followed by a sly grin. "You're not the only one with friends in high places. Bron's Nana likes me, and her people have been helping out with trying to trace this thing too. All I have to do is call and I can get permission to use the portal I used before in Minneapolis. Remember?"

"Bloody hell, I forgot about that. All right—if you can get access to that portal and meet me there, I'm happy to have you along."

"Great. Are you serious about leaving right away?"

"As soon as possible. I need to go home and gather a few things first, and it will take you some time to get back to San Francisco. Call me when you're home, and we'll leave then." He didn't like waiting even a few hours, but as he reminded himself before, the proverbial horse had well and truly left the barn quite some time ago, so another short wait wasn't likely to make any appreciable difference. He nodded toward the door. "Don't hurry, though, if you'd rather stay and visit for a while."

Her sly smile returned. "I think those two want to be alone anyway, so I'll just stay long enough to be polite and then head back."

Before she could turn away, he gently gripped her shoulder. "Verity…"

"Yeah?"

"I wanted to thank you again for pounding all that healing stuff into my head. Believe me, you're every bit as responsible for that child's continued existence as I am."

Her expression softened, and she covered his hand with hers. "I don't know if that's true, but I'm really glad I could help." She gave his hand a squeeze and backed off. "I'm looking forward to meeting this little girl."

"Ah—so they told you too? Worst kept secret ever, apparently."

She grinned. "Nah, they didn't tell me. But Amber did let me do a scan a couple weeks ago. Can't hide stuff like that from me."

Of course. Verity's sensitivity about that sort of thing had always been higher than his. "All right, then. I'll just—"

His phone buzzed with an incoming text. He pulled it out, expecting to hear from Eddie or Ward, or perhaps Gina, since most of the others who routinely texted him were nearby.

But it wasn't any of them. *Dr. Stone? It's Jennifer from the coffee shop.*

He glanced at Verity, then back at the phone. Why would Michele Berry's roommate be texting him? Had Michele changed her mind about not pursuing her threat against him? Was Jennifer texting to warn him? *What can I do for you?* he sent back. *Is everything all right?*

There was a long pause as the little dots cycled. Finally, the message popped up. *I'm sorry, but it's not.*

The dots cycled for several more seconds, so long that Stone almost sent a reply, but then the next message appeared, and his whole body went cold.

Verity must have caught his shocked expression. "Doc?"

He jerked his head up. "I've…got to go," he said dully.

"What's wrong?"

"One of my students—the one I told you about, from the seminar—has attempted suicide. Sleeping pills. Her housemate doesn't know if she's going to make it."

CHAPTER TWENTY-SIX

S TONE TEXTED JENNIFER half an hour later when he returned to Encantada. *Can I meet you somewhere?*

Yeah. I'm at the hospital. Her parents are flying in. She sent him directions to the hospital cafeteria. *Our other housemates are here too, waiting for news.*

I'll be there in twenty minutes.

Hospital cafeterias always struck Stone as strange places. Most of their clientele consisted of either hospital staff carrying on their normal days, or nervous friends and relatives killing time while they waited for word about whatever was being done to their loved ones. Nobody ever went to a hospital cafeteria because they loved the food.

He found Jennifer seated at a table near a window, her aura morose and dejected. She looked up as he approached. "Hi, Dr. Stone." Her voice was as lifeless as her posture. "Thanks for coming."

He took the seat across from her, noting that her hands were wrapped around a half-full cup of coffee that was no longer steaming, and a half-eaten croissant lay on a paper plate in front of her. "How is she doing?"

She shrugged. "Don't know. They won't let us in to see her yet. The doctors are doing their thing, and the rest of the girls are in the waiting room."

He considered how to ask his next question, and spoke with care. "How…did you…"

"Find out?" She stared into her coffee. "I found her. This morning. Went to see if she wanted anything for breakfast, but she wouldn't wake up." Her voice hitched, and tears appeared in her eyes. "I found the empty bottle on her nightstand."

"I'm so sorry," he murmured. Even as he tried to comfort her, though, he wasn't sure why she'd contacted him in the middle of this crisis. Later, sure, to let him know what was going on, but surely she must have more pressing things on her mind than keeping him up to date.

She nodded, head still bowed. Then she drew a deep, shuddering breath and met his gaze. "She…left a note, Dr. Stone."

He went still. "Did she?"

"Yeah." She pulled out her phone and tapped it. "I read it…and took a photo since I didn't want to mess with it." She found what she was looking for and shoved the phone across the table toward him.

He didn't want to read it, but of course he had to. He pulled it closer and peered at the photo. The note was written on a piece of binder paper, only a few words in a rounded, looping hand.

I'm sorry. I can't live with what I am anymore, and I can't make it go away. This is the best way.
—Michele

He read it over twice, then pushed the phone back.

"Do you know what she was talking about, Dr. Stone?" Jennifer's voice held pleading, almost desperation. "What does she mean, 'what I am'? What *is* she?"

He wished he could tell her. Instead, he shook his head. "I've got no idea."

"Did she talk to you? You know, after you and I talked?"

"She did, yes."

"Did she say anything that made you think she might be…thinking about this?"

He replayed the conversation. "No. She seemed sorry for what she'd done. She told me she wouldn't have gone to anyone, even if you hadn't shown her the video, and I told her I believed her. She seemed a bit upset at first, but…more at peace when she left. I think she was worried I was going to show that video to someone and get her expelled." He didn't tell her about giving her Gina's number, but now he wondered if she'd ever used it.

Jennifer nodded several times, processing what he'd said. "She did seem unhappy lately…but I thought it was just the whole college stress thing. Maybe it was boyfriend trouble. All those guys who were interested in her lately…maybe she didn't know how to handle it." She dropped her hand to the table. "I don't know. I don't have any idea. I wish she'd come and talked to one of us about it—or *somebody,* anyway. We would have helped. Hopefully the doctors will help her, and somebody can ask her what she was—"

A snatch of a pop song cut her off. She picked up her phone and peered at it, then her shoulders sagged.

Stone's body went cold again. "Is it…?"

She gave a weary nod. "That was Emma, one of our other housemates. The doctor just came out, and…and…" She dissolved into fresh tears.

Stone sat there on the other side of the table with no idea what to do. "Jennifer, I—"

She shook her head, swallowing hard and trying to pull herself together. "It's okay. No…it's…not okay," she amended quickly. "But you don't need to be here. I just wanted to…show you the note. To see if you had any idea why…"

"I'm sorry," he repeated softly. "I wish I could help you."

Jennifer stood. "Thanks, Dr. Stone. Thanks for coming. I'd...better go back. We should be there when her parents get here."

Stone remained seated as she gave him a wan wave and trudged off. He watched her until she disappeared through the door, and stayed there for several more minutes, deep in thought, before preparing to leave. Before he got up, he took out his own phone. He'd pulled up his conversation with Verity before a thought struck him. Instead, he switched to Gina's number. *Are you there?*

She answered quickly. *Hey Doc. How's Amber?*

She'll be fine. Should be coming back tomorrow.

Yeah that's what J said. I'm really glad everything worked out OK. Sucks about the accident tho.

He didn't reply to that. Instead, he sent, *Gina, remember I recently asked if I could give someone your number?*

Yeah sure.

Did she ever contact you?

He waited while she typed, but he was sure he already knew the answer. *Nope, never heard from her. Why?*

He thought of Michele Berry—so confident and cocky during their first encounter, so lost and confused during their second. He remembered what Gina herself had said, along with Wayne Carter, and even Eddie and Ward: that the people who'd experienced the change were happy about it, that they felt content as if they were waking up to what they'd always been meant to be.

Not every time, he thought bitterly.

Just wondering, he sent. *Thank you, Gina.*

Seriously, tell her to get in touch. I'm happy to talk to her. A few of us are having another meeting in a couple days if she wants to come. At Harry's Hofbrau.

He put the phone back in his pocket without replying, because he had no idea what to say.

CHAPTER TWENTY-SEVEN

VERITY FIGURED OUT something was wrong instantly when she showed up at the house later that afternoon. She didn't even make it inside before her eyes narrowed and she regarded him with concern. "You okay?"

"Not really." He headed back in and slumped onto the sofa.

"What happened? You don't look ready to go." She eyed the table in front of him, noting the pair of empty Guinness bottles. She wore her jeans and leather jacket, and carried a tote bag over her shoulder.

"Eh, give me a few minutes." He still didn't move, though.

His thoughts had been in turmoil ever since he left the cafeteria, his guilt over Michele Berry's suicide—even though in his rational mind he knew it hadn't been his fault—warring with his growing desire to find out if he was right about the source of the changes. If he *was* right, he wanted nothing more than to locate the fissure, close it, and hopefully reverse the course of the strange phenomenon. His rational mind had a few things to say about that, too, reminding him of what Eddie, Ward, and Dr. Schubert had said about it not being reversible, but he refused to listen to it. Contrary to what some said, the affliction—*yes, it is an affliction*—wasn't universally welcome, and the sooner the magical researchers could figure out a way to stop it, the better.

But even as he wanted more than anything to do that, he couldn't drag himself off the couch. He'd been using Verity's absence as an excuse—*can't go until she gets here*—but now she *was* here and he couldn't lie to himself any longer.

Verity sat next to him, glancing at Raider as if to ask the cat what was wrong with his human. When she got no answer, she twisted back around to face Stone. "Oh, no," she said, frowning. "This is about your student, isn't it?"

He nodded without looking at her.

"She…is she—"

"She died, Verity. The doctors couldn't save her."

"Oh, God…" She leaned closer, pulling him into a hug. "I'm so sorry."

He returned the hug, but then stepped back. "Think of that next time someone like Gina tells you this mess is all bloody kittens and rainbows. Michele got hit with it, and it did something to her she couldn't cope with. And now she's dead because of it."

"Doc—"

"We've got to stop it. We've got to find a way to reverse it. Some people might be happy about it, but if they're putting out some sort of…contagion…they can't be allowed to keep doing it."

"Doc—" More insistent, but still soft.

"What?"

"You…kinda sound like me. You know, back when I was all hot and bothered about organizing the mages. I'll tell you what you told me then: it's probably not possible. From what it sounds like, the best thing we can hope for, if you're right about one of Jeremy's rips being the source, is to stop whatever it is from coming in. But I don't think we can stop the people who already have it."

"Not yet," he said bitterly.

"Maybe not ever." She put a gentle hand on his arm. "I'm really sorry about Michele. It's horrible, if you're right and this messed with her head, and that's what caused her to…do this. But the more of them there are out there, the more they're going to get togeth-er…help each other through it. Gina's already doing that. I'm sure lots of other people are too, like those ones you told me about up in the City." She paused when he didn't reply. "Doc…some people can't cope with having magic, right?"

He dragged his gaze up. "What?"

"That's right, isn't it? You told me that once. Aren't there a few people who find out they have magic and they…don't deal well with it, for whatever reason? End up with mental illness? Sometimes even die?"

"Yes, but—"

"Isn't this the same thing? I know you don't want to see it, but…I think for some people, whatever this is, it *is* kind of like having magic. It changes them, yeah, but it makes them feel *right*. It makes them *better*. You think it's worth the risk for magic because you know how awesome it is to have it. Maybe…" She spoke hesitantly now, as if afraid of setting him off. "Maybe…most of these people think the same thing, but you can't see it any more than a mundane can see it about magic."

Stone didn't want to listen to her. A part of him wanted to tell her to leave him alone so he could wallow in his guilt. But it was only a small part, and it was already receding. He wasn't always rational, but he tried to be—and Verity was making sense, damn her.

"Fine, then," he muttered, pulling himself to a more upright position. "I suppose you've got a point. And whatever we do—whatever we *can* do—if there really is a fissure out there, our first step is to find it and close it."

"That's the spirit." She hugged him again, then pulled back. "Come on. Let's go. I called Bron's Nana and she got me permission to use the Minneapolis portal, so I need to drive down to Sunnyvale. That should give you time to get yourself together and get there on your own."

He looked at her, than at Raider. The cat was watching him as if to say *listen to her, idiot. She's talking sense.*

And, much as he hated to admit it, she was.

He tucked in his T-shirt and ran a futile hand through his hair. "Text me using the Mullins number when you arrive. And keep a good thought that I'm not out of my mind about this, because if I am, I haven't got any other ideas about where to look."

CHAPTER TWENTY-EIGHT

WHEN VERITY TEXTED STONE an hour later, he was on the second level of the parking garage of the same IKEA near the Mall of America where they had made their final stand earlier that year, helping Daphne Weldon and her son return to their home dimension. He'd been pacing around the area for the last twenty minutes, to the point where the security guard had driven by twice in his little golf cart to make sure he wasn't breaking into cars or accosting shoppers. The store was open this time of day, so it meant there were a lot more cars to deal with.

Where are you? she sent. *I just got here.*

He called her, talking as he continued scanning the space. "I'm at the IKEA parking garage. Haven't found anything, though. I'm fairly certain there's nothing here to find."

"Started without me?" She sounded more amused than annoyed.

"Didn't have anything else to do. Going somewhere and getting pissed off my arse is tempting, but counterproductive."

"Do you have a car?"

"No. I took a rideshare over here." He'd remembered to bring the phone connected to the fake ID Kolinsky had arranged for him this time.

"How about I rent a car and pick you up? Do you know where you want to go next?"

"Not really. If Jeremy was agitated while Daphne was driving, the damned thing could be anywhere between here and Rochester. *If* it even exists at all. I've got no idea what sorts of things might have set him off."

"Let me get over there, and we'll talk about it some more, okay?"

"Yes. Get here soon. I've got to stop looking around before this overzealous rent-a-cop tries to arrest me for trespassing."

"Just bribe him. Trust me, most mall cops will hand over their own mothers for a hundred bucks in cash."

"I'd rather not test that. Get over here, will you?"

She showed up half an hour later, driving a rented Toyota mini-SUV. He hurried over and climbed in. "About time," he grumbled. "Did you take the scenic route?"

"Oh, hush, Dr. Grumpy." She turned the car around and headed for the exit. "Maybe you Scrooge McDuck types can rent cars fast, but us normal peons have to go through the line like everybody else." She indicated the garage as she drove down the ramp toward the ground floor. "Still didn't find anything?"

"Not a bloody thing. I suppose I should be glad about that, though: we closed that fissure, and apparently it stayed closed. So score one for us, I guess. But that puts us right back at square one for finding anything."

She looked his way. "You're stressed, which means you're not thinking as clearly as usual. I can tell. Take a few deep breaths, and try to remember back to what happened that night."

He almost protested that he was *too* thinking clearly, but he didn't. She was right. Even as he'd been prowling around the garage, he couldn't get Michele Berry's death out of his mind. He kept going over the likely scene in the hospital waiting room when her parents arrived, and the doctors and her tearful housemates had to fill them in on what had happened. "Yes. All right. Just...drive around a bit, I guess."

He leaned back in his seat, closing his eyes and pulling in a few slow, centering breaths. He even used a meditation technique to clear his mind, shoving the thoughts about Michele off to a corner where he didn't have to focus on them. He could mourn her later, but right now he had a job to do.

"Just start talking," Verity murmured. "Tell me about everything you remember about that night, before I got there."

He let his thoughts drift, visualizing the night he'd traveled to Minnesota in pursuit of Daphne Weldon and her strange son. He'd done a ritual in a small town in the southeast part of the state that had led him to Rochester, where he'd found Daphne and Jeremy holed up in an abandoned bed-and-breakfast. While he and Daphne had talked, Jeremy had been asleep in an upstairs room— or so they'd thought. Daphne had finally given Stone the whole story of what was going on with her and her son, and he'd convinced her Jeremy was causing the fissures and that they'd have to find a way to send him home before Stefan Kolinsky took matters into his own hands. However, when she'd agreed to accompany him back to California and stay in his house while they worked out the details of sending Jeremy home, the boy had taken off and stowed away in a vehicle bound for Minneapolis. They hadn't caught up with him until he'd reached the IKEA parking lot where Stone had been searching.

"You think he could have gotten upset while he was riding in the back of the truck?" Verity asked. "You know—spawned one of those things while he was traveling?"

Only then did Stone realize he must have already been speaking aloud while he'd organized his thoughts. "Possibly. But if he did, I don't think there's any way we're going to find the fissure." He kept his eyes closed while he talked, to keep his concentration laser-focused. "I'm inclined to think he didn't, though."

"Why not? Why do you think that?"

"Educated guess, that it would be more difficult to do it while he was moving."

"You sure you're not just trying to convince yourself?"

"Well, there's that too. But let's look at every possibility before we start considering that one."

Her sigh came through in the silence. "Okay. So my thought is he probably didn't do it in Minneapolis."

"Why?"

"Just a hunch. He already created a big one, and even for somebody like that, magical energy is a finite thing, right?"

Stone nodded. "Good thought. Yes, it's reasonable to assume he didn't spawn two of those things in close proximity. Even if he didn't realize he was doing it, or didn't do it on purpose, he'd still need time to recharge."

"Yeah, exactly. So if we don't think he did it in Minneapolis and we don't think he did it while he was stowed away in that truck, that leaves Rochester. Was he agitated there?"

Stone almost said no, but then he sat up straight in his seat, jerking his eyes open. "Yes! He was. I'm not certain, but I'm fairly sure he must have heard us talking downstairs—discussing sending him back home."

"Why would he get upset about that, though? You said he *wanted* to go home."

That was a good point. Stone closed his eyes again, trying to recall the rest of the conversation and identify anything else that might have triggered Jeremy.

"Wait!" Verity said suddenly. "You said you told Daphne that Kolinsky planned to hurt Jeremy, right? Could he have heard that?"

A thrill of dread passed through Stone. "Yes! That's got to be it. If he heard that, it's no wonder he got upset. That was probably what caused him to sneak out and run, but it's possible he might have spawned a rift without even realizing it before he left. I'm sure he had no idea what he was doing."

"Me too. When we went inside his mind, I got the impression he was sad, and didn't want to hurt anybody."

Stone gripped the arm of his seat. "Okay. That all makes sense. So we need to go to Rochester."

They were approaching the freeway entrance now. Verity made a quick turn onto the onramp, and didn't speak again until the Toyota was settled into the flow of traffic. "Where will we look, though? It could be anywhere."

"Maybe not. They didn't spend much time there, and I don't think Jeremy's range was that long. It would have to be somewhere close to that abandoned place they were squatting in." He pulled out his phone and called up the Google map of Rochester, hoping he could remember where the place was.

"You think it's in there? That would make it really easy—probably *too* easy."

"I don't." He spoke distractedly while he prodded at the small screen, trying to zoom in and locate anything familiar.

"Why not?"

"Eddie and Ward and the others are convinced whatever this thing these people have, it's contagious. If that's true, in order to spread it would need contact with other people—and not just *any* other people, if their researchers' hypothesis is correct and it can only affect people with magical blood who aren't mages."

She glanced his way. "When were you going to tell me *that* part?"

"Sorry—things have been a bit mad lately, with Amber and Michele. I forgot to mention it. But yes, that's their current thought. So if it was going to spread, it would need to come into contact with susceptible people."

"Yeah, but what's its range? If it has a big range, it could affect a wide area around that place."

That was true. Stone had no idea how potent the hypothetical fissure was, and how far out it could range with its influence. "Hang on—I think I've found the place. Let me take a look at this for a moment."

Verity concentrated on driving while Stone bent over his phone, zooming in as tightly as he could and scrolling around to examine the area surrounding the abandoned house. The map didn't provide a lot of detail, but it appeared the place was surrounded by a small strip mall, a few other residences, and what looked like a pair of vacant lots. Nothing that stuck out as a place for a fissure to affect a lot of people.

On a whim he pulled the map down, allowing him to view the area behind the house. There was a parking lot, another vacant lot, and—

"There!" He stabbed his finger down on the phone.

"What did you find?"

"A possibility."

"What is it?"

"A place called the Halcyon Hotel. It's less than a quarter-mile from the house where they were staying, along a larger street to the north."

She shot him another quick glance. "You think it could be *there*?"

He was already pulling up the hotel's website. "Look at this. They advertise that they host a lot of wedding receptions, and niche-type conventions that appeal to nerds. You know—gamers, the blokes who like to dress up as furry animals, Japanese anime fans, that kind of thing. There's one there now—what the hell is *My Favorite Monster*?"

She laughed. "You're out of the loop, Doc. It's only one of the most popular cartoon series around. It's a whole cottage industry:

videos, toys, stuffed animals, a collectible card game. Really big with young boys and geeky college students."

"Brilliant," he muttered.

"But it is. If the place is known for hosting conventions, it makes sense it would attract a decent amount of people from out of the area. Maybe that's why there was a bigger concentration around this area, but how it also got out to other parts of the country so fast."

That did make sense. Stone leaned forward, wishing he could force the car to go faster.

"Are there any other likely places around the same area?"

He checked again, more carefully. "Nothing nearly as large. Everything else looks like houses, strip malls, and small-scale industry."

"I think we've got our best place to check, then."

By the time they reached Rochester, Stone was ready to try levitating the car so they could fly to their destination. He looked at his watch: nearly five p.m. already.

"You want me to go to the hotel right away?" Verity asked as they exited the freeway.

Even though he was nearly certain the Halcyon was their destination, Stone still wanted to cover the other likely location. "Let's drive around the area first, and check the house. I doubt it's there, but Daphne and I were in such a hurry I didn't think to look when we left."

It took them a while to find the house. The last time Stone had been there it had been dark, and he'd been following the tracking spell he'd used to located Daphne without paying much attention to his surroundings. He directed Verity to three wrong turns before he finally recognized the strip mall where he'd parked his car that night.

This time, they parked in front of the house. It looked even worse in daylight, tumbledown and dilapidated with gaping holes in its roof, boarded-up windows, and a big yard full of overgrown weeds and cast-off junk.

"Nice place," Verity said, wrinkling her nose.

Stone looked around to make sure nobody was paying attention to them, then pulled up a disregarding spell and headed for the door.

Inside, the light was dim, the boarded windows blocking most of the sunlight. Stone raised a light spell, shining it around. He recognized the room where he and Daphne had talked; it looked the same as before, except now a dirty blanket and two shredded sleeping bags lay spread across the splintered wooden floor next to a pile of beer cans and fast-food wrappers.

"Somebody's living here," Verity murmured.

"Probably squatters. Be careful."

They quickly examined the lower floors, using magical sight to ensure no fissures or rifts had remained behind after Daphne and Jeremy left. They did find more hints that squatters were using the place as a temporary home, though.

"Upstairs?" Verity pointed up the staircase. "Is that thing safe?"

"It was three months ago." Nonetheless, Stone didn't take chances and levitated to the second floor. After a moment, Verity did likewise.

There were six bedrooms upstairs. Stone started with the one where Jeremy had been sleeping. The mattress from before was still there, now joined by two more sleeping bags, an old camp stove, and a tarp tacked to the wall to make a makeshift tent.

"Hey, Doc?" Verity's voice came from down the hall. It sounded strange.

He hurried to join her. "Are you all right? Did you find—"

He stopped in the doorway as he saw what had captured her attention.

A woman and two small children, both well under ten, sat huddled on another dirty mattress. They were pressed against the wall, the kids clutching their mother and looking at the intruders with big, scared eyes.

"Don't worry," Verity told them softly. "We're not going to hurt you."

"Are you cops?" the boy, who looked about eight, asked. "Or bad guys?" He was obviously trying to sound brave, but his voice shook.

"No," Stone said. "Neither one. We're just—looking for something. We won't bother you, we promise."

"You better not hurt my mom or my sister, or I'll hurt you."

"Doc?" Verity whispered.

"Yes?"

"Look at them."

For a second he was confused—obviously he *was* looking at them—but then he caught her meaning. He shifted to magical sight.

Instantly he saw what she was referring to. The mother and the girl looked the same as before, their flickering auras a similar shade of pale blue. But where the boy had been, in his dirty jeans and oversized Mickey Mouse T-shirt, a wolflike creature now crouched on the mattress. He had gray fur, a long snout, and glittering brown eyes fixed on Stone and Verity. His hands ended in furry, clawed paws.

"Bloody hell…" Stone murmured. Then, louder to the boy: "We aren't going to hurt anybody. And I can see you're ready to protect your family. Good on you." He slid his hand into his pocket and pulled out a small, folded sheaf of twenty-dollar bills. "We're sorry we invaded your home. I hope you'll accept this with our apologies." He was talking to the mother now, and stepped forward to offer the money.

Immediately, the woman and the girl shrank back, and the boy moved in front of them, waving his claws and baring his teeth. "Stay away." His voice was deeper now, and held a warning growl.

Stone stepped back, raising his hands in a gesture of surrender. "All right. All right. No trouble." He tossed the money gently on the floor in front of them. "Come on, Verity—let's leave these people in peace."

They quickly searched the remaining bedrooms, finding no sign of any magical anomalies—aside from the wolf-boy, anyway. If Jeremy had spawned another fissure, it hadn't been here. They descended the stairs and headed out through the front door.

Stone paused, turning back toward the house. "That poor kid. I wonder if he's even had a chance to look at himself in the mirror—and what he thought if he did."

"Don't feel too sorry for him, Doc. It sounds like he's found a way to keep his mom and his sister safe, and trust me, when you're homeless, that's a big deal. Come on—let's go check out the hotel."

As they left, Stone couldn't help thinking of Michele Berry again. This young boy had found a way to deal with his change—even embrace it, to protect what he loved—while Michele had paid the ultimate price because she couldn't come to terms with it. Regardless of what they did or didn't find at the hotel, this situation wasn't going to be an easy problem to solve.

The Halcyon Hotel wasn't as big as some of the chain places, but it was big enough to host a healthy-sized convention. When Stone and Verity walked through the revolving door at the front and into the lobby, they both had to stop and stare.

The whole place had been transformed, hung with colorful banners and peppered with life-sized replicas of bizarrely cute creatures that looked like a combination of classic monsters and some kind of cuddly animals. *My Favorite Monster Fest! Welcome, MFM Fans!* the biggest banner read. It was bright yellow, printed in comic-book-style blue letters. Another pair of the furry monsters flanked either side of the message, pointing proudly at it. The whole area was full of people: hyperactive children, bored-looking parents, and groups of college-age men and women, all of them either standing around chatting or hurrying through on their way somewhere else. A good percentage of the children wore handmade costumes, and a surprising number of the college students did too—though most of theirs looked like the products of many hours of loving labor rather than parental desperation.

"Bloody hell…" Stone murmured. "And I mean that literally this time."

Verity chuckled. "Come on, Doc. They won't hurt you. Let's go look around." Her grin widened. "Besides—it might be an omen. We're the biggest 'MFM' fans around, right?"

They passed through the lobby, moving past placards on easels pointing the way to various conference rooms, a larger one that proclaimed *MFM Dealers' Room This Way!,* and a few flat-panel TV screens set up to show episodes of the cartoon on endless loop. Stone paused for a moment to watch, and shook his head in amazement. This loud, brightly colored, hyperkinetic presentation was the visual and aural equivalent of dosing a kid with several cups of sugar.

"Don't say it," Verity warned. Despite the gravity of their situation, she seemed amused at his discomfort. "I bet you watched some pretty horrible stuff when you were a kid."

"We didn't have a television at home, so all I saw was whatever somebody put on in the common room at Barrow, or else when I could sneak over to Aubrey's flat. And *none* of it was like this, I can guarantee."

He was about to resume walking when a college-age man in a fluorescent orange *I'm a Little Monster!* T-shirt hurried up to them. He wore a badge that said *STAFF* on a lanyard around his neck, along with a colorful drawing of a creature that looked like the unholy union of a chubby pink piglet and Frankenstein's monster.

"Excuse me," he said breathlessly.

Stone stopped. "Yes?"

The guy looked them up and down, and his thoughts couldn't have been more obvious: *you don't look like you belong here.* "Uh—you need to wear your badge at all times."

"We haven't got badges. We're just looking around."

The young man appeared uneasy, clearly not comfortable with potential conflict. "I'm sorry, but you can't be in here if you're not a registered attendee. You can buy a one-day badge at the registration desk."

Stone glanced around, for the first time noticing that all the other people hurrying around wore similar badges, except theirs had dates on them instead of *STAFF.*

Verity prodded his arm. "C'mon, Doc. Guess we'd better get badges."

The man smiled, relieved they weren't going to give him any trouble. "Just over here. Follow me. We'll get you set up. Hey, who's your favorite Monster?"

Stone gave him a *Don't push it, kid* look and didn't reply.

"Don't mind him," Verity said, grinning. "He's old and grumpy. And *my* favorite Monster is Cthul-Hoo the Great Owl One."

"Awesome choice!" He returned her grin and something in his expression changed, as if he'd just noticed she was attractive, female, not much older than he was, and actually *had* a favorite Monster. He pointed at his badge. "Mine's Frankenswine. Hey, after you get your badge, if you want I can show you a table in the dealer's room where they have some *great* Cthul-Hoo merch."

"That's quite all right," Stone said quickly before Verity could reply.

The guy shot him a sour "*I wasn't talking to* you" glare, but continued across the lobby to a long folding table with *Registration* across the front. "Here you go," he said curtly. "They'll get you set up." Without waiting for a reply, he stalked off.

Five minutes later, they had one-day badges hanging around their necks. Verity's sported a swarm of gray, X-eyed hornets, and Stone's had a long-armed, clawed creature with twinkling eyes and a black void where its mouth should have been.

"Sweet," Verity said, tweaking Stone's badge. "You got Azasloth, and I got Zom-Bees. Bummer that they ran out of Cthul-Hoo."

Stone glared. "You're getting entirely too caught up with this nonsense. Shall we get moving? If that fissure is here, the sooner we find it, the sooner we can close it. Even though I strongly doubt that will reverse whatever's changed these people, maybe we can slow it down, at least."

"You are *no* fun, Doc."

"Not at present. Or do I need to remind you that this thing's been responsible for the death of at least one person—probably more?"

She sobered. "Yeah, you're right. I'm sorry. Should we split up?"

"The place isn't that big. Let's just wander about and see what we can find. Keep magical sight up as much as possible."

They walked around the hotel for nearly an hour. They checked the dealer's room (even more colorful and chaotic than the lobby), the conference rooms where the panels and collectible-card-game contests were taking place, and the restaurant on the ground floor, then rode the elevator all the way to the top floor and systematically checked the hallways and public areas of each floor on the way back down. Stone even found the entrance to the roof and, using a disregarding spell and magic to pop the lock, took a quick detour up there. By the time they reconvened in the lobby, both he and Verity were losing hope.

"Maybe it's just not here," she said, slumping into a vacant chair and watching three costumed kids spread out a card game on the floor near the wall. "I mean—it was a good idea, and it makes a lot of sense, but I didn't notice even a hint of anything. Except for that one guy."

"That one guy" had been coming out of one of the rooms on the fourth floor, his furled wings and hawklike profile visible to magical but not mundane sight. Stone and Verity had decided not to stop him.

"Yes." He leaned against the column next to her chair. "You may be right—but I can't shake the feeling that it's got to be around here somewhere. It would mean a long incubation period— somewhere around two months—but we're dealing with a new phenomenon here. We can't make too many assumptions about how it behaves."

"If only there was a way to tie this place to any of the people who got affected. Then, maybe we could—what?"

Stone had jerked his head up at her words, and yanked his phone from his pocket. "Maybe there is. Hold on."

Curious, she rose. "What are you doing?"

He didn't answer, but didn't try to hide the phone screen from her. Instead, he called up a search engine and tapped in *halcyon hotel event schedule*.

A calendar popped up. He scrolled back to the April-May timeframe, then zoomed in. "Wedding…wedding…retirement party…Wait. This might be something. Biff-Con."

"What the heck is Biff-Con?" She leaned in closer for a better look.

"Damned if I know." He tapped the link, bringing up a series of photos of people in costumes. "Looks like the same sort of thing, though. And the date range is right."

Verity frowned. "Okay, but I don't see what you're going to learn from that."

He flashed her a wicked grin. "You should pay more attention to your brother." He closed the search engine, then switched to his text app and sent a quick message: *Are you there?*

The reply was almost instant. *What's up, Doc? I've always wanted to say that, by the way.*

Can I call you?

You old people. Always with the calling. :) Sure.

He immediately switched to the phone and tapped the number. "Hello, Gina."

"Hey. What can I do for you? I'm hanging out here at the office, cleaning up the case files until Jason gets back tomorrow. I'm *so* glad Amber and the baby are okay."

"I need some information about the people you've been collecting. I assume you've been building a database?"

"Oh, yeah, for sure."

"Brilliant. I need to know if any of them attended something called 'Biff-Con,' at the Halcyon Hotel in Rochester, Minnesota."

"Why?"

"We're tracking our Patient Zero, and we think they might have been here."

"Here? You're in Minnesota?"

"Yes. Verity and I are both here. Long story. Best if you don't ask too many questions."

"This *is* me you're talking to, you realize. Questions are my life. But I'm gonna guess this is some magic thing, right?"

"Got it in one. Could you do that check for me?"

"Sure. Might take a little time, though. Can I call you back?"

"How long are we talking?"

"No way to say. Depends on how easy the info is to get. I figure an hour, tops, if it's available."

Stone grimaced at Verity, but didn't say anything. "Fine. Please make it a priority—this is important."

"You got it, Doc. Hold onto your butts, and I'll get back to you ASAP."

Impatiently, Stone stuffed the phone into his pocket and watched more of the colorfully-costumed kids—and more than a few college students—trooping through the lobby. He wondered if a costume contest was about to begin, or if they just dressed this way all day. "Come on. Let's get a cup of coffee—or something stronger, if they've got it. I've had about enough of this place."

"You're in luck—I saw a bar while we were looking around."

Gina called back in twenty-two minutes, as they were sitting in the bar sipping drinks and picking at a plate of breaded calamari. "Okay, Doc. I got a hit for you. That wasn't as hard as I thought it would be."

"You do?" Stone glanced at Verity, surprised. "Who is it?"

"Dude named Darrell Gronsky, from San Diego. I checked out his Facebook page, and he posted a bunch of photos of him and his friends at the con." She snorted. "His nickname is 'Spunk.' I do *not* want to know how he got that."

Stone ignored that. "Er—brilliant. So he *was* here."

"Yeah. He's a LARPer, it looks like."

"What's that when it's at home?"

She laughed, and spoke as if addressing a small child. "Live Action Role Player. LARP. It's like…when people play things like Dungeons and Dragons in real life. Quite a few of the pics on his Facebook are of him and his friends dressed up like wizards and shit, going on a treasure hunt."

Stone almost discounted that and went on to his next question, but then something occurred to him. "Treasure hunt? In the hotel?"

"Looks like it, yeah. He says the treasure ended up being hidden behind a curtain in one of the unused conference rooms."

He shot a significant glance at Verity. "So you're saying they were poking about all over the hotel looking for this treasure?"

"Yeah, that's it. Doc, what exactly are you looking for?"

"It's…hard to explain. Gina—could you gather up those photos and send them to me?"

"The Facebook ones?"

"Yes."

"Why don't I just send you a link to his page? He doesn't have it friends-locked, so you can see it on your own page."

Sometimes Stone felt like the world was moving on without him, and this was one of those times. "I…er…don't have a page."

There was a long pause. "You don't have a Facebook page? I mean, come on, Doc. All the old people have Facebook pages!"

"All right, that's quite enough with the 'old people' thing. And I haven't got one."

"I do," Verity said quickly. Louder, she called, "Gina, send me the link. I'll get 'em."

"There you go. Bam—it's on its way. Good luck, you two."

Verity was already pulling up the page on her phone as Stone put his away. "I can't believe it either—you're a college professor and you don't have a Facebook page? I know Facebook does kinda skew older these days, but…"

"Look—I've got better things to do with my time than spend it with my nose buried in some screen, all right?"

She cocked her head at him and gave him a look. "Aren't you supposed to be immortal these days? You've got nothing *but* time."

"*Plus*," he continued firmly without acknowledging that she'd spoken, "there's a reason they call it 'social media,' and it's the same reason I avoid it. I've *also* got better things to do than post photos of last night's dinner for people to *ooh* and *ahh* over."

"Sheesh, grumpy." She grinned to take the edge off her words. "Besides, nobody wants to see photos of your Chinese takeout and empty Guinness bottles. You could post a pic of Raider—they'd be all *over* that. Anyway, okay, here we go—she's right, he *did* post a lot of pics." She set the phone down between them and slowly began scrolling through the images.

Most of them included some subset of four people, taken by two of them. 'Spunk' Gronsky was dressed in a red velour robe tied with a golden rope, a pointy wizard hat with stars on it, and a fake beard. He carried a purple pool noodle with a silver-painted softball duct-taped to one end. The other three appeared to be roleplaying an elven thief (pointy ears, tunic, tights, and dagger), a warrior (plastic armor plates, sword, and shield), and a barbarian (fake fur cloak, plastic mace, and horned helmet).

Stone gave Verity a withering glance. "Seriously? These people look old enough to have proper jobs."

"Hey, don't knock it if you haven't tried it."

"You've tried it?"

"Uh...yeah, once. A girl I was seeing for a while when I was eighteen was into it. It wasn't fantasy like this, though. It was more like...angsty vampires and politics. Goth stuff. It was fun. I lost touch with the people who did it after we broke up, though."

Stone didn't reply, but turned his attention back to the photos and tried to focus more on the backgrounds and less on the ridiculous costumes. "Most of these areas look familiar. This is the lobby...this is where the dealer's room is..."

She pointed. "I think this is out behind the hotel. We haven't looked there yet."

"And the men's room? They expected to find treasure in the men's room?"

"You never know. Maybe they—"

Stone held up a hand. "Wait. Stop. Scroll back one."

When she did, he leaned in to peer at the photo. "I don't recognize this one."

"It looks like some sort of...storeroom or something."

She was right. The light was dim, but shelves lined the walls. He zoomed in, trying to identify the objects on the shelves. "Why would they look in there? What are the rules to this game? Can they go anywhere they like?"

"Not usually. Only public places, or ones specifically designated for the game." She tapped it, bringing up the caption. "*Oops. Read the directions wrong and ended up in here. No treasure unless you're into TP and cleaning products.*"

The two of them exchanged glances.

Stone slipped off his barstool, finishing the last of his drink. "That might be our spot. Let's check it out."

"We should check the back, too. If nobody can see this thing, there's no reason it can't be outside."

It wasn't outside. They walked all the way around the outside of the hotel, earning them odd looks from the parents shepherding groups of kids in from the parking lot. Then they went back inside, flashing their badges toward the eagle-eyed college students scanning for gatecrashers.

"Where do you suppose the storeroom is?" Verity asked, looking around. "I don't remember seeing it when we were checking in here, do you?"

"No, but it can't be far. If they just stumbled into it, it's got to be fairly accessible."

The convention was more crowded now, so they had to shove their way through knots of people and take care not to step on anybody's card game on the floor. Three staff members dressed in the professional-looking costumes of menacing but somehow still cute sheep (one with a sign around his neck reading *Beware the Sheep Ones*) were drawing a lot of attention. Stone and Verity took advantage of the chaos to duck down a cordoned-off hallway, and were rewarded with a door labeled *Storage*. It was locked, but the simple lock was no match for Stone's magic.

Switching on the light revealed a staircase down, ending in a long, narrow room lined on either side with shelving units. Another freestanding unit in the middle bisected the area into two aisles.

Verity looked around. "This looks like the same place from the photo. Toilet paper, cleaning supplies, linens, old junk—"

Stone was already stalking down the nearest aisle toward the back part of the room, magical sight active. By this point, he was mostly convinced this would be another wild-goose chase, but he was determined to check everywhere he could. The fissure could just as easily be in one of the guest rooms or some other hidden part of the hotel, but—

He almost missed it, even when he was nearly on top of it. Only a faint ripple at the corner of his eye alerted him to its presence. "Verity!"

She hurried over. "What? Did you find it?"

"Look!" He pointed.

"I don't see anything." Even with the narrow-eyed, fuzzed-out look of magical sight, she was gazing around as if nothing was out of the ordinary.

"It's low to the ground. Very hard to see." He crouched, still examining the area. No wonder no one had noticed it. Even most mages would have missed it, since it was obviously doing its best to remain concealed, blending in with the wall behind it. It was roughly three feet long and one high. As he narrowed his focus, he spotted faint hints of sparkling air drifting out of it and creeping across the floor like dry ice vapor at a rock concert. Oddly, it didn't reach far, though, dissipating well before it reached the door. "Do you see it now?"

"I…think so." She crouched next to him, peering at the space. "I see…*something*."

Stone had no doubt that they'd found what they were looking for. What he wasn't so sure of, though, was how dangerous it was. Obviously this room wasn't safe, but if the energy didn't make it outside, how had it affected so many people? Was the only reason the energy got out at all that Spunk and his buddies had blundered in here and carried it out? Were the maids and other hotel personnel spreading it?

Reluctantly, he acknowledged what some part of him had believed all along: that even if they closed the rift now, the damage was done.

There was no rolling this back.

Four schlubs in bad fantasy costumes had likely set into motion one of the biggest changes the modern world would experience in not-so-recent memory.

Except it wasn't them. Spunk and his crew of ersatz adventurers had only served as the final catalyst. If it hadn't been them, it would have been a housekeeper, or a maintenance person, or a chef. *Somebody* out there with magical blood would have come into contact with it eventually. It was inevitable. But whoever it was, whatever happened after wouldn't have been their fault, either.

Jeremy had caused this—but even he hadn't been responsible. He was a child, brought unwillingly into an unfamiliar world, coping as best he could. Stone shook his head with a bitter chuckle.

"Doc? You okay?" Verity had risen too and was looking at him with worry.

He didn't answer.

She touched his arm. "Alastair?"

"We aren't fooling anyone, you know. We're not going to make a bloody bit of difference. All of this was for nothing."

"What?"

He indicated the rift. "We could close it. We *will* close it. But you don't honestly think it's going to make any difference, do you? It's not going to cure the people already affected. It probably won't even stop it from getting out. It already *is* out." He ran a hand through his hair. "I wonder how Daphne would feel if she knew what a major effect she's had on the world—and not even just once, but twice."

Her eyes widened. "You're right. I didn't think of that."

"I can't think of anyone else who's had such a far-reaching effect. I suppose a few monarchs, heads of state, those types could make a claim. But she's right up there, isn't she?" He let more bitterness creep into his voice. "And she'll never even know it."

"Doc…"

He snapped his head up and clapped his hands with a briskness he didn't feel. "Right, then. Let's get to it, shall we? Let me take a few readings, and then close this thing. With any luck, this shouldn't take long. Anticlimactic, even."

Verity looked like she didn't know quite what to make of him and his sudden, odd mood. "What do you want me to do?"

He eyed the rift. It didn't look like much. Such a small, insignificant thing to be responsible for so much chaos. "I think I've got this. Keep an eye on me—and it. If anything changes, be ready to pop in and help. And don't get too close to it."

"You got it."

Confident that Verity had his back, Stone faced the fissure and crouched, shifting to his deeper version of magical sight to help him keep an eye on the thing's edges. If it flared up, he wanted to know it. He began by performing a thorough examination of the fissure, at least to the limited extent he could. He wished Eddie and Ward were here to help, and a small part of him wondered if their hypothesis had been correct—*was* the fissure only dangerous to people with magical blood, not mundanes or full mages? If they were wrong, standing here bathing themselves in the ground zero emanations could be altering him and Verity without them even realizing it.

A bit late to worry about that, he thought sourly. If it was going to happen, it probably already had. He had no choice but to go on.

After jotting down a few notes about the fissure's structure, he reached out, summoning power and carefully shaping it around one of its edges. Unless it behaved otherwise, he planned to close it the same way he did any other extradimensional rift: by stitching it together from one end to the other. At least it was small.

Small, yes—but also powerful. He figured that out fast, as the little thing immediately began putting up significant resistance against his efforts to bring it together. Beads of sweat popped out on his forehead as he struggled to firm his mental grip on it.

This wasn't going to be as easy as he'd hoped. This thing wanted to survive.

"You okay, Doc?" Verity's voice came from far away.

"Fine," he said through gritted teeth. "Just…keep watch and don't distract me."

He had no idea how long he'd been concentrating, but he didn't think it was long, when a *click* sounded behind them.

"Hey!" called a voice. "What are you two doing in here?"

CHAPTER TWENTY-NINE

STONE DIDN'T SPIN AROUND—if he did, he'd lose his fragile progress toward sealing the fissure. He struggled to split his concentration, trying to spare a bit for what was going on back there. He'd have to count on Verity to deal with it.

"Uh—" She sounded startled and uncertain. "What are *you* doing in here?"

"I've been following you." Pride, and triumph. "You've been acting weird. And now I see why."

The fissure pushed back, and Stone was forced to devote more of his focus to it. Even so, now he was sure he recognized the voice: the young man who'd initially accosted them about their lack of badges.

"What are you talking about?" Verity demanded.

The young man snorted. "It's pretty obvious, isn't it? You two were looking for a place to hook up. That's disgusting! There are *kids* here!"

"What the *hell*?" Now she sounded indignant. "In a *supply closet*?"

"Hey, I don't care what kind if kinks you have. Some people get off doing it in public places. But you're not gonna do it here. Get the hell out before I call security."

Stone had no doubt that the young man was still smarting from earlier, when his clumsy advances toward Verity were rebuffed. He'd seen enough of the same behavior among some of his students—spurned young nerds of both sexes could turn vindictive on a dime, and that wasn't something he and Verity had time to deal with right now. He didn't have much brainpower to spare, but they needed to find a way to get rid of the guy without causing a full-scale disturbance.

Unfortunately, Verity's customary social skills seem to have taken a brief holiday, probably due to her shock and annoyance at the young man's accusation. "Come *on*," she said with contempt. "If we wanted to hook up, it wouldn't be here in the middle of Kiddie Central. And even if we did, we'd get a real room."

"Yeah, right. Okay, then, if that's not it, what *are* you doing in here? And if you don't give me a good reason in the next five seconds, I'm calling hotel security. If you give me any trouble, I might even call the cops."

Great. Drunk with power, this one was. The fissure hiccupped again, sending a blast of tingling energy through Stone. He braced himself to keep from falling over backward. *Come on, Verity, say something.*

But she didn't. Stone could picture her glaring at him, but she remained silent.

"Okay, then," the guy said. "I'm gonna—"

"We're LARPing!" Stone blurted without turning.

"*What?*"

That apparently busted through Verity's momentary paralysis. "Yeah," she said, fast and earnest. "That's right. We're LARPing. We didn't want to say it because that's part of the game. We're— hunting for a secret treasure. The map said it would be in here somewhere."

Stone couldn't see the guy's expression, but he didn't have to. Their lame explanation, combined with the fact that they were both still fully dressed, had clearly taken the wind out of his self-righteous sails.

"Uh—what's he doing over there?"

"Him?" Verity was pedaling fast now. "He's—uh—casting a spell, to open the way to the treasure chamber."

Stone, playing along, began making "magical" gestures and muttering nonsense Latin under his breath.

The guy was silent for a few seconds, probably watching. "Guys, I'm serious, there's no treasure in here. You're not even supposed to be in this part of the hotel. This door should be locked."

"It wasn't. And look!"

Stone wasn't positive what Verity was doing, but if it had been him, he'd be showing the guy an illusionary map right about now. He dug in harder, fighting against the small, powerful fissure. Unlike the others, this one apparently hadn't grown in size, but perhaps it had grown in potency instead. Sweat trickled down his back, dampening his shirt. He only had about a quarter of the thing sealed, and could barely spare the concentration to follow what was going on behind him.

"Well, damn," the guy said, sounding surprised. "Where'd you get this map? I didn't even know there was a LARP going on at this con. Nobody told me."

"It's kind of a secret, like I said. It's not just this con. We've been to a couple others, like Biff-Con a couple months ago. This what we're looking for now is only part of the treasure. We—uh—have to find the whole thing to win." Verity was clearly tap-dancing as fast as she could, piling lie on top of lie until she hit on something the guy would believe.

"Whoa. That's cool." His whole demeanor had changed now, his fascination with this new game overwhelming his resentment at Verity's rejection. And besides, she was talking to him *now*. Maybe he still had a chance. "Can you tell me more about it?"

"Uh—I kinda need to keep an eye on him. This is hard work."

Footsteps sounded, and a shadow fell over Stone as the guy approached. "Wow. He's really into this. He looks like he's about to faint."

"Yeah. He…uh…he's into method acting. Really gets caught up in his role."

"How come you're not wearing costumes?"

"We are. We're—modern-day magic users hiding among the normals. I mean, come on—how many normal guys have you seen wearing a long black coat like that?"

Stone thought she might have pushed it too far that time.

Apparently not, though. "That is…*awesome*. You guys look like you're straight outta one of those urban fantasy novels, like *The Dresden Files*. I'd love to play this game. I mean, I love *My Favorite Monster*, sure, but my real love is RPGs. Do you think I could join your team and help look? I'm off duty in half an hour. I don't think they'll miss me. My name's Paul, by the way."

Verity had recovered her tact by now. "Ooh…no, I wish you could, Paul, but I don't think so. The teams are already set, and we could get penalized if we get outside help. But after we finish here, I can give you more information about the game so you can get started."

"That'd be great." His voice held more than a hint of another kind of interest. "Maybe we could…team up on the next one? You know, you and me?"

"Maybe. We'll see. Look—I really need to keep an eye on my friend. He…tends to go overboard sometimes."

"Yeah, okay." Back to the reluctant grumble.

"You won't tell on us, will you? We should be out of here soon."

"I guess not. I guess you don't look like the type who'd steal cleaning supplies or set the place on fire or anything."

Stone hoped the latter wouldn't end up being true. The fissure was still fighting him, harder now. Every inch he gained was hard-won, and he had no idea what it might start doing when it felt truly threatened.

"I won't tell on one condition."

Uh oh.

"…Yeah?" Verity had apparently reached the same conclusion Stone had.

"I want to watch. If the treasure really is here, I want to see it when you find it. Is that cool? I promise I won't get in the way."

Stone let his shoulders slump a little. At least Paul wasn't going to try taking advantage of Verity to get his way.

"Doc? Can you hear me? Is it okay?"

"Doc?" Paul moved in closer. "Ooh, is that your magic name? Like Doctor Strange? Or Doctor Who? Oh, wow, you *do* kinda look like that guy who played Doctor Who a few years ago…I was like six back then…"

Stone kept his teeth gritted around a swallow. He had the fissure about a third of the way closed now, and the tingling energy was starting to hurt. Here he was, worrying that this stuff was rewriting his magical DNA, and he had to deal with King of the Nerds, too. Still, he didn't see a way around it. If they sent Paul away, he would certainly come back with friends. They could use magic to keep him in line, but that had its own dangers.

"Sure…" he rasped. "But keep quiet."

"Yeah, yeah. Quiet as a mouse." But he didn't step back. Stone could still hear his loud, excited breathing, and smell the onions on his breath. "Thanks…Doc."

Stone didn't answer. The farther he got with the fissure, the more of his energy he was having to devote to keeping the closed part closed while fighting against the part that was still open. He was burning up now, his whole body soaked in sweat. Impatiently, he shrugged free of his coat and flung it aside.

"You need help, Doc?" Verity's voice came from even farther away, like she was standing at the other end of a long tunnel.

"No…no…I've got it…" He hoped he had it. She didn't have much experience closing rifts, and this one was proving both tricky and unconventional. He remembered back to when they'd sent Daphne and Jeremy home—even Kolinsky had had trouble with the last one. He wished the dragon were here now. Hell, he even halfway wished *Aldwyn* was here, if his ancestor was willing to help.

They're not here, though. This is all you. Focus.

His strength was ebbing, either because of the energy he was putting into closing the fissure, or because the fissure itself was sapping it. He dropped from his crouch to his knees, fighting not to sag. He heard Verity and Paul talking softly in the background, but could no longer devote any of his attention to following their conversation. He must look strange to Paul, who couldn't see any sign of the fissure he was working on. Like a lunatic making strange gestures at a dirty, stained old wall.

Halfway done now. The fissure bulged, trying to push its remaining energy through the smaller opening. The tingling sensation grew stronger still, pumping painful pulses along Stone's nerve pathways. His whole body felt now like his hand had when he'd accidentally touched a live amp cable while setting up for a Cardinal Sin show. The pain wasn't debilitating—yet—but it was stronger than before. And he still had another half to go.

This would be easy, he'd thought. He reminded himself *never* to think that. Either it wasn't true in the first place, or thinking it insulted the Universe into thwarting his puny plans.

He pulled in more Calanarian energy, forcing himself to take it slow and easy. While it was highly tempting to try moving faster, if something went wrong the whole thing could blow up in his face. Possibly literally. Whatever this thing was putting out, it was potent. He wished he knew what dimension the fissure was pointing at—not that it would help, but even now his curiosity hadn't deserted him.

Around him, the shelving units started to shake. A few packs of toilet paper and stacks of linen shimmied over the edge and hit the floor.

"What the heck?" Paul sounded even farther away than Verity had, but the fear in his voice was evident. "What's happening? Are we having an earthquake?"

"No, I think it's just—part of the game."

"How can it be part of the game?"

"It's all—uh—very high tech. Trust me. We're good."

Stone wasn't so sure, though. The more the fissure's opening decreased in size, the more the stuff coming from the other side intensified. It was the same effect as putting a thumb over the end of the hose, turning a gentle stream into a focused blast. His whole body was trembling now, as he continued directing the Calanarian energy to stitching up the fissure's edges. He wouldn't run out of energy—Harrison's magic-rich dimension was a boundless source—but eventually he would reach the limits of his body's ability to channel it. It was a race now, and he wasn't sure it was one he could win.

"You sure he's okay?" Paul sounded worried now.

Verity hesitated a moment before answering. "He's...really devoted to this. He'll be fine. Just don't distract him. He—Doc!"

Stone had barely been listening to her before, registering her and Paul's conversation only on the most superficial level. But her sudden cry of surprise broke through and caught his attention. He bobbled the fissure for a terrifying second, allowing a couple of stitches to slip, and struggled to get it back under control before replying through clenched teeth. "What?"

"Look—do you see something moving on the other side?"

His blood turned to ice water as he shifted his perceptions. He'd been laser-focused on the fissure's edges, paying no attention to what was happening beyond them. But now, as he looked past the boundary, he spotted a shadowy, amorphous figure approaching the opening. *No, no, not now...*

"This is so cool!" Paul was saying. "It's like you guys are putting on a show for me! Wait till I show my buddies!"

"No photos!" Verity barked.

Stone almost turned around, picturing the young man pulling his phone from his pocket and preparing to snap a selfie.

"What—why not?" Now Paul sounded surprised and annoyed.

"Uh—you can't. You'll get us in trouble. Like I said, nobody's supposed to help us."

"But I won't show anybody but—"

"No photos or you can't stay and watch." Her voice was firm. "Put it away, Paul."

It seemed for a moment as if he would push back, but finally he grumbled, "Okay, fine. Jeez."

Immediate crisis averted, Stone turned his full attention back to the real one. If he couldn't get this thing sealed before whatever that was reached the opening, he had no idea what it would do. Would it just look? Would it try to come through? Would it attack? He didn't even know if it was alive—it might be merely another floating clump of energy pulled in by the increasingly intense flow.

He didn't want to find out, though.

Nearly three-quarters done, but his strength was flagging hard. His body sagged, fighting to remain upright as he directed trembling hands at the diminishing aperture. The pain was nearly constant now, the energy buffeting him. He spared a thought to wonder if anyone else at the convention would be affected by the growing power, but that was a minor consideration at this point. A few more lizard-people or ogres would be a small price to pay.

Verity was next to him now. He felt her hand on his shoulder and smelled the leather of her jacket. "You need help, Doc? What is that thing?"

"Don't—know." His breath came sharp and fast now. "Can't—help." He wished she could, but at this point, if she tried inserting herself into the working, she was much more likely to do more harm than good.

"You're bleeding."

Was he? That was news, but now that she said it, he could feel liquid trickling down from his nose. He'd thought it was sweat from his forehead, but the copper smell gave it away. "Can't—be helped…"

"Wow…" Paul murmured from somewhere far away. "You guys weren't kidding about method acting…"

Verity ignored him. "Doc—you can't keep this up. You're gonna pass out, and then what?"

The amorphous *thing* was getting closer. Stone still couldn't tell if it was alive, but it was definitely separate from the ambient energy on the other side of the fissure. And it had definitely noticed them now. It picked up speed, approaching the opening. Stone forced himself to stitch faster. It might not be the best idea, but letting that thing through was a worse one.

"It's getting closer." Verity's voice shook now. "Doc—"

"Hush!" He couldn't spare any more concentration for her, or Paul, or anything on this side of the rift. He was almost there now, but he'd have to give this everything he had. More blood trickled from his nose, slipping past his clenched teeth to fill his mouth with a coppery-sweet taste.

Just a little further…

The thing reached the edge.

Before Stone could stop it, it slammed into the opening. Part of it, like a living shadow, poked through and snaked toward him. He threw himself backward, but not fast enough. The shadowy appendage slipped around his throat and began to squeeze.

Verity yelped. "Doc!"

Stone barely heard her. He clawed at his throat with both hands as the thing began to constrict his airway. Through slitted eyes, he saw his careful stitching was beginning to slowly, inexorably unravel. He had to get his focus back! But already, black dots were blooming in his vision. Another part of the shadow-creature was poking through, and the part around his neck was trying to drag him toward the opening—

And then, suddenly, a rush of energy slammed into him. He had no idea where it came from, but he didn't care. It was there, and he had no other choice but to use it. He gripped the ropy, shadowy thing around his throat and poured his magical strength into it. If this wasn't enough, he didn't have any other options.

In his mind, he heard something scream—a sharp, grating sound that felt like it was pulling his brain apart. But then the appendage dropped away and retracted back through the unraveling opening. The other one joined it, and the shadowy creature moved a few steps—or whatever it used for movement—away.

Stone gulped great lungfuls of air, on his hands and knees now, but he couldn't stop. If the thing got its second wind and decided to go for another attack, he knew he couldn't stop it. He pulled in more Calanarian energy, not caring what it did to his body, and combined it with the remainder of the mysterious infusion, and directed all of it in one last, desperate shot, knowing if this one failed, the whole thing would pull apart again.

It was sort of a magical Hail Mary, which Stone supposed was funny given his relationship with both sports and religion.

With a loud yell of rage and defiance, he let the power go.

This was it. Either it would work, or it wouldn't.

Something white-hot lit up in his brain, submerging his sight and his consciousness at the same time.

CHAPTER THIRTY

"So...you're *sure* you got it all."

They were in a motel room on the outskirts of Rochester an hour later. Stone was stretched out on one of the two queen beds, and Verity was propped on a pile of pillows on the other one. This wasn't the first time Verity had asked that question.

Stone nodded wearily. He still felt as if he'd been run over by a train and hung off the side of a building, but his energy was slowly returning.

They'd both thought it wouldn't be a good idea to try driving far, but they had to get away from the Halcyon Hotel. Verity had been a trouper, concealing them under illusions so they could sneak out after Paul had gone to get help.

"I'm sure. It's gone." He pushed himself up to a slightly more elevated position. "Don't know what good it will do, but it's gone."

He closed his eyes, thinking back over the events of the last hour. He hadn't blacked out for long; when he woke, he was flat on his back with a worried Verity and Paul both hovering over him, trying to revive him. Paul, terrified and fascinated in equal measure, had been effusive with his compliments about the "show" they'd put on, but had insisted on leaving to bring back the con's first-aid staff to check Stone over. He'd refused to take no for an answer even after they'd both tried to convince him the performance had been fake, so they had let him go. After a quick healing spell from Verity to get Stone back on his feet and another to neutralize the blood spatters on the floor, the two of them had slipped away and were gone before the young man had returned. They'd exited through one of the back doors and limped to Verity's rented SUV. She'd picked the first motel she spotted once they were away from the Halcyon.

Now, she twisted to give him a sober glance. "Yeah. I'm not even sure it was worth it, to be honest. It doesn't change anything, does it?"

"I doubt it. Unless the researchers figure out a way to reverse the effect, it sounds like the world's on the way to changing permanently." He gave up trying to sit up straighter and settled back on the pillows. "Still, though, I feel good about finding the source and closing it. Who knows what might have happened if one of those shadow-things—or more than one—had found the fissure and managed to get through when no one was around to stop them?"

"That's a good point." She didn't sound convinced, though.

"In any case, good job with the energy at the end. You might have made all the difference. I'm sure you did for me, anyway. Even if I can't die, getting dragged back through to that thing's home dimension wouldn't have been pleasant."

As they'd driven away in search of a spot to rest, Verity had explained the sudden surge of power that had bolstered Stone's efforts. She had made a desperate attempt to focus her healing, combining it with her own magical force to provide him with a last-minute jolt. "Thanks. I didn't know whether it would work—never did anything like that before—but I figured it couldn't hurt." She looked pensive. "I have no idea if Paul snapped any pics while I wasn't looking, though."

"Eh, it's all right. The best he might have got was the two of us from the back. The fissure won't show up, so if he wants to show his mates some photos of two strange people waving like idiots at a wall, good on him."

She flashed a wan grin. "Well, *he's* happy, anyway. Maybe we should charge for putting on a show like that."

"That was my swan song performance, I think." He tried sitting up again. "In any case, it's time to head home. I want to update Eddie and Ward on what we've found out, and send them my notes so they can pass them on to their flock of researchers."

"You really think they'll figure out how to cure this?" Her expression was troubled and skeptical.

"Honestly? No. And you're probably right—maybe it's not something that *should* be cured. It's a shame about Michele, and I do wish she'd reached out to Gina's group for some help, but…" He shrugged and shook his head. "I suppose we can't resist *every* bit of change in the world."

Verity swung her legs around and sat on the edge of the bed. "What will you do now?"

"About this? I'm not sure I'll do anything. If this condition truly is as contagious as it seems to be, and *if* it only affects people with magical blood, I suppose there's no stopping it from eventually infecting whoever it's going to infect. Since we can't identify them, we can't even put them in quarantine bubbles to prevent it. And if it's not up to mages to cure them, I don't think it's up to us to try organizing them, either."

"No, I guess not. I guess that's almost as arrogant as thinking we *should* try to cure them."

Stone nodded, looking at his hands in his lap. "This isn't our business. It's theirs. Took me a while to get that through my thick skull, but I see it now. Though I do worry about how the world's going to change, and how we're going to have to change with it. It will be an interesting period to live through, if nothing else."

"For us, anyway, and for the people involved. It's going to be weird, though, that all the mundanes and other people who aren't affected by it will just go on about their lives with no idea anything's changed. Even if somebody tells them, they aren't going to believe it. Not with no way to prove it."

"Oh, I don't know—that's rather what they do now, with mages, isn't it? They can't see *us*, either, and even if we do magic under their noses, most of the time they rationalize it away like our friend Paul did."

He stood, testing his balance. "Come on—I've had about enough of Minnesota for the foreseeable future. Let's go home. I'm glad this is settled, at least as much as it can be. I'm looking forward to getting in a bit of rest before Aubrey's wedding next month."

She grinned. "Oh, right. Crazy as it sounds, I almost forgot about that. Aubrey's wedding, and Jason and Amber's baby coming soon after that." She reached out and took his hand. "Think about that, Doc—the world hasn't changed too much. Normal stuff like babies and weddings still happen."

And funerals, Stone thought, but didn't say. Verity seemed to be shaking off her despondent mood, and he didn't want to do anything to upset that. "Right, then. Off we go, back to the land of Normal for a while. I've still got to figure out a proper wedding gift for Aubrey and Susan."

CHAPTER THIRTY-ONE

I T WAS THE NIGHT BEFORE THE WEDDING, and Stone was feeling not only comfortably tipsy, but utterly content.

The group had taken over Aubrey's favorite pub in the village, which was now full of a combination of the caretaker's old friends, his and Susan's fellow parishioners from their church, a few of Stone's crowd including Verity, Jason, Eddie, and Ward, and of course Selby from the house.

Ian hadn't shown up, but Stone hadn't expected him to—he'd promised to be there tomorrow last time they'd spoken, but his father didn't hold it against him that he didn't want to attend a gathering where he barely knew anyone and most of the guests were at least three times his age.

Amber wasn't there, either. She still found it amusing that Jason was so overprotective, but after the accident, she'd decided to humor his reluctance to have her traveling through portals in her condition. She'd only agreed after insisting he himself had to go, though, since he was much closer to Aubrey than she was. Verity planned to take him home through the portal tomorrow following the ceremony and reception, so he wouldn't be away for long.

Stone leaned against the wall, a half-finished pint of Guinness in front of him, and watched the festivities without much comment. Mostly, they consisted of Aubrey, Susan, and their friends reminiscing about past adventures, and Stone felt no need to join the conversation. A warm feeling had been growing inside him all evening every time he noticed his old friend's craggy, smiling face, at the loving way he and Susan looked at each other, and at how healthy and happy he appeared while surrounded by the people he loved. Aubrey deserved this kind of happiness. He'd spent his entire life watching over Stone's family and their rambling estate, and now it was time for him to take a rest and focus on his and Susan's own happiness.

Stone hadn't revealed what he'd chosen for a wedding present yet. That was on purpose, because he was sure Aubrey would try to turn it down and he wanted to be well away before that happened. The gift was in two parts: the first was a lavish, around-the-world tour with first-class accommodations. He'd left the details open so the couple could choose the destinations they'd like to visit, and arranged everything with the travel agent—after he'd managed to *find* a travel agent, since everybody did everything online these days—so Aubrey and Susan could stop in at their leisure and firm up the itinerary when they were ready to go.

The second gift was monetary, and substantial. He'd thought about buying them a house, but decided against it when he realized Aubrey loved his flat above the garage, and Susan had her own place in the village. The two would probably decide to live in one of those two locations, and Stone didn't presume that he knew better than they did about where they'd like to end up. The monetary gift was large enough to make a significant dent in the cost of another place, though, if they did decide to move.

He sat now, finishing his Guinness and watching the happy couple as Aubrey related a funny story that had the rest of the elderly group in stitches. He smiled too, even though he hadn't been listening to the story. All was right with the world tonight.

"Hey, Al." Jason slid onto the bench seat across from him, setting his own pint on the scarred table. "You look like you have something on your mind."

"Not really." His smile didn't fade as he continued watching Aubrey. "For the first time in a long while, I've got nothing on my mind except what's happening right here and now."

Jason laughed. "I wish I could say the same thing. My mind's on the future—specifically, about a month from now."

"That's certainly understandable. I assume Amber is doing fine."

"Oh, yeah. She's got a friend staying over tonight, and they're watching movies and scarfing popcorn. She practically shoved me out the door to get me to come here." He looked around, taking in the pub. "I'm glad I did, though. This is nice."

"It is. There's something to be said for slowing down."

"I don't know. I can't see you slowing down for anything, actually."

"Probably not. Not for long, in any case. But tonight, I'll make an exception." He shifted his attention to Eddie and Ward, who had moved to another table and were chatting with Verity. He'd talked with them earlier that evening, comparing notes and getting the latest updates about the magical affliction, which the people affected were starting to call "the Change." The research at Caventhorne had spread out to several other hubs around the world in the previous month, and so far none of the researchers had found any indication that the Change was reversible. All of the evidence they'd gathered supported the hypothesis that the condition only affected those with magical blood, but to Stone's relief no actual practitioners had succumbed. He'd been concerned after the Halcyon incident, keeping a close watch on himself for any signs his aura was shifting, but so far everything had remained as expected.

Gina had been doing her bit to help with the research, too. Her message board had grown to several hundred members all over the world, and others had started similar ones. She maintained her database when she wasn't working at the agency, and shared her findings with Eddie and Ward so they could pass them on to the others. Last Stone had spoken with her, she'd gathered a small local group of fellow "Changelings" who found it amusing to get together for activities, hiding among the "normies." Stone hadn't told her what he'd discovered about the source of the Change; in fact, nobody knew the whole truth except Verity, Eddie, Ward, Jason, and Amber. He'd asked them to keep the details to themselves, since knowing Daphne and her son had been behind it wouldn't alter the situation. As far as the magical researchers knew, the phenomenon had originated when a reclusive and now-dead mage had lost control of a summoning and opened a portal, which was now safely closed. He felt a little dishonest about it, but it wasn't something that kept him up at night.

"World's changing," Jason mused, finishing his pint.

"Indeed it is, on many levels." He looked up to see Aubrey, who'd apparently finished his story, pushing carefully through the crowd toward him. He raised his glass in greeting. "Having fun, Aubrey?"

"Oh, yes, sir."

"Come on—tonight, at least, stop calling me 'sir.' You're the star of this show. You and your lady love."

Aubrey's lined face crinkled in a smile. "I hope you're having fun too, and not getting too bored among my old crowd."

"Not in the slightest. I don't think I can convey how happy I am right now. You enjoy yourself. Just don't get too potted, or poor Susan will have to drag you down the aisle."

"Not much chance of that, sir. I'm just glad you could be here for it."

"I wouldn't miss it for the world, my friend. Not for the world."

The next day couldn't have been more beautiful. It was as if someone had called God, or the Universe, or whoever was responsible for perfect days and ordered one full of sunshine, mild weather, and cool breezes.

The ceremony was as beautiful as the day. Stone, in his black tuxedo, watched with satisfaction as Aubrey and Susan exchanged their vows, feeling as proud of them as he would have if he'd been Aubrey's son. He didn't cry—he didn't cry at weddings, not even a sniffle—but he was sure his small, happy smile didn't leave his face all through the ceremony.

It wasn't until Aubrey and Susan were pronounced husband and wife, shared a decorous but heartfelt kiss before the assembled crowd, and departed for the reception at a local hall that Stone realized he hadn't seen Ian all day.

He waved to Verity, who'd been sitting with Jason, Eddie, and Ward on the groom's side of the church. When she came over, he looked around again. "Have you seen Ian at all?"

She looked startled. "No. Was he supposed to be here?"

Stone remembered that he hadn't specifically told anyone else his son was coming. Aubrey no doubt had been too busy to notice, as Stone had apparently been himself. "Last time we talked, he promised to come. I told him Aubrey would be unhappy if he missed it. Maybe he forgot, or got caught up in something with Gabriel."

Verity didn't miss his disappointment, and she didn't try to tell him he was wrong. "Maybe so. Can you text him?"

"I'm not sure I should. He's already missed the ceremony." He shook his head in frustration, allowing her to take his arm and lead him out of the church toward the car park. The truth was, he wasn't sure he wanted to talk to his son right now.

"I think you should. At least give him a chance to explain himself."

"I'm not exactly in the right frame of mind to listen to his explanations."

"Maybe he's sick."

"He lives on his bloody phone—he couldn't have sent a text?"

She tightened a gentle grip on his arm as they reached Stone's car. "Come on, Doc—just send him a quick text." Her expression sobered. "Remember what happened with Amber…"

A quick jolt of worry went through him. He pictured Ian lying injured on the side of a road somewhere, or more likely at the foot of a mountain or at the bottom of the ocean. Normally, he tried not to concern himself too much with his son's and Gabriel's daredevil lifestyle, which had grown easier when he'd found out Gabriel's true nature.

But now…

"Fine. But if he's sleeping off a hangover somewhere, we're going to have words." He slid into the driver's seat, pulled out his phone, and dashed off a text: *Missed you at Aubrey's wedding.* There. A bit snarky, but there was no helping that.

He stared at the phone, willing for *Read* to appear below his text, and the dots to start moving.

Neither happened.

"Nothing?" Verity leaned on the frame next to Stone, and stood up straighter to wave at Jason. The two of them had planned to drive to the reception together.

"Nothing. Hold on, I'll try calling him."

The phone rang a few times, then went to voicemail.

"Bugger. No answer there either."

Verity frowned as Jason arrived. "Do you have Gabriel's contact info?"

"No. I never needed it for anything. I always reached him through Ian."

"Something wrong?" Jason's gaze shifted between the two of them.

"Ian didn't show up to the wedding," Verity said. "And he didn't leave word or anything. Doc's either worried or annoyed."

"Both, actually." Stone swung his leg into the car and started it. "I should get going, though. I can't be late to the reception as the best man. I'll try again when I get there."

"I'll try too," Verity said. "Jason, you drive."

They hurried off, leaving Stone alone, the space below his text still empty.

Stone made it to the reception on time, but not by much. Fortunately, the caterers were efficient and highly competent, so his only essential duty was to deliver the best man's speech.

As soon as he got inside, he checked his phone again, but there was still no sign Ian had seen his text. Verity and Jason approached, this time followed by Eddie and Ward. All of them looked concerned.

"Verity says Ian 'asn't shown up," Eddie said, looking around. "Didn't know you were expectin' 'im."

"He promised to come." Stone looked around too, half expecting his son to be lounging near the bar, flirting with the bartender. No guests were there, though; everyone was in the process of finding their seats at the small, round tables. Aubrey and Susan were holding court at the head table, surrounded by their friends. Stone would have to make his appearance there soon.

Ward shook his head. "I'm sure he's fine, Alastair. You no doubt know better than the rest of us—the lad is a bit…flighty."

"I know. But it's not like him to skip out on something this important. He's always been very fond of Aubrey, and Aubrey of him." Even as he spoke, though, he wondered if he was overreacting. Ward was right: Ian *could* sometimes be "flighty," a gentler synonym for "self-absorbed and flaky." Stone certainly understood it, even though he didn't entirely sympathize. He himself had exhibited no shortage of self-absorbed behavior in his life, so it was no surprise his son had inherited similar tendencies. Almost certainly, Ian had got caught up in some adventure with Gabriel and his crowd of young, jet-setting mages, and forgotten all about the date.

I should have reminded him. Except that wasn't true, either. Ian was an adult, and Stone couldn't always be there to clean up after him. The boy would just have to explain things—and apologize—to Aubrey when he finally turned up.

Right now, Stone had obligations, and there was no way he was going to disappoint Aubrey by not giving them his full attention.

He mostly succeeded in putting the matter out of his mind during the meal, and afterward delivered his toast—a gently mocking but otherwise heartfelt tribute to the man who'd been one of the most profoundly influential presences in his life from the day he was born. By the time he finished, both Aubrey and Susan had tears sparkling in their eyes, and Verity was dabbing at hers with a tissue.

"In closing," he said, raising his glass, "I wish Aubrey and Susan many, many years of happiness, love, and pleasure together, and…" He flashed a wicked grin. "I'm so incredibly lucky to have had this grumpy old curmudgeon in my life. I couldn't be gladder that he's found such a wonderful woman to put up with him. Cheers, you two."

Aubrey's eyes twinkled. Susan laughed and put her arms around him, leaning in to kiss his cheek. *Thank you,* she mouthed at Stone.

"And now," Stone called, "let's see about getting this party started, shall we? Aubrey and Susan will start things off with their first dance."

On cue, the band began to play a slow waltz, and couples rose from their tables and gathered around the small dance floor, leaving an opening for the newlyweds to come through.

Stone watched from the sidelines, standing next to Jason and Verity and smiling at the happy couple. He doubted either of them saw anything around them as they danced, gazing into each other's eyes as if no one else was present. By the time they finished and more couples began to join them, Stone had nearly forgotten about Ian's absence.

Until he glanced up and spotted Gabriel standing among the elderly guests on the other side of the dance floor.

Nobody else appeared to acknowledge or even notice him, not even Verity or Jason. When he caught Stone's gaze, he made a quick head motion. His expression was unreadable.

"Er—excuse me a moment," he told his two friends. He skirted the dance floor and followed Gabriel outside. It was dark now, the moonlight and the fairylike lights along the walkways giving the place an otherworldly air.

The young dragon waited, leaning against the side of the building. He wore an immaculate black tuxedo.

"What are you doing here?" Stone asked. He looked around, expecting to see Ian. "Is Ian with you? I won't lie, I'm a bit annoyed at him for missing Aubrey's wedding, so I hope that wasn't your doing."

Gabriel's solemn gaze settled on him for a moment before he spoke. "He…is missing, Dr. Stone."

Stone blinked, shocked. "Missing? What are you on about?"

"He was supposed to meet me this morning for some magical instruction before heading to the wedding, but he didn't arrive."

CHAPTER THIRTY-TWO

"**D**IDN'T ARRIVE?"

Stone fought to quell his growing sense of panic, as visions of Amber's accident rose in his mind. "And you don't know where he is? How is that possible?" He lowered his voice to a harsh whisper. "You're a bloody *dragon*. How could he have hidden from you? You didn't have a row, did you?"

"No, nothing like that. And I'm not sure he's hiding."

Stone had never seen him look anything but perfectly calm and vaguely amused at the world, as if there was nothing it could throw at him that he couldn't deal with, so his current expression of concern was even more terrifying than it might have been in anyone else. "What's that supposed to mean? Did you look for him?"

"I did. I began with mundane means—texts and phone calls, to both him and some of his close friends. When those didn't get me anywhere, I searched several of his favorite locations, but no one there had seen any sign of him. And then I performed a tracking ritual."

A cold jolt of dread crawled down Stone's back. "*You* did a tracking ritual. And you didn't find him." *Oh, dear gods...* "Does that mean he's—" Guilt wracked him: if he hadn't been so sure Ian was being flaky and blowing off his responsibilities in favor of his own pleasure, perhaps he could have begun a search earlier.

But Gabriel is a dragon...if he couldn't find him, what makes you think you—

"I don't think he's dead," the young dragon said soberly. He pushed gracefully off the building and began pacing, staring out into the lights of the reception hall's garden.

"Why not? How do you know?" Stone remained where he was, following Gabriel with his gaze and trying to calm his suddenly pounding heart. "If you can't find him, how can you be sure—"

"I just know. Call it dragon magic. Our tracking spells don't work like a human mage's would. We get more information."

Stone wheeled on him. "All right, then—what information did you get? Tell me everything!"

"That is what I'm trying to tell you, Dr. Stone—I know he's not dead. He's…out there, somewhere. I'm certain of it. But I don't know where. Something is blocking my spell."

A hard lump in his stomach joined Stone's icewater veins. "What could be doing that? What could block a dragon?"

"I don't know. Before, I would have said nothing. I'm young, but my magic is among the strongest of our kind. Even another dragon would have difficulty blocking me." He stopped pacing. "But that isn't why I've come to you."

"You didn't just come to tell me? Why, then?"

"I need your help. Perhaps between the two of us, we might have more success."

"Of course. Anything! But if you couldn't find him, how do you think I'm going to—" He stopped as the answer came to him. "Ah. Blood."

Gabriel inclined his head. "Exactly. As his father, your blood might succeed where my ritual alone failed. Between the two of us, we might have a better chance."

Stone remembered another time, when he'd used his own blood to track Ian when Trin Blackburn and the demon were concealing him. "Of course. Let's do it now! Come on—we can do it at my house. I've got a big circle."

At that moment, Verity poked her head out through the door. "Doc? You okay?"

Stone realized she didn't appear to even notice Gabriel's presence. The dragon must be concealing himself from everyone else. "Er—yes, I'm fine. Just—getting some air."

She tilted her head. "Have you tried reaching Ian again? I tried texting him but still no answer."

Stone glanced at Gabriel, who shrugged.

Verity started. "Gabriel? Where did you come from?"

"Verity—" Stone spoke before he could answer. "Listen—I think something's wrong, and so does Gabriel. Ian's missing. We're going back to the house to try a ritual using my blood. Can you please tell Aubrey something came up and I had to leave? I don't have any more duties—it's all just dancing and drinking now. Please give him my apologies, but don't tell him what's happened. I don't want to ruin his wedding day over what might be nothing but a misunderstanding."

Her brow furrowed. "Doc—"

"Please, Verity." His heart was racing; he wanted to *move*. "Come by the house if you want, after you take Jason home. But I've got to go."

She hesitated, but then nodded. "Okay. Good luck. Please let me know if I can help."

He was already heading for the car park. "Thank you," he called back over his shoulder, lengthening his long-legged stride to a near-run. Unfortunately, none of the three ley lines that crossed through the Surrey house also passed through the village, so he'd need to drive home the old-fashioned way. "Come on, Gabriel. I'll drive."

They both remained silent on the short trip back to the house. Stone's thoughts careened madly in his head, trying to recall anyone who might want to abduct, hide, or hurt Ian. He couldn't think of anyone. The boy had a lot of friends, and no enemies he was aware of. He thought again of Amber's unfortunate accident, and wondered if something similar could have happened to his son.

But if he's hurt somewhere, Gabriel should have been able to find him.

Stop speculating. Let's just get home and do something.

They reached the house. He drove the little black convertible up the graveled entrance road and slammed on the brakes at the front, slewing tiny rocks in every direction. Gabriel easily kept up with him as he took the steps to the front door two at a time, flung it open, and dashed inside.

"When was the last time you saw him?" he demanded on the way downstairs to the hidden basement area and his massive inlaid circle.

"Early last night. We attended a dinner with some friends, but he begged off the party after. He said he wanted to prepare for the wedding the following day, and didn't want to be too hung over."

Stone swallowed hard. So Ian *hadn't* forgotten the wedding, and had been planning to attend. "And he didn't turn up for a lesson this morning?"

"It wasn't a lesson—just some quick technique instruction. We were to meet for lunch, and then he planned to take the Prague portal here in the early afternoon."

"Bloody hell..." They reached the circle, and he skidded to a stop. "Okay—here we are. I assume you want to take point on the ritual?"

"Yes. Please give me some of your blood. I'll try to use the connection between the two of you to augment my own magic."

Stone was already heading to the shelves lined with ritual materials. He used magic to pull a small beaker and a knife down. Without bothering to sterilize the knife, he raised it in a shaking hand and slashed it across his palm with barely a wince.

Gabriel hurried over, holding the beaker steady until it was half full, then gently pulling it from his grasp and using a healing spell to seal the slash.

Stone began gathering more components to customize the circle, but Gabriel waved him off. "We don't need to change the circle. I don't really need it at all, but it will help me focus the energies. Please step inside with me."

"Why? You've got my blood—"

"Yes, but if I can establish a physical connection to you, that will make the spell more potent." His expression sobered again. "I'm not certain our search will be confined to this dimension."

Stone's body went cold again. "You think someone's taken him to another dimension?" He thought of the people he knew who could do that, but none of them had any reason to abduct his son. It had to have something to do with Gabriel—perhaps one of his enemies had decided to get back at him through his apprentice.

"I don't know," Gabriel said. "I know very little right now, and that troubles me. Come—let's begin the ritual, and perhaps we can gain more information."

Stone stepped without hesitation into the center of the circle. "What do I need to do?"

Gabriel poured the blood into the brazier. "Clasp hands with me, and focus on your connection to Ian. And don't be surprised if the sensations are a bit uncomfortable."

"Do whatever you've got to do, but find my son."

He reached out, and Gabriel took his hands in a strong grip. The young dragon began a low, chanting invocation in a language Stone was certain he'd never heard before. He wondered if any non-dragon had ever heard it.

As the chant continued, Stone's hands began to tingle. The sensation crawled up his arms, bringing with it a nearly overwhelming compulsion to break the grip and scratch it—but he knew that would be a very bad idea. He gritted his teeth and did what he'd been asked to do, concentrating as hard as he could on his mental image of Ian, their past relationships, the conversations they'd had. He also tossed in a plea to the Universe to help Gabriel trace him, wherever he was.

The tingling sensation didn't get any worse, but it did take over more of his body, creeping to his shoulders and then downward, settling in the center of his chest. His magical tattoo began to thrum, as if it were being infused with power, and then the same thrumming sank deep into his body until it seemed to grip his heart. It was a profoundly disquieting feeling, unpleasant and frightening but not painful. Stone clamped his eyes shut and kept concentrating. *Come on...come on...*

And then, suddenly it was over.

Gabriel stepped back, releasing the grip and letting out a loud breath as his shoulders slumped. Though he wasn't sweating or shaking, and every line of his perfectly-tailored tuxedo was still in place, Stone got the strong impression the ritual had tired him.

Either the ritual...or the lack of result.

"Did you find him?" he demanded. "Do you know where he is?" He was afraid he already knew the answer.

Gabriel shook his head, not meeting his gaze. "No."

"But the blood—"

"The blood helped. I got more than I got before. I'm certain he's alive now. But I'm also certain he isn't on this dimension."

Stone stared at him, shock rendering him momentarily speechless. He managed to sputter out, "But you don't know which one he's on? Or why? Or who put him there?"

"No. Every time I try to reach out to him, his consciousness eludes me. He may be imprisoned, or in an altered mental state."

"But—" Stone couldn't believe what he was hearing. Gabriel was a *dragon*—one of the most powerful magical practitioners on Earth. "What are you saying? We can't find him? We can't get him back?"

"Not yet." He took a deep breath and squared his shoulders. "But I won't quit, Dr. Stone. I promise, I'll find him."

Stone hesitated, but the loss of his son drove away any remaining sense of tact. "What about the other dragons? What about your father, or Madame Huan? Do you think *they* could find him, if you asked them? Do you know where they are?"

Again, Gabriel shook his head wearily. "No. I do know where they are, but it won't help to contact them."

"Why not? They're older than you are, more experienced—" An edge of desperation crept into his tone.

"They are. But in this case, none of that will matter." He raised a hand when it seemed Stone would protest again. "My magic is every bit as strong as any of theirs. That isn't boastfulness or a false sense of my own worth. Objectively speaking, I'm a bit of a prodigy in the magical arts. But that isn't the main reason why they won't be able to find him."

"Why not, then?" Stone's voice rose to a near-shout.

"Because they have no connection to him." Gabriel paced the chamber, alight with restless energy. "You're his father, bound to him by blood. He and I have a…significant relationship."

"You're sleeping with him."

"That's part of it—but as you well know, the master-apprentice relationship is a strong one as well. The point is, you and I have a far stronger connection to Ian than any of them do. If the two of us combined can't find him, they'll have no chance."

"So you can't—I don't know—join forces with them? With your father?" He narrowed his eyes. "If this is because you two don't see eye to eye—"

Gabriel shook his head. "That isn't it. If I thought it would help, I would go to him and beg for his assistance, no matter what he might force me to agree to. But it won't."

"Then…what do we do?" Stone stalked over and got in his face. "What do we do, Gabriel? Because I'm not going to stop trying to find him, either. I'll do whatever's necessary." He thought of Trevor Harrison, whose dimensional knowledge rivaled—and possibly exceeded—the dragons'. Perhaps if he could travel to Calanar and find Harrison, he could—

Gabriel was staring at the floor, smooth brow furrowed, deep in thought. "I don't know," he said at last, and his despair was clear. "There's only one stronger connection to him than you, but there isn't any way to access it."

Stone stopped, tensing. "A stronger connection? What is it?"

"Ian is a scion, the same as you are. His—and your—line's sire would have a direct connection to him. It's impossible for scions to hide from their sires. But I don't know who the sire is. Some of the older ones might, but I doubt they would reveal it to us."

Stone was barely aware Gabriel was speaking. The cold sensation that had settled into his blood had turned to solid ice. "Oh, dear gods, no…"

"Dr. Stone? What is it?"

"I do."

Gabriel's gaze sharpened. "You know who the sire of your line is? It's not my father, is it? Is that why you two have grown so close?"

Stone couldn't believe this. "I only wish it were Stefan. That would make things a lot easier."

New excitement showed on the young dragon's face, and new passion filled his voice. "But don't you see? This *does* make things easier. If you know who your sire is, we can approach them. They might require you to agree to something, but they would have a vested interest in helping to recover their scion. Scions are rare these days, as you well know. Tell me who it is, and I'll arrange it. If I have to knock down the doors and gatecrash their little conclave, we'll get through to them."

"That…won't work." Stone spoke dully now.

"Why not? Who is your sire?"

He met the dragon's eyes, watching him closely for any reaction. "Aldwyn."

Gabriel jerked like someone had run an electrical jolt through him, and he fixed Stone with an intense, penetrating stare. "You're...sure."

"I'm sure. You know who he is, then."

"I do. I had heard rumors he might have returned from his exile, but I wasn't certain."

"Oh, he has. And it wasn't exile. It was being buried under this very house for two hundred years."

"I...see. There isn't any chance you could be wrong about your relationship to his line, is there?" He looked as if he were grasping desperately for any potential way out of this.

"No. I've...spoken with him. Told him to go to hell, in fact. But both he and others have confirmed it, including your father. Ian doesn't know any of this, of course."

The young dragon bowed his head. "Then...we must find another way."

Stone glared at him. "Why? You said you'd do anything to get Ian back. Does that only hold true until you've got to request something from someone you find distasteful?"

Gabriel didn't rise to the bait. "That isn't the problem. Not...entirely, anyway."

"What the hell does *that* mean?"

"It's more complicated than you know." He began to pace again. "Dragon society is...highly regimented, as you're well aware. We have many rules and strictures that govern us and our interactions with each other. I've stepped away from all but the most important of those, which they tolerate because I'm young and I don't involve myself in their affairs. Aldwyn has...stepped away from all of them."

"So? You've said before you don't give a damn about that bunch of hidebound fossils and their rules."

"That's true…to a point. But Aldwyn is very powerful, and in the days before his exile, through a combination of that power, sheer hubris, and skating on the edge of defying the rules—not to mention suspected insanity—he managed to avoid punishment. If he truly is back and the others haven't dealt with him, I'm sure there's a reason for it."

"What, are they *afraid* of him? Is he that much more powerful than the others?"

"No. But I suspect they've made the mutual decision to continue their old course of action: avoid him, as long as he doesn't actively oppose them. And he's too smart to do that."

Stone's anger rose. "I don't give a damn about any of your gods-damned rules. All I want is my son back. If it means finding Aldwyn, then let's find him. Come on, Gabriel. This is *Ian* we're talking about. Believe me, I hate Aldwyn as much as you do. Probably more. But if he can help me get my son back, we've got to at least *talk* to him."

"I can't, Dr. Stone. I don't know where he is. I don't know how to find him, and that's the truth. I give you my word. I didn't even know he was back until you told me. He has always been notorious for his secrecy."

Stone almost protested, but then remembered Aldwyn had told him during their recent conversation that he'd chosen not to attend the dragon conclave.

Gabriel was continuing. "All is not lost. I told you I wouldn't give up, and I won't. My next step is to go to the conclave. Perhaps someone there will have an idea, either how to find Ian or how to contact Aldwyn. My magic is strong, but their greater experience might provide a solution we haven't considered."

"How long will *that* take? Your lot don't do anything quickly, you know that. That's part of why you don't get on with them."

The dragon's expression showed he knew that all too well. "I'll leave immediately, and do my best to impress upon them the necessity for haste. It's the best I can do, Dr. Stone. I'm sorry. I will be in touch as soon as I can."

Before Stone could say anything—and there was a lot he still wanted to say—Gabriel had vanished, leaving the circle with its spent brazier of dried blood behind.

For a long time, Stone could do nothing but stand there, his body numb, his mental gears spinning but gaining no traction. Gabriel was gone, and he had no way to contact him. He had no way to get hold of Kolinsky or the other dragons at the conclave, and no way to know how much longer they'd be at it. He almost physically felt the time ticking away, every second another one his son was imprisoned on some other dimension, possibly in pain or distress. Who could have been responsible for taking him? The only entity he thought possible, the demon Razakal, was dead. Perhaps another demon had learned of Ian, and—

"Doc?"

He turned slowly. Verity was standing in the doorway, still in her formal dress and heels, watching him with worried eyes. He let his shoulders slump. "Verity."

"Are you…all right? Did you and Gabriel figure out where Ian is?"

"Not yet. Not…exactly."

"What does that mean?" She entered slowly, as if afraid he might order her away.

"Where's your brother?"

"Uh—I need to take him home, but I wanted to check with you first. Do you need him for something?"

He shook his head. "No. You two can't help with this."

"We can try. *I* can try. Doc, you know I'll do everything I can."

"I know, Verity. And I appreciate that. But this isn't something you can help with. Please—just go take Jason home so he can get back to Amber. I've got to think."

She hesitated. "Doc…"

"Go. Please. I'm not fit company right now. I'll call you if there's anything you can do."

Still she hesitated, watching him as if she wanted to say something else. But then she bowed her head. "Okay. I'll go. But you have to promise to call me if I can help. Give me your word and I'll go."

"You have it." He was barely aware of what he was saying.

She remained a moment longer, then withdrew. The soft *click-click* of her heels receded down the hallway and faded.

What could he do? He couldn't stay here, standing in an empty room. He had to do *something* to try finding Ian. Another ritual? Maybe get Eddie, Ward, and Verity together to try the combined one again?

He snorted in disgust. Who was he fooling? If he and a bloody *dragon* couldn't find Ian, four human mages, three of whom had no close connections with him, weren't going to do it on their own.

There was only one answer, and he knew it.

He'd have to talk to Aldwyn.

The thought made him shudder with distaste, but he'd done distasteful things before in his life, for far less compelling reasons. If he couldn't talk to Kolinsky or Madame Huan until they returned from the conclave, and he didn't know how long that would be, he couldn't afford to wait.

But how was he to contact Aldwyn? He couldn't exactly ring the dragon on the phone, or send him a letter. Aldwyn had been very careful about hiding his location, and Stone had no illusions about his ability to penetrate those protections. So how was he to—

The memory came to him suddenly, of the last time they'd spoken.

Aldwyn had given him a way.

Press your thumb to the center of the card and picture my name in your mind. I will respond at my earliest convenience.

He'd told the dragon not to hold his breath at the time. Terror rose as he realized he couldn't immediately remember where he'd put the card. He'd jammed it carelessly into his pocket, certain he would never use it, but that had been weeks ago. Had he tossed it into the laundry? Thrown it in a drawer somewhere?

With barely a thought, he pictured the pattern in his mind and gathered energy, pacing impatiently as it built and then releasing it, sending him streaking along the ley-line pathways to the Encantada house. A startled Raider dived out of the way as he pounded up the stairs toward his office, loosening his tie as he went.

Another bright shard of panic struck him when the featureless black card wasn't where he expected it to be. He'd tossed it on the edge of his desk—he knew he had. He often off-loaded the contents of his pockets to a little caddy there, then searched through them later to separate the important bits from the trash. The caddy still held a few coins, a couple receipts, and a dry-cleaning stub, but no matte-black card.

A little voice spoke in his head: *when you can't find something it's probably Raider's fault.*

His heart thudded harder as he dropped to his knees and peered under the desk.

The black card was there, peeking out from beneath a dust-bunny. *I've* got *to find a housekeeper,* he thought, and snatched the card.

Once he had it in his hand, though, he hesitated.

This was *Aldwyn* he was preparing to contact. Not just contact, but beg a favor from. The man who had committed numerous atrocities in the past to further his own power. The man who had already hit him twice with the *join me and we'll rule the world as father and son* routine, and whom he'd already told twice to pound sand. Would Aldwyn even be *willing* to help, or had he tired of his insolent scion who didn't show the proper respect? And if he *did* agree to help, what would he ask in return?

It doesn't matter. This for Ian. Nothing matters more than him.

Decisively, before he could second-guess himself out of doing it, he pressed his thumb firmly to the middle of the black card and pictured both Aldwyn's name and his image in his mind's eye.

Nothing happened.

I will respond at my earliest convenience.

That could mean anything. Aldwyn *was* a dragon. His "earliest convenience" could be five minutes, a week from next Tuesday—or ten years from now.

The clock on the bookshelf ticked away in the silence. Raider jumped onto the desk and butted his head against Stone's arm, purring.

Stone scratched the cat's head, looking into his wide green eyes. Raider was the perfect companion for this sort of situation: quiet, comforting, and he didn't ask questions Stone couldn't answer. "I don't know, mate," he said softly. "I haven't got a bloody idea what I'm doing here."

His phone rang. The landline on the desk, not his mobile.

Stone almost didn't answer it, since the majority of the calls he actually cared about came on the mobile these days. Finally, before the voicemail took it, he snatched up the receiver. "Yes, hello?"

"Return home," said a voice.

Stone tightened his grip. The voice was male, but unfamiliar— certainly not anyone he knew. Definitely not Aldwyn. "Why?"

But the caller had already hung up. The dial tone buzzed in his ear, almost mocking him.

He looked at Raider again. Part of him—the rational part— tried to convince him not to do it. If this was Aldwyn getting in touch with him, responding to his dragon ancestor's call could lead him places he didn't want to go.

But on the other hand, he reminded himself, this was for Ian. He couldn't wait for the other dragons. Ian could be dying some- where, held captive by an enemy Stone didn't even know existed.

And besides, the best he'd get if he waited, or went back to Kolinsky's shop and somehow managed to convince him to show up, was the same thing he probably already had: a way to contact Aldwyn. If Gabriel was right and the other dragons didn't have enough of a connection to Ian to help find him—at least not quickly—then Aldwyn was his best bet.

He pulled a sheet of paper from his desk and dashed off a quick note to Verity: *Found a possible clue to finding Ian. Don't know how long I'll be gone, but if I don't return, find Gabriel. -AS.*

He folded it, wrote *Verity* on the front, then enchanted it so magical sight would be required to read it and put it in the center of his desk.

With a final glance at Raider, he stood next to the desk, visualized the pattern in his mind, and took the ley line back to the shadowy great room at the Surrey house.

"Good evening, Alastair," said a pleasant voice from the sofa in front of the unlit fireplace. "Thank you for arriving so promptly. How may I be of service?"

CHAPTER THIRTY-THREE

ANOTHER SHOT OF APPREHENSION rippled through Stone at the sound of that voice, but he didn't let it show. "Aldwyn. Thank you for responding so quickly." He gestured, bringing up the sconces lining the wall.

Aldwyn sat with his back to Stone, facing the fireplace. "I provided you with the means to contact me should you desire it, though I must admit I didn't expect it to be so soon. Your words at our last meeting were rather…definitive regarding your feelings on the matter." Without turning, he waved him toward one of the chairs. "Please. Sit down and tell me what you wish of me. I make no promises, of course, but you have my attention."

Stone took the seat, regarding his ancestor. Aldwyn wore a dark brown suit of the finest cut, a white shirt, and no tie. He appeared relaxed and attentive, with no sense of mocking or amusement at his scion's discomfiture.

"My son is missing," he stated. Might as well get right to it.

"Your son."

"Yes. Please don't insult my intelligence by implying you didn't know I've got one. He's your scion too."

"I'm aware. The seventh in the line." He raised an eyebrow. "You say he is missing? Why would you come to me with such a thing? Surely with your blood bond and your level of magical power, you should have no trouble locating him on your own."

"Normally, that would be true." Stone wanted to pace, but forced himself to remain seated and calm. Showing weakness to Aldwyn—any dragon, really, but this one in particular—was not a good idea. "Do you know of Gabriel?"

Aldwyn snorted. "The young one. He is a fool."

"Maybe so—we'll have to agree to disagree about that—but he's also Ian's master."

"Indeed."

"You didn't know that?"

"I did not." He made a dismissive gesture. "As your friend Kolinsky might have told you, and my absence from the conclave certainly demonstrates, I deliberately avoid embroiling myself in the tiresome bureaucratic activities of my fellows unless they directly affect me."

Stone wasn't sure whether to believe him, but he let it go. "Well, he is. He was the one who came to me about it. Ian was supposed to attend a family wedding today, but he didn't arrive. Gabriel last saw him last night, when they attended a dinner together. He didn't arrive for a planned lesson this morning."

Aldwyn looked bored. "I am sure you find all of this very fascinating, Alastair. I, however, do not. Please get to the point."

Stone quelled a rise of annoyance. "The *point* is that both he and I did tracking rituals to look for him—Gabriel first, on his own, and then the two of us together, using my blood-bond with him."

"And you did not find him? Perhaps he is dead." The dragon's voice held no shred of sympathy or compassion.

Again the annoyance—closer to full anger now—rose, but again Stone drove it down. He wasn't going to get into a pissing match with a rude dragon. It was possible Aldwyn was just trying to wind him up, perhaps to get a little revenge for his scion's previous insolence. If it meant getting the dragon's help, Stone could take a few digs. "He's not dead—though I'd think you would care at least a bit, given that he's your blood as much as I am."

"He is young, and far less interesting to me at this point in his life and level of magical experience. But I remind you that you still have not told me why you have contacted me."

"That should be obvious. But if you want me to come out and say it, fine: I want you to help me find him."

"What makes you think I could—or would be willing to—do that?"

"Why do I think you could? Because Gabriel told me sires can locate their scions, no matter where they are. I assume that's how you keep managing to find *me*, even though I do my best to avoid you." *Careful, Stone. Don't piss him off until you find out if he's willing to help you.*

Aldwyn inclined his head. "Your knowledge of our people grows each time we speak. The young one risks much by revealing such things to mortals."

Yes, about that, Stone thought but didn't say. A thrill of hope rose in him, though. "Is it true, then?"

"It is true, yes. A simple ritual is required—we are not constantly aware of our scions' locations. That would be exhausting and annoying."

Stone remembered the story Kolinsky and the other dragons had told him, about how Aldwyn had mated with numerous magically talented human women over the years to produce scions. According to Kolinsky, he (and Ian, obviously) were the last of Aldwyn's living scions. But he wondered how much the others truly knew. If Aldwyn had attempted to hide any of his scions, could he have done it? Stone supposed it didn't matter, though. He didn't need to know the gritty details of dragons' relationships with their descendants. Nothing mattered right now but getting Ian back.

"Then that's why I've come to you. Because the best Gabriel and I could determine was that Ian is still alive—and Gabriel thinks he might be on another dimension, which is why he's so difficult to find."

Aldwyn frowned thoughtfully, his brow furrowing. "Why would your son be on another dimension?"

"I've got no idea. It doesn't make sense to me, either. Especially not the night before he was supposed to attend this very important event. It leads me to believe someone has taken him."

"Does he have enemies?" The dragon's tone was still a little distracted, as if he were only giving Stone's words part of his attention.

"I don't know. He did, sort of—an enemy of mine made a pact with a demon and they took him to lure me—but the enemy is dead and the demon was disrupted."

"You are certain?"

Stone thought about it. He *had* allowed Razakal to take Trin's shattered soul as a consolation prize. But he also knew Nick Happenstance and Bron Broome had destroyed Razakal in Los Angeles. "As certain as I can be."

Aldwyn nodded. "Is there anyone else who might be interested in him? I trust you haven't received any messages from anyone who might be trying to reach you through him, as they did before?"

"Nothing." Stone realized he hadn't checked his voicemail or email, though he doubted any magically powerful entities would bother trying to contact him in such a mundane way. He pulled his phone out now and looked to be certain, but his most recent messages and emails were either related to the University, or spam.

"I haven't heard from anyone." He clenched his fists in his lap. "I'm asking for your help, Aldwyn. As you're no doubt aware, that isn't easy for me."

"I am sure it is not." The dragon regarded him with a level gaze as the seconds stretched out. "I might be persuaded to provide some assistance, since you are my blood and so is your son. But it will not be without a price."

A little knot settled in the pit of Stone's stomach. This was nothing new—Stefan Kolinsky had made a cottage industry out of trading favors—but he suspected Aldwyn's request would not be as relatively benign as Kolinsky's. "What do you want?"

Aldwyn rubbed his chin and looked thoughtful. "What, indeed?"

"Look—let's not be coy about it. You've got me where you want me. I can't find Ian without your help, so you have the advantage on me. But as you continue to point out, we're also blood. I might not be a dragon, but I also don't have the constraints you do."

The dragon gave his chin a final stroke and turned to face Stone. "You are correct on all counts. And in truth, although I have found your previous behavior toward me to be disrespectful and insulting—I would have killed any other human who spoke to me in such a way without a second thought—I cannot say I entirely blame you for your feelings toward me, based on your knowledge of my past activities. Perhaps I might take this opportunity to change your opinion about me."

Stone refused to allow himself to believe Aldwyn would show mercy. Not even because it was their own shared blood they were talking about. "What's that mean, then?"

Aldwyn's smile showed no mirth. "What it means is that I will help you. What it does *not* mean is that I will do so without a price. Merely that I will adjust my price to the circumstances. A...blood discount, as it were."

Stone remained silent, and didn't take his eyes off the dragon. It couldn't have been clearer to him that his ancestor was practically reveling in this new development.

"What do you say, Alastair? Do you wish my help or not?"

Stone continued to hold Aldwyn's gaze, but his mind was spinning. After all these years, he trusted Kolinsky not to take advantage of their relationship by demanding a price he wasn't willing to pay. Aldwyn had no such strictures. What would the dragon ask for? Would it be something he wouldn't do?

Was there anything he wasn't willing to do to get his son back?

He took a slow deep breath. "Once again, I say: what do you want? I can't agree to your terms if I don't know what they are."

"My terms are simple: You will swear a magically binding oath that, if my assistance results in the safe return of your son, you will ally yourself to me for a period of five years or three unspecified tasks, whichever comes first. The tasks to be determined at my discretion in the future, after your son is returned. You will also agree to tell no one about this association or the particulars of the oath."

Stone stared at him in shock, forgetting he'd intended to be respectful. "You have *got* to be having me on, Aldwyn! I'd be a fool to agree to that!"

"Perhaps so. But unless you have another way to locate your son, I am not certain you have much room to bargain. Be thankful of our relationship: my normal price for such assistance would be an oath of permanent association."

"Servitude, you mean."

Aldwyn made a dismissive gesture, but didn't deny it.

Stone glared. "Do you know where he is?"

"I do not."

"How do I know you didn't grab him in the first place?"

Aldwyn's expression darkened, growing dangerous. "You tread on very thin ice, scion, making such an accusation. I have far better things to do with my time than to waste it toying with you *or* your son. You are my blood, true, but never overestimate your value to me. You come seeking my aid, and then give me insult."

In spite of his resolve not to show any weakness, Stone couldn't help flinching slightly. He'd grown so used to dealing with Kolinsky and Madame Huan that he sometimes forgot how powerful and alien the dragons were, and how dangerous, Aldwyn perhaps more than any of them. He wasn't going to help Ian if his ancestor burned him to a cinder, or shipped him off to yet *another* alternate dimension in a fit of pique. He wasn't even sure his confusing immortality would stand up against the wrath of a fully mature dragon. Spending eternity as a lump of coal was in no way appealing.

"Okay," he said. "I'm sorry. But my other comment still stands: I'd be a fool to agree to your terms. Three unspecified favors? You could force me to do anything. You could tell me how to find Ian, then turn right around and order me to kill him once he's safe."

The smoldering fire in Aldwyn's eyes settled. "You make a reasonable case. Allow me to alter the agreement slightly, then, to make it more palatable: I give you my word I will not ask you to kill, injure, or otherwise interfere with any of your human friends or family members, nor will I ask you to do anything of which you are not capable." He gave Stone a withering look. "If you think I have any interest whatsoever in your insignificant human associates, you do not know me even as well as I might have thought. If I wanted to interfere with any of them, I would not need you as my proxy to do it."

Stone didn't like any of this. He didn't like it one bit. He was tired of dragons and their machinations, and tired of feeling like a pawn being tugged around between beings far older and more powerful than he was.

But this was Ian they were talking about.

He turned Aldwyn's words over in his mind. *"Nor will I ask you to do anything of which you are not capable."* Did that mean he wouldn't become Aldwyn's assassin, sent to kill Kolinsky or one of the other dragons? The dragons' agreements meant they couldn't interfere with each other directly, and Gabriel had said that even though Aldwyn didn't follow them, he still preferred to keep a low profile. If Stone agreed to his terms, would Aldwyn send him to do what he himself chose not to?

This was pointless. The dragon could ask any of a countless number of things of him, and there was no way he had any chance of anticipating them all. As much as he didn't want to acknowledge it, what the question ultimately came down to was simple:

What am I willing to do to save my son?

And the answer to that was clear, unambiguous, and immediate.

That didn't, however, mean he was a complete fool.

"Find Ian first," he said, fixing what he hoped was a resolute stare on Aldwyn. "I want to know he's alive and that you *can* help me get him back. Then we'll talk."

Aldwyn's face was like granite. The seconds passed, to the point where Stone expected any moment for the dragon to take some sudden and brutal action against him. Neither of them moved or broke the gaze.

Finally, Aldwyn's shoulders released their tension, and his smile this time was almost a gesture of respect. He inclined his head. "That is a reasonable request, and I will grant it."

He stood. "Remain here in my absence. I will not be away for long."

Stone narrowed his eyes. "How long?"

"No more than half an hour."

He sighed. "Fine. Do what you need to do. I'm not going anywhere."

Aldwyn nodded once and vanished.

Stone slumped back against the chair, suddenly tired to the point of exhaustion. He realized he'd been holding his whole body stiff throughout the entire conversation with Aldwyn, and only now allowed himself to let it ebb away.

How had his life spiraled so far out of control so quickly? Things had finally settled, at least as much as they ever did with him. They'd found the fissure and closed it. Aubrey and Susan were safely married and no doubt heading to their honeymoon by now. Jason and Amber's daughter was weeks away from being born. Verity and Hezzie were making a success of their new shop. Sure, the Change was still out there looming large over the world, but every bit of evidence he or any of the researchers had found so far indicated it was permanent and irreversible, which meant it would be a source of study, but not necessarily a problem he could solve.

Something to accept, in other words.

He could do with getting comfortable with a little acceptance now and then. He didn't always have to fight against everything.

But this new development—the idea of becoming oathbound to Aldwyn, the most dangerous of the dragons—that wasn't something he would ever be comfortable with accepting.

The fact that he might not have a choice didn't make it any easier.

He pulled out his phone and scrolled through his list of contacts as the house, mostly silent without Aubrey's and Selby's presence, made its familiar settling noises around him. Should he contact anyone? Once again, his accursed scorecard tripped him up. Nobody he could contact even knew about Aldwyn, except as a name on an empty crypt in the family mausoleum. They didn't know he had been the "fiend" imprisoned in the caved-in room under the house, nor that he was still alive. Jason, Verity, Eddie, and Ward didn't know anything about the dragons. What would he say if he contacted them? "I'm about to agree to a Faustian bargain with an ancient dragon who also happens to be my many-times-great grandfather to save my son, and I'm not sure I should do it?"

What was the point? Even if he did that, he couldn't explain the situation in half an hour. All it would do was cause his friends distress on his behalf. Kolinsky had told him the one thing dragons—even Aldwyn—took deadly seriously was their word. And Aldwyn had given him his word that he wouldn't be asked to do anything that would cause his friends or family members harm. There was a lot of wiggle room in that, but at this point, assuming Aldwyn *could* reach Ian, his only choices were clear: accept the agreement, or refuse and try to find another way to locate his son.

He bowed his head, wanting to scream or punch something. Despite apologizing for his insulting words, he still wasn't completely certain Aldwyn *wasn't* behind this whole thing. He replayed the conversation, realizing the dragon hadn't come right out and denied his involvement. Was he truly insulted, or was his response carefully calculated? Did he dare ask again and risk not only Aldwyn's wrath, but losing his help? Or was Stone overthinking the whole thing, trying to find a reason that would allow him to rationalize turning down the bargain even if it meant Ian's death?

Did it even matter?

If he had more time, he might have a chance at working through this, at coming up with another solution. But he didn't have more time. Cursing himself for acting so quickly, for seeking out Aldwyn before he'd had a chance to talk to his friends or wait for Gabriel to reach the other dragons, was pointless now. He couldn't take it back, so all he could do was go forward with things the way they were.

When Aldwyn returned, reappearing in the same position on the sofa that he had vacated thirty minutes ago, Stone was slumped in the chair, staring into the massive, yawning opening of the dead fireplace.

"Did you find him?" he asked in a monotone, without looking at the dragon.

"I did."

Now he did look. "Is he all right?"

"He is not injured, but his strength is fading. As you suspected, he is imprisoned on another plane—one which is not entirely hospitable to human life."

"Did you go there? Did you talk to him?" Stone snapped to an upright position.

"I did not."

"Then how do you know?"

Aldwyn's eyes narrowed dangerously. "My tracking methods are not the same as yours, scion. But if it will ease your mind, I give you my word that I am aware of both his location and his current state. That will have to suffice." He leaned back, relaxed, and crossed his ankle over his knee. "This is the point when you have a decision to make. Do you accept my terms?"

Stone swallowed. There it was again: a dragon's word. If Stone chose to believe what he said, then his son might be dying. There were other ways to die than injury, and foreign dimensional energy could have a detrimental effect on humans—even human mages. Especially if they weren't prepared for it.

Still, he had more questions. "Do you know who took him?"

"Not specifically. Although I did get the impression of possible demonic energy. I cannot guarantee the energy was related to his abductor, though." He made a mocking little clucking noise. "Come now, Alastair. You can continue to ask me questions, but at some point—some point soon, I might add—my patience will be exhausted. I sympathize with your concern over your son, but I have many things to do. Make your decision, please. Do you accept my terms?"

Stone's heart beat faster. His every instinct was telling him not to do this—but the alternative was losing Ian. Did he even *care* about his own safety if it meant letting Ian die?

"One more question," he said firmly. "If I do agree to your terms, what will you do then? Will you go to this place and bring Ian home? Will you take me there?"

"I will do neither."

"What?" Stone blinked in surprise.

"This dilemma of yours is not my concern, Alastair. I will not subject myself to even a minor risk on your behalf—not without considerably stronger inducement."

"Then—what *will* you do? What am I getting in exchange for my agreement?"

"I will send you to where he is, and provide you with the means to return home. What you do there when you arrive is up to you."

The cold little shiver crept up Stone's spine again. "So you're saying that you give no guarantee of safety."

Aldwyn's expression was unreadable. "No."

"But yet you said Ian would be returned safely."

He shook his head once. "No. I said your oath would take effect upon the safe return of your son. If he—or you—do not return safely, the oath is, of course, null and void."

Stone let his breath out. "You aren't making this easy, are you? I think you're enjoying watching me squirm."

Aldwyn didn't answer. He sat, hands clasped in his lap, and waited.

All Stone could think about was Ian, held captive on some other dimension, his life force draining from him. Would that kill him? He didn't know. What was this "possible demonic energy" Aldwyn had mentioned? *Was* there a chance Razakal had survived the disruption? He hadn't been there to see it, so he had only the word of Nick and Bron that the demon was gone.

If it *was* Razakal holding his son captive, the demon would learn a few things about Stone's power level since they'd last encountered each other.

If it wasn't, he was going into this blind.

Even so, regardless, he knew what the answer had to be.

What it always had to be.

He could have saved himself the trouble of the long conversation, because it didn't change anything.

He stood, and drew a deep breath. "All right, Aldwyn. *If* you help me return my son safely home, I agree to your terms."

Aldwyn inclined his head gravely, then stood as well. "So be it."

Stone looked at him.

He looked at Stone.

"Well? Don't we have to do something? Cut our palms and shake hands? State our names and the terms of the oath?" He recalled a similar oath he'd made with Stefan Kolinsky, the one that prevented him from revealing the existence of the rifts.

"No. Your statement of agreement is sufficient."

The chill in Stone's body increased intensity. "You mean I'm already oathbound?"

"Yes. Although it will not take full effect until my part of the bargain is fulfilled. Are you ready to go?"

This was moving too fast. "Now? Right here?"

"Is there a better time? You do want to rescue your son, do you not?"

Stone thought about it—about all the preparations he could potentially make, weapons he could gather, people he could consult.

But he had no idea what he was getting into, and every moment he hesitated was another for Ian's life force to drain away.

When it came down to it, his wits and his magic were and always had been his own best weapons.

"Okay," he said. "You're right. I'm ready."

Aldwyn nodded again, as if he expected it. He reached into his suit pocket and withdrew a golden ring with a black, faceted stone. "Put this on. Press the stone when you wish to leave. When you have found your son and are ready to return, clasp his hand and press the stone again. It will return you here."

Stone took the ring. It was heavy, substantial, and felt oddly warm. Magical sight revealed a hard, glittering silver aura around it. Potent magic indeed. He slipped it onto his finger, where it immediately adjusted to fit him as if it had been made for him. "That's it?"

"That is all. I will be in touch with you when you have returned. I must consider carefully the tasks I wish to assign to you."

Stone shivered, but tried not to show it. He didn't say anything—he couldn't bring himself to thank Aldwyn for his assistance, and might not even be able to do it after he'd returned. He realized he had no more to say to his ancestor.

With a shaking finger, he pressed the ring's black stone.

Instantly, the world faded around him.

When it came up again, he was standing in a tiny, featureless room. The walls, floor, and ceiling were all white. The only furniture, a bed with a white frame and white sheets, took up most of the space, barely leaving enough room for Stone to stand.

Ian lay on the bed, dressed in a white T-shirt, pants, and socks with no shoes.

As soon as Stone appeared, he jerked up to a seated position, his eyes wide and full of fear. "Dad. Oh, gods, why did you come after me?"

CHAPTER THIRTY-FOUR

A T FIRST, all Stone could do was stare at his son in shock, drinking in the sight of him. Then he strode forward and pulled Ian into a hard embrace. Relief flowed through him. Whatever else was going on here, his son was alive, and appeared to be uninjured. At least it was easy to see, in this white room, that no blood stained his clothes or the bed.

Ian returned the hug, but his whole body felt tense, primed for something. "Why did you come after me?" he repeated.

"Why wouldn't I come after you?" Stone pulled back and swept his gaze around the room, but saw nothing that caught his interest. The white walls were blank and featureless, and the room had no windows and no door. "When you didn't show up at Aubrey's wedding, I'll admit at first I thought you'd forgotten about it. But then Gabriel turned up at the reception and said you were missing."

Ian slumped back to the bed. "Yeah. I got tricked. This is a trap, Dad. A trap for you."

"What?" Stone looked around again, spinning in place, half-expecting something else to appear in the room. But it remained as serene and unsettling as before. "Why? Who did this?"

"I don't know." He bowed his head. "I got played. I can't believe they fooled me."

"*Who* fooled you? How?"

"I don't know who. I know *how,* though." He rested his elbows on his white-clad knees and plowed his hands through his spiky hair in a gesture reminiscent of his father's. "Early this morning—I guess it was this morning, anyway, since I've lost all track of time—I got a text from you."

"From me? I didn't send you a text this morning."

"Yeah, I get that now. But I didn't know it then. It asked me to come to the house early, because you had some stuff related to the wedding you wanted to discuss with me."

Something went cold in the pit of Stone's stomach. "So what did you do?"

"I was in Prague at the time. Gabriel and I had gone to a party last night. He was off doing something else until later that morning because he wanted to show me some stuff before I left for the wedding. I didn't even leave him a note, since I knew I'd be back before then. I got my clothes together and went through the portal to the one at the Surrey house. Except I didn't."

The chill in Stone's stomach intensified. "What did you do?"

"I stepped through the portal like normal, but when I came out, I wasn't in Surrey. I was—" He gestured around the small room. "—here. I've been here ever since. I'm sorry, Dad."

"Don't be." A suspicion was already starting to form in the back of Stone's mind. "Did anyone speak to you when you got here? You said this was a trap for me. Why do you think so?"

"They only spoke to me once. I didn't recognize the voice, though—I'm sure I never heard it before. I'm not even completely sure whether it was a man, a woman, or something else."

"What did they say?"

Ian reached under the pillow and withdrew a single sheet of what looked like vellum. "They said I should give you this when you arrived. I don't know what it is—it looks blank to me, even with magical sight." He bowed his head. "I'm sorry."

"Don't be sorry, Ian. I think I might know who's behind this, and if I'm right, there's no way you could have seen through it."

"Who?"

He took the sheet of vellum. "Let me see if I'm right first."

Contrary to what Ian had said, the sheet was not blank. One side was covered with text, written in a bold, old-fashioned but fully legible hand. As Stone ran his gaze back and forth over the lines, his fist involuntarily clenched.

"What is it?" Ian demanded. "Do you see something there?"

Stone didn't answer. Instead, he read the note again.

Alastair,

As you no doubt suspected, I am responsible for your son's disappearance. Do not ask my reasons, as they are my own.

This is what you will do now.

Say nothing to your son about my existence or my responsibility for these events, nor about the existence of dragonkind. If you do, all agreements are null and void and your son is lost.

The ring I have given you will perform exactly as I described: pressing its stone will return you safely home. However, it will return only one of you—the wearer. The other will remain behind.

It is your choice, Alastair. If you wish to save your son, give him the ring and tell him you must clasp hands and it will return you both home.

If you do not—if you choose to sacrifice your son and return to seek retaliation against me, simply press the stone and you will be returned alone, leaving him behind.

I give you my word that the ring's wearer will be returned, safe and unharmed, to the place from which they left.

The choice is yours, Alastair. Make it quickly, as the ring will rapidly lose potency. If you hesitate too long, both of you will remain.

—AAES

As soon as he read the last words, the sheet vanished from his hand.

"Dad?"

Ian's voice barely broke through Stone's thrashing thoughts. He stared at his hand that had held the message, and didn't answer.

"*Dad?*" Stronger this time, followed by a firm grip on his arm. "What's going on? Who was the note from? Were you right?"

Stone jerked his head up as if coming out of a trance. "What? Oh—er...no. I wasn't right."

"Then who was it? What's that note say?" Ian was standing next to him now, his gaze intense and concerned.

"It...doesn't matter. We've got to get out of here."

"But how are we going to do that? I've tried every kind of magic I can think of, and investigated every inch of this place. There's no way out of here."

"There is." He held up his hand, slipping the ring free. It came readily, loosening enough to offer no resistance when he pulled it from his finger.

"What's that? Who gave it to you?"

Stone's thoughts continued to whirl. *Say nothing to your son. All agreements are null and void.* Did that mean the ring would stop functioning? Would they *both* be trapped here if he revealed anything about Aldwyn? He tried to think of a way, any possible way, to give Ian a clue, but his brain seemed to be stuck in molasses. If he did this wrong, he could doom his son.

"Gabriel gave it to me," he lied easily. "He's the one who figured out you were here, and sent me here to retrieve you. We're on another dimension."

Ian's eyes widened. He started to say something, but instead looked at the ring. "What does it do?"

"It will get us out of here. Return us home."

"And after that?"

"After that, I'm going to see about tracking down the one responsible for this." He held out the ring in his palm, shifting to magical sight. Aldwyn was right: already, the jagged silver aura around it had diminished somewhat. Stone had no idea how long it would remain powerful enough to perform its function.

Damn you, Aldwyn…

All that rubbish about oaths and unspecified tasks had been nothing but smoke and mirrors—something to trouble his mind enough that he lost sight of the other way Aldwyn could trap him.

But why? Why would Aldwyn even *want* to trap him, or kill him? Was he truly vengeful enough that Stone's refusal to ally himself with him had led to this?

He had no idea.

At this point, it didn't matter.

"Dad?"

"Don't worry about it, Ian. Right now, our first priority is to get the hell out of here. After that, we'll re-assess."

"I'm all for that. Let's go. I've had about enough of this place. What do we have to do?"

Stone held up the ring. His hand didn't shake. He was proud that he didn't even have a second's thought about slipping it back on his own finger and leaving Ian behind. No *you could come back for him* or *you could track down Aldwyn and* make *him release him* or anything like that.

He didn't know either of those things were true anyway, and he wouldn't take the chance.

This was the time to test whether a dragon's word—even Aldwyn's—was inviolate. If it wasn't, they were both screwed anyway.

"Take this," he said. "Put it on."

"But what about you?"

"Once you've got it on, take my hand and hold on tight. Then press the black gem. It will take us both home." Stone was glad he was a good liar. He dropped the ring into his son's outstretched hand.

Ian looked at it, then back at his father. His eyes narrowed. "Wait. How do I know you're really my dad?"

Stone blinked. "What?"

"I got into this by believing you the first time—that you texted me. How do I know this place isn't playing tricks on me again?"

A rush of pride fluttered through Stone. *That's my boy.* But right now, Ian's distrust could do nothing but hurt them. He shifted to magical sight again. The ring's silver aura had dimmed a little since the last time he'd looked. He doubted they had more than a few minutes. He struggled for a way to convince Ian, something he could tell him to make him believe, but his mind refused to settle on anything. Finally, he blurted, "Ask me anything. Anything at all. Something only you and I would know."

Ian's gaze burned into him. His hand closed around the ring. For several seconds, the two of them did nothing but maintain the increasingly tense staring contest.

Then, inexplicably, Ian smiled.

"Okay," he said. "Tell me what you dressed up as with Mom, the night you went to the midnight show at the movies in London."

The knot in Stone's stomach made a little sideways lurch. "*Seriously? That's* what you want to know?"

"Yep."

Tick. Tick. Tick. The silver aura was fading.

"Damn. I forgot Verity told you about that."

"Come on, Dad—time's wasting, and I want to get home and apologize to Aubrey for missing his wedding."

A quick rush of regret sluiced through Stone at his words. If he did this, would he ever see Aubrey again? Would he ever see Jason and Amber's baby? Eddie and Ward? Verity?

But none of that mattered. Not as much as his son did.

Damn you to hell, Aldwyn.

He took a deep breath and looked into his son's eyes. "I dressed up as Frank N. Furter, from *The Rocky Horror Picture Show.* And no, there aren't any photos, so don't ask. Now put the bloody ring on and let's get out of here."

Ian hesitated for only another few seconds. Then he slipped the ring on his finger and quickly grasped Stone's hand. "You'll let me help you look for who did this, right? I'm involved now too."

"I promise," he said softly, hating himself for lying to his son. He nodded toward the ring. "Press the stone." His voice did shake a little, then.

Fortunately, Ian was too stressed out to notice. He reached across with his other hand, squeezed their clasped hands, and pressed down on the black stone.

Instantly, he faded away.

Stone got a second's glimpse of his horrified face as he realized he was leaving his father behind, and then he was gone.

A soft, familiar chuckle sounded inside Stone's head.

The white room around him brightened, and continued brightening until nothing was visible but unrelieved, impossibly bright white light.

Alastair Stone Will Return in
AWAKENING
Alastair Stone Chronicles
Book Twenty-Eight

Look for it in Winter 2021

WE LOVE REVIEWS!

If you enjoyed this book, please consider leaving a review at Amazon, Goodreads, or your favorite book retailer. Reviews mean a lot to independent authors, and help us stay visible so we can keep bringing you more stories. Thanks!

If you'd like to get more information about upcoming Stone Chronicles books, contests, and other goodies, you can join the Alastair Stone mailing list at **alastairstonechronicles.com**. You'll get two free e-novellas, *Turn to Stone* and *Shadows and Stone!*

WHO IS THIS R. L. KING, ANYWAY?

R. L. King lives the kind of exotic, jet-set life most authors only dream of. Splitting her time between rescuing orphaned ocelots, tracking down the world's most baffling cheese-related paranormal mysteries, and playing high-stakes pinochle with albino squirrels, it's a wonder she finds any time to write at all.

Or, you know, she lives in San Jose with her inordinately patient spouse, three demanding cats, and a crested gecko. Which, as far as she's concerned, is way better.

Except for the ocelots. That part would have been cool.

You can find her at *rlkingwriting.com*, and on Facebook at www.facebook.com/AlastairStoneChronicles.

Printed in Great Britain
by Amazon